Love the Bright Foreigner

Born in Gillingham, Kent in 1937, Anita Burgh is the author of *Distinctions of Class*, her successful semi-autobiographical novel also published by Pan. Until recently she owned and ran an exclusive hotel in the Northern Highlands of Scotland. She now writes full-time and lives in Bristol and near Land's End. She has four children.

Also by Anita Burgh in Pan Books
Distinctions of Class

ANITA BURGH

Love the Bright Foreigner

Pan Books
published in association with
Chatto and Windus

First published 1988 by Chatto and Windus Limited
This edition published 1989 by Pan Books Ltd,
Cavaye Place, London SW10 9PG
in association with Chatto and Windus

9 8 7 6 5 4

ISBN 0 330 30808 4

Printed and bound in Great Britain by
Richard Clay Ltd, Bungay, Suffolk

For Sarah Portley
with love

'Love is the bright foreigner, the foreign self.'
Ralph Waldo Emerson, *Journals*

One

1

Stored deep within her, petrified for all time as if in a mental deepfreeze, were the noises, sights and smells that had surrounded her seconds before the telephone rang.

Insignificant, innocent, barely noted, they were part of the background of her life, until the phone rang, interrupting them and stripping them of their unimportance for ever.

Their neighbour's motor mower was coughing and spluttering its idiosyncratic way across the lawn. The blue smoke billowing from the exhaust wafted the acrid smell of petrol into her kitchen. The machine was a mild irritant which had to be endured for the sake of neighbourliness, until that day, when it became a harbinger of fear.

From the cooker a surge of blue flame was followed by the familiar soft plop, as the calor-gas cylinder sighed its emptiness to her, seemed to sigh for her lost security.

The busy chattering and chirping of the house martins, wheeling about the eaves, endlessly forming and re-forming into squadrons, had always been an omen of good luck upon the house. In an instant the whirring of their fine wings mirrored the bleak, black circles of panic in her mind.

The red-and-white gingham curtains flapped gently, lifted by a slight draught in the somnolent air, and like a metronome, clicked against the bamboo support of the bright geranium which so exactly matched the red of the curtains. The rhythmic clicking, like a giant clock, ticked away the moments of her happiness.

A bumble bee buzzed, urgently searching for an escape into the garden. The lattice shapes of sunlight on the newly polished tiles made them appear redder. The lush perfume of the roses and the insistent scent of the herbs mingled with the sweet smell of the newly mown grass. Summer was everywhere.

That Friday in June was the start of a precious weekend when, for a short time, Ben was to be hers without interruptions. Ann stood at the worktop, carefully and methodically chopping bright, shining green and red peppers. She brushed back a strand of hair: hair that had once been blonde but had now faded into a light brown. All her life she had worn it long until six months ago when, to her husband's fury, she had, on a whim, had it cut short. Its length was now at that awkward in-between stage so she had caught it back with a child's slide. She peered at her glossy cookbook, propped up against the flour jar. With a sigh of exasperation she turned, searching the kitchen for the newly prescribed reading spectacles which she had not got used to using. She perched them on the end of her nose and the clear blue eyes focused on the writing. Large eyes that had a look of innocence to them: the eyes of a person whom life had treated kindly.

She was not tall. She had once been petite but the years and her own neglect had allowed a little too much weight to settle upon her. Her rounded curves were not unattractive, rather her shape was unfashionable. Ann was aware of this fact and wished she had sufficient self-control to rectify it. It was a subject she gave a lot of thought to but rarely did anything about. Her face, however, belied her years. Her perfect skin had the bloom of a much younger woman; the only lines on her face were those etched by laughter. Its smooth curves gave a gentleness to her expression, accentuated by a full and generous mouth.

The motor mower gave an aggressive grunt and stopped. Ann looked up. She stood waiting, expectantly, for the noise to begin again. Any other day of the week the neighbour's mower might have irritated her but not on Friday. Nothing was allowed to spoil Ann's Friday.

The day had not always been special. For years, as her husband had laboriously worked his way up through the hospital hierarchy, a free weekend to spend with his family had been a rare treat. Now, as a consultant, Ben's weekends were his own, only to be interrupted by the most serious emergency. There were often weekends when he was away. With his experience in his field, he was much in demand at medical conferences all over the world. Often she wished he would take her with him. '. . . you'd be bored out of your mind. I like to think of you here to return to . . .' he always said, with his disarming smile. As she had been a dutiful daughter, so she was a dutiful wife, and complied uncomplainingly.

But this was not one of those weekends; this weekend he was to be at home. Ann had bought an expensive claret, a Château Latour, recommended by the wine merchant. She would have liked to cook something special to go with it, but Ben only ever wanted steak and salad, so she contented herself by producing the most exotic salads she could find. During the week, when Ben had operations to perform, they rarely drank alcohol, but at weekends they had grown into the habit of having wine with dinner and a fine brandy afterwards. Ann loved the wine and secretly regretted that they could not have it more often, not just because she enjoyed it but, more importantly, because it made Ben relax, made him easier to please and less critical. Now there were just the two of them, the closeness of these weekends was important to her.

The ringing of the phone interrupted her. She wiped her hands on her apron as she crossed to the wall phone.

'Midfield 2433,' she answered automatically. It was the hospital. She leaned against the wall, wondering what her husband wanted: he rarely phoned during the day. She listened to the familiar antiquated wheezing of the hospital exchange. She glanced out of the window. What a summer it had been for the roses. Their blooms seemed larger, their colours more vivid this season. Strange how some people hated roses, thinking them vulgar. Confident was a better description, she thought, that's what produced their amazing colours – their confidence in their own beauty.

'Ann?' She recognized the voice of her husband's best friend.

'Paul, what a pleasant surprise,' she said, hoping that she didn't sound too disappointed that it wasn't Ben. There was silence on the other end. 'How's Amy?' she asked politely, already wondering why Paul and not his wife should be phoning her.

'Ann . . .' It was not a question. It was as if Paul were trying to start a sentence and was not sure how to finish it. 'Ann . . . Oh, God! I don't know what to say!' For the first time she heard the strain in his voice and small tendrils of fear flickered through her.

'Paul. Is something wrong? Paul?'

'Ann, love, it's Ben. He's had . . . Oh, Christ!'

'Paul, what are you trying to tell me?' She was surprised how calm her voice sounded compared with the hysteria which was beginning to bubble up within her. 'Paul!' she said sharply.

'Ann, I'm sorry. I don't know what to say, perhaps I should have come round. Perhaps I . . . Ann, it's Ben, he's had a heart attack . . .'

'No, that's not possible, Paul,' Ann said briskly. 'He's so fit. He looks after himself, he really does. And he's always nagging me about the few cigarettes I smoke. Gracious, he still weighs exactly the same as he did the day we married.' The words gushed out of her. 'No, Paul, you've made a mistake, it's probably indigestion!' She forced a brittle laugh, hoping that laughter would destroy the mounting fear.

'Ann, I'm so sorry. There's been no mistake. He's dead, Ann, I can't begin to tell you how sorry I am . . .'

She stood, leaning against the wall. She looked at the mouthpiece of the telephone, her head to one side, a look of disbelief on her face. She could hear Paul's voice relentlessly saying all the words she did not want to hear. Words were jumbling about in her brain, words that, if she used them, would stop Paul saying these dreadful things. She felt her mouth opening and shutting but no sound came out.

'Ann, Ann . . .' Paul was still speaking to her.

'Thank you for calling.' With superhuman effort she managed to get the words out; all sharpness, irritation and fear had left her voice, to be replaced by her customary politeness. Gently she replaced the receiver. She leaned against the tiled wall. How pleasantly cool the tiles felt against her cheek, she thought, outlining the grouting with her fingertip. There was something she should be thinking about, something important . . . But she would much rather not think.

The mower spluttered into life. The chasm of her mind was filled once again. She remembered. From a long way away she heard a strange noise which grew louder and louder. She put her hands over her ears in an effort to shut out the horrifying sound. The kitchen door flew open and Meg, her cleaning lady, burst in, a look of terror on her face.

'My Gawd, Mrs Grange! What on earth's the matter?'

But Ann was past hearing and was not to know that the strange animal noise that she could hear came from herself as she hurtled, screaming, into her pit of despair.

The bee droned, the bamboo cane clicked against the latticed window – innocent sounds which were to become indelibly printed on her mind, inescapably linked with death.

2

Later, try as she might, Ann could not recall clearly what had happened in the subsequent hours, days and weeks. That whole period of her life had become a blur. If she tried to remember she would see herself as an indistinct shadow moving wraithlike in a misty other-time. Like a dream but not quite like one, for dreams could be faced and analysed, whereas she could not look at what had happened from any angle.

Everyone had been kind, too kind. She remembered that, though what she had wanted was to crawl away like a wounded animal, to find an isolated, secret corner. But it was not to be. An army of friends and relations had prevented that. She was never alone, never allowed to be. Sleep was induced by pills from her well-meaning doctor, pills she did not want, but did not seem to have the energy to refuse. Always in the morning there would be the smiling face, the too brisk voice of a loving friend, and more pills to see her through the day.

Arrangements must have been made, but she didn't know by whom. There must, at some point, have been a funeral, for later everyone told her how wonderfully she had stood up to the ordeal. But she knew her behaviour was a sham, since she could not even remember being there.

And then, as if by organized conspiracy, all the friends became brisk and practical with her. '. . . you must pull yourself together . . .'; '. . . life must go on . . .'; '. . . get out more . . . take a holiday . . . join a club . . .' Ann felt she was floating in a sea of platitudes.

She would look at them with dazed incomprehension. How could she 'pull herself together' when everything within her was shattered and she could not think long and hard enough even to sort the pieces out – did not know if she wanted to try? 'Life must go on . . .' they said, but she could not think of one good reason why it should. Why go out? Where? What for? There was no joy for her out there without him; she felt safer here in her home, surrounded by his possessions, where his presence remained. She was certain too, although she told no one, that he would return. One day the door would open and he would enter and their life would continue just as before. She could not leave the house, ever. What if he came back and she was not there?

She smiled politely at the banality of their comments, realizing that they could not begin to comprehend the emptiness she felt.

The days turned into weeks. Slowly, despite herself, she started to return to her family and friends. The grief that had been lying in wait began to get to grips with her, and insidiously clawed its way, day by day, into her consciousness to fill the emptiness.

Seeing Ben's friends was both difficult and a joy. She enjoyed hearing him spoken of, his name in the air. She felt pride as they extolled his virtues. She laughed when they told her anecdotes about him she had not heard before. And yet, there was only so much she could hear, as if inside her was a meter which allowed her to hear only a preordained amount before she would feel the grief welling up; her face would become like stone and her eyes would take on a faraway, glazed look, and it was as if she could not hear what they said. Embarrassed, they would change the subject, but it was too late: they had lost her again.

She could not remember how many dinner parties, drinks parties, she had been taken to during those months. She had never explained that these occasions were the hardest – the loneliness she felt when surrounded by people was the worst of all.

At last she found the courage to refuse the invitations. The grief had again altered course. Now there was a burning need to come to terms with what had happened to her. She wanted to cry; she felt that if only she could she would alleviate the dreadful weight of misery that was heavy within her, like some malevolent tumour that she realized was destroying her.

She chose to spend her evenings alone, rejecting her children's offers to visit. She did not even pause to wonder if she hurt their feelings for these adults no longer seemed to be the children she had nurtured and raised; they seemed to have become strangers.

On these lovely evenings, she tried to read but the words would fade in front of her eyes. She could never find one programme on television to interest her. But she found that music helped and would sit at night, a drink in her hand, letting the sounds wash over her. She would sit gazing with unseeing eyes into the past, dreaming of the time when she had been happy. But it all seemed so long ago now – those golden days when the children had been small and the sun never stopped shining. It must have rained sometimes, she reasoned, but she could not recall the rain. And she would wake from her sunlit reveries to face the drab greyness of her world.

She insisted that all Ben's things remain untouched. She took some comfort from sitting in his study at his desk, stroking the arms of the chair that he had used, conscious that his hands had rested there. She would caress his pen, his blotter, his telephone, as if in touching his possessions she was able to touch him again. At night she lay on his side of the bed clutching a jacket on which his smell still lingered.

As the day he had died was clear in her mind, so was the day, over a year later, when reality finally returned.

There had been a phone call. She replaced the receiver, leaned against the wall and looked across the kitchen. It was a glorious, warm summer's day. The red tiles glowed on the floor, a gentle breeze lifted the bamboo blind which clicked against the window frame, the bees buzzed in their hurried search for pollen. Suddenly, next door, the chug-chug of the mower started up. Ann's hand shot to her mouth: everything was the same and yet so different!

Suddenly she knew – the waiting had been in vain, he was never coming back. She stood rigid against the wall as the knowledge seeped through her.

'Oh no!' she cried. 'Oh, Ben, how could you?' Unheeded tears began to fall. She sank on to the cool, tiled floor and a long, racking sob shook her body. 'How could you leave me like this?' she shouted. She beat the floor with her fists, anger filling her. 'I can't forgive you for leaving me. Never. I can't forgive you!' she screamed to the empty room. 'You bastard, why did you have to go?' She moaned and rocked herself back and forth as the grief which had lurked for so long within her at last began its escape into the open.

Her tears of anger mingled with her tears of sadness as she acknowledged that Ben had gone for ever. As they flowed, as her body shook in its lonely agony, so, at last, the final healing process began.

3

Ann returned, as if from a long illness. She felt disbelief that so many months of her life had slipped through her fingers while she had lived in a twilight zone. She might just as well have been in a coma, she thought, as she realized how much had happened of which she had been unaware: not only large events such as a new government, another war in the Middle East, there were the small things too. An apple tree had fallen down in the worst storm in living memory – a storm she did not recall. There was a new vacuum cleaner in the house which she presumed she had ordered. And someone must have discussed with her the need to paint the back of the house, for it had been painted, but when? Christmas and Easter had passed her by. There was a new curate, and new people had moved in to the Mill House: she was told that they had called.

She collected all the bottles of pills and hid them at the back of the medicine cupboard. She began to take an interest in her house again. It seemed like a house whose occupants had been away for a long time. There was a mustiness about it and it felt unlived-in. She began, with Meg's help, feverishly to clear out rooms.

At last she drove herself to the shops. She kept her car permanently in the driveway, unable to enter the garage and face Ben's gleaming new Mercedes. He had been so proud of it. It would have to be sold eventually, but at the moment this was something which Ann could not bring herself to organize.

Almost shyly at first, she began to venture out to visit friends. As in the past she often dropped in unannounced on Karen Rigson, her best friend in the village. Karen lived in the old rectory, a large, rambling Victorian house which, now that her children had grown up, was too big for her and John, her husband. Although they often discussed moving to something smaller, everyone knew they were settled in their ways and never would.

Ann sat in Karen's kitchen. She had always liked this room. It was a powerhouse of activity. In the past the notice board had been full of children's drawings, *aides-mémoire* for dental appointments, choir practice, school pick-up rotas. The children had long left home but the notice board was still a riot of pinned-up information. Herbs swung from the ceiling in large fragrant bunches. The smell of newly baked bread hung in the air. There was always a pleasant clutter which was absent from Ann's kitchen, for Ben had been a stickler for tidiness.

With a cup of coffee in front of her and a plate of Karen's excellent shortbread, Ann watched her friend, who with lips pursed in concentration was decanting last year's wine into bottles. One by one these were corked and labelled with Karen's personalized label, which proclaimed in swirling gothic print 'Château Rigson'. As each bottle was finished it was racked in the larder. From where she sat, Ann could see shelves of home-made jam, all with neat gingham lids, and Karen's own printed labels. She's a one-woman cottage industry, Ann found herself thinking, to her surprise.

With a satisfied smile on her face Karen joined her at the table and while she drank her coffee talked rapidly of the proceedings at the last Women's Institute meeting, of the planned autumn agenda. Ann listened – she was told that, if this weather held, it promised to be a bumper year for blackberries, how she must start collecting jam jars for the glut of strawberries there was sure to be – till she wanted to scream. She wanted to scream so badly that she had to turn it into a cough. The room seemed to be pressing in on her. She quickly stood up, scraping the kitchen chair on the ceramic-tiled floor, and, making excuses to a surprised Karen, quickly left the house.

Ann parked her car around the corner. She switched off the engine, sat looking at the timeless view of their beautiful village and was puzzled. What on earth had come over her? Karen was her best friend. She had spent hours in that kitchen talking of nothing in particular and had enjoyed it. Yet, today, there had been something about her which had caused this over-reaction in Ann. She no longer gave a damn about the WI or how many bloody blackberries there were going to be. Even more surprising, she had found the pots of jam, the bottles of wine and those labels ridiculous. She had seen them a hundred times: why should they suddenly have irritated her? With a jolt, Ann acknowledged that it was Karen's sense of smug security which had put her on edge and – she faced the fact – bored her to screaming point.

A couple of nights later, as in the past, she accepted an invitation to bridge with friends with whom she and Ben had often played. Another couple was there. To her embarrassment Ann saw that, as the odd one out, if she was to play someone would have to give up their hand. She said she had a headache and would prefer to watch. When the rubber was over and drinks were served she sat listening to the village gossip. It seemed that the new curate's wife was frowned upon – she was a social worker in the city, and the word was out that she might be a little bit too pink in her political views to suit the inhabitants of Midfield. Everyone agreed that it looked too as if the Church Fête was going to be a disaster this year. Ann smiled to herself, they always said that. She did not know why she lied when, asked if she would be manning a stall, she said that she would probably be away on holiday – even though she had no plans to go anywhere. She listened, and the same restless boredom that she had experienced at Karen's began to swamp her. Pleading that her headache was worse, she left.

At home she sat for a long time wondering what was happening to her. She had been doing the things she had always done with the same people in the past. Ann could never remember being bored before. It was an uncomfortable feeling, an unknown quantity for her. But why? It was as if she had come back from her grief a different person.

She began to worry. What should she do? She did not want to become a recluse again, but at the same time she knew she could not live the rest of her life with these people as her only social contacts.

Lydia rescued her. Lydia was comparatively new in the village and had not been a close friend while Ben was alive. Ann had met her at odd sherry parties, at the community council meetings, at the Fête, but could not say she knew her. Now, it was Lydia with whom she felt most at ease; in her company she was never bored. Perhaps because she had not been part of Ann's past it was easier for Lydia to become part of Ann's present.

Lydia lived just outside the village in an inventively converted pair of cottages. Her husband was something in the City, but what that something was Lydia never clarified. Lydia was one of those fortunate women who never have to work at looking elegant. In faded old jeans, T-shirt and sneakers she still had a sleek style, not surprising perhaps, since for years she had worked as a fashion editor on a bewildering number of magazines and papers. She was always elaborately vague about why she had resigned – she hinted darkly of boardroom conspiracies, of ruthless competitors. Ann thought that the truth was that Lydia had become bored with the routine of her editorial role. She had not totally retired, however: she did a lot of freelance work and when the new collections were being shown Lydia always had a writing commission that entailed her flying off to Paris or Milan, or disappearing to London for weeks at a time. Ann envied Lydia the ability to work when and how she wanted. To have opinions that people were willing to pay to hear.

Her house reflected the same effortless stylishness. At total variance was her raucous laugh, her voice with more than a hint of Cockney to it and a vocabulary which, when she was roused, would not have shamed a squaddie. There were many in the village who did not like Lydia and thought her brittle, hard and, if the truth were told, rather common – Ben had been one of them. As Ann forged this new friendship there were times when she felt a sense of disloyalty to Ben for choosing someone of whom she knew he had disapproved. But Ben had been wrong; Lydia, beneath that urbane shell, was one of the kindest people Ann had ever known. And, with her matter-of-fact approach to life and wry sense of humour, she was the ideal companion at this time.

Ann had been invited by Lydia for lunch and by cocktail time was still there.

'You know, Lydia, I begin to wonder if I haven't been slightly mad this past year.'

'Of course you were, my old love.' Lydia laughed at the expression of shock on Ann's face. 'What did you expect me to say? Bloody hell, it's not surprising, is it? You had to handle Ben's death, and there was nothing to help you fill the void, was there? The children grown up, no job, heavens, you haven't even got a dog, have you? There was nothing to force you to pull yourself together. It had always been you and Ben and the house, so naturally you slunk back to where you felt safest. 'Nother gin?' She poured their drinks and settled down again on the sofa. 'Perhaps you should get a dog, marvellous company – aren't you, my precious Pong?' She crooned to the Pekinese which lay on the cushion beside her.

'I would have liked a pet, but Ben didn't like animals in the house, said they were unhygienic.'

'Unhygienic!' Lydia spluttered. 'Typical bloody doctor's comment, that. Your Ben sounds a right bastard some times.' 'Ben?' Ann sounded puzzled.

'Get a dog, not a cat – they're too unreliable.' Lydia swept on, ignoring Ann's surprised expression.

The idea appealed to Ann, the thought of something small and dependent upon her. 'I don't have enough to do, that's half my problem. I must think of something. It was bad enough after the kids left and there was just Ben and me, I was hardly overworked but now – it's worse . . .'

'Well, I wouldn't know. I'm not famous for doing housework. I've said to all my husbands, "I'll do whatever you like in bed but for goodness sake don't expect me to bear you brats or do the cleaning." I must say, they've all been most understanding on both counts.' She laughed her loud laugh.

Ann smiled at Lydia. The truth was that Lydia's house worked like clockwork, her dinners were always the best cooked, the most elegant. Lydia was a perfectionist in everything she did.

'I did wallow, though. Remember Judy Planter when her husband was killed in that car crash? She coped very well and was back to normal within a few weeks, not moping around like me for over a year!'

'Perhaps she didn't like her husband very much,' Lydia said practically.

'Oh, Lydia, what a thing to say. They always seemed very close.'

'*Seemed* could be the operative word.' Lydia's loud laugh rang out again. Her laugh punctuated everything she said like a living exclamation mark. It should have grated, but instead Ann found it endearing. 'You're a more sensitive soul, that's all.'

'I think, with me . . . it was . . .' Ann searched for the words to describe how she had felt. 'It was physical, that shock, not just mental. I felt as if I'd been knocked out, it was as if I had concussion for all those months.'

'But you've made a total recovery, that's the important thing, love.'

Ann smiled ruefully. 'About bloody time. Grief is such a selfish thing, Lydia, you really don't care about anyone else.'

'I can imagine. I know divorce doesn't compare but in a way it's a kind of bereavement too, isn't it, grieving for lost dreams and hopes? My first divorce I was in a dreadful state, wandering about like a zombie for ages, totally self-centred. Then the second time, being acclimatized, it wasn't nearly as bad. Now I think if George and I split up I'd be right as rain by the weekend.' Lydia snorted with amusement.

'Lydia, don't you even dare think of such a thing. George is a darling, I couldn't bear it if anything happened to you two. You're so perfect together.'

'Because the silly old codger lets me get on with my own life and boss him around.'

'No, I realized ages ago that's just a game you two play.'

'Blast, found out.' Lydia guffawed, knocking back the remains of her drink. 'Changing the subject, would you like to come to dinner on Saturday? Very small. The new people from the Mill House. They're good fun, she paints and really well. He's an accountant but quite amusing despite that. One of George's old army friends is coming to stay. He's just got divorced,' she said meaningfully.

'Trust you, Lydia!' Ann laughed. 'I could have bet money you'd be the first to start matchmaking.'

'Ann, you've got it all wrong. As if I would do anything so heavy-handed! Me? All I meant was that he would be miserable too.'

'No you didn't, you were meddling,' Ann chuckled.

Lydia grinned sheepishly. 'Oh, all right, I confess, but it was only a little try. I just can't bear the idea of a good woman like you, and a good man like him, going to waste. I mean a little fling would do you the world of good.'

Ann thought a moment. 'That's a strange idea, you know. I just can't see myself with another man.'

'Rubbish. You can't live alone for ever. And after all . . .' She paused, looking at Ann curiously. 'I mean, you must get the odd twinge, surely?'

'Twinge? What are you talking about now, for heaven's sake?'

'You know, lovely – sex. You remember – nooky, screwing, call it what you will. I mean, surely you can't possibly have a regular diet of it and then have it suddenly stopped without the old body giving you the odd twinge to remind you.'

'Trust you to ask.' Ann chuckled. 'I admit I used to wonder how widows coped. But, you know, it isn't a problem. I rarely think about it.'

'Heavens, if I was in your shoes I wouldn't think about anything else. I'd be going bonkers by now.'

'Perhaps sex is more important to you. In the past, if Ben had to go away on one of his trips, it never bothered me. After all, sex is only a small and rather unimportant part of a relationship.'

'Small part,' Lydia shrieked. 'I don't believe it. George thinks you're such a sexy bundle, too.'

'Me? You're joking.' Ann's astonishment at such an idea sounder in her voice. A 'sexy bundle' was a description of someone young, she thought, but Ann had never, at any time in her life, regarded herself as sexy. She had always endeavoured to look smart – Ben had set great store on neatness. When she had looked into a mirror it was to make certain her seams were straight, her make-up matt, her hair tidy. Even now, with Ben gone, these were the criteria she looked for. And although she realized, from the waistbands of her skirts, that she was losing weight, she did not look at herself in terms of physical attractiveness. She was therefore blithely unaware that she was emerging from her grief with a good figure and that, with the fining down of her face, she was evolving into a beautiful woman whom Lydia longed to advise on make-up and clothes.

Ann looked sad, and suddenly burst out. 'No, it's not sex I miss. You know what I really miss? Being cuddled. At night in bed, it's so empty and he's not there to snuggle up against like spoons in a cutlery drawer.'

'Ann, I'm so sorry. I should never have asked you. My bloody big mouth, forgive me,' Lydia exclaimed, concerned.

'I'm all right, Lydia. It's good for me to talk, that's what I need now. And I love the way you say exactly what you're thinking, you're the one who does. Don't you ever change.' She smiled at her friend.

'Well then. What about this dinner?'

'It's very kind of you, but not just yet. I'm having problems enough relating to people I know let alone meeting new ones.'

'I suppose you know best, but . . . oh, well, next time. You will stay to dinner tonight, though? George will hit the roof if I let you go.'

As so often recently, Ann found herself staying the evening. But after this particular visit she lay in her bed, unable to sleep, thinking about sex. She herself had wondered whether this strange restless boredom she was experiencing was something to do with it. But she had rejected the idea for she had spoken the truth to Lydia. Sex never had been important. She had enjoyed it but in the last few years when Ben seemed to have lost interest, this had not bothered her unduly. So she had not given a thought to another man in her life. What was the need? She had money, a beautiful home – she didn't need sex. She lacked companionship, she decided, the sort of quiet companionship that grows over the years within a good marriage. That would be difficult to replace. No, the idea of another man was a pointless preoccupation.

She started going to church again, less for the solace of religion, for her faith had taken a hideous blow from which she doubted it would ever recover, but more because it was part of a comfortable routine from the past. She finally enjoyed a couple of sherry parties in the village, even though everyone was a little too solicitous, telling her to sit down all the time, as if she were an invalid, as if by taking the weight off her feet she could ease the ache in her soul.

She was pleased with her progress as she experimented with living again. And, while she was certain her loneliness would never go away, she felt that she could learn to live with it – it had become second nature to her so that she could no longer remember not being lonely. It was as if this loneliness had always been part of her and had only been biding its time before it revealed itself.

At last she was able to sort through Ben's things. She bundled his clothes up for Oxfam, all except the old jacket that she still took to bed with her.

Picking up the threads of her life, she discovered, was like doing a large jigsaw puzzle. Slowly and inevitably the pieces began to fall into place. Each day now she allowed herself the hope that she could survive without Ben.

4

Ann sat at the pine table in the cluttered and unfinished kitchen of her son's house, and felt sad. They had once been such a close and loving family, but now the ties of childhood had been broken, her children seemed to have bolted from her, as fast as they could. She had become used to seeing them rarely, and to feeling grateful when she did.

She watched her daughter. How slim and smart Fay was – so immaculately groomed that everything about her shone as if newly polished, even the dark, intelligent eyes. Such a self-assured young woman, so unlike the shy and introverted child she once had been. It always amazed Ann that she could have produced this elegant, confident creature. Like her twin brother, Fay was ambitious with a single-mindedness that fascinated Ann since she herself had never had any ambition at all. All she had wanted was to marry and raise a family – a role that was now defunct. Though she did not understand Fay, Ann could envy her. She envied the self-confidence and independence, but most of all she envied her daughter's job. After the Slade everyone had presumed that Fay would gravitate to the world of theatre and films; instead she had opted for the competitive and hectic world of commercial design. One month she could be working on the interior of a boardroom in Manhattan, the next in the searing desert heat as she planned a sheik's palace. Fay lived in a welter of fabrics, woods, paint, fine crystal and colour – a job that Ann instinctively knew she too would have enjoyed. But it seemed a price was being exacted for this glamorous career, for there was an edginess and brittleness about Fay which frequently worried her mother. She had never been as close to Fay as she had been to her son, but there were times now when she felt that between them there was a barrier, like a shield of plate glass through which Ann could not pass but could only observe.

Peter laughed. Ann jumped with surprise. Peter's laugh was a rare sound these days. They might be twins and share the same dark hair and colouring – so unlike her own – but in character they were totally different. Fay had been the quiet one while Peter was always the extrovert of the family. A noisy, delightful boy to whom life was an endless joke. But it was a long time since he had been like that. These days he had a sour and brooding expression, and Ann's sadness was that she did not know why and felt too distant from him to ask. He should be happy: he had this house, a wedding present from Ben and herself; he had a good degree; his Ph.D. had been well received; he was now a junior lecturer in Economics, it would surprise no one if he were offered a Fellowship at his college. Then why the look of discontent? Perhaps he was unhappy with Sally. Ann tried to suppress the little glimmer of excitement and hope that this thought gave her. That was no way to think! How could she wish the misery of divorce on her son, especially now that they had told her there might be another baby on the way? Nervously she lit another cigarette.

Sally had been just one of a long parade of girls whom Peter had brought home. She was quieter and less attractive than most of his girlfriends, and at first no one in the family had taken her seriously. Ann had put her lack of co-operation down to the thoughtlessness of youth, and her silence to shyness, but as the months passed she was forced to the unpleasant conclusion that the girl did not wish to be friends – least of all with Ann. There were times, it seemed, when those large, dark brown eyes surveyed her with a challenge in them.

Ann's relationship with her son had always been a warm, affectionate one, and it had surprised her that Peter should be attracted to someone so cold and undemonstrative. Ann had not worried too much: at twenty-one her son had been too young and too fond of the girls to contemplate marriage. She was certain the affair would never last.

It had been difficult, therefore, to appear pleased when Peter, who seemed blithely unaware of the animosity building between his girlfriend and his mother, announced he was going to marry Sally.

Confident in the closeness of their family, Ann had always smugly presumed that, when this day came, she would be pleased to welcome a new member to it. Unfortunately, the one thing she had not prepared herself for was the possibility that her son would marry a woman whom she disliked and who in turn disliked her, someone whose last wish, it seemed, was to become part of the Grange family.

The wedding had been large, white and formal and the only one Ann had ever attended, where she longed for someone to find some 'just cause or impediment'.

There had been no row. Nothing had been said. Sally was never rude but when Ann and Ben called on the young couple Sally's welcome was sufficiently cool to make certain that they soon stopped calling. For the first year Peter would drop into his old home fairly frequently. If Ann invited them to dinner or for a family celebration Peter would always arrive alone, the excuses for Sally's absence so weak that Ann was almost relieved when he stopped making them: it was less embarrassing all round. Since any invitation to their house was never forthcoming, Ann learned to cherish the hour or two Peter spent with her. But the visits became fewer and fewer and there were times when she felt almost as if the meetings were clandestine. It had become the custom for neither of them to mention his wife. Ann was frightened to discuss her in case she said too much and risked losing her son for ever.

For months after the wedding she had worried, analysed and fretted over what was happening. Ben's attitude had been quite straightforward – Sally was a spoilt, unpleasant little bitch whom he had not liked in the first place and just because she had married his son he could see no reason why he should change his attitude towards her. As to his son, Ben had died regarding Peter as weak and ungrateful.

'You have to let them go. They're not children any more, they're adults now,' Ben had said, brusquely, one night when Ann once again had raised the subject. She was hurt by his words.

'But I don't want to keep them. I just don't want to lose either of them. And suddenly, it seems, it's all over. I'm not needed any more. There are barriers between us. And I don't know what I've done wrong.'

She could see herself now, in her mind's eye, quite clearly, standing in the middle of their drawing room, the tears beginning to tumble down her face.

'Pull yourself together, Ann, for Christ's sake. I've had a pig of a day. The last thing I need is your histrionics about that ungrateful little beast. Kids grow up!'

'I know, I know! But does that mean they have to stop loving you, seeing you?'

'Perhaps they never loved you,' her husband had snapped.

'Ben, how could you say such a thing? I can't believe that. I won't. I know they loved me, especially Peter.'

'Well, he doesn't appear to any more.'

More tears poured down her cheeks. 'Then where has all that love gone?' she implored.

'You didn't so much love them as smother them. No wonder they wanted to get away from us,' Ben snapped.

'That's a cruel thing to say, Ben.' She wiped her eyes. 'How could this be happening to me?' she said, more to herself than to him.

Ben suddenly seemed to regret his words, crossed the room and put his arm about her. 'Oh come on, Ann, you mustn't let yourself get this upset. You've always got me, haven't you?' He had put his arm about her. 'There's no point in us rowing about it, is there? It's you and me now.'

He was right: there was no point in their falling out. It was then that she had firmly resolved to bury the hurt. She had made herself get on with her own life and fill the void which the children's going had created by concentrating entirely on her husband – but now he was dead, and she felt completely alone.

She looked about the table. It seemed a happy enough gathering. Maybe she had been invited to try to mend the rift with Sally, make a new start in their relationship. Certainly, since Ben had died they had been good to her – all of them. Why, she had seen far more of them than she had for a long time. Fay had come down from London for several weekends, Peter had often popped in and Sally had done her shopping and cooked the odd meal. Then the tables had turned on them during the worst of her grief when she had not wanted them near her. But now? She looked at the three of them, her children talking earnestly about politics, Sally clearing the dishes . . . but the thought persisted – what was she really doing here?

'Brandy anyone?' Peter asked.

'Lovely,' Ann replied, lighting another cigarette.

'You smoke too much, Mother.'

'Not smoking didn't do your father much good, did it?'

Their collective embarrassment hung in the air. She was sorry for the remark, it had been meant as a joke and as such she realized it was in dubious taste. 'If I didn't smoke or drink I think I'd go mad these days!' She smiled. They looked even more embarrassed and turned hurriedly back to their conversation.

It annoyed her how freely they talked amongst themselves and yet when they spoke with her it was as if they weighed each word carefully – no one but she had mentioned Ben. She did not know if this was to protect her or themselves.

She watched her children. How silly it was to continue to think of them as children now that they were adults. Would she go to her grave referring to her 'children'?

'You look very thoughtful, Mummy.' Fay smiled at her, almost guiltily, as if she had suddenly realized that they had been leaving Ann out.

'I think a lot these days, Fay. I never did before . . . Sometimes I didn't know what I really thought about something until I actually said it.' She laughed, re-arranging the cutlery before her. 'But now . . .'

'And what were you thinking about so hard this time?'

Ann toyed with her spoon, uncertain what their reaction to her thoughts might be. 'I was thinking how sad it is that we all seem to have drifted so far apart. I used to have a family, now I don't seem to have anything.'

An awkward silence greeted her words.

'Now, come on, Mum, don't get maudlin,' protested Peter, eventually. 'Of course you still have us.'

'Do I? I don't think so, Peter. I sense a distance that has built up in the past few years – it wasn't there before. I look at you both and I can't even seem to see any of your father in you – you might look like him, but that's all. There's nothing of his character in you, it seems. It

31

would be nice if there was, then it wouldn't seem as if he had gone for ever,' she continued relentlessly, turning her spoon first one way then the other, concentrating on its shiny bowl rather than look at the faces of her children.

'I think we should change the subject, Mummy. You'll get upset talking like this,' Fay said, concerned.

'But I don't want to change the subject, I want to talk about him, especially to you both who knew and loved him.' Ann finally looked up at them, the urgency in her voice reflected by the expression in her eyes.

'Mum, you've had a rough time. You're doing so well, Fay's right, let's drop it, there's a good girl.' She felt a flutter of irritation as Peter spoke to her as if she were the child.

'I don't wish to "drop it".' She heard the slight shrillness in her voice which she could not control and which made her children look up sharply. 'For goodness sake, are we to spend the rest of our lives never talking about your father?'

'You've got to look forward, Mum, not back,' Peter said, with exaggerated patience in his tone.

'I'm sick to death of platitudes. Not you too, please. Surely you can understand how I feel? How can I not look back? Ben was my life for twenty-five years. He filled every waking hour of my day. Everything I ever did was for him, and I'm supposed to forget and not talk about him? You might just as well ask me not to remember or talk about my own life!' Her voice had thickened with emotion. She had to make them understand. It would be as if she had lost them for ever if she could not get through to them now.

'I think you should let your mother talk if she wants to,' Ann was astonished to hear Sally say. 'She's right, you can't just turn your back on all those years. And why should Ben be swept under the carpet as if he had never existed? For good or bad he did.' Sally leaned, almost nonchalantly, against the dresser as she spoke.

32

'You keep out of this, Sally. It's none of your bloody business,' Peter snapped angrily.

'Suit yourself.' Sally shrugged, stood up straight, and collected the rest of the plates. 'We all know how endearingly selfish you are, Peter, but just for once can't you forget how you feel about your father and help your mother you profess to love so much?' she said, over her shoulder, as she crossed to the sink.

'You bitch!'

'Peter!' Ann said, shocked. 'You mustn't talk to Sally like that. She was only trying to help.'

'Was she, Mother? You sure?'

'Of course I'm sure. That was unwarranted.'

'Pete, Sally,' Fay pleaded, a deep frown momentarily marring her face. 'I think we should be careful . . .'

'What do you mean, careful?' Ann asked, quickly.

'I just meant, Mummy, that if people start losing their tempers things could be said that we might regret.'

'What sort of things?'

'Nothing, Mummy.'

'Nothing!' Sally snorted in a derisory way. 'That's a laugh!'

'I warn you, Sally. Just shut your mouth.' Peter glowered, across the room, at his wife. The unfinished row simmered, frustrated in the air.

'I don't understand. What's going on?' Ann asked puzzled.

'Honest, Mum, nothing. Come on, let's have our coffee in the sitting room,' Peter said, getting up and leading the way, followed by Fay.

'I'll help you with the dishes, Sally,' Ann volunteered.

'It's all right, you needn't bother. I've got a dishwasher now – at last,' Sally said.

'They are wonderful machines, aren't they?' Ann attempted to make conversation, as she cleared the last of the meal. 'Sally, what was all that about?'

'You heard Peter, nothing,' Sally said without turning, continuing to load the machine.

'There must be something. Are you two all right, Sally?'

'What do you mean?' Still Sally's back was turned.

'I mean is everything all right between you and Peter? Can I help?' She felt awkward to be asking her daughter-in-law such personal questions.

At last Sally turned and looked at her. 'I don't think my affairs are any of your business, Mrs Grange, do you?' Her voice echoed the cold expression in her eyes. Ann stepped back, involuntary, to escape the icy stare.

'I didn't mean to pry. I just . . . couldn't you call me Ann, after all these years?'

'If you wish,' Sally said in an expressionless voice.

'I've always wanted you to.' Ann stood feeling rather ridiculous in the middle of the kitchen, a dishcloth in her hand. 'Would it be all right if I crept up to see Adam? I haven't seen him for months.'

'If you must. But please don't wake him. He's hell to get back to sleep again.'

With relief Ann left the kitchen and the malevolent atmosphere that Sally seemed so expert at creating. Upstairs she quietly opened the nursery door and crept across the bed where Adam, her only grandchild, slept. She smiled at the ungainly bundle lying in the cot. His bottom stuck in the air, his face turned to one side, thumb and comforter firmly placed in his mouth. Despite Sally's warning she gently twisted the child round, enjoying the feel of his warm, solid little body, inhaling the sweet young child smell of him, and then re-covered him. He did not wake, merely clutched the comforter to him and immediately rolled over and stuck his backside up in the air again. Ann laughed, softly, despite a lump in her throat. It was sad that she saw so little of him, especially now when she needed her family. Quietly she left the room, and entered the bathroom and hurriedly repaired her make-up. She did not know why but it was important that tonight she should look her best.

Ann opened the door of the sitting room in time to hear Peter say, 'Well, someone's got to tell her . . .' but he stopped in mid-sentence as she appeared. Fay beckoned her to a chair by the fire.

'I've saved this one for you, Mummy.'

'So, Peter, what have I got to be told? I assume you were referring to me,' she said without preamble, accepting a cup of coffee from Sally.

'Well, if you think you would like to hear . . . ?'

'Of course.'

'We've been talking and we think you should sell the house.'

'We?'

'Fay and I.'

'Hang on, you've only just this minute mentioned it to me,' Fay butted in.

'Well, you agreed, didn't you?'

'In principle, but I would need to know how Mother feels.'

'Thank you, Fay, that's very considerate of you,' said Ann, unaware how sarcastic she sounded. She sipped her coffee, biding her time, for she suddenly felt threatened, the atmosphere oppressively charged.

'It's far too big for you, Mother.'

'I agree, Peter.'

'The garden is huge.'

'Yes, it is.'

'Good, so you'll sell it then? I've a friend who works for Hockeys, he says it's worth a bomb now, and sensibly invested . . .'

'So you've talked to an agent?'

'Just in passing. They'd be very happy to handle it for you.'

'I'm sure they would, but no thank you.'

'You mean you'd like another agent to deal with it?'

'No, Peter, I mean I don't wish to sell.'

'Why on earth not?' demanded Peter.

'Because I don't want to.' Carefully she replaced her coffee cup and saucer on the table, not trusting herself to hold it without making it rattle.

'But the maintenance must be enormous.'

'It is, but I can afford it.'

'But think of what you would save,' Peter persisted.

'What for?'

'You could take nice holidays.'

'I can do that already.'

'Well, for you old age then.'

'Are you sure you don't want me to sell it for *your* old age?' Ann snapped, her patience rapidly disappearing. Three pairs of eyes looked at her with astonishment: they were not used to her taking the offensive.

'Mummy,' said Fay, 'that's an awful thing to say.'

'Is it? I think in the circumstances it's a perfectly reasonable question. I love the house, you both know that. I don't want to live anywhere else. I can well afford it, so what reason is there for me to sell?'

'I know you love it, Mummy. But it does seem a bit unhealthy mooning about in that enormous house on your own. And you could buy a nice little cottage in the village . . .' Fay continued.

'And see strangers in my house? No thank you.'

'Well, a cottage somewhere else . . .'

'It's not so easy to make friends as you get older, you know. I really would get morose then.'

'Forget it, Fay, there's no point in beating about the bush,' Peter interrupted impatiently. 'No, Mother, I'm not thinking about my old age. I'm thinking about now, if you want to know. I'll be honest with you – it was one hell of a shock to find that Father had left Fay and me out of his will . . .'

'Peter! You speak for yourself. It doesn't bother me!' Fay shouted at her brother, reddening with embarrassment at the tack the conversation was taking.

'Bully for you, Fay.' Sally spoke bitterly. 'You haven't got a child and another on the way. And look at how much you earn with only yourself to think about. Of course it's all right for you. Do you know what Peter earns? Do you know what we exist on, yes, exist – it's hardly living.'

'No one asked him to be an academic, and you knew the score when you married him. I'm sure if he got off his arse and went out into industry he could double if not treble his salary. But of course there wouldn't be so much kudos in that, would there?' Fay retorted with an equal amount of spirit.

'Selfish bitch!' Sally said, quietly, but loudly enough for Ann to hear.

'For goodness sake, can't we discuss this without the conversation deteriorating into a brawl?' Ann said, exasperated, her sadness at what was happening swamped by the anger she was beginning to feel. 'Right, Peter, you think it was unfair that your father left you no money, and you think it is unfair of me to continue to live in my home?'

'Yes.' Peter glowered.

'Have you thought this is what your father wants? You'd no right to expect anything, you know how your father feels that inherited wealth stultifies people? He gave you this house . . .'

'I knew that would come up . . .' Sally sneered.

'He gave you this house,' Ann pointedly repeated. 'And obviously he knows how strongly I feel about the house and he wants me to stay there . . .'

'*Knew*, Mother, *wanted*! He's bloody dead, don't you understand, dead!' Peter shouted loudly. Ann reeled back from the anger in his voice.

'I think it's time I left,' she said, in a subdued voice, getting quickly to her feet.

'Mummy, you can't go like this,' Fay said concerned.

'Yes, I can, Fay. I'm getting tough, these days.'

'We've noticed!' her daughter-in-law interjected.

In the hall, with shaking fingers, Ann buttoned her coat. She returned to the sitting room where the others seemed frozen in the same positions, like children playing statues. 'Such a shame that the evening should end like this,' she said, opening the briefcase she had brought with her and removing a sheaf of papers. 'I'd planned this as a surprise for you. Silly of me that I didn't

37

mention it earlier – think of all the bother we would have been saved. I've put a large insurance policy your father left me into a discretionary trust for all my grandchildren born or unborn. The income will be divided between you and Fay, Peter. It's primarily for their education. Or you can spend it on cars, pictures, furniture, anything that can be regarded as an object. You can't take holidays or buy food with it. If Fay has no children, then the whole lot reverts to your children, Peter. You see, I knew your father wasn't leaving you anything. I was shocked too. I argued with him but he wouldn't listen to me. This seemed the fair thing to do.'

She wouldn't have been human if she had not enjoyed the look of shamed astonishment on all their faces. 'If you could both sign these documents and send them to the lawyer . . . Thank you for a lovely dinner, Sally.' She turned to go.

'Mother, what can I say? Oh, Christ, I'm so sorry.'

'Yes, Peter, I expect you are.' She smiled her sweet smile and let herself out of the room.

5

The following morning Ann lay in bed listening to Meg enthusiastically hoovering downstairs. In the days just after Ben's death she had often lain in bed half the day, but she had pulled herself together since then, making herself get up early even if she had nothing to do, for she knew the risk to her spirit if she hid away. But today she felt a new grief, if not as strong, sufficiently daunting for her to want to face anyone.

Last night had shocked her. To her son she was a source of money, no longer of love. She remembered a friend with a wealthy mother and how he would often refer with longing to the day when he would get his 'black-edged telegram'. She had laughed with the rest at his cynicism, little thinking that either of her children would ever regard her in such a light. Was that how they had viewed Ben? Had he been nothing but a cheque book, a collection of insurance policies, a repository of expectations to her son? She was certain Fay felt differently – Fay had adored her father. In fact, if anyone had asked Ann which of her children loved her most, she would, without thinking, have said Peter. Now she knew that this was not so.

All that investment of love, and what was she left with? A sad emptiness, a feeling of loss almost as if Peter had died too. For so long all she had thought was necessary to receive love was to give it in abundance. It was all so simple: 'nothing to bringing up children', she had said. She laughed to herself. 'Well, that's you wrong again, Ann Grange!'

She stirred in the bed. And Fay? She had loved Fay but to be honest she had to admit that it was her son she had favoured as Ben had favoured his daughter. She had regarded that as perfectly normal. Dear God, now she was to rely on the child who probably thought she had been neglected by her mother!

Perhaps if he had not married Sally, things would have been different. Or was she committing the crime of an over-indulgent mother, searching for a scapegoat for the horrible reality that her son was not as she had thought and would have behaved this way no matter whom he had married?

'Ben, Ben, God how I wish you were here . . .' she sighed and turned her face into the pillow where he should have been. She lay there allowing the longing for him to wash over her. She had learned that the easiest way at moments like this was to ride the wave of grief just as a woman in labour rode the wave of pain. As with the pangs of birth so with her grief – if she fought it she found the hurt was stronger. The moment faded.

Sell this house! It was an impossible idea. She had not even told them last night that, if the house was security for her, within it was a greater emblem of security – this huge, impractical, beautiful bed. Ben had been such a predictable individual who lived his life to such a rigid routine that she had been surprised, one anniversary, returning from the hairdresser's, to find him standing in the hall and behaving like an over-excited schoolboy. He had led her upstairs, insisted she close her eyes and had then shown her this wonderful, four-poster bed, with its beautiful gold and cream silk curtains. Used to either cheques or flowers for presents, usually sent by his secretary, she was overwhelmed by this gesture, the unexpected romanticism. '. . . Move into a cottage . . .' Fay had suggested. How could she ever move into a cottage? She would never give up her bed and as it would never fit into a cottage she would have to stay where she was and they would have to put up with it.

Yes, no question. She swung her legs over the side of the bed. They would just have to wait until she was senile or dead before they got a hand on a penny more. At least she now knew where she stood. So, she was alone, thousands of women were alone. She would do something, get a job, take a course. She would cease being lonely!

She quickly showered and dressed and raced down the stairs to Meg. 'Sorry, Meg, I felt lazy, just couldn't get up.'

'A lie-in never hurt anyone, Mrs Grange. I expect you were tired after the excitement of going to your Peter's.'

'You're probably right, Meg.' She smiled with affection at the stout little woman who had been such a friend to her. 'Mind you, I can't imagine you ever indulging in a lie-in.'

'Well, I don't like bed myself. Beds are for sleeping in and being ill in, and since I'm never ill I just sleep in mine. But I have heard tell that lie-ins can be nice.'

'Mrs Webster's coming for lunch. I quite forgot, mooning away up there. Do you know if I have any steak or something like that?'

'If you ate properly, Mrs Grange, you would know, wouldn't you?'

'Yes, Meg. I know.'

'Too many sandwiches can't be good for a body.'

'No, Meg,' Ann said obediently.

'I do know your Sally put some fillet steak in the freezer when you didn't fancy shopping. And there's plenty of salad and I could always make you one of my nice vegetable soups if you wanted?'

'That's kind, Meg, but you've enough to do.'

In the kitchen she found a tin of consommé far more to Lydia's taste than one of Meg's hearty vegetables soups made so thick the spoon stood up in them. Meg, having lit the fires, and been assured that there was nothing else she need do, waddled off home.

Lydia arrived punctually, immaculate in tweeds which hung sveltely on her slim body. Her blonde hair, its colour helped these days by the hairdresser's skills, was beautifully cut, so that fronds of it caressed her cheek, accentuating the fine bones. She engulfed Ann in an expensive-smelling embrace.

'You look well, Ann,' she purred. 'The weight's just falling off you, isn't it? You ought to go to my hairdresser, you know.' She looked closely at Ann with the expert, sweeping gaze of a beautiful woman sufficiently confident of her own charms to take an almost professional interest in the appearance of other women.

'I do seem to be losing weight. I'd have thought I'd be putting it on.'

'What? On a diet of sandwiches and gin.'

'How did you know?'

'It's what any sensible woman does in a catastrophe, straight to the gin. Speaking of which?' She archly raised her eyebrows.

'So what's your excuse?' Ann laughed at her.

'I always maintain that my life is one dreadful balls-up from one day to the next and then people automatically think – "must give the poor bitch a drink".' Her loud laugh rang out as Ann busied herself with mixing their drinks. 'So, how was last night at the dreaded Sally's?' Ann pulled a face at the question. 'Bad as that?'

41

'Worse!' Ann, at length, began to tell her friend who sat silently listening. 'This morning I was thinking about it all and suddenly I thought nothing is really different – only me. I've come out of my fog, and I suppose I expected everything to be the same, but it can't be, can it? I'm different. I think I feel surprise more than anything.'

'I'm not surprised at all. I have to be honest, Ann, I've always thought Peter completely self-centred.'

'My biggest shock is, I don't think I like him much. I think I still love him, I suppose nothing can stop that. Do you know what I mean?'

'Luckily, no, never having had children. But I don't think it's dreadful. There must be masses of parents who can't stand their offspring.' She waved her glass expectantly in the air. Ann refilled it.

'But Fay seems just as distant.'

'Of course you're having to deal with one hell of a lot of jealousy flying around, aren't you? You've got that sweet charming Sally crazed with jealousy over you. You've got Fay probably resentful that you loved Peter more. And Peter, who always hated Ben, is left with no money, and no father still to hate. Christ, it's positively Russian in its dark complexities.' She hooted with laughter again.

'Jealousy?' Ann asked, amazed.

'Of course, it's rife in all families. Always carries on beyond the grave. Gracious, a death in the family is an ideal time for all the nasty emotions to come crawling out of the woodwork. Christmas too, it happens then, doesn't it? I hardly know of a family that doesn't have the most stupendous rows over Christmas.'

'We didn't.'

'Then you're getting all the bottling up of the past years in one go.'

'Seems you can't win as a parent.'

'Good Lord, no. If you love them too much you're smothering and destroying them and they want to get away. If you don't love them enough then you've wounded them and given the poor little brats a deprived psyche! I tell you, the things I see I'm bloody relieved I was never a parent. I think it has to be the most unrewarding job in life – divine when they're little, a pain in the arse when they grow up.'

'Lydia!' Ann laughed. 'You're so good for me. You know I never wanted or needed to confide in anyone in my life before, there was always Ben, but now . . . I don't know what I'd do without you.' Tears sprang to her eyes.

'Hey, come on, don't you cry. You'll start me off, and my eyelashes need dyeing and I had to use mascara this morning,' Lydia airily announced. 'But bless you, Ann. I think you're the only person who has ever confided in me. Most people run a mile. I'm honoured, you know,' she added, for once serious.

'Lunch?' They made their way into the kitchen, the dining room seeming too formal. They chatted non-stop of this and that and the time passed so quickly that Ann felt almost surprised when Lydia announced she had to go.

'You listen to Aunty Lydia. Let the little monster stew. If you want to keep this house, then keep it. You think of number one for a change. It's the only way to survive, and that's the name of the game.' And with a squealing of tyres she was gone.

6

In the past neither Ann herself nor anyone who knew her would have regarded her as a strong person. Her friends would have described her as easy-going, kind or compliant rather than strong. For Ann's life had been an easy one and she had not needed the reserves of strength most people have to call upon to survive. After the first years of marriage, when being hard up had almost seemed a game for them to play, money had not been lacking in her life; her children had never been seriously ill; her husband had not beaten her, been a drunk, spendthrift or gambler. Her worries had been restricted to what she should cook for dinner, whom to invite, what seeds to plant this year, and in what style to wear her hair.

But, unknown to everyone, not least herself, within Ann was a great pool of strength, totally untapped, which now, first with Ben's death and then her son's attitude, she began to draw from like a prudent nomad at his well.

She wished, in the days after the family row, that she could have seen Fay. There were things she would like to clarify. She phoned Fay but she was abroad.

Peter called once, inviting her to his house to 'talk things over'.

'Not yet, Peter. Next month perhaps, I'm very busy at the moment,' she replied hurriedly, knowing that it was too soon for her to return to his house and Sally's cold presence. It was one thing to rationalize how she felt on her own ground, but back on enemy territory, this new-found strength might desert her; she could not be sure how she would feel, and was not prepared to risk losing it.

'Doing what?' She could hear the disbelief in his voice.

'I've got stuck in to the garden. It really has become a shameful tangled mess. I can't think what your father would say if he could see it.'

'I'd have thought it was more important to see me and sort things out than fiddle around with your bloody garden.'

'It depends really on what it is you want to talk about. If it's to nag me to sell the house, then thank you, Peter, I'd rather do my garden.'

'No, it's not that. You're right, we *have* drifted apart. I'd like to see you, that's all.'

'Fine, then pop over whenever you want. And why not bring Adam? I'd love to see more of him.'

Later, as she worked in the garden, she grudgingly admitted to herself that she did not care whether or not Peter came. It was Adam she really wanted to see.

The following weekend, Peter and Adam visited her. She was happy as she prepared a nursery tea. It was a long time since she had needed to make jelly, trifle and chocolate sponge. When they arrived, it was Peter who seemed nervous and awkward. Ann kissed him warmly and hugged Adam hard. In the drawing room she had a box of Peter's toys which she had unearthed from the attic and which Adam swooped upon. The toys saved the afternoon, for mother and son, unsure of what to say to each other, talked about the toys and the afternoon rang with 'do you remember'. As they left Ann promised Adam, faithfully, that she would be at his birthday party in December.

It had not been a lie to say there was much to do in her neglected garden. The weather was on her side as each day dawned with bright autumnal sunshine. She did not garden so much as attack. Weeds were pulled, undergrowth hacked, anything that could be pruned was pruned to its limits. The leaves were swept, the compost scattered, the lawn was treated, the bulbs were planted, and each day a bonfire celebrated the scope of her efforts.

At first she had ached from head to toe with the unusual exercise. Ben had always done the hard work, saying it was the only exercise he got. She had always been the planner and weed picker of their team. It had been her especial delight to plan the garden. The beds were planted in carefully selected colour graduations. Frequently Ann used unusual combinations of colour, planting scarlet asters mixed with purple and cerise. She mixed oranges with pinks, yellows with blues. Her special pride was the area she had designated for every shade of white, cream and silver. The Grange garden was famous in the area for the colour mixes that Ann had contrived.

As the days wore on she found she ached less and she could tackle more. Each evening after a long bath, she would fall into a deep sleep, too tired to think or to worry.

After several weeks of this regime the garden looked well and truly put to bed for the winter. She was almost sad when her task was finished and the garden slid into its deep winter sleep and she began immediately to long for spring and its reawakening. She was looking forward, she realized with a jolt – at last, she had a future again.

7

'Mrs Grange, you're a wonder!' Meg informed her one cold November morning, as they enjoyed a quick coffee break. 'That garden's going to be a treat next spring. And you've done it all on your own. A real treat it will look, you mark my words.'

'I didn't think I was going to manage it on my own, that garden had been sorely neglected. But I've really enjoyed myself, Meg. I feel sorry it's finished. Mind you, I wish it could have been kinder on my hands!' And she looked ruefully at her broken and grimy fingernails.

'Good soaking'll soon put them right. Wash a couple of sweaters in Lux, that's all they need. And what's a few broken nails when you see the good it's done you? We've got to think of what you can do now.' She folded her arms over her ample breasts, and looked sternly at Ann, like a bossy mother.

'I've got lots of plans.' Ann laughed at Meg's stern, no-nonsense expression. 'We'll start on the house.'

'But we've scrubbed it from top to toe.'

'I know, but now I want to decorate it. There's so much that could be done with this house. I've always longed to do it but my husband liked it just as it was. Also, I plan to turn Peter's old room into a studio. The light is good in there, and I'd like to try my hand at painting again.'

'I didn't even know you could paint, Mrs Grange.' Meg looked very impressed.

'I'm not very good. I used to dabble, years ago. But you know what it's like, Meg – with the family – I just never seemed to have the time to waste. But now . . . well, my time's my own, isn't it? I might even do a course, interior design, something like that. People say I'm good with colour.'

'Well I never! A course would be a very good idea. It would get you out and about . . . meet some people . . . some nice men . . . you never know.' She looked archly at Ann, an expression that was totally at odds with her homely, bulky appearance.

'Oh Meg! Don't be silly. I'm too old for that sort of thing.'

'Umph,' sounded Meg, sipping her coffee. 'You can't have been looking in your mirror for some time, that's for sure. I was saying to my Bill only the other day, that's a shocking waste of a very pretty lady, never going out nor nothing.'

'Meg, you'll make me blush. And I do go out, I'm very good now.'

'Yes, but you don't go to the right places. I mean, if you went to a nice dance or something . . .'

'Meg, sweetie, I don't think they have dances like we used to go to.' Ann laughed. 'And I don't see myself in a disco somehow! And I'm a bit past being picked up.'

'Don't you believe it. There are many woman your age would give anything to look like you. I know I would,' and Meg sighed and glowered at her thick and swollen ankles.

Later, Ann stood naked in front of her mirror, and studied herself. She had been rather pleased with Meg's compliments. She turned this way and that. Certainly her body had tightened up from her hectic gardening. Her skin was clear and glowed with health. The fresh air had made her eyes sparkle in a way they had not for a long time. She peered at her face closely: she had more lines. Had Ben's death caused them or had they appeared because her face was so much thinner? She did not mind them, rather she thought they made her face look more interesting – she had always felt she looked too bland. She liked her new slim figure, and she grinned at her reflection, amused by her new self-interest. It was time to get new clothes, she decided. What was the point of this new svelte body if it was disguised by loose clothing? She turned her attention to her hair – she would have to do something with it. It was too long now and, since it had no natural curl, tended to hang limply about he face unless she pinned it up in a bun. She had been growing it since Ben had died. He had been so angry when she had had it cut short, but she had liked it. Maybe she would have it short again. There was the odd grey hair too, she could not remember when they had appeared. She would ask Lydia for the name of her London hairdresser: if she was going to have it done she would go to the best.

She wrapped her dressing gown about her. Dear Meg, everything was so simple to her; if only she knew. She frowned at the memory of the large party she had gone to last week, at Sheila and Roger's, old friends. She had been enjoying herself until she had popped upstairs to the bathroom and had found Roger outside the door when she emerged. She had smiled at him and then . . . involuntarily, she wiped her mouth at the memory of his whisky-laden breath as he, clumsily, had tried to kiss her. She had laughed at first, thinking he was just tipsy and being silly. She stopped laughing as he grabbed her by the shoulders and pushed her firmly through a half-open door, and backwards across the room, finally throwing her roughly on to the bed where she sprawled amongst the coats piled high upon it. She had begun to feel rising terror as he tore at the buttons on the front of her dress and for the first she saw the blazing lust shining in his eyes.

'Bloody hell, Ann, don't act coy. Open your legs . . .' His voice came thickly as if he spoke through layers of cloth. His legs was pushing between hers, prising them open. She turned her head away and opened her mouth to scream but his large hand clamped firmly over it, suppressing all sound. She began to tear helplessly at his heavy body as he lunged on top of her, pinning her to the soft swelling bed.

'Come on, old girl, you must be desperate for it by now!' And he laughed. It was his laugh that had saved her, for it made her fear disappear to be replaced by a burning anger.

With ice-cold fury, she lifted her knee and with precision brought it up sharply.

'You filthy bastard!' she hissed at him as he rolled from her, his hands now safely between his legs as he grunted with pain, floundering about in agony. Desperately she searched through the coats for her own, throwing the others on the floor in her haste, and rushed from the house, saying goodbye to no one.

She had stopped the car once on the way home to vomit. Her hands were still shaking as she put the key into the lock, rushed upstairs and began to brush her teeth roughly. She had lain, sleepless, tossing from side to side, anger, hurt, indignation, sorrow and self-pity taking it in turns to ebb and flow through her mind. They had all been such good friends the four of them. Roger had spoilt everything.

At two the phone rang and a tearful, drunken Sheila began to scream at her, 'You filthy cow, you stinking bitch!'

'Sheila, I . . .'

'I don't want to hear any excuses from you, Roger has told me everything.' The tone of her voice changed to the whining wail of self-pity. 'Ann, how could you? We were friends!'

'But Sheila, you don't under—'

'Don't you bloody lie to me.' The screeching was back. 'Just because you couldn't keep your own husband there's no need to take other people's.' And before Ann could protest the line went dead. She lay frustrated that she couldn't explain. She picked up the phone to re-dial Sheila, but replaced the receiver. What was the point? The woman was too drunk to listen to reason and even if she were sober would she believe Ann rather than her husband?

No, she couldn't explain to Meg that that was the reason she had decided not to go to any large parties. Small dinner parties were safer. She slipped into her nightgown and into bed.

But was one ever safe? Just two days ago, Harry, their solicitor, had appeared at the door on his way home from work. Ann was surprised but pleased as she welcomed him and poured him a drink. They talked of nothing in particular until, suddenly, Harry stood up, his back to the fire, his thumbs looped into his waistcoat pockets.

'You look every inch the successful solicitor, now, Harry,' she remembered teasing him.

'I have something serious I want to discuss with you, Ann.' Ann looked at him expectantly. 'It's a bit difficult to put into words.' He paused. 'You see, I've been thinking . . .' Another pause, one which threatened to continue indefinitely.

'You've been thinking?' she said encouragingly.

'You know how marriages are, Ann. You know one gets a bit down in the dumps. It's the routine, really. Yes,' he nodded, 'the endless routine.'

'I'm not sure what you mean, Harry.'

'Boredom, I suppose. That's what I'm trying to describe. Familiarity and all that . . .' He drifted into an awkward silence.

'Do you mean you're not happy with Deidre?' she asked kindly.

'I'm not happy, but then I'm not unhappy. I'm just not as happy as I used to be. If you get my drift.'

'Oh, Harry, I'm so sorry. I'd no idea.'

'No, no one has . . . It's quite common, I gather. This sort of, well, restlessness,' he said, helpfully.

'Is it?' Ann asked, nonplussed.

Harry stood on her hearthrug, staring at a point a long way beyond her shoulder.

'I've given it a lot of thought and I really think the best solution is to have a mistress.'

'But, Harry,' Ann said with dismay, 'that wouldn't be right. I don't see how that can solve anything. I mean, if Deidre found out, your marriage would be in an even worse muddle.' She felt that 'muddle' was the only word possible to use as she watched Harry frowning into the middle distance as he struggled to unwrap the mystery of his thoughts.

'I would be very discreet, I've worked it all out, Deidre need never know. I have a little flat in town we could use whenever you could get away.'

' "Whenever I could get away . . ." Harry, I don't think I quite understand this conversation . . .' Ann looked at her hands with embarrassment mixed with a growing sense of anger.

'Sorry, typical of me I suppose. I'd planned everything I was going to say, too. I've always found you very attractive, and we get on so well, and, let's face it, with Ben gone you must get lonely, if you know what I mean. I'm not so bad-looking, am I? And I'd be very generous.'

Ann looked up sharply. He suddenly looked so silly, pompously swaying back and forth for all the world as if he was in court instead of her drawing room. She wanted to laugh at the absurdity of the situation, her amusement blowing away her initial anger. 'Harry, how could you? Harry, really!' she admonished. He began to look sheepishly at the floor, took his thumbs out of his pockets and, seeming not to know what to do with his hands which now hung limply at his sides, promptly put them back again.

'I don't wish to insult you or hurt your feelings, Ann, that's the last thing I want to do. I really am rather lonely, my marriage isn't all it seems and after all – merry widows and all that.' He smiled but to Ann his expression looked more like a leer. The situation seemed so funny that this time she could not stop herself from laughing.

'Harry, for an intelligent man, you can be very dumb!' she finally managed to say. 'Isn't it obvious that I'm not the "merry widow" type? Don't you realize that I can't ever imagine myself with another man – the idea is ludicrous to me. And why do men seem to think that widows are desperate for sex? I'm desperate for my husband, yes, but not sex!'

'I've made a fool of myself, haven't I?' Harry said, miserably staring at his shoes.

'Yes, Harry, you have. I've never heard such rubbish. You sound to me like a man who's reached the male menopause and that can be a dangerous time. Go home and we'll forget this ever happened. I'm too fond of you and Deidre to risk our friendship in this way. And I don't believe that your marriage is so bad that you can't do something to pep it up and get rid of your boredom. Really, Harry, what a thing to suggest.' Harry stood before her like a small schoolboy discovered scrumping apples. 'How would you feel if you discovered that Deidre was planning to take a lover?'

'Oh, I don't think she'd ever do anything like that!' He sounded affronted at the very idea.

'And what makes you so sure? I think you'd better get home now, don't you?' she said more kindly. Hurriedly he bundled himself into his coat.

'Ann, I don't know what to say!'

'Nothing, is the safest.'

At the door she kissed him gently on his cheek. But as she let him out she knew that another friendship had ended. She knew Harry too well, he would be too embarrassed to face her and so riddled with guilt that he would no doubt confess his thoughts to Deidre. And how would she feel it she were in Deidre's shoes? Bitter, probably.

Now, two days later, she lay in her bed, a lot more disillusioned than she thought possible and certainly no wiser.

8

Late on Friday night, Fay arrived. Inevitably, when the girl came, she slept the whole of Saturday, emerging in time for supper. This weekend was no exception.

'Recharging my batteries', she called it but Ann could not help worrying about what stress she must be under to need a sleep of such abnormal length to recover.

'It's unhealthy, sleeping that long.'

'I must need it or I wouldn't do it, would I?' Fay smiled patiently at her frowning mother across the dining table, the debris from the meal still surrounding them, as they enjoyed a port with their Stilton.

'But what do you get up to that makes you so tired?'

'It's a demanding job, Mummy. I do it wholeheartedly, and then, wham, I just need a good sleep.'

'Probably play wholeheartedly too!'

'Mummy, you're sounding middle-aged and crabby.'

'Hardly surprising, I am middle-aged.' Ann sipped her port thoughtfully. 'You know, Fay, I just don't know where all the years have gone. Apart from having you two and being married to Ben, what the hell have I done with my life?'

'That's menopausal talk.'

'Shut up!' She playfully aimed a bread roll at her daughter. 'Why is it when a woman of my age starts to think about her life, everyone thinks she's menopausal? As far as I can make out your generation do nothing else but think of themselves and their role in the scheme of things.'

'Touché, Mummy.'

'With your father dying, it's inevitable, isn't it, that I should think of what's been and what's to come? I just seem to have drifted through life. Why, it's only since Ben died I've even had to pay household bills, he did all that. I'm like a child really. You know more about life than I do.'

'But that's to do with generations, Mummy. Things were different when you were young.'

'No, it's not. Lydia knows everything and she's the same age as me. I've been so protected all my life I don't know a bloody thing.' And she started to tell Fay about Harry and Roger.

'Oh, dear, poor Mummy. Of course that sort of thing is likely to happen, isn't it? You're a very attractive woman which means you're sure to get the odd pass.'

'But from good friends?'

'Friends are often the most dangerous. Perhaps they think they can presume upon that friendship in the first place. And men are intrinsically lazy creatures, it's such a bore and expense to search out new crumpet. They're all the same.'

'But if you can't trust your friends – that's too awful. You see what I mean, you're so wise compared with me.'

She drained her glass. 'At least we can be grateful your father wasn't like that.'

Fay twirled her glass absent-mindedly. 'I'd love some more of that port, Mummy.' Ann picked up the decanter. 'You drink more since Dad died.'

'Lovely, isn't it?' Ann giggled. 'I shudder to think what he would say about me, he did so disapprove of excess in anything. But the odd drink and my cigarettes have helped enormously. The trouble is I feel so guilty doing it . . .' She looked at the decanter in her hand. 'Oh blow it,' she laughed as she poured them both another glass.

'You are sweet. You're just like a little girl let loose in a sweet shop.'

'That's exactly how I feel sometimes. And I'm beginning to do silly things. I nearly bought a red dress the other day.' She looked anxiously at Fay.

'So? What's silly about a red dress?'

'Well, the point is, your father never liked me wearing bright colours, he said they didn't suit me and that I should stick to black or pastel. But I've always longed for a red dress.' She took a sip of her port. 'Then he dies and I find myself looking at red dresses.'

'Oh, Mummy. Don't be draft. You buy it. Red would suit your colouring marvellously. Dad was such a dandy, he probably didn't want you to outshine him.'

'A dandy?' Ann looked up sharply. 'That's not a very nice thing to say. He was always smart and enjoyed good clothes; that doesn't make him a dandy.'

'He was. It suited him to keep you looking dowdy. He was probably frightened that if you looked too attractive someone else would run off with you.'

'Fay, don't be ridiculous. And thank you for thinking me dowdy,' she pouted.

'Sorry, dowdy's the wrong word. You always looked very nice, but that was the trouble – you could have looked fantastic. Maybe he didn't do it consciously but . . . Come on, Mummy, be honest, he kept you down dreadfully. You always seemed to be sitting here waiting for him – no life of your own. He was always nagging you, if not about your smoking then about the house being untidy or something equally unimportant.'

'Really, Fay, what else would you expect a doctor to say? Smoking is bad for you, and I think he was very patient. It must be dreadful, if you don't smoke, living with someone who does, even if it's only one packet a week.'

'He made you feel guilty about it, admit it.'

'Ha!' Ann laughed gaily. 'Well, I used to smoke a lot under the extractor fan in the kitchen. I used to feel so daft too.' She giggled and with a small gesture, almost of defiance, lit a cigarette, inhaling deeply and watching the smoke curl into the air with pleasure.

'And he didn't like you drinking.'

'Ah, that's not true, he didn't mind, we always had wine on Fridays.'

'Big deal. I should think most of your friends have wine every night. I bet Lydia does.'

'I'm sure if I'd wanted to he wouldn't have said anything. It just didn't seem fair somehow if he couldn't drink because of his work.'

'Mummy! He would have hit the roof!'

'Still, I'm making up for it now,' she chuckled.

'Don't get me wrong. I loved Dad but honestly this house is a much more relaxed place to visit these days, and you're a much more relaxed person in it. He was too demanding. Look at us now, the plates all over the table, there's ash on the hearth, the bookcases are in a muddle. For the first time ever I don't feel I've got to keep my bedroom neat and tidy all the time. Dad would be up in arms if he could see us.'

'He would!' Ann giggled again. 'I suppose I *am* letting things slide a bit but you see, Fay, I'm not naturally tidy, whereas your father was such an exact and orderly sort of person. I'm a muddler really. It looks as if I'm reverting to type now, doesn't it – the slut re-emerges!' She snorted as she refilled her glass.

'You're not a slut, you're normal. Dad went too far. Remember how hysterical he became if anything got broken? How often did you hide things in the bottom of the dustbin? Come on, how often?'

'I understood that. He had had to work, and damned hard, for everything we owned. Nothing came easy, therefore the value of things meant a lot more to him.'

'There you go, still making excuses.'

'But I loved him, Fay.'

'So did I, but it didn't blind me. He was too bossy, Mummy, too finicky, he swamped you. Towards the end of my schooldays he drove me potty. I couldn't live with him any more – I had to get away, and fast!'

'You left because of your father?' Ann's voice brimmed with surprise.

'Yes.'

'I thought it was because of me.'

'You! But you're the easiest person in the world to get on with.'

'But your father said I smothered you both with too much love. And as a girl you'd want to get away from me. He was very upset when you left so suddenly and he always blamed me.'

'That's typical, he couldn't ever accept that he might be in the wrong, could he? Don't look so surprised, you must have known how I felt.'

'No, darling, I didn't. I just presumed it had to be me since you loved Ben so desperately.' She shook her head. 'You know, Fay, so much is going on – I'm having to look at everything differently and I don't want to, but it keeps happening. There are those wretched men, and Peter, now you, and all the odd things that make me feel guilty – the red dress, the wine, my friendship with Lydia – all things he would have disapproved of. When he was alive I thought we were a couple, but now, it sounds dreadful to say, I think I was an adjunct to Ben. I hadn't realized there was so much I didn't do or say because of him. And I don't like it, I wish I could go back to the way everything was before.'

'You were a wonderful and patient wife to him. It's dreadful that he died. Had he lived no doubt you would have gone on in the old way. His dying changed everything, but there is good coming from his death – you're beginning to be your own self. Ann Grange is emerging, a kind of re-birth really.'

'Well I never!'

'You sound just like Meg!' Fay laughed. 'Would you ever marry again?'

'Me?' Ann looked up, surprised by the sudden question. 'Who would ask me?' she laughed, dismissively.

'Quite a few, I should think. You're a very attractive woman. If you changed your style of dressing, got your hair cut – it looked super when you had it short – you would look stunning.'

'Do you think so? Lydia said I ought to have it streaked.' Ann patted her hair.

'Lydia's right. Bet you anything you'll be snapped up in twelve months.'

Ann assumed a surprised expression but was secretly pleased by her daughter's assessment. 'What a preposterous idea. I wouldn't mind a male friend, someone to go out with, take me to the theatre, that sort of thing. But to live with someone – no, I don't think so. I'm getting used to my independence. Quite honestly, I'm enjoying it. And having to go back to considering someone else, clearing up after them, washing their socks. No, thank you.'

'Heavens, Mummy, you've changed. I'd have thought you would long to be married again. I'd have said you were programmed for it.'

'Thank you very much, Fay.' Ann smiled indulgently. 'How patronizing you sound. It just shows how little you know me then, doesn't it? No, I plan to do a course in something – art probably, I might even try design. I might end up in competition with you. And what about you, lecturing me? You're nearly twenty-six, what about you getting married, or aren't you programmed for it?' Ann chuckled.

'Not for me. I like my career far too much and what it gives me. I'm a selfish, dedicated career woman.'

'What about children?'

'I look at Sally and Peter and the way they live. Adam wrecks everything, Sally looks permanently tired. The thought of them stops me getting broody. By the way, did I tell you I've seen a wonderful warehouse? I'm thinking seriously of buying it. I'd convert it into flats, keeping the penthouse for myself.'

Ann listened with amazement as her daughter talked knowledgeably of house prices, finance, mortgage payments, the investment potential in converting and selling or leasing flats. It was after one o'clock when they began to clear the dirty dishes away and together loaded them in the dishwasher.

'What did you mean, just now, about seeing Peter differently too?' Fay asked cautiously.

'Oh, nothing, darling.'

After Fay had gone to bed, Ann stayed up a little longer. In the past she felt she had never really thought deeply about anything; these days she seemed to do little else. Nothing had gone as she had planned. She had wanted to talk about Peter to Fay, but when the opportunity arose she had ducked away from it. It seemed such a shame to spoil the evening.

Since Ben had died everything was turning topsy-turvy. Fay had adored her father, everyone said so, and yet tonight she had listened to a young woman talk about her father quite clinically. She might have loved him, but it hadn't sounded as though she had liked him – just as Ann had revised her feelings about Peter. She felt Fay had been too hard on her father. Of course he had liked everything his own way, but didn't most men? That was Fay being naïve: wait until she married. But somehow Ann could not see her strong-willed daughter being the dutiful wife she herself had been. She had enjoyed the evening, she had felt so close to Fay tonight, as if she had a new friend. She felt elated to discover that Fay had not left home so abruptly because of her. Ben had been wrong. Perhaps there were other ideas and attitudes about which he had been wrong.

Ann would love to have him back with her, there was no doubt of that, the longing for him was as strong as ever, the loneliness always at her shoulder. But the difference now was that if she could turn the clock back she would like to be wearing a red dress, a drink in one hand, a cigarette in the other.

Purposefully she plumped up the cushions. Part of the problem was that she had not enough to do: too much time for thought and worry was no good for anyone. She would go to London next week, sort out the decoration of the drawing room; get her hair cut; maybe visit some art colleges and find out if there were courses for mature students. Then she would learn to paint properly.

Activity, that's what she needed, she said to herself firmly as she switched out the lights.

Two

1

Ann sat contentedly on the train to London. She had always loved train journeys. There was an excitement about them that was lacking in travelling by car. She had hated the diesel engines at first, for daring to replace the romantic stream trains, but now she was used to them and was just as excited by their rumbling and purring as she had been by the clatter and hissing of the old trains. She felt secure, cocooned, on a train: for the length of the journey an observer of life, not a participator.

The regularity of the landscape never failed to fascinate her, the open fields with the occasional farm or cottage. The cottages becoming more frequent as a village approached, then fading back to the scattered buildings of a farm. Then the ribbon development as a town drew near. First the modern estates, with picture windows designed for a view but looking out instead on the railway. The modern houses gave way to rows of Victorian terraces. It was rare to see one these days, but she always looked out for a blue-grey, coffin-shaped tin bath hanging on its hook on a whitewashed wall.

Even the new looked small, she thought. It wasn't right for whole families to be forced into such close proximity, while she was lucky enough to rattle around in expensive isolation. 'Lucky' she had thought herself, she realized with a pleased surprise. Would she and Ben have been as happy living in such houses, in a city? Could their love have weathered the claustrophobia of this kind of living or was it nurtured by space, privacy, beauty and a large garden? Was that all it took, she wondered. She realized that for the first time she was questioning the love she had always taken for granted.

By mid-morning Ann had chosen new wallpaper, curtains and upholstery fabric. She had completed in a couple of hours a task which, in the old days, might have taken her days of dithering. She noticed that with only herself and her own tastes to consider, she could make decisions faster.

She sat in front of the peach-coloured mirror of the hairdresser's salon where Lydia had made her an appointment. The epicene young stylist held a strand of her hair aloft, sucking in his cheeks and making a tutting noise of disapproval.

'It's in a deplorable condition,' he eventually pronounced.

'Sorry,' Ann said apologetically.

'The colour's all wrong too – dull. And . . . Oh, my Gawd!' he shrieked, peering closely at her hair. Ann's heart pounded as she wondered what he had found. 'You're going grey,' he went on in a barely audible whisper as if her greyness was some obscene disease that the other clients must not hear about.

'Yes.' Ann slid down in the chair.

'And you've done nothing about it?' He sounded shocked.

'Well, no.' By now completely disheartened, Ann wished she had not come here but had gone as usual to the local hairdresser's.

The man held her head in his hands twisting it from side to side, studying her reflection in the mirror. Ann tried to smile but was too intimidated to succeed.

'Chin's good.'

'Thank you,' Ann whispered.

'Cheekbones too.'

She was inordinately pleased that something about

her was right. He stood tapping his comb against his other hand.

'All off,' he announced, grandly. 'And highlights. Masses of highlights.'

'But . . . I . . .'

'Yes?' he asked, tapping his foot impatiently in time with the comb.

'Well, I was wondering about a pageboy . . .'

'Pageboy,' the stylist snorted. 'Went out with the ark, that style did. No, short, it'll knock years off you, ducks. Marlene,' he shouted. A young woman, her hair an alarming bird's nest of blonde spikes tipped with emerald green, sashayed towards them. Together they studied her hair. 'I should use three colours, Marlene. At least it's rat-coloured enough to do something with. See you later, duckie,' he said to Ann and minced off, leaving her with Marlene the colourist.

In silence, Marlene laboriously painted the thin strands of hair and wrapped them carefully in silver paper. When she had finished and Ann's hair had been washed, she studied her woebegone appearance in the mirror and wondered if she had made a dreadful mistake. She was returned to the stylist who was called Wayne. With gusto and much clicking and flashing of scissors he started on Ann's hair. Her heart thumped with dismay as her hair grew shorter and the pile on the floor grew larger. In contrast with Marlene, Wayne talked non-stop. The pop music blared – everything was so unlike Maison Barry in the local market town.

Like a juggler Wayne deftly manipulated blow-dryer and brush. Ann was stunned by the image that began to emerge. The new style, short on top, smooth at the sides, removed years from her face. The silver-blonde colour lightened her face. She clapped her hands with delight.

'See, Wayne's always right. You look really stunning, ducks. What you want now is a facial – your make-up's all wrong. Where you been all these years?'

'I don't know,' she replied nonsensically, still stunned by the transformation.

'Never wear blue eyeshadow, it's ageing.'

'Is it?'

'Gawd, yes. Stick to the greys and pearls.'

'I'll remember that.'

'See you in a fortnight,' he announced airily. Ann looked puzzled. 'You need a light perm, give it more body, more hold . . .' He stood back, studying her, evidently pleased by his creation.

'Fine, see you in two weeks,' Ann said meekly.

At the reception desk Ann nearly fainted at the size of her bill. She could not possibly afford a perm here as well, she decided. She began to write the cheque, and caught sight of herself in a mirror. Oh what the hell, she thought, adding a fifteen-pound tip and making an appointment to return for the perm.

She toyed with a salad and a glass of white wine at Fortnum's, feeling isolated in the crowded restaurant. She realized she would have liked to have someone sitting opposite to admire the new look. Her elation began to dissipate.

Her plan had been to visit some art colleges and enquire about courses but she was overcome with shyness at the audacity of what she was attempting. Surely they would laugh at her presumption that, with only an O-level in Art and a meagre collection of sketches and watercolours attempted over the years, she had the talent to attend a college. She would write to them instead, she determined, but she didn't want to return home until the evening. She would treat herself instead to a visit to the Tate Gallery. As an aspiring art student, she should start learning now.

The steps of the gallery were littered with couples enjoying the weak winter sunshine. As she made her way up the steps between them she felt as if she were the only person in London on her own. The feeling passed, as she had known it would, once she was inside the gallery. Often, on trips to London, Ann visited the Tate, the

National or the Courtauld. This had been the one small area of her life where Ben had had no influence. Galleries and art had bored him, so she went by herself. In each gallery she had her particular favourites and would go straight to them and spend ages staring at them, enjoying the physical and mental pleasure their colours and form gave to her. She would peer closely at them, marvelling at the differing techniques, always curious as to how different effects were produced.

Over the years her tastes and loves had altered, changed in a way that she would not have thought possible when she was eighteen. At that age the Impressionists had been her passion. Then for a couple of years abstract art had engrossed and puzzled her. But then her tastes had seemed to travel backwards, she wearied of abstraction and for a while it had been the work of the Romantics she chose to look at. That phase had coincided with her rediscovery of Wordsworth – a poet for whom she had had no time as a girl. She had wallowed for several years in the delights of the Italian Renaissance, fascinated by the blues and reds they had used, so skilfully that the vibrant colours never unbalanced the paintings as a whole. Her flirtation with pop art had been short-lived. She now realized that she had only pretended an interest to shock Ben out of his entrenched conservatism. In fact the swirls and patterns had given her a headache, and she had scuttled back to the calm serenity of the Florentines, preferring their games with perspective.

Now she stood in the busy entrance hall and wondered which gallery to go to. It was some time since she had looked at the Pre-Raphaelites and the wallpaper she had just ordered, with its distinct Burne-Jones influence, decided her.

A couple of hours later Ann sank on to a banquette, exhausted, not from walking but from the intensity of her reactions to the works she had seen. On the opposite wall, a large painting seemed to loom at her as if insisting she should study it more closely. A luminous twilight glowed from it, contrasting with the darkness of the exposed earth where two nuns were digging a grave. The young novice appeared to be moving as she swung the glinting spade into the heavy soil. How could such movement be created from something as static as paint, Ann wondered, admiringly. But it was the face of the other nun that captured her attention: there was such an expression of calmness and resignation, an acceptance of death in her face. Whose death? Her own? The picture did not make it clear, but Ann felt a sense of calmness and peace flow over her. She sighed.

'That is what art is for, to calm the soul,' she heard someone say in a deep, slightly accented voice. She turned quickly to find a man had sat down beside her on the banquette and was looking gravely at her.

Ann hesitated for a moment. 'It's beautiful, isn't it?' she replied. 'It's a picture of death and yet it makes me feel totally at peace with myself.'

'Ah, I understand,' he said, gently.

'My husband,' she answered plainly, as if explaining to him was the most natural thing, she began to tell him of the day Ben died, the months that followed, her loneliness and the new longing to live again. Throughout, he sat patiently and listened to her outpouring, his large, clear grey eyes studying her face as she spoke.

A child began to cry, breaking the spell. 'Oh, my God! I'm sorry. What must you think of me going on like this . . . a complete stranger . . . I must have bored you to tears . . .' Ann jumped to her feet in flustered confusion, immediately dropping her handbag and gloves.

He bent and retrieved her things from the floor, and when he stood up Ann found he towered above her. He was broad-shouldered and muscular. The hand that returned her handbag was large and tanned, a strong, well-manicured hand. She was acutely aware of standing before someone who was very strong, not just physically but mentally too. Suddenly she felt small and very vulnerable. As he moved towards her to return her bag, she smelled a combination of cologne, tobacco and masculinity that her senses had not noticed for years.

'Please, I was not bored. Not for one minute.' He smiled. 'Sometimes it is necessary to talk, and sometimes it is better with a stranger. I do understand.' He spoke with a deep, warm voice with just a trace of an accent which Ann could not identify but which she found intriguing and which contrived to make her own language sound more interesting. He was not handsome in the conventional sense, but his face was an arresting one – wide, with high cheekbones, which made her certain he came from the East. Above a strong chin his lips were full, beside his mouth ran two deep lines, which gave a hardness to his face that disappeared the instant he smiled.

'Well, thank you so much, Mr . . .?' she enquired.

'Georgeopoulos. But please call me Alex.'

'Ann Grange,' she said, awkwardly holding out her hand. 'Thank you – Mr Georgeopoulos.' She smiled shyly. 'I must be going.'

She started to walk to the entrance, aware that he had fallen into step beside her. As they reached the door Ann was startled to see that it was already dark.

'Good heavens, I must have been in there for hours!' she exclaimed, more to herself than to him.

'Would you have dinner with me tonight?'

She looked at him, startled. 'I . . . but you see . . .' she faltered.

'Please,' he interrupted her. 'It would give me such great pleasure.'

Her thoughts raced; the only clear ones to emerge were that she had a train to catch and that she was wearing blue eyeshadow. With astonishment she heard herself say, 'Yes, thank you, I should like that.'

'Good. I shall pick you up at seven-thirty. Where are you staying?'

'At the Rembrandt,' replied this other voice that seemed to have nothing to do with her.

He called a taxi and handed her in. 'The Rembrandt,' he said to the driver. 'Until seven thirty then, Mrs Grange,' and he smiled again, the smile making him almost handsome.

Ann slumped back on to the seat as the taxi edged its way into the traffic. What on earth had induced her to accept an invitation from a total stranger? And where the hell was the Rembrandt Hotel? She hadn't even known such a hotel existed; it had simply been the first name to come into her head. She had no clothes or make-up with her . . . she ought to tell the driver to take her to the station, immediately, get her home fast. He could be anything, a rapist, a murderer! But not with those kind eyes, her other voice argued. And what had she to go home to? Some soup, the television . . . Come on, Ann, just this once, the inner voice persisted. We'll be in public places. I'm old enough to look after myself. She leaned forward and slid open the little window behind the driver. 'Where is the Rembrandt?' she asked, feeling foolish.

'Just along from 'arrods, miss.'

'Would you drop me off there, at Harrods, I mean?'

'Right yer are, miss.'

Within an hour, Ann, who had intended to buy only a toothbrush, toothpaste and face cleanser, was loaded with shopping bags. The girl selling her favourite cleanser had had little problem in persuading her to buy the makings of an entirely new face. And Ann, thinking she was only idly browsing, had found herself in the dress department where she had fallen in love with a smart, black, full-skirted silk dress which just happened to fit perfectly. So shoes were required, and a handbag, and a change of underwear. She was on her way to the street before she realized that it might look odd to arrive at a hotel laden only with carrier bags – like a middle-class vagrant, she thought, as she made her way to the luggage department.

<h1 align="center">2</h1>

In the hotel foyer Ann waited her turn at the reception desk. A large party of Americans had just arrived, their matched sets of baggage scattered about the large hallway. The women were all dressed in Burberrys, the familiar checked scarf and trilby almost like a uniform. Those men who wore spectacles all seemed to be wearing the same steel-framed model as if there was only one optician in the whole of the United States. They waited their turn good-naturedly as their harassed courier tried to make sense of a folder stuffed with papers. Their happy noisiness was infectious except to the solitary businessman who kept peering anxiously at his watch as he waited his turn. It was going to be a long wait. Ann sat down until the desk cleared.

This was a mistake, for, as she did so, another large party arrived. A dozen women whose fresh complexions, discreet make-up, sensible low-heeled shoes announced them as countrywomen in town for some early Christmas shopping, and staying overnight to take in a show. Ann had done it often enough. She recognized, in their aura of staunch respectability and unflustered command, so many of her friends. There was a decisiveness about their actions, an expectation that they would be obeyed which made even the Americans move to one side as the women loudly demanded their keys, efficiently signed in and bossily organized a porter for their luggage. Ann watched them and wondered if one day she might become like them: maybe to outsiders she already appeared so for she too wore a tweed suit and sensible shoes and clutched a camel-hair coat. She smiled to herself: she might look the height of respectability, but what she was planning this evening would fill these stalwart women with shocked dismay.

Finally she was registered and shown to her room. By six she was running her bath. As she watched the pearls of bath oil burst, filling the water with milky-coloured, sweet-smelling perfume, and felt the satin smoothness as she swished the water back and forth with her hands, she was certain she had never bought such a luxury before: it was the sort of thing one was given as a Christmas present. Strange that she should have picked up the bottle in Harrods, but then today everything she did was strange.

She stepped into the bath and lay luxuriating in the perfumed water, enjoying the unfamiliar, sensuous feel that the bath oil gave to her skin. Feeling strangely elated, she thought about Alex Georgeopoulos. He must be Greek, with a name like that, she thought, picking up the soap provided, courtesy of the hotel, and sniffing it absent-mindedly. Did he live in London, or was he just visiting? What was he doing in the Tate? And how long had he observed her before she noticed him? He had beautiful grey eyes, as clear as a young man's with none of the yellow flecks of age. And the strange way his smile transformed his face. He . . .

This was foolish. Ann sat up quickly and began, vigorously, to soap herself. The oil made the soap lather into a froth of bubbles and though she rinsed herself repeatedly her skin still felt slimy. Disgusting stuff, how stupid to have bought it, she remonstrated with herself. She pulled the plug out and, standing up, she slid on the slippery surface of the bath – and dangerous too, she told herself sensibly as she regained her balance. Angrily she turned on the shower to wash off the last of the oil and soap.

Wrapped in a large white bath-sheet, she padded into the bedroom and began to unpack her new case which was full of bulging Harrods carrier bags. She hung the black dress on a hanger and enjoyed the silky sensation as she smoothed the skirt. She sat on the bed and admired her shoes – so elegant in their shiny, patent-leather newness, such thin spindly heels, so unlike any other shoes she owned. She had heard that such shoes did dreadful things to one's back and unspeakable damage to the uterus, but . . . she knew he would like them, appreciate their femininity. She had thought so the minute she had seen them. 'Rubbish!' she spoke aloud to the empty-room. 'I bought them because *I* like them!'

Sitting at the dressing table she began to unwrap the packages of make-up. Soon the wastepaper basket was full of cellophane, boxes, inner packing and instructions. Such a waster of trees she tutted as she lined the pretty bottles and boxes on the table. She had bought far too much. Ann had always prided herself on resisting the make-up assistants' sales pitch, their ability to make one feel guilty of neglect, then full of deluded hope. But this time, she had fallen for it all. She opened a flat box and, perplexed, studied the small block of powder, its fat brush nestling neatly beside it. Blusher. What the hell was she doing with blusher at her age? She would never put it on right, never.

She glanced in the mirror and was shocked. The face reflected back at her was radiant with excitement, the eyes sparkled, lips curved in a secret smile.

'No!' she whispered, covering her face with her hands. 'No! I'm being stupid. Stop it, Ann, stop it. What do you think you're playing at?' She peeped through her fingers, then slowly lowered her hands, but still her face was an image of glowing anticipation.

Half rising from the stool, she decided to phone Lydia, who could talk some sense into her. Slowly she subsided back on to the stool. But what could she say? 'Lydia, I got picked up by this man, Greek I think, and I'm going out to dinner with him.' It sounded too ridiculous. She started to apply the make-up. 'I could never face Lydia again,' she berated herself, rubbing the cream into her face and gingerly experimenting with the blusher. She looked at her face critically. The blusher made her face look thinner, her cheekbones finer. Carefully she painted her eyelids with the soft, charcoal-grey eyeshadow, shading it out with the soft brush to merge with the lighter shadow, just as the assistant has instructed. She outlined her full mouth with the red lip-crayon and filled the frame it made with a coral lipstick applied with a small brush. The way she handled the unfamiliar miniature brushes – like the artist she would like to be – made her laugh with delight. Carefully she combed the new but unfamiliar hairstyle, sat back and looked again at her image.

Ann barely recognized herself. The new hairstyle and make-up made her look years younger. It was not just a trick of the light which made her eyes look so much bigger, the grey shadow accentuating their blueness. The mascara she had laboriously painted on, twirling her lashes carefully, instead of with her normal, perfunctory stab, made her lashes denser and longer than ever before. Ann liked what she saw.

She shook her head at the glamorous reflection – 'I won't go,' she muttered to herself. 'That's the sensible thing. I'll phone reception and leave a message.' Quickly she crossed the room and picked up the phone, and as rapidly replaced it. That was not fair. He had been nothing but kind to her: she owed it to him to explain in person. She would say she had made a mistake, all because of a sentimental painting.

Whatever the outcome, she thought, as she slipped the new dress carefully over her hair, the dress had been a good buy. Its clinging polo-necked bodice made her waist look tiny. The full skirt flared out, its silk lining making a pleasingly soft and expensive swishing sound as she moved. She buttoned the cuffs of the tight-fitting sleeves and thanked heaven she had worn her pearls and matching earrings: they looked perfect against her pale skin which contrasted dramatically with the dense black of the dress. Picking up her camel-hair coat, for a moment she wished she had invested in a new one more suitable for the evening. But that would have been a stupid additional expense. And what did it matter whether or not she had her pearls – she was not going out with him. On the other hand, it would be a shame to waste all this finery, she thought. She would go to the Italian restaurant in Beauchamp Place to which Ben had taken her once. In any case, if she could think it all a silly idea, wasn't he likely to think the same? That was it. She doubted if he would even bother to turn up, and that would solve everything.

At seven-thirty on the dot she slipped out of the lift, and there he was. He had changed out of the well-cut grey suit of the afternoon into an even smarter dark one. As the lift doors clanged he turned from the desk and saw her. Immediately his face broke into a smile which transformed his features and he moved across the foyer towards her.

'Mrs Grange. How lovely you look.'

'I hope I'm not late,' was all she could think of to say, and together they walked out into the London night.

3

In the taxi they sat in a silence which was agony to Ann, who racked her brain for something to say. She had always, even as a child, regarded such silences as her responsibility, something she should have been able to avoid. Thus, throughout her life she had indulged in inane conversations with taxi drivers, people in lifts and in railway carriages. But now, with this stranger, her mind was a complete blank; no useless prattle would rise to the surface to rescue her. He looked at her; nervously she smiled at him.

'It's not far,' he said, and she could have hugged him just for speaking.

The taxi drove up in front of an elegant town house in a Georgian square. No restaurant signs adorned it, few people walked the pavement. Ann's heart lurched with fear. He was taking her to his house where she would not have the protection of other people. She swung around to step back into the taxi but already it was moving away from the pavement. He took her arm and led up her the steps.

'I don't know if I want to go in there.' Her voice emerged high-pitched.

'But I can recommend it highly, the food is excellent,' he replied, still firmly holding her as he rang the doorbell which was immediately answered by a young man in grey livery.

'Mr Georgeopoulos, such a pleasure.' A razor-thin woman, in a long black dress, bore down upon them, her heavily ringed, long-nailed hand outstretched in greeting. Her lips were a bright red gash in a face that appeared almost white. 'It's been too long. How we've missed you.'

Ann watched, mesmerized, as the woman, with what amounted to professional coquetry, gushed over him, while she led them into a large, opulent, chandeliered hall. This was a very odd restaurant, she decided. There were no people, no bustle, no waiters, no smell of cooking. And this woman's flirtation was a parody of a young woman's. Oh my God, Ann thought, memories of her mother's warning of white slave traffickers flooding into her mind, what if it were a brothel, and this the Madame!

'Madame.' Ann started as his voice echoed her thought. 'Might I introduce my friend Mrs Grange?'

The heavily made-up eyes flashed in Ann's direction. With one swift sweep they had taken in all aspects of her appearance. She barely touched Ann's proffered hand and imperiously waved to the footman to remove Ann's coat, which had changed mysteriously from a good camel coat into a garment to be disdained. The woman's attention returned immediately to Mr Georgeopoulos.

'I've put you in the green room Mr Georgeopoulos, your favourite.' The woman simpered. Her large teeth, yellow as a horse's, flashed menacingly. 'But of course you'd prefer a drink first?'

He nodded. Ann looked about her desperately for the footman to recover her coat, but he had disappeared. Alex grasped her arm tightly and purposefully guided her to a room at the side of the hall. He stood talking to the dreadful woman, seeming to loom over Ann whom he had seated in a corner chair. She felt trapped by his bulk.

The room was decorated with beautiful understatement. Everything was in grey and cream with discreet touches of gold. Huge vases of flowers filled the air with heavy perfume, but Ann was not in a mood to appreciate any of it. Perhaps it was a 'house of assignation'? Her mind raced – she had read about them in novels. What a bloody cheek he had, just because she had allowed herself to be picked up . . .

'Martini, Mrs Grange?' she heard him ask as if from a long way away.

'Gin and tonic, please,' she replied, noticing the woman's lip curl with disapproval. The two of them suddenly broke into fluent French far too fast for Ann's schoolgirl variety to grasp. She caught the odd word, enough to realize that they were discussing food. She began to relax a little, blaming herself for over-reacting. Another handsome young footman appeared with their drinks, the rapid conversation ended and the woman left them alone. Ann looked at her escort warily; he smiled, his expression so unthreatening that she relaxed visibly and settled back in her chair.

'That's better. I thought you were going to bolt, back there in the hall. And you've been sitting on the edge of that chair like a frightened schoolgirl about to run away from some unspeakable horror.' He laughed.

'I wasn't. I was trying to catch what you were saying.'

'So you approve?'

'Approve of what?'

'Of Madame Pétin's and my choice of dinner.'

'No, I mean I couldn't understand what you were saying, you spoke so quickly,' she said, flustered.

'I apologize. Perhaps I should have consulted you. It's just that I always rely on what Pétin recommends, she's always right.'

'I'm sure it will all be lovely,' she said, resenting her own gaucheness. 'In any case, I never know what to order, no matter what I get I always think everyone else's looks more appetising.' She attempted, unsuccessfully, a bright smile. 'It's a lovely room, isn't it?' she added quickly.

'Yes, the French certainly have a unique style.' One of Ann's dreaded silences descended upon them. 'What is it, Mrs Grange, you seem so ill at ease?' he asked, gently, after a pause.

'Do I?' she laughed nervously.

'Have I done something to upset you, Mrs Grange?'

'Nothing, really. But please, call me Ann.'

'I would prefer Anna,' he smiled.

'As you wish.'

'But you still haven't explained what is bothering you.'

'Nothing, really.' She sipped her drink and fumbled in her handbag for a cigarette. By the time she had found the packet, he was ready with a heavy gold lighter. 'Thank you.'

He sat back in his chair and calmly studied her. She found herself unable to return his stare, to search for what expression there might be in his eyes.

'You speak beautiful French.'

'And you are beautiful, Anna.'

Ann choked on her drink, hurriedly delving back into her handbag in search of a handkerchief. 'Take mine,' she heard him say and looking up saw he was offering her a large white one.

'No, no thank you, I'm fine, the drink went the wrong way. What was I saying? Oh yes, your French, it's so good.'

'Thank you.'

'How many languages do you speak?'

'Apart from my own, three well and three badly.'

'Which three?'

'English, French and Italian.'

'And which do you speak badly?'

'English, French and Italian.' He laughed.

'That's rubbish. You speak the first two brilliantly. But which is your mother tongue?'

'Greek of course. With a name like mine, what else?' He continued to laugh but Ann had a strange feeling that he was laughing at her more than with her, as if her discomfort amused him.

'I've never met a Greek before.'

'Then I hope I will be a pleasurable experience for you.' As he smiled she noticed for the first time that he had a small gap between his front teeth which lent an endearing charm to his smile. She began to feel embarrassed as he continued to look at her long and hard. She changed the topic.

'This is a strange sort of restaurant.'

'Yes, I suppose it is.'

'It's very discreet.'

'Very.'

'Do you always go to discreet places?'

'If I can.'

'Why?'

'It makes life simpler,' he replied enigmatically.

She took a deep breath. 'Is it a brothel, or a house of assignation?' she asked in a firm voice, deciding to take the bull by the horns.

'I beg your pardon,' he said incredulously, sitting bolt upright in his chair. 'A brothel? A house of what . . .? What on earth are you talking about, Anna?'

'It's too discreet, and there are no signs for American Express or Diners. I mean, whoever heard of a restaurant without credit cards?'

His laugh exploded loudly from him. 'A brothel! Oh my God, what would Pétin say to that!' He laughed so much that the tears began to roll down his cheeks and it was he who then needed the large white hanky. She watched him. The laugh had been so instantaneous that she knew, with relief, that she had been wrong. Slowly she began to chuckle and soon she too was laughing. The woman reappeared.

'Your table is ready, Mr Georgeopoulos,' she announced eventually, having to raise her voice about his loud bellowing. 'Might I be permitted to ask what is the joke?' she asked a shade huffily.

Ann looked with mute appeal at Alex. 'One day, my dear Pétin, I'll tell you, but not tonight . . .' he managed to say through his laughter.

Madame Pétin led them into a room as beautiful as the first but smaller. There was only one table, covered with the finest damask on which creamy wax candles glowed, reflecting on the silver and fine crystal, making the waxen petals of the bowl of camellias gleam. Two waiters settled them, fussing about like agitated hens, and reverently, like acolytes at a communion, placed the plates of quail's eggs in aspic in front of them. Alex tasted the wine and the fluid glinted light gold in the fine glass. He lifted his to her.

'To new friends.'

'And happiness,' she replied.

'Most certainly happiness.' His transforming smile and the glow of the wine made Ann at last felt at ease.

The eggs were delicious, and she had to tell him. So was the wine and she had to tell him that too. And how soft the napkins were, how perfect the candlelight, the flowers. She had to share her enjoyment of it all with him.

'And you don't think it's necessary now to search for a bed?'

She feared she might blush. 'Oh please! I feel so silly.'

'Not silly at all. I'm used to this place, I've been coming here for years, and I suppose it is rather unusual. And you did take a risk coming with me. After all, you don't know me.'

'I don't think I'm taking a risk,' she found herself saying, having already forgotten her initial panic.

'Then I shall not betray such trust in me,' he said seriously.

The second course arrived. It was Madame Pétin's recommended noisette of lamb, rosy pink in colour. The vegetables were small and evenly matched. The wine this time glowed deep red in the many facets of her glass. Ann ate with enjoyment. She looked at his plate and realized that whereas she was half finished he seemed barely to have touched the food.

'You eat very slowly,' she said, as if to excuse herself for eating too fast. He picked up his wine glass and looked at her over its rim.

'I don't think we should ever hurry the important pleasures in life,' he said softly.

This time Ann did blush, deeply. There was no escaping his meaning and a delightful shiver ran down her spine. She looked at her plate.

'Don't you agree?' he persisted. She dared to look at him and saw the merriment in his eyes.

'But I'm English, I can't possibly forget my puritan antecedents,' she countered.

'Then I must teach you otherwise. What do you think?'

'Maybe I'm too old to learn,' she replied, feeling she was losing control of the conversation, indeed in great danger of losing control of herself.

'One is never too old to learn anything. Ask Madame.' he said, and laughed again, loudly. Ann felt that some sort of danger had passed, but perversely she also found herself feeling disappointed that it had done so.

She forced herself to eat more slowly, even though the food was growing cold and though she sensed him watching her.

'What do you do?' she asked.

'A little of this and a little of that,' he replied non-committally.

'As a Greek you should be something to do with the sea.'

'Less so these days. The whole business has got very risky.'

'You don't look Greek.'

'Don't I? How do you think I look?'

'Oh, you shouldn't look any different, I think you're lovely as you are!' The minute she spoke she was blushing again, this time with confusion.

'Why, thank you,' he smiled.

'What I mean,' she tried again. 'You're so big, and tall, your eyes are grey and your skin . . . you don't look as I imagine a Greek to look,' she finished lamely.

'We are not all short, fat, dark and greasy. We come in all shapes and sizes, you know.'

'Oh dear, I've offended you. I didn't mean to be rude, really, I'm sorry.'

'I'm not offended. How could I be if you think I'm lovely?' he said very softly. For one heart-hammering moment she thought he was about to take her hand, but the moment was broken by the arrival of the waiters to remove their plates.

He was disappointed that she did not want pudding, but he insisted she try the cheese. 'It tastes different when it comes from France and Madame had it flown in daily,' he explained as he selected several different cheeses for her to try. He almost cried with laughter again when she told him that the Brie definitely tasted different from the Brie she bought in Sainsbury's.

'Don't you dare tell Madame Pétin that,' she whispered urgently. 'She obviously thinks I'm suburban enough already and despises me for it.'

'What makes you say that?'

'The way she looks at me as if she's sneering at me.'

'Ah, that's because she's French and you are beautiful. Had you been fat and ugly she would have been charming to you. French women are all the same from the cradle to the grave – all attractive women are a threat to them.'

'Do you know many French women then?'

'Yes.'

'And English and Italian?'

'Of course.'

'Is that how you learnt so many languages?' she said lightly.

'On the pillow you mean?' He grinned at her. 'No, I had an English nanny, and a French governess, but I confess that I learnt Italian the most beautiful way.'

She had meant to tease, to banter with him, instead she suddenly felt an intense loathing for those Italian women.

They dawdled over coffee and liqueurs and he talked of the countries he knew, the meals he had had, memorable wines he had drunk. She listened intently, enjoying his subtly accented voice, the ease with which he made her laugh, but all the time longing to ask if he was married, how many children he had. But she dared not ask because, as the evening progressed, she realized she did not want to hear the answer.

Madame was as effusive as ever in her farewells to Alex and as dismissive of Ann. The hall was still empty, she saw no other patrons, no noise came from behind the closed doors and no money changed hands.

Since the night was fine they walked back to Ann's hotel. Alex slid his arm into hers. It was such a natural action that it was some time before Ann realized she was walking arm in arm through the night streets of London with a man she hardly knew.

Too soon they reached the Rembrandt.

'Would you like to come in for a nightcap?' she asked, suddenly shy, but not wanting the evening to end.

He glanced at his watch. 'I should love to, but I'm afraid I'm late for an appointment.

Her heart sank with disappointment that she tried to keep out of her voice as she said, 'Ah well, never mind. But thank you for a lovely evening – in France!' Politely she extended her hand. He took it in his but leaned over and kissed her gently on the cheek.

'Would you do me a great favour?' he asked.

'I'll try.'

'It's silly, but in all the years I've been coming to London I've never been to Hampton Court. Would you come with me? Please?'

'I'd love to,' she answered quickly, immediately regretting that she had sounded far too eager.

'Marvellous. I'll call for you at ten-thirty, if that's not too early.' Again he lightly kissed her cheek, turned away and with a wave was gone.

She switched off the bedside light and settled back contentedly on the pillow. It was then that she became aware that she had not thought of Ben once, all evening. The realization was a shock. She had not spent one day, since he died, when he had not monopolized her thoughts. Yet she had spent hours with another man and Ben had not entered her mind. What would Ben have thought of her? She would like to think he would be pleased for her, but she doubted it. She knew she should be feeling guilty; in an uncharacteristic way, she was not, she could not. The evening had been too perfect and now, tired from the excitement and the wine, she soon began to drift into sleep. Just as sleep took hold of her one thought loomed large – who has an appointment at this time of night?

4

Ann awoke, startled by the unfamiliar sound of the London traffic beginning its early morning crescendo to the day's cacophony. She studied the innocuous white ceiling as if it could solve the tumult which already, in the first moments of waking, filled her mind.

By going to the Tate, by talking to a stranger, by accepting his invitation – everything in her life could change, perhaps was already changed. For the first time in months she had been truly happy. For the first time ever she had enjoyed the company of a man other than Ben. She could not remember, in her whole life, being made to feel as feminine as this man made her feel. There was such an aura of sensuality about him. Yet he had not forced the issue, had made no physical advances, nothing had been said. However, it was there between them, real and tangible, almost like a challenge. Strangely, she felt he had left the decision to her – the decision of what was to happen in their lives.

What had started as an innocent little adventure now loomed as a large and far from innocent one. She had two choices, it was as simple as that. She could pack her bags, leave him a note, slip out of the hotel and back to the safety of Midfield with the memory of her little adventure, a memory that would probably fade quickly. Or, she could stay and meet him and have an affair, which would no doubt be short-lived, and then return to the security of her house with memories of a greater adventure which would take longer to fade and might leave regrets that would never pass.

If she stayed she would no doubt be hurt. It would seem inevitable. He must be married. He was a foreigner who must sooner or later return home. And what if she were imagining all this and the last thing he wanted was an affair with her? He was attractive, he could have any young girl he wanted. What made her think he was attracted to her? It wasn't her imagination, she was sure. Inexperienced as she was with men she knew he had wanted her last night – it was in the air, his smile, the look in his eyes . . .

Hell! What had she got to lose? A little pain – had she not learned to deal with pain this year? She could cope. It was *her* life now, to do with as she pleased. She would meet him, she would grasp at this chance of happiness, however brief.

She jumped out of bed, showered, dressed and by ten-thirty had checked out of the hotel, depositing her bag with the hall porter. Ann sat in the foyer, heart fluttering like a young girl on her first date. Looking at the party of middle-aged women paying their bills, she knew for certain that she would never become one of them.

'Good morning, Anna.' His voice behind her made her start. She leaped to her feet and, with his arm about her shoulder, he seemed to envelop her, as he guided her through the throngs of people who parted at once to let them through.

It was a glorious late November day, briskly cold in the bright sunshine. He led her to a metallic-grey Mini, parked on double yellow lines with a traffic warden already in attendance. Alex helped her into the car and waited patiently for his parking ticket, which to the warden's amazement he accepted with a pleasant smile and a 'thank you'. Seated beside her he leaned across and opening the glove locker, stuffed the ticket in to join a pile of others.

'Is collecting parking tickets a hobby of yours?'

'Damn things. I haven't the patience to find parking places so I just leave the car and accept the tickets.'

'I always feel like a criminal when I get one.'

He chuckled. 'How very English – so proper, so law-abiding. I can't say it ever bothers me. Now, to Hampton Court.' He put the car into gear and eased it out into the Knightsbridge traffic. He obviously knew London well for he drove speedily, weaving in and out of the traffic, taking short cuts along side roads.

'Would you light a cigarette for me, please?' he asked.

She lit two cigarettes and handed one to him. She had seen Bette Davis do that in a film once; it had meant nothing to her then, but now she understood the intimacy the action created. 'Thank you, darling,' he said. The endearment was a delightful shock. She looked at him quickly. Momentarily he glanced away from the road, smiled at her and blew her a kiss. She leaned back contentedly in the seat: she had imagined nothing.

'So, Anna, tell me all about this Hampton Court.'

'It's beautiful, the most wonderful rosy-red colour. The oldest part is Tudor. It was built by Cardinal Wolsey but his king, Henry VIII, lusted after it. He made the mistake of making it grander than anything the King owned, you see.'

'Stupid mistake. Is this the king with all the wives?'

'That's him.'

'Did he get the palace?'

'Oh, yes. But then he always got what he wanted.'

'Not much point in being a king if you don't,' he said matter-of-factly. 'You have a lovely voice. It's so soft and low I could listen to you for hours.'

'No one ever told me that before.' She felt pleased and embarrassed at the same time.

'I wonder what else you haven't been told about yourself.'

Because it was early and a weekday in November, they had the whole place to themselves. Her nervous system gave a pleasurable jolt as she felt his hand take hers. It seemed, however, right that he should. They wandered through the lovely rooms. He asked many questions, as if he had a desperate thirst to know everything.

'I just don't know, Alex,' she confessed for the umpteenth time. 'If we ever come here again I shall have to study the subject beforehand.'

'We'll come again. It's beautiful and there's so much to see. I'm afraid I'm naturally inquisitive; I've always been the same. If something interests me then I want to know everything. Just as I want to know everything there is to know about you.'

'That won't tax your mind too much,' she replied as they emerged into the grounds. They walked along the wide, gravelled paths.

'And this king – Henry VIII, wasn't it? Why do you know so much about him and so little about the others?'

'I suppose I've always found him more fascinating than the others. Charles I aways sounds so boring, and William of Orange positively unpleasant.'

'You love him?'

'Hardly!' she spluttered. 'I shouldn't think he was particularly lovable, but intriguing: so huge and dominant. Who was it said that power was an aphrodisiac?

'Henry Kissinger, and he was right. So, What am I to do? I'm big, that's one thing in my favour. So

you would like to be dominated, little one, would you?'
he teased her.

'A little bit. Don't most women?'

'Not these days, my sweet, where have you been?'

'I think I'm too old to pretend an independence, I
don't feel.'

'There you go again saying you're too old. You must
stop that. Nor must you let anyone hear such views on
women's liberation, you'll set their cause back years.
And you'll find ruthless men like me lying in wait ready
to exploit you.' He stood in the sunshine, laughing with
delight at her. And Ann signed. 'My darling, why do you
sigh? Are you cold?' he asked anxiously.

'Because . . .' and she stretched her arms above her
head in an expansive gesture. 'Because I'm so happy.
Because I'm with you.'

He quickly stepped forward and put his hands either
side of her face. 'My darling,' his lips brushed hers, 'I
wanted you to say something like that. I was too afraid to
rush things, you seem so frightened of me.'

'I'm frightened at what is happening and so quickly too,'
she confessed.

'Have no fear, my love,' and he took her in his arms and
this time she felt the force of his full, sensuous mouth upon
hers. They clung to each other in the morning sunshine,
the old rose-brick building, the birds, and any ghosts that
wandered the only witnesses to their first kiss.

They broke apart and both stood, grinning happily at
each other.

'So, Mrs Grange, my English lady?'

'So, Mr Georgeopoulos?'

'Lunch, Mrs Grange?'

'Why, thank you, Mr Georgeopoulos.' Hand in hand,
they ran to the car through the cold morning air, their
breath trailing behind them in wispy white tendrils.

Ann stood warming herself by the large log fire in the
riverside pub they had found. She watched him at the

bar, the sour-faced barmaid visibly melting at his effortless charm. She watched and did not mind, cloaking herself with the knowledge that soon, very soon, they would be lovers. They chose a table in front of a huge bow window which seemed to hang over the river itself, and ordered their steaks.

'Now, I want to know about you. Tell me everything about your life,' he said, pulling his elbows on the table and cupping his chin in his hands as he watched her intently.

'There's not much to tell.' She laughed, nervously, unused to such attention from a man. 'My father was a doctor, a GP. I met my husband while I was still at school and he was a medical student. Our parents were friends. I left school at sixteen, and did a cookery course, flower arranging, that sort of thing. When I was eighteen we were married. I had twins – a boy and a girl, very organized,' she said in a rush. 'That's it really, the story of my life.' She shrugged her shoulders. 'Not much, is it?'

'You were very young. Weren't there things you wanted to do? Travel? A career?' Still the intent gaze was focused upon her.

'I had no idea what I wanted to do, none whatsoever. It sounds silly, I suppose, to someone like you. But I'd never been much good academically. I like English and Art. Perhaps if I hadn't met Ben I would have worked harder to go to art college, who knows?' Again she shrugged her shoulders almost self-deprecatingly. 'Mind you, I don't think my parents would have let me go. I can just imagine their horror at their precious daughter mixing with all those dreadful beatniks.' she laughed at the idea. 'Most of all, I wanted to be married. My parents were idyllically happy – I suppose I wanted to be like them. After all, in those days, wanting to be married was a respectable career for a girl. Then when I met Ben I knew I had found the right man, so there seemed no point in waiting,' she explained, and was puzzled that she should be sounding almost defensive. He said nothing, so she continued. 'It was a struggle when we were first married. Ben had only just qualified and we had very little money. Perhaps I should have thought of getting a job then, to help out, but my mother had never worked, I didn't know any married women who did. To be honest I don't think the idea crossed my mind. But, in a way, I think that not having much money made us appreciate everything more when we could afford to buy things.' He nodded agreement. 'And then I had the twins, a boy and a girl. And I kept the house, and that's all really. It makes me sound very boring, doesn't it?'

'And were you happy?'

'Of course.'

'It doesn't always follow.'

'No, but I was lucky. Ben was a good husband.'

'What makes a good husband?'

'He was considerate, generous, I enjoyed his company.'

'Was he faithful to you?'

She looked surprised at his question. 'But of course.'

'Said with such confidence. Then you really were fortunate, a most unusual husband!' She wondered if there was sarcasm in his voice but if there was it was negated by his smile. 'And what did you do, your husband and you?'

'Not much really. Our home was our main interest. Ben played golf and when he was younger he played rugby. I used to go to watch the matches, but I never enjoyed golf. We would have friends to dinner and we would visit them, that sort of thing. Ben didn't enjoy concerts or galleries so sometimes I would go to London with a girlfriend or by myself.' She fell silent for one moment. 'There were times I wished Ben enjoyed the same things as I do. But he didn't and that was that . . .' She half smiled and remembered the many times she had returned home, her mind full of pictures she had seen or the music she had just heard, bursting to share them with him, and how quickly her elation had disappeared at his lack of interest. 'It used to get me into trouble too. You see, I sometimes popped into small art galleries and bought pictures. Oh, nothing too expensive, but it would annoy Ben. He saw it as a waste of hard-earned cash . . . Mind you, he never stopped me buying what I wanted,' she added hurriedly. 'You see he worked so incredibly hard and got so tired.' Again she heard the hint of apology in her voice. Apologizing for Ben now.

'I like opera and I also collect paintings – it becomes a compulsion doesn't it?'

'It does.' She laughed with pleasure that he understood. 'I see a painting and my stomach does a flip, and I just have to have it. And you like opera too?' She checked, almost disbelievingly.

'Yes. My company has a box at Covent Garden – it's yours to use whenever you wish.' He put out his hand and touched her, so gently that she was at first unsure he had done so: only her own nervous shiver assured her that he had.

'Were you content with this life?'

'Yes, of course.' She looked at her plate and then across the table at him, as he leaned forward, intent on what she was saying. 'Actually that's not strictly true. I used to get restless.' To her surprise Ann found herself confessing something she had never told a living soul. But his unwavering interest in her flattered her, made her feel that to tell him anything but the strictest truth would be insulting.

'Everything was so planned, you see. It would have been nice now and and then to do something on the spur of the moment. How strange, I've never told anyone that.' She shook her shoulders as if shaking the traitorous confession away. 'But, as Ben pointed out, I should count my blessings. With such a lovely home and family what had I to complain of? He was right,' she said emphatically. He sat silent. 'I read a lot and years ago I used to try and paint. In fact I've been thinking of taking that up again. And I had the garden. I'd never known any other kind of life.' She listed the advantages she'd had. 'But what else is a wife for?' she added lamely.

'It sounds idyllic.' This time she was sure she heard the irony in his voice but when she looked up sharply he was smiling her again. 'And you never travelled?'

'Oh, yes. We went to France a couple of times. And once to Spain – holidays, you know. But he didn't like me to go to conferences with him, which was a shame – he went all over the world.'

'And why was that, do you think?'

'He thought I'd be bored.'

'Maybe he was frightened you'd prove too much of a distraction.' He looked at her kindly.

'Me? I shouldn't think so for a minute,' she said, laughing good-naturedly.

'And the house you spent all your time in, tell me about that.'

'Since you like old places, I'm sure you'd love it. It's in a village about an hour from Cambridge called Midfield. The village was mentioned in the Domesday Book. I shouldn't think much had changed since then, apart from the council estate.' She smiled wryly. 'Part of my house is Tudor and the most modern part is Queen Anne.' Her face glowed with pleasure as she described her home to him. 'Buying it was the maddest thing we ever did. It was in a dreadful mess. It took us years and every penny we could spare to restore it. But I guess we couldn't help ourselves: it was a case of love at first sight.'

'Ah! Love at first sight, dangerous.' He poured more wine. 'And now, with no Ben, you are happy to stay there?'

'Oh yes, I feel safe there. But my son wants me to sell it.'

'Why?'

'He says it's too expensive and too big for me.'

'And is it?'

'It's too big, but I can afford it. Ben left me well provided for.'

'Then keep it. It's nothing to do with your son. It's your life.'

'That's what I say, but he doesn't see it that way. He thinks I'm wasting what should be his money.'

'A son should want his mother's happiness.'

'Well, I had a perfect husband, I suppose it's too much to expect a perfect son too,' she said lightly. 'But don't let's get bogged down talking about Peter. I want to know about you. What do you do? Where do you live, in Greece?'

'I live wherever I am. A true cosmopolitan, you see,' he mocked himself. 'I have a place in Greece, but I'm rarely there, sadly. I always seem to be too busy elsewhere.'

'And how long will you be in England?'

'Tonight I leave for New York. In fact,' he said looking at his watch, 'we should be going now, I have a couple of meetings I must attend before I fly out.'

'Oh, no, Alex,' she made no effort to hide her disappointment.

'I'm sorry too, my darling. Just as we meet, just as we get to know each other – but I cannot cancel this trip. I would if I could, I assure you. I shall only be gone a week however. Will you be waiting for me?' He asked the question without a hint of smile.

'Of course,' she found herself replying.

The traffic back into the city was heavy and at the hotel they had to rush the porter to get Ann's baggage. She said she could get a taxi but Alex was insistent that he must see her on to her train. He hurled the little Mini down side streets, taking short cuts he said, but to Ann they seemed only to prolong the journey. His fingers never seemed to be off the horn and he cursed the other drivers in a multitude of languages.

At Liverpool Street station Ann's train was about to leave. They raced down the platform and Alex opened the door of the nearest first-class carriage. The guard's flag was already raised and they had time for only a quick kiss.

'I'll phone you. You will be patient, you will wait for me, won't you?' he said with a strange urgency. 'There's so much to say . . .' The train began to move. Alex walked along beside it, quickening his pace as the train gathered speed, all the time, to Ann's delight, blowing her kisses. She was certain he would have run to the end of the platform but for a British Rail trolley blocking his way. She hung out of the window waving until she could no longer see his tall figure.

She picked up her case and made her way from the almost empty first-class carriage into a crowded second-class compartment. She found a seat and sank back on to it. Still, she smiled to herself, she had the memory of his kiss, his hand touching her, the secure feeling of his arm about her, and the sound of his voice as he called her darling. She sat contentedly wrapping these memories about her.

'Excuse me. Is this seat taken . . . Ann . . . Ann Grange. What a wonderful chance, meeting you. I do get so bored on train journeys, don't you? Been shopping?'

With a sinking heart Ann looked up to see Karen Rigson standing above her and stowing plump carrier bags on to the parcel rack.

Karen sat down noisily in the seat opposite. 'I do so like to get the Christmas bits and bobs in early, don't you, before the crowds. Mind you, it was bad enough, wasn't it? I thought I was going to suffocate in Selfridges, thought I might pass out . . .' Ann smiled sympathetically, at the same time doubting if tough Karen was capable of fainting anywhere. 'Gracious, Ann, you've lost weight,' Karen's loud voice rang out, making the other occupants in the carriage turn to stare at her with curiosity. 'Haven't seen you for ages. What have you been doing?'

'Nothing much,' Ann lied, longing to say, 'falling in love with a bright and wonderful foreigner.' Instead she smiled patiently.

'Have you had your hair dyed?' Karen's voice boomed out. Again the curious passengers turned and stared.

'Lydia's hairdresser highlighted it for me.'

'Oh, yes. I'd heard you'd been seeing a lot of Lydia.' Karen's thin lips pursed in obvious disapproval.

'She'd been a very good friend to me. I like her,' Ann said sharply, hoping in some way that by defending Lydia she could shut Karen up and return to thinking about Alex. Karen's conversations were insistent at the best of times, but tonight she surpassed herself, seeming hardly to draw breath on the whole journey. Still, thought Ann, she had the car ride when she would be alone to concentrate her thoughts on him.

The train pulled into Cambridge.

'Got the car? Fancy giving me a lift? I didn't have time to phone John and the local train takes such an age.'

'Of course,' Ann replied with a studied pleasantness she was far from feeling. 'Here, let me help you.' She took a pile of Karen's parcels. The two women walked through the large car park, Karen still in full spate.

5

The euphoria with which Alex had left Ann had been relentlessly chipped at by Karen Rigson's company. Now, as Ann let herself into the silent house, it disappeared completely. She wandered aimlessly about the house, goaded by the uncharacteristic restlessness. The place was so empty, she thought, as she drifted from room to room, forgetting all those months when she had cherished and chosen that self-same emptiness.

If he had not had to leave she might have been in his arms now, even perhaps in bed. Mundanely she put the kettle on to make a cup of tea, realizing, as she did so, how amused he would be at the very Englishness of making a cup of tea to calm the unfamiliar raging ache in her body. The telephone rang. Eagerly she answered it, hoping for the sound of his voice.

'At last! Where the hell have you been? I've been

worried sick.' She was disappointed to hear her son's voice.

'I went to London to do some shopping.'

'You might let people know in future. I rang all day yesterday and today.'

'I'm sorry, I should have phoned. I didn't think. I didn't plan it.'

'Plan it? Plan what?' he asked sharply.

'I mean staying on. I'd done my shopping and decided to stay overnight.'

'You didn't stay with Fay,' he said accusingly.

'No, I stayed in a hotel.'

'Which hotel?'

'Really, Peter, does it matter? Just a hotel.'

'Well, it's odd, very odd. You've never done anything like this before.'

'Maybe I should have done. I've been spending too much time alone recently.'

'So, you weren't alone?'

'Don't be stupid. Peter. I simply meant I should get out and about more instead of rattling around here on my own.

'Ah, going off the house then?'

'Peter, don't you ever give up?'

'Just a joke, Ma.' He laughed but it sounded hollow to Ann. 'We wondered if you'd like to come to lunch on Sunday.'

'Does Sally want me to come?'

'Of course Sally bloody well wants you to come. You are neurotic. Ma.'

'What's today?'

'Christ, Ma, it's Friday.' She could imagine the irritated expression on his face as he spoke through clenched teeth. 'What the hell have you been up to that you don't even known the day of the week?'

'Let me see . . .' She rustled some papers as if she were leafing through a diary. Her thoughts were tumbling in panic. She could not go. What if Alex phoned and she

93

missed his call? How could she face her son with this inner excitement which must show on her face? 'I'm lunching with friends,' she lied.

'Who?'

'I don't think you know them.'

'When can you come then?'

'I am not sure, I'll have to give you a ring.'

'Great!' he shouted. 'Now I have to make an appointment to see my own mother!' and she heard the receiver at his end slam down. She sighed as she replaced the receiver, wondering if he was ill, or worried about something. Maybe he had always been like this, and she, thinking him perfect, had simply never noticed.

She collected her tea tray, crossed the drawing room, put on a record, kicked off her shoes and lay back on the sofa, consciously removing thoughts of her son and settling back to think, at last, about Alex. A secret little smile played about her mouth, the music filled the room . . .

'Oh, no!' The words broke from her in an agonized wail and in rage she threw the cup she was holding across the room. The tea splashed down the wall, the pretty cup shattered into pieces. 'Oh, no,' she repeated. How could they have been so stupid? In all the rush of leaving each other they had forgotten the most important thing – her address and telephone number.

Ann sat staring bleakly into space as she imagined this new-found potential happiness disappearing from her grasp. What on earth could she do? Phone his embassy, Pétin? But were they likely to give away information like that over the phone? In any case where was Pétin's? No doubt ex-directory to ensure its ludicrous discretion.

She brightened at the thought that he might have contacted her hotel but, almost immediately, her shoulders slumped. Hotels of that calibre would surely not divulge clients' addresses, she thought sadly. She tried to remember if she had mentioned the name of her village.

She had talked about the house but had she described the village, let alone named it?'

Two days ago she had left this house a woman who had conquered grief, reasonably content with her life and with no thought of finding another man. She had returned infatuated by a foreigner who had entered her life by chance. A man who, in such a short time, had reawoken a physical need in her body. So that now all equilibrium had left her again and she was racked with frustration and disappointment.

Despondently she stood and wandered aimlessly over to the drinks tray. She picked up the familiar dark green bottle and poured herself an enormous measure of gin.

The doorbell woke her. She looked about her, dazed. It was morning. She was still on the sofa, the lights were on, the record still spun silently on the turntable. She sat up too quickly, her head reeling from too much gin, her mouth dry from too many cigarettes, her clothes crumpled. She decided to ignore whoever it was. At least it was Saturday and Meg would not be in. The ringing persisted, followed by heavy hammering on the knocker. Barefoot she tiptoed to the door and looked through the spyhole. Outside stood the familiar green of a Harrods van. Puzzled, she opened the door.

'Mrs Grange? Special delivery.' The man disappeared to the back of the van and re-emerged carrying an enormous basket of yellow roses. He handed them to her, grinning at her astonished face, disappeared and came back with another. 'Someone thinks a lot of you,' he said cheerily as she signed for the flowers.

Ann backed gingerly into the hall. She carried the baskets through the kitchen and, lowering them on to the floor, searched feverishly for a card. Finding it, with trembling fingers, she tore it open.

Anna,

Did you think you could escape me?
Do you know the language of flowers? These are for all the people you see, speak to, and smile at until I return!

Alex

She read the note again and again, tenderly tracing the bold black writing with her fingers. How on earth had he found out her address? What on earth must it have all cost? Special delivery, too, not Interflora. The language of flowers? She raced to the study. Somewhere she had a book on Victorian etiquette, picked up years ago in a jumble sale. At last she found it and returned to her flowers, leafing through the book. 'Yellow,' she read, 'the colour of jealousy'. She sat on the floor by the opulent flowers and laughed and cried at the same time.

'How magical. You beautiful, lovely things,' she said to the flowers. She rocked back and forth, hugging herself with joy.

She sat up straight. There was so much to do. She had a week in which to organize herself, get some new clothes, try to restore her nails. But first the flowers . . . she collected every vase she could find. Arranging the flowers took her an hour, by which time vases stood all over the house. She wanted to see them wherever she went.

Later, in her bedroom, she sat gazing at a large arrangement of her roses. What sort of lover would he be, she wondered. She remembered a friend, who had had an army of lovers, once telling her that she always looked at a man's lower lip – if it was full he would be sensuous lover. It was infallible, the friend had claimed. Ann remembered his mouth, the full lower lip, and smiled with satisfaction.

She stood up and went to study the contents of her cupboards. She had been right: she needed a whole new wardrobe. Everything she owned looked safe and dull; nothing was suitable for the adventure on which she was about to embark. And shopping would help her get through the week until he returned.

The familiar roar of Lydia's car interrupted her ruthless pruning of the clothes that forty-eight hours ago had pleased her.

'Ann, I love the hair!' Lydia enthused. 'Isn't Wayne a genius? You don't mind me popping in, do you? I had to see the result.' She tripped into the hall. 'Good God, it looks like a bleeding florist's!' she exclaimed as she saw the flowers.

'It does a bit, doesn't it? I've run out of vases,' Ann said sheepishly.

'How many are there, for heaven's sake?'

'Two hundred and eighty-eight, I counted them.' Ann giggled as she led Lydia into the drawing room.

'All is revealed. How exciting. Such profusion – it's positively vulgar! Who is he?'

'A man.'

'I realize that, silly. I didn't think you'd turned gay in your old age. Come on, tell me, I can't wait . . .' she insisted, elegantly draping herself on the sofa, and picking up the empty gin bottle from the floor with a questioning look.

'I was depressed last night.' Ann blushed, hurriedly picking up her debris. 'I forgot to tell him where I lived, and I thought I'd never see him again,' she explained.

'Oh, Ann, you're hopeless. So then what?'

'The flowers came. Special delivery from Harrods – imagine all that way, and on a Saturday. He'd found my address from somewhere . . . Oh Lydia, I'm so excited!'

'I can see that, but it's not telling much, is it?'

'He's gorgeous, very tall and broad and . . . I'm so frightened that Peter will find out and spoil it all,' Ann burst out.

'Don't tell him then. You're right, he'd have kittens at the very idea of his precious mama with a feller! Where did you meet him, I thought you were going to buy wallpaper?'

'I feel stupid telling you, but well, I met him at the Tate. We happened to be looking at the same picture and we just got talking. It sounds so corny.'

'I think it sounds lovely.'

'He invited me out to dinner. He took me to his fabulous restaurant. It was more like a house and there was a ghastly French woman who made me feel very provincial . . .'

'Pétin's?'

'Yes, that was her name.'

'My, I am impressed. Ludicrously exclusive and it costs an arm and a leg just to have a pee in there. And?'

Next day we went to Hampton Court and had lunch and just talked and talked. He's not handsome, more ugly-interesting. He's about our age, might be a bit older. And he's Greek.'

'Greek! Darling, I don't want to put you down, but do be careful. I had a friend married one but it didn't work: he was positively feudal. Married?'

'I don't know, he didn't say, and I couldn't bring myself to ask.'

'What's he do?'

'I'm not sure.'

'Darling, you are too naïve to be allowed out on your own! Let's think, he must be rich to take you to Pétin's and then there are the flowers, that's a plus.'

'Lydia, don't be so cynical. I couldn't care less if he's rich or poor.'

'Then you're making a mistake. If you're going to have an affair it must be with a rich man. Imagine if he were married and poor – it would be too sordid. Married and rich, at least he can commit adultery in style.'

'Lydia, you're impossible. Don't you take anything seriously?'

'Hardly anything. Have you slept with him yet?'

'Of course not. We've just met.' Ann tried to sound shocked. Lydia chuckled, not for one moment deceived by Ann's attempts at righteous indignation, and arched an elegantly plucked eyebrow. 'He had to rush off to New York, otherwise . . .' Ann spread her hands and shrugged.

'Oh you lucky girl, all that delicious anticipation! How I envy you.'

'Don't tell anyone, will you? I mean at my age, it's all so silly – allowing myself to be picked up.'

'If you were twenty you wouldn't think twice about being picked up, so why should you feel different about it now? But don't worry, I won't tell a living soul, not until you tell me I can.'

'It's very odd, Lydia, but you know I expected to feel guilty, and I don't.'

'Why should you feel guilty?'

'Guilty to Ben's memory.'

'Ben!' Lydia looked at her with a mixture of affection and concern. She took Ann's hand and grasped it hard. 'Don't let anybody get in the way of this happiness, not anyone, least of all Ben, you promise!'

'I promise.' Ann started to laugh but there was an intensity in Lydia's voice that stopped her. 'I expect you'll have Peter on the phone to you, snooping. He's already suspicious that something's up.'

'I shall just tell him he must expect strange behaviour from his menopausal mother,' Lydia said airily. 'Any gin left?'

The next couple of days dragged by for Ann. The longed-for phone call did not materialize. The new clothes had to wait, she did not go shopping, she did not leave the house, fearful that she might be out when he rang. She was convinced there was something wrong with the telephone and kept picking it up to check the dialling tone. She laughed at herself, remembering how, as a teenager waiting for Ben to call, she had done the self-same thing. That was really how she felt, just like a kid again.

Late on Tuesday afternoon the phone rang. She heard the bleeping of a call box.

'Mrs Grange?'

'Alex!'

'I'm here, can I come and see you?'

'Oh, yes,' she answered immediately, breathless with excitement. 'Where are you? How long will you be?' But there was no reply: the phone was dead.

She raced upstairs. Looking in the mirror she wished she had gone to the hairdresser's again. Perhaps she had time to wash and dry her hair. She was irritated to hear a ring on the front door bell. Who the hell? Exasperated she ran down to open the door.

'Hullo, my darling.'

He stepped in and swept her into his arms, covering her face with kisses. 'I've missed you so much. Isn't that marvellous?' he announced with a surprised pride.

'But where have you come from? I thought you were in London. I'm such a mess!' she complained through her laughter.

'You look perfect to me. I phoned from the village, I wanted to surprise you.' His arms were around her and he was kissing her and through Ann's body swept an excitement she had never felt before.

6

They clung to each other, as if fearful to let go, and Ann led him towards the drawing room, thankful that she had lit the fire.

'Mind your head,' she warned. He ducked his head as he entered the low doorway.

'Perfect!' he exclaimed. 'It's just as I imagined it would be. It's so English – the great fireplace, the beams, the leaded windows, the chintz. I must see all of it, then when I'm away I can imagine you anywhere in your house.'

'I can't believe you're here.' She turned, looking up at him. It seemed so strange to see him standing in her drawing room. 'Would you like a drink?'

'No. I want tea. Proper English tea, with cucumber sandwiches, fruit cake, in front of this log fire.'

'I've no cucumber,' she said, worried.

'No cucumber. How remiss, Anna.' He laughed, kissing her lightly. 'Poor darling, such an anxious expression. Who wants cucumber?'

'Gentleman's Relish?'

'Splendid. Even more English.'

He insisted on following her into the kitchen and perched on a stool as she prepared the tea and toast. She felt oddly clumsy as she laid the tray, for his eyes were constantly watching her, and the expression of longing in them made her nervous. Each time she passed close to him his hand would reach out to touch her, to stroke her hair. She found she kept dropping spoons and banging into things.

'I didn't thank you for my lovely flowers,' she said, dropping a teaspoon on the floor for the second time, and bent, flustered, to pick it up. 'I thought you'd never find me. I even thought of trying to find Madame Pétin.' She was annoyed to hear the nervousness in her voice.

'How brave of you,' he smiled. 'It's easy to find anyone in the world, if you want to badly enough. But you were particularly easy. I had your name, the name of the village. I wouldn't let you go once I'd found you.' He stroked her cheek fondly, as if he too was unsure that he was really here. Ann liked him constantly touching her, but at the same time, it made her feel gauche. She was unused to it and was unsure how to react. Nor was she used to the close proximity of a man who disturbed her physically – that too was a new experience.

In the drawing room she indicated a chair for him, purposely avoiding Ben's favourite chair. She sat on the floor, at his feet, and poured the tea.

'How was your trip?'

'A disaster!'

'I'm sorry.'

'It couldn't be helped. I couldn't concentrate. I lost all interest in my work.' He leaned forward in his chair. 'All I could think of was what you were doing, who you were talking to. I was frightened you might meet someone else. I didn't dare telephone, I felt if I heard your voice I would drop everything and rush to you. I made everyone very angry with me.' He took the cup she offered him, the fragile bone china looking even more delicate in his large hands.

'I'm sorry,' she repeated, not in the least sorry for the turmoil she had caused him and hardly daring to believe what he had said. She was incapable of taking her eyes off his hands which she longed to have touching her again.

'Then, last night I decided it was useless trying to get anything done. So I left my assistants to cope.' He leaned down and gently took both her hands and kissed them.

'I hope your bosses won't mind too much.' She found herself smiling despite her concern, it was as if he had read her thoughts.

He laughed, 'No, I don't think that's likely to happen. But I should have taken you with me. Next time I will.'

'Me? To New York! You're joking.'

'No I'm not. At least I'd get some business done!' He took another slice of toast. 'Did you speak to lots of people, did they feel my furious jealousy?'

'I don't think so,' she laughed. 'My son phoned, my cleaner came, and Lydia my friend visited.'

'And did you tell them about me?'

'I told Lydia.'

'I see,' he said, stroking her hair. 'You're ready to tell your confidential friend of me but not your son? Why not? Would he disapprove of me?' She listened for a hint of laughter in his voice but did not hear it.

'I don't think he would approve of anybody in my life just yet. I think it's too soon for him,' she said seriously.

'But not for you?' His tone matched hers.

'No,' she replied firmly, 'I thought it was until last week, but, I don't know how, you changed all that,' she added simply.

'I missed you, Anna, it was like a pain that would not go away. You are like a fever to me. I never expected to feel like this again, ever.'

'Isn't it wonderful?'

He turned her to him, cupping her face in his hands, and studied her face for what seemed a long time. 'I want you, Anna, I can't play games. I need you, I want you in my bed, I want to make endless love to you. I should court you, flirt with you, shower you with presents, be the romantic suitor, but this longing for you is too strong. Do you understand? Can you accept?'

'Yes, Alex. I feel the same way. But . . .' she paused. 'Not here, not in this house.'

'Of course,' he replied gently. He looked at her with undisguised passion in his eyes and kissed her hungrily. 'London or the country?'

'The country,' she answered without even having to think.

'Can you get away for a week?'

'Oh yes, easily.'

'Right, if I might use your telephone I'll make arrangements.'

While he was on the phone Ann ran upstairs and hurriedly began to pack, throwing a random selection of clothes into her case. She quickly washed her face, brushed her hair, changed into fresh trousers and sweater and rushed from the room without realizing that she had not once looked at the big double bed. There was no reply when she phoned Meg so she called Lydia whose voice bubbled down the phone with ill-concealed curiosity. Ann talked quickly, giving nothing away, asking Lydia to arrange with Meg about the house, and to let Peter know she was going away for a few days. The prospect of speaking to her son and dealing with his questioning was too daunting.

She had expected to see the silver-coloured Mini, and was surprised and stunned to find, instead, a gleaming silver Maserati in the drive. He drove fast but she felt safe cocooned in the car's leather luxury. It all seemed impossible. Last week she had been alone, concerned with her wallpaper; this week she was swept away at speed, in a powerful, expensive car, by an intriguing man. A man she hardly knew and yet to whom she could talk easily about herself and her thoughts. A few days ago she had not even known he existed. What the future held she did not know, nor did she care. She wanted to savour and treasure every moment of this electrically charged present.

After several hours the car slipped through ornate iron gates, along a mile-long drive and stopped in front of a large, white Georgian mansion, ablaze with lights.

'Is it a hotel?'

'No. It's called Courtneys. I didn't want people around us. I want to be alone with you.'

They crossed the hall, her heels clattering on the black and white marble floor, and he led her into the most perfectly proportioned room she had ever seen. It was furnished entirely in period style and a fire glowed in the Adam grate.

'Now for that drink,' he said, crossing to an intricately inlaid side table and mixing their drinks from the decanters on the heavy silver tray.

'This room is lovely. Those mouldings, this furniture and the paintings . . .' Surprise made her tongue-tied.

'I'm glad you're pleased with it. But I would rather have yours. This is too perfect: instant furnishing, care of the designers. It was all right until I saw yours, then I realized it lacks soul.' He handed her a drink. The glass shook in her hand. Feeling as nervous as a young girl, she shivered, suddenly chilled to the marrow. She took a large gulp of her drink, desperate to steady her nerves. He approached her, took the drink from her, and, wordlessly, taking her by the hand, led her out of the room, across the hall, up the sweeping staircase, and to the end of a landing where he opened a door into a large, softly lit bedroom.

She had expected him to take her in his arms immediately, and was surprised when he said, 'I just have to fetch something. You should find everything you need in your bathroom.'

In the bathroom Ann leaned against the door. She was filled with a strange mixture of excitement and fear. She had wanted this to happen but now it was so close she felt a dreadful shyness. The thought that he was to see her body, the body that only one other man had caressed, filled her with near terror. She stripped and on the mirror-lined walls she saw a dozen reflections of her naked body. Involuntarily she covered her breasts with embarrassment as if he were in the room with her. She turned away hastily and stepped into the shower. When she emerged, she decided against a silk négligé which was draped on a chair, and wrapped herself instead in a large bathtowel. She returned to the bedroom to find him lying unselfconsciously naked on the bed. Shyly she sat on the very edge.

'I thought we should have champagne.' He indicated the tray and bottle beside him. She accepted the glass from him. 'Don't be frightened little one.'

'It's silly, isn't it? I feel like a young girl.'

'You look like one, my darling.' Very gently he folded his arms about her. 'Anna, my sweet Anna, at last.' Slowly he removed the towel from her and she, feeling totally vulnerable, lowered her eyes. 'Beautiful,' he whispered, gazing at her breasts. 'This first time, Anna my darling, is for me. Forgive me, but I need you desperately. But after will be for you, I promise.

He kissed her passionately with a hunger that frightened her and then he was upon her, his body thrusting into her with an urgency she had never experienced before. She cried out, but either he did not hear her or did not want to hear as he continued to possess her, but his cry as he took her made her want to hold and protect him.

He kept his promise that afterwards was for her. Slowly, languorously, he began to make love to her again. Under his skilled hands her body was alive and she was clinging to him and begging him to enter her again. But he laughed.

'We have the whole night, my love.'

'Please, please . . .'

He ignored her pleas and time and again he drew her into a frenzy. She thought she would faint from the pleasure he gave her body. At last they climaxed together and she could feel a torrent of relief flood through her. She slumped exhausted on the pillow.

'But I thought you wanted me?' he laughed.

'I did. I mean I do! Oh Alex, I didn't know it could be like that. I'm totally exhausted.'

'You needn't think you're going to sleep!' he said commandingly and unbelievably he was making love to her again and even more unbelievably she found herself responding to him. She lost count of the number of times they made love but each time he took her body he took a little bit more of her soul.

There was no past, there was no future, there was only this moment of loving present.

7

'*Agapi mou*, wake up. *S'agapo*, Anna, *s'agapo* . . .'

The strange words drifted into Ann's waking mind, the voice soft and persistent. '*Agapi*.' She opened her eyes and smiled contentedly, remembering where she was.

'*Agapi*?' she repeated. 'What does it mean?'

'Darling.' He kissed her.

'*Agapi*, I like it. What do the other words mean, there were other words, weren't there?'

'Ah, that's pillow talk, my sweet. See, I've made you tea,' he announced proudly.

She shifted on the pillow and took the cup he offered. She tasted it and grimaced. 'Alex, you may be the most marvellous lover in the world – but you make the worst tea!'

'I never made it before. What have I done wrong?'

'Most people prefer to boil the water,' she said, laughing happily at him. The sheet which had covered her slipped and quickly she recovered herself.

'No, no, my darling.' Gently he took the sheet from her hands and pulled it down to reveal her nakedness. 'Please let me look at you. After such a night of love, what is more natural than to want to look at your body?'

'You embarrass me. I'm not used to . . . and her voice trailed away.

'You must learn, my love. When we are alone like this I want to see you naked all the time, remembering, anticipating . . .' He leaned forward, kissing her, and she felt her body begin to stir with excitement beneath his touch. Suddenly she began to laugh and he stood up, abruptly.

'I'm sorry, but it just struck me as so funny – what if the other members of the Midfield Church Fête Committee could see me now?' She shrieked at the idea. 'They'd have a fit, I'd be drummed out of the church. An outcast,' and she sank back on the pillows, still laughing. He stood, hands on hips, towering above her, with no flicker of amusement on his face. 'I'm sorry, so sorry. I wasn't laughing at you but at me!' she added, quickly seeing the expression, bordering on affront, upon his face.

'I'm hungry,' he announced abruptly. 'I have some calls to make, perhaps you wouldn't mind cooking me some breakfast?'

'Have I time for a quick bath?' she said, trying to keep the laughter out of her voice.

'Be quick,' was all he said as he strode from the room.

She lay in the bath wishing she hadn't laughed. She seemed to have hurt his feelings. She did not want anything to spoil this week, but it was such a silly thing for him to get upset about: after all, it *was* funny.

She looked about the room, which was larger than her own bedroom, with curiosity. The thick white carpet covered even the steps up to the sunken bath. Water gushed from large gold dolphins whose bodies arched elegantly over the bath. She could see no light fitments and yet the room was diffused with light. There were armchairs, tables with ornaments and books, a telephone, a television, even a silver tray with a selection of drinks. It was as if the room could not make up its mind whether it was a sitting room or a bathroom.

Wrapped in an enveloping white bathrobe, she crossed to the dressing table which was a large slab of white marble, supported by two golden eagles, their wings outstretched. The top was laden with various bottles of perfume and bath oils. She looked at the bottles, studying the labels, so many of her favourites – Patou's 'Joy', Givenchy's 'Le Dé', Hermès's 'Calèche'. She unstoppered the bottles, reminding herself of their various smells, unsure which one to use. To the other side was a range of make-up and skin-care products – everything she could possibly need. But to whom did it all belong . . .? The bottle of Calèche clattered from her grasp, an expensive rivulet of perfume snaking across the white marble. She wrenched a Kleenex out of the box and desperately staunched the stream, convinced that it would mark the marble – show she had been here . . .

She sat down heavily on the stool. Her face in the mirror was woebegone, all the joy she had woken with erased as she surveyed the armoury of another woman's weapons.

What on earth did she think she was doing? What the hell did she mean playing this sort of game? What right had she to be here in another woman's bathroom, with another woman's possessions, and worst of all sleeping with her husband? She was now everything she normally despised – the other woman.

She had allowed herself to be borne along on a wave of excitement and glamour that had suddenly invaded her dull life like a shaft of light. She had sat in her house in Midfield and weighed up the effect on this affair on her, and what it would do for her, but she had not once thought what it would mean for his wife. She had not given that more than a passing thought. It had been easy in her own home to ignore this unknown woman and her feelings but now, surrounded by her things, it was impossible.

She looked with distaste at the silk négligé that she had spurned last night. She had thought Alex a sensitive person, but bringing her here was not the act of such a man.

And now his remark that he wanted to be alone with her began to make more sense. She had thought it romantic but now it took on an entirely different meaning – he did not want, or could not risk, being seen with her.

She remembered last night and her body tingled at the memory. How wonderful it had all been, what a selfless lover he was. But now that could only be a memory. She had to leave, she had no right to be here. She knew she would never be able to be happy with him with this feeling of guilt growing rapidly within her like a child's crystal garden.

She began to dress, taking her time. She did not look forward to telling him she wanted to go home. On the one hand she was certain he would be angry; on the other she knew that once she stood before him, was close to him, it would be a difficult thing to say. She knew she would be in danger of changing her mind, would want to put out her hand and touch him, feel his lips on hers . . .

Carefully she applied her own make-up. She felt an illogical dislike for his wife. She shook her head at her own reflection in the mirror. How stupid of her, how unintelligent to dislike someone she did not know and was never likely to meet. Jealousy, she presumed. Efficiently she clicked her make-up case closed and rapidly collected her few things together and placed them in her case.

Downstairs she searched for him. In each room a fire glowed in the grate, but there was no sign of Alex. From behind a door she thought she heard a voice. Tiptoeing to the door, she heard only silence, but she sensed there was someone in the room. Softly she knocked; there was no response, so she quietly opened the door and entered a study. Alex was at the desk, his back towards her, listening intently to a conversation on the telephone. She stood waiting for him to notice her.

'You absolute bloody fool,' he suddenly shouted into the receiver. 'What have I told you time and again, Nigel? Check, you stupid bastard. Think! Or aren't you capable of logical thought? Get me Yianni,' he roared. Ann decided she had better leave, but before she could, he swung around in the chair. She was shocked by the expression of cold anger on his face, the blazing fury in his eyes. He did not even seem to notice her standing there as he began what was obviously an angry torrent of Greek into the phone. Ann backed from the room.

She passed through a green baize door and found the kitchen. Still shaken by the new Alex she had just seen, and uncertain what else to do, she began to cook the breakfast. Really, she told herself, she had no cause to be surprised: she could not claim to know him. There was obviously another side to him, an Alex whose anger she would prefer never to have directed at her – not that there was any risk of that now.

It was a good half-hour before he joined her. He did not speak but instead stood, looking out of the window, a deep frown on his face, and with his hands thrust deep into his pockets. She did not know what to do, whether to speak to him, whether to ask what was wrong. It did not seen the best time to tell him she wanted to be driven home. Instead she decided to say and ask nothing and began to fry his eggs. The breakfast ready, he still stood in the same position.

'Alex, your breakfast's getting cold,' she eventually ventured to say, and gently touched his arms.

'Thank you,' he responded, still frowning. He began to eat. She poured the coffee. 'Darling, I'm sorry,' he suddenly said. 'I hadn't wanted anything to spoil this week, and then this happens. I am beset with bloody fools!' He angrily banged his fist on the table.

She realized that she felt an illogical relief that he had called her 'darling', that his anger wasn't because she had laughed. What on earth did it matter now? She looked at his frowning face, at his fine hands, remembered the pleasure those hands had given her in the night, and despite herself and her good intentions, found herself taking hold of his hand and lifting it to her mouth and kissing it, '*Agapi*,' she said shyly.

He smiled, all anger disappearing, a gentle expression returning. 'That's what I need, a calm woman to keep me in order, to keep a sense of perspective. But, my darling, you don't eat?'

'I never have breakfast.'

'But you must, you had no dinner and, as I remember, a very busy night! Here, take this,' and he fork-fed her some of his food despite her protests. Then he pushed the plate away. 'Come here,' he ordered and pulled her towards him. She resisted but he was too strong for her and she found herself on his knee as he nuzzled her neck.

'You smell of soap.' He looked up, sounding surprised.

'I forgot to pack my perfume last night, it was all such a rush.'

'Didn't you like those in your bathroom?'

'I'm sure they're lovely,' she said stiffly.

'Why didn't you use them then?'

'I don't know who they belong to,' she answered primly, but he began to laugh.

'So that's why you came to my bed wrapped in a towel instead of that becoming négligé. You're jealous!' he declared triumphantly.

'Of course I'm not jealous. Don't be ridiculous, Alex. What right have I to be jealous? It's just that I would never use another woman's scents and clothes, just as I wouldn't

111

like another woman, and a stranger at that, to use mine!'
Still he laughed at her.

'Who do you think those things belong to, then?'

'I don't know, how could I?' she snapped.

'Come on, Anna, whose are they?' He sat grinning at her.

'I presume they belong to your wife, and I certainly had no intention of using them.'

'Oh, such a prim and proper English woman you are. You will share my bed but not the perfume. I find this strange.'

'That's different,' she said, getting flustered.

'I think it's worse. Tut, tut, Mrs Grange!'

Ann began to feel angry. It was bad enough having to face up to reality without him teasing her like this. It was all a game to him, one he was probably adept at playing, she thought bitterly, a deep frown creasing her forehead.

'Oh, my darling, I'm sorry, I shouldn't tease you. Don't frown so angrily at me.' He tried to kiss her but she turned her face away from him. '*Agapi*, my sweet. They are for you, my love, they don't belong to any one else, I bought them for you. Precious, I don't have a wife.'

'You don't?' she asked, her voice full of suspicion. She looked at him tentatively.

'No. On my life, darling, there is no Mrs Georgeopoulos. You don't believe me?'

'Yes, I do,' she said, the uncertainty in her voice betraying her distrust.

'I should have spoken of this sooner. I apologize. My wife died, Anna, over ten years ago,' he said seriously.

'I'm sorry,' Ann lied, knowing full well that she felt only relief and could feel no grief for this dead woman.

'That's how I knew in the art gallery that you had been touched by death. You had a certain look about you.'

'It seems to be disappearing very fast, that look. I wonder if it goes too fast.'

'Never. It's good that this is happening to you. I can assure you ten years is too long to wait for it to happen.'

He smiled. 'But – the day is disappearing, let's go for a walk.' He let her slip from his lap.

'I'll just wash these plates.' She turned towards the sink.

'No need. The servants will do that.'

'What servants?'

'There are servants here, I told them to keep out of the way.'

'Just like Pétin's.' She laughed with pleasure. 'What a secretive man you are, Alex.'

'No, possessive. Come on.'

'Upstairs I thought you were having to keep me secret.' She was laughing now.

He took her hand and led her from the kitchen. 'Who owns this house? It's so beautiful,' she asked as they crossed the hall.

'The company I work for – it's used for business entertaining normally.'

'And they let you use it? You must be very important to them.' She looked at him questioningly, but he ignored her comment and burrowed into a cupboard searching for raincoats for them both.

They walked through the rain-soaked garden, clinging to each other like limpets. They passed through the dripping, winter skeletal trees of a small beech wood and emerged into a cove. The sea was whipped wild with the December wind, large foam-flecked waves pounded on to the shore with a loud echoing boom, to be followed by the greedy sucking noise as the sea attempted to steal the pebbles from the beach. As each wave crashed water flew in the air and they were soon drenched. They ran with difficulty across the sliding pebbles and sat between two large rocks which, whilst allowing them to see the water, sheltered them from the spray and muffled the noise. 'I love the sea,' she said, flinging her head back to shake the water from her hair.

'I hate it,' he said with venom. 'Loathe it,' and he angrily threw a pebble into the water.

'Why?' She sounded surprised.

'I was a reluctant sailor for years. You have to love the sea to be a sailor. But me? There was nothing else I could do and I had my mother and sister to support.'

'Did your father die?'

'My father!' and he laughed with irony. 'My sainted father got through his money, then my mother's, and only had the decency to die when there was nothing left. He was a compulsive gambler, he even lost our family home in a game of cards. So I joined the Merchant Navy. Cargo ships can be hell, you get a bastard captain and first officer and life hardly seems worth living. Weeks and weeks at sea, no women, and then you get to port and who wants to know a sailor? So you land up in a brothel with stinking prostitutes.

'So why hate the poor prostitutes, Alex? I doubt it most of them do it from choice.' She spoke with spirit, annoyed by his chauvinistic assessment of these women.

'Anna, you've never met women like that. You don't know what you're talking about, I assure you.' He looked so angry that she was puzzled by his vehemence, and wondered what could have caused such antagonism. 'Anyhow,' he continued, his voice again normal, 'I got promoted to passenger ships. The conditions were better, but if you were halfway good-looking then every un-attached woman, and even some with husbands, regarded you as a stud included in the fare. I worked the ships until I was thirty when my mother died and my sister married.'

'But surely you could have left sooner if you hated it so much? Your mother would not have wanted you to be unhappy.

'My mother did not know how I felt. It was my duty to support her, I could not risk losing my income while she lived.'

'Couldn't your sister have helped' Ann asked practi-cally.

'We Greeks do things differently from you English, my darling. My sister was also my responsibility until she married. Her dowry had to be supplied. Once she was married then I could take risks with my life.'

'How unfair.'

'Not at all. Without responsibilities a man is alone – a sad state of affairs. I was proud to be able to set my sister up in style.'

'Then what did you do?' Ann asked, unconvinced of the fairness of the Greek system.

'I opened a shop selling perfumes to rich Athenian women. The joke was, they didn't know that all the early stock was smuggled.' He threw back his head, laughing loudly at the joke.

'Smuggled?'

'Yes, didn't I tell you, I'm a desperate criminal,' he said in a poor imitation of James Cagney. 'Being in the navy it was the easiest thing to do.' His sour mood seemed to have passed completely. 'I met my wife in the shop. She came in as a customer and left as my girlfriend.' He looked out at the sea and for a while was silent.

'Was she beautiful?' Ann ventured to ask, and wondered why she wanted to know.

'Very. One of the most beautiful women I have ever seen,' he replied.

Ann felt a shimmer of loathing for such beauty and wished that she was years younger and very beautiful.

Still Alex stared out to sea. 'She was everything a man could desire,' he said, a hardness in his voice, and with an angry gesture threw a pile of pebbles into the water. 'I worked as I have never worked in my life. I needed to succeed you see, for her. Everything I did was for her. I wanted to cover her in jewels, furs, buy her the finest clothes, build her the best house . . .' He gave a short, half-strangled laugh, as he continued to throw the pebbles.

Ann played with the buttons on her raincoat, suddenly aware of how dishevelled she looked. Her hair, wet from the rain and sea, lay plastered against her skull. The raincoat was several sizes too big. All her make-up was washed away. She was painfully conscious of the contrast she must make to the woman of whom he was thinking and about whom she wished, vehemently, she had not asked.

'I was a success. Soon I had several shops and I began to branch out in other businesses. By now, Nada was my wife. Such a proud man I was. I had everything.' He paused. Ann was uncertain whether to speak or to remain silent. 'Then she died,' and he hurled another handful of pebbles at the steel-grey sea.

'Poor Alex.' She gently took his hand. 'How did she die?

'Having a baby.' At last he looked at her, his grey eyes appearing almost black with the shadow of his memories. 'Shall we go back?' he said abruptly. 'You're getting cold.'

A violent thunderstorm began just as they reached the house. They ducked into the doorway, water dripping all over the porch as they took off their soaking clothes. As they ran up the stairs water still dripped from their hair and shoes, marking their passage across the thick carpet. In the bedroom she turned to go into the bathroom to remove her still damp clothes.

'No. Here,' he ordered. 'Undress here.' He sat sprawled in a chair and indicated a spot in front of him where she was to stand. 'Undress,' he hoarsely commanded. Slowly she began to unbutton her blouse, conscious that his eyes never left her.

'I can't with you watching me. I feel so awkward.'

'You'll get used to it. Now undress, I want to see your body,' he ordered huskily.

'As best she could, and with trembling fingers, Ann removed the rest of her clothes until she stood before him. He sat silently. As he watched her she began to feel a wave of sexual excitement rise within her. As if aware of the effect he was having upon her, he slowly smiled at her. 'Come here, darling.'

Later, she lay back on the carpet and looked at him contentedly. 'What a strange man you are, Alex.'

'Am I?'

'Your moods change so quickly. One moment you are so considerate and then you behave like a Pasha.'

'A Pasha! Oh I like that.' He laughed his appreciation of her description.

'There's something else. I didn't know what it was like to be a woman until now.'

'I know,' he answered, a contented and lazy smile spread across his face.

8

They were content with each other. Easily they created their own routine. Alex seemed to require little sleep and would rise early, while Ann, exhausted by their nights of love-making, would sleep late. Each morning she would find him in his study. He used the early mornings to make his necessary business calls, for he did not work once she was awake, and the telephone never rang.

She would cook them a late breakfast. And then, no matter what the weather, they would walk, arms about each other, deeply engrossed in each other, barely noticing the countryside about them. They would return to lunch which, each day, was laid out, prepared for them by the unseen staff. Then the need for each other would become too great and they would go to their rooms and make love, and sleep, long, deep, rejuvenating sleeps. Each evening they dined in the candlelit dining room on food once more prepared by the invisible servants.

Only once did Ann see one of these servants ahead of her on the stairs but the figure hurriedly disappeard, like a wraith, into a room, as she approached. The illusion that the fires were lit, the beds made and the food prepared by magic persisted. She felt she was living in a dream world. They talked endlessly, deeply, delighting in discovering each other, which books they liked, what music, and making jokes, evolving their own language of love – exploring each other's minds as at night they explored each other's bodies.

In a small sitting room they sat, side by side on a Persian rug, light from the flames of the log fire bathing them in its warm and golden light. This room was smaller, less ornate, than the formal drawing room. The clutter of books and magazines, of records and videos, made it more homely than the rest of the house and was the room they used the most.

In the firelight he took her hand. 'Anna, darling, I love you.'

She looked at him and smiled. 'You haven't said that before.'

'I have, in Greek, often.' He smiled. 'I have known it from the beginning. Maybe I was frightened to say it in English, in case you might not feel the same way.'

'But I do, I do,' she burst out, ingenuously, her face aglow with happiness. 'I didn't trust the feeling at first, but this week . . . Oh Alex, I love you. There, I said it too, isn't it wonderful?' She laughed with delight.

'It has been a time of total magic. Such love, such tenderness. I never dared dream that it could happen like this.'

'Do you feel young again?'

'Totally, just as I did in my twenties.'

'Me too, it's crazy isn't it? Absolutely crazy.'

'But wonderful,' and he kissed her, gently. 'But we have to talk, my darling. It seems so simple and yet it isn't.'

She settled herself comfortably against him. 'I think it's as easy as pie, loving you.'

'But it may not be easy to continue loving me. I am the problem. I'm a difficult, demanding man, Anna. You may find, in time, you cannot tolerate me.'

'Oh, Alex, don't be so silly. I love you, I just said so.'

'You don't know the dark side of me, you have only seen this happy side. I am selfish, impatient, my temper is dreadful. I can be insanely jealous and possessive . . .'

'Darling,' she interrupted him, pressing her finger against his lips. 'I don't want to hear you say such things. Come on, don't spoil the evening.'

'I have to, Anna. You must know what I am truly like, how demanding I am. I want you to think about it. Weigh everything up. Then you can decide if you want to share my life.'

'Alex, you exaggerate, I'm sure. We all have bad habits. You don't know me, either. I'm dreadfully lazy. I've got a temper too. I can be indecisive which I can imagine will drive you mad, but I'm unlikely to change now. And, of course, I always forget to put the cap back on the toothpaste,' she concluded with a laugh.

'Anna, I'm being serious. You must listen. I'm a Greek. I'm not like the Englishmen you are used to.'

'I've noticed!' She grinned with delight.

'Anna,' he said sternly. 'Listen. I have to travel a lot with my work. I may not always be there when you want and need me, but I'm unreasonable – I shall expect you to be available whenever and wherever I am. I will accept no excuses.'

'But Alex, I should only want to be with you, anyway. Heavens, my whole adult life has revolved around a man.'

'But I shall want you to the exclusion of everybody and everything,' he said urgently, taking her hand in his.

'That's what relationships are about, Alex,' she answered lightly.

'I shall not be faithful to you.'

'Oh, darling, don't say such a thing,' she said with a frown, her voice at last losing its light and bantering tone.

'I must. It's the truth: you have to be warned. I shall not seek to be unfaithful nor, when I am, will it be of any importance, but I cannot live without sex and when we are apart I shall be unfaithful. It's only fair you be told, now, at the beginning.'

'What's sauce for the goose is sauce for the gander,' she tried to joke.

'What does that mean?'

'It means if you're unfaithful, it gives me the right to be too.'

'No, Anna,' his grip on her hand tightened and began to hurt, 'you must never, if you do, just once . . . I don't know what I would be capable of doing.' He shook his head.

'Oh, Alex . . . you're being melodramatic.'

'No, Anna, you are treating this too lightly. I feared you would. I've watched infidelity amongst people I know, here, the easy way it is accepted. I could not accept that, ever. I'm like my forebears in such matters – I shall want, expect and demand your total devotion and fidelity.'

'But, Alex, that's how I think. I can't imagine what people you have been mixing with but I can assure you infidelity is certainly not condoned in my village.' She laughed at the very idea. 'And I wouldn't want anyone else, darling. To me, loving you means that you have me totally, I'm not one for playing games. But I feel strongly too. I don't accept it's necessary for you to be unfaithful to me. You can't have it both ways, Alex. You're being very unreasonable.'

'I am as I am. That is the whole point of this conversation.'

'Then I shall make certain that you won't want any other woman,' she said with bravado and a defiant shake of the head, knowing as she spoke that, with her lack of experience, she had no idea how she was to achieve this state of affairs, but determined to try.

'How many men have you slept with?' he asked suddenly.

'Two, of course: you and Ben. I thought I was content with the one, but if you left me, I don't think I could ever be content again.'

'I shall never leave you, you have my solemn oath on that.'

'I shan't even ask you how many women you have slept with, I bet you can't even remember,' she said, looking sideways at him, desperately wanting the conversation to return to safer ground.

'Better not to ask.' At last he laughed.

'But, Alex, why me? I don't understand. A man like you, you could have any young girl you wanted, not someone like me.'

'What on earth do you mean, like you?'

'Well, middle-aged, even if you do make me feel like a young girl. And past my prime . . . you know,' she said awkwardly.

'Oh you English, you English, as bad as the Americans with this accent on youth. Good God, woman, young girls bore me to tears with their vacuous minds. Young women belong with young men. If one goes out with me, I know damn well why: because there's more money in my pocket, that's the only reason. And you're not past your prime, you're in it. Your maturity is beautiful, it gives you grace and dignity. It makes your face lovelier than it could ever have been in youth. You are the most beautiful woman in the world, to me. But it is not just your beauty, it is your honesty, the openness and warmth of your character, the strength I sense there, your sensitivity. And, you make me laugh!' He kissed her, gently outlining her lips with his tongue. 'Such a generous, sensuous mouth – it shows everything about you, your kindness, humour, tolerance. There's so much about you, that wonderful silky hair, your smile, the way you wrinkle your nose when you laugh. Your thighs . . .'

'My thighs?' She sat bolt upright with surprise.

'Oh, yes, I adore your wonderful, smooth thighs,' he said, laughing at her astonished expression.

'My thighs? But I've never liked my legs.' She looked at them critically.

'You are so strange, Anna. You don't seem to have any idea how attractive you are. You have beautiful legs. Perfect . . .' He began gently to caress them, when the sudden thrill of the telephone interrupted. 'Damn!' he said, leaning across her to answer it.

She watched him as he talked, in Greek. She thought of what he had said and she remembered how shocked she had been that first morning when she had seen him angry on the telephone, and knew that he did not exaggerate his temper. So was she to believe his complete assessment of himself? She did not know men. Was his passion different because he was a foreigner? Or did other Englishmen make love as he did? She did not know for she had only her life with Ben to which to relate her new-found sexuality. She found what he said and her reaction to it perplexing. On the one hand she felt enraged at his presumption, at his arrogance. But then there was a part of her which was excited by his attitude. She knew she wanted to be completely his; she felt that only then would she feel safe and secure. Fay and Lydia would throw up their hands in horror, but that was how she was, with a deep need in her to be part of someone else. And if there was love, then how could there not be possessive jealousy – surely the two went hand in hand? By declaring his jealousy he was, after all, only declaring his love.

He put the phone back on the receiver.

'We have to go, don't we?' she said sadly.

'Yes, my love, tomorrow. I told them not to call until it was absolutely necessary and Yianni, my assistant, needs me now.'

'Ah, well, it's been a perfect week. The call might have come days ago.'

'There's no need to look so sad. You're coming with me, it's simple.'

'Where to?'

'New York.'

Her eyes widened. 'Heavens, I've never been to America. But I couldn't, Alex. It's impossible. I've so much to do.'

'What do you mean? What is more important than being with me? Of course you must come. What have you just promised? We shall only be gone a week, ten days. We shall be back in plenty of time for Christmas.'

'Darling, I can't go with you. I'm sorry. It's my grandson's birthday on the twelfth and I promised him I would be there. I can't let him down.'

'But you can let me down? You promised me. You said you would always be there when I wanted you. So much for your promises,' he shouted angrily at her.

'But Alex. You can understand, Adam can't, he's only a child. He's three, for goodness sake!'

'You promised.'

'Good God, man, I'd forgotten the birthday,' she shouted back. 'I'm sorry, but there it is – there's nothing else I can do.'

'So, you won't come?'

'I can't. Don't you see?'

'I see your promises to me mean nothing already!' he roared.

'Oh, for God's sake, Alex. Grow up,' she yelled back in exasperation. Alex glowered at her, leapt to his feet and stormed from the room, slamming the door shut behind him.

She sat alone, fuming, waiting for him to return. The phone clicked and pinged as he made call after call, but he did not come back. She wearied of waiting for him, turned off the lights, and went to their room. At the sight of the bed where they had spent so many happy hours she felt a sadness that took away her anger. How could such happiness be so easily destroyed? She flung herself across it, and thumped the pillow with frustrated despair.

'He must understand,' she said desperately.

The thick carpeting muffled his footsteps. She jumped as she felt his arms encircling her.

'Sweetheart, I'm sorry. You're right. I was childish and inconsiderate. You see how selfish I am? And bad-tempered?' He laughed. 'Of course the little boy wouldn't understand, of course you must go to him. It's just that, having found you, I'm terrified to lose you, and of the thought of all that loneliness returning.'

'Darling, I'm as disappointed as you. But you won't lose me. Trust me. We can talk on the telephone everyday.'

'Of course, of course. But what about Christmas? Your family, will they demand you then?'

123

'No, darling, we shall celebrate it together. I promise.'
Even as she said it, she knew that such a Christmas was likely to be difficult to arrange.

The following morning they drove to London. She wanted to shop not only for Adam's birthday but for Christmas presents too, and for clothes if she could find the time. They clung to each other as they said goodbye in the car.

'I'll return as soon as possible. Be waiting, my darling.' And he waved as the car slid into the London traffic.

Later that evening, she let herself into a bitterly cold, darkened house. She tried to light the fire in the drawing room but each effort failed. Instead she made herself a pot of tea, soaked in the bath, and went to bed. Twice the phone rang, but each time, knowing it could not be Alex, she ignored it, wanting only to speak to him.

9

It had been a restless night. In a week, Ann had become used to the feel of Alex's warm body beside her, the security of hearing him breathe in the dark, the weight of his arm protectively about her.

She lay in the grey, sluggish light of the winter dawn and ached for him. The silk-canopied bed that for so long had been her oasis of calm had become a lonely, alien place.

The woman who had slept there the week before and the woman she now was were two entirely different people. She could have been excused in thinking that, by her age, there could be no changes in her life. But what was she to make of herself now? She had abandoned the ways of a life-time and was turning her back on all her previous standards and moral codes. In doing so she would lose her friends, her family. Maybe only Lydia, her new friend, would understand. She would be leaving the only way of life she knew and venturing out into an entirely new one that led she knew not where.

She would have to sell the house. That decision which she had resisted so vehemently was, after all, an easy and logical one to make. She could no longer expect to live in this village, the mistress of a foreign man and expect everything to go on as before. She was too fond of the village and its inhabitants to allow the embarrassment that her behaviour would cause. She felt no resentment, she understood them: had she not been one of them until now? Living in sin might be all right for the liberated youth in the cities but such social revolutions had not yet reached Midfield and were certainly not for the respectable, stalwart woman she was thought to be.

Yet, strangely, she was not afraid. Nor was she full of regrets. How could she be, blessed as she was by this all-consuming love that filled her, obsessed her, as no other love had done?

Ben! What would he have thought of her? She would like to think that he would be happy for her to have found such joy. Regretfully, though, she wondered whether he would, in fact, have been one of the first to condemn. What really shocked her was how little thought she had given him in the past weeks. It was as if he had faded from her life, almost as if he had never been, and yet only a short while ago she had been certain she would never stop grieving for him. Maybe, subconsciously, knowing how he would have felt, she had shut the memory of him from her mind. But she was thinking of him now and still she felt no guilt.

Instinctively she knew the reason why. Had Alex not been such a lover, had they found only companionship, she might, illogically, have felt guilt at her disloyalty to Ben. But Alex was a superb lover, had given a new dimension to her life. If she were honest, she felt that for all those years with Ben she had been cheated. It was not that she had not loved him; she had, but with a gentle, quiescent love, not with the passion she now felt. When Ben had made love to her, she had enjoyed it but with an enjoyment bred of ignorance. It seemed, now, as if during every minute of her waking day she longed for Alex, was ready for him and full of desire. All those years her sexuality and her passion had lain dormant. It was as if she had been half alive and now wanted to scream to the world how totally alive she was, how completely loved and desired, how much a woman she had become.

And what of her children? Ann felt that Fay might understand, but Peter, never. Already she could imagine his face scowling with disapproval. But she couldn't live her life for Peter. Her children were as much part of the past as Ben had been: she could not and would not allow anything to mar her present.

But what of herself, she reflected. What had happened to all that talk of bright, new independence? She had promised to give her time, attention, her life – just as if she were his wife. Had she been deceiving herself before, had the longing to be her own woman been something she had manufactured to fill the void of her empty life? She no longer knew. What she did know, though, was that she relinquished it willingly.

She swung her legs over the side of the bed, shivering in the early morning chill. Dear God, how she had changed! Ann Grange, ignoring her past, facing the future as mistress, wanton! She laughed. The ringing of the phone made her jump. Glancing at the clock and seeing it was only seven, she knew it had to be Alex. Quickly she climbed back into the warm bed, cradling the phone beside her.

'Alex?' she answered breathlessly.

'I'm sorry it's so early, but I had to hear your voice, I miss you so.'

'I was awake. I was sitting on my bed thinking what a wanton I was,' she laughed.

'Wanton? I don't know the meaning of this word.'

'It means I'm irresponsible, unchaste, licentious!' She laughed merrily at her own list of words.

'No, I don't like these words for you – they're bad. You're not bad. Making love to you has been like

126

making love to an innocent, so much to teach you, such joy in teaching!'

'That's exactly what I've been thinking. All those wasted years and I didn't know what love could be like.'

'Not wasted, you were waiting for me. Are you up so early?'

'No, no. I knew it was you and I crawled back into my bed with the phone. Oh, Alex, such a lonely bed . . .'

'Darling, don't. Oh my God, the thought of you in a bed without me. My darling Anna, I want you so badly, right now, this minute – the agony is unbearable.'

'Alex! Just the sound of your voice and I'm ready for you . . .' She shivered with delight at her own boldness.

'Then you really are mine, my prisoner,' he said softly. 'Touch your breasts, my little one, caress your nipples. Press harder . . .' his voice ordered huskily . . .

When Meg arrived it was to find Ann busily moving her belongings from her bedroom to the room across the landing.

'I've decided to move into this room, Meg.'

'That's nice. It's as big as yours and it's got its own bathroom. Mind you, if you're wanting that big bed moved we'll need my Bill and a couple of other strong men to help us.'

'No need. I've decided to sell it.'

'You'll get a good price for that, I'm sure,' was Meg's sole, sensible comment. If she felt surprise, it was not echoed in her voice.

'I do wish I'd time to decorate it and get new curtains. It's so dowdy.'

'What nonsense. It's a lovely room, lighter and quieter, too.'

'You don't understand, Meg.'

'Don't I? You might be surprised, Mrs Grange,' she said, smiling slyly at Ann.

Three

1

As Ann parked her car outside Peter's house, she realized with mounting annoyance that she was nervous. She repeated to herself what was now becoming her refrain, 'It's my life'. She rang the doorbell and for the first time in their relationship she was relieved to see Sally.

'So, you made it. I'd just been trying to explain to Adam that you probably wouldn't be coming.'

'I couldn't let Adam down.'

'You look very well, I like your hair like that. Your break has done you good,' Sally said as she ushered Ann into the hall, and Ann chided herself for wondering if she detected a sharpness in the young woman's voice. Along the narrow hall her grandson came charging at her like a little tank.

'See. I said Granny would come,' he announced triumphantly to his mother, giving Ann an excited wet kiss, grabbing his present and seeming to tear it open in one movement. Immediately the bell rang again and Ann was saved from being alone with Sally as the small guests arrived and the afternoon slipped past in the deafening row of a toddlers' party. By six both women stood, exhausted, amidst the debris that only three-year-olds can make.

'When's Peter due back?' Ann asked, as nonchalantly as she could.

'About half past. He delayed on purpose. Kids' parties aren't his scene,' she explained. Adam began to cry from fatigue.

'You get him bathed, Sally. I'll straighten up before

Peter gets back. His father could never stand the chaos of kids when he returned from work either.' For once, Sally smiled companionably at her mother-in-law.

The sitting room tidy, Ann began on the kitchen and was so engrossed with the washing-up that she didn't hear Peter's key in the door.

'So you condescended to come!'

'Peter! You made me jump.' Purposely she ignored his remark. 'You missed a grand party. Adam had a lovely time but he's tired himself out. Sally's putting him to bed.'

'Drink?' asked her son. She nodded. He poured them both a gin and tonic, silently concentrating on measuring out the drink. Ann watched him with a nervousness that both irritated and alarmed her.

'What on earth have you done to your hair?'

'Oh, I had it cut and some highlights put in.'

'It looks ridiculous.'

'I like it,' Ann replied defiantly.

Sally reappeared. 'Hullo,' she said in an off-hand way to her husband as she crossed the room. Ann watched them, noting how distant from each other they seemed, and was saddened that a greeting between a couple could be so cold and uninterested.

'I forgot, I bought some wine for dinner.' She fetched the wine from the carrier in the hall. 'I should open it now, Peter, let it breathe a bit.'

'This is expensive,' he said, studying the label. 'Going up-market in your tastes, aren't you?'

'I've always enjoyed good wine,' she replied, a mite too quickly she thought.

Mother and son sat in silence with their drinks as Sally finished preparing their meal. Ann toyed with her glass. She made patterns on the tablecloth with her fork. She lit a cigarette, took a couple of puffs and then extinguished it, almost immediately lighting another one.

'You seem edgy, Mum?'

'Me? No, I'm fine.' Nervously she choked on the smoke she had inhaled. Her son, with irritation in his movements, waved the smoke away.

'The amount you smoke is stupid, Mum. You never used to smoke like this.'

'I know, I should cut down. Silly habit.'

She looked about the kitchen, always so cluttered, she thought tetchily, and wished to God the food would come – no matter how awful it was. It was odd that Peter who enjoyed food so much should have married someone who couldn't cook. But at least if they were eating, her son would be concentrating on his plate and not on her.

'Sorry everyone, you must be starving,' Sally said, at last ladling out the food, an appetizing chicken casserole instead of her usual ubiquitous lentil stew. Peter poured the wine. For a few minutes they ate in a silence broken only by their appreciative remarks on the food – Peter sounded as surprised as she.

'So where have you been, Mother?' Peter asked just as Ann had put a forkful of chicken in her mouth. She patted her mouth, excusing her inability to reply, futilely hoping he would have forgotten the question by the time she had stopped chewing. He waited, she said nothing. 'So?'

'I just went away for a week. I felt I needed a break.'

'Couldn't you have phoned?'

'I asked Lydia to tell you,' she replied defensively.

'She did. And a right fool I felt being given messages about my mother's whereabouts from someone I barely know.'

'Peter, you've met Lydia several times. She's hardly a stranger.'

'That's not the point. I think you should let us know yourself where you are. You didn't even leave a telephone number.'

'I'm sorry, I should have called. I left in such a rush . . . spur-of-the-moment decision . . .'

'You had time to phone Lydia.'

'But I had to phone her anyway, so I killed two birds with one stone. In any case . . .' She wished she hadn't said that and hoped he had not noticed.

'Any case, what?'

'Oh, I don't know, silly of me really. I just didn't think you'd understand my needing to get away like that. I didn't want to worry you.'

'I'd have understood. Just wish I could take off into the blue like that sometimes.'

'Ah, that's all right then.' She smiled, feeling released from a potentially difficult conversation, and neatly arranged her knife and fork on her plate. Peter stood to refill the wine glasses, and smiled at Ann as he retook his place.

'But with whom, Mother? That's what's really occupied our minds. Who could it possibly be?'

Ann felt herself blushing and was furious with herself and furious with him for making her blush.

'What on earth do you mean, Peter?' she blustered.

'Peter, I don't think this is any of our business!' she heard Sally admonish him.

'It's very much my business, and you keep your bloody nose out of this!' he snapped.

'Peter, what has got into you? Just listen to yourself. That's no way to speak to Sally.'

'Where were you, Mother?' he continued, as if there had been no interruption.

'I went to stay with friends in Hampshire.'

'You don't have any friends in Hampshire, Mother.'

'You don't know all my friends,' she retorted sharply.

'Evidently.'

'Peter, this is ridiculous. I do wish you would stop calling me Mother, it's so formal,' she said, laughing nervously. 'You're making me feel like a naughty child. I don't expect you to explain your comings and goings to me. What right have you to question me like this?'

'Because just recently you have been behaving most oddly, Mother, and I have been worried.' His tone was pointedly patient and his continual use of 'Mother' made an ominous shiver go down her spine.

'That's sweet of you, but really I'm fine, there's nothing to worry about. Gracious, don't you think I'm old enough to look after myself?'

'It depends on what you're up to, Mother.' He turned his attention back to his food, and Sally began to talk about Adam – should she buy bunk beds with the new baby on the way? – and Ann felt herself relax as the mundane conversation whirled about her. Refusing cheese, she lit a cigarette and asked for another glass of wine.

'Who is he, Mother?' The question caught her off her guard and she started, knocking over her glass and spilling the red wine across the tablecloth.

'Sally, I'm so sorry, how clumsy of me!' She jumped up to get a cloth.

'Mother, sit down, stop fussing, Sally will clear that up. More wine?' Smiling weakly, she proffered her glass to him. 'I repeat, who is he?'

'I don't know what you're talking about,' Ann mumbled, playing for time.

'Come off it. Since when has one of your girlfriends driven a Maserati, like the one seen outside your house last week?'

Ann sat stunned, knowing that her mouth had dropped open in surprise and yet seeming unable to close it.

'So, who is he?'

'How dare you, Peter? You've been spying on me!'

'No, I wasn't spying. A friend happened to pass by the other day, saw the car, and mentioned it to me out of interest, as any man would. So, who was it?'

'I'm not going to tell you,' she said defiantly.

'Ah! So you admit there was someone?' He almost shouted with triumph.

'And if there is, so what?'

'I think I have a right to know.'

'And I don't think you do.'

'Oh, Mum.' He was smiling at her; Ann looked at him suspiciously, unsure whether the change in his attitude was genuine or was simply a change in tactic, a trap he was setting her. Still he smiled, put out his hand, took hers and squeezed it affectionately. 'Why are you always on the defensive with me? Good heavens, you've had a dreadful year. There were times when I worried for your sanity. What's more natural after all that worry that I should be concerned? I'm sorry, Mum, I didn't mean to upset you, honestly.'

Ann felt ashamed that she had felt such suspicion of her son, when all the time he still loved and cared for her. She had been stupid: of course he had a right to know what she was doing and who she was seeing – that's what families were all about. She smiled at him warmly.

'I must be getting neurotic in my old age. Yes, I have met someone: his name is Alex. I met him when I went up to London.'

'I see. Where did you meet?'

'It sounds so silly to tell you, but we met in the Tate. The Pre-Raphaelite room actually.' She was trying to inject a lightnesss into her voice but succeeded only in sounding embarrassed.

'You did what? You allowed yourself to be picked up in the Tate Gallery! Good God, Mother, what were you thinking about?' Peter exploded, no semblance of pleasantness in his tone now.

'Death, actually.' She laughed nervously, her apprehension returning. 'I know it must sound odd, but really, it seemed the most natural thing, at the time – getting into conversation with Alex the way I did. We just started talking about this picture, you see, it was the . . .'

'Good God, how undignified.'

'It wasn't, you weren't there, you don't understand,' Ann said a shade angrily, wanting to protect the memory of that first meeting.

'Mother, you are so naïve, you're too vulnerable at the moment. Heavens above, he could be anyone, a crook, Christ knows what.'

'Don't be silly, Peter. He's a very respectable businessman. A crook, really!' Her laughter at the preposterous idea was genuine.

'What sort of business?'

'I don't know, I haven't asked. But he's obviously successful, he's got a Mini as well as the Maserati, and he sent me such lovely flowers, and he took me to . . .'

'You mean he didn't tell you? There you are, if he was a bona fide businessman, he'd tell you, wouldn't he? I tell people what I do, but then I have nothing to hide.'

'It just never came up. We have so much else to talk about. You know I've never been interested in business or anything like that.' She could feel the old defensiveness returning, matched, this time, with anger.

'I suppose he's young?' her son asked unpleasantly.

'I don't like the implication behind that question. If you must know, he's older than I am, in his mid-forties,' she snapped back with spirit.

'I suppose that's something to be thankful for.'

'He can't be that badly off if he runs a car like that,' Sally added helpfully.

'It doesn't prove a thing. Maybe the Mini's his car and he borrowed the other to impress my stupid mother.'

'Impress me? Well off? What the hell are you both going on about? What does it matter if he's rich or poor? I'm happy with him. I'd have thought that was the important issue.'

'Christ, Mother. Don't you understand anything? You're a good catch! God knows what this man's intentions are. You allow yourself to be picked up by any Tom, Dick or Harry and expect us to think it's all soft lights and roses. Bloody hell, you could have been set up. There are people who read up wills in the papers, you know, then stake out the widows. It would be the simplest thing to find out where you live and follow you.'

'Don't be so bloody stupid. Good heavens, who's being paranoid now? He's a wonderful man, extraordinarily generous, and he's made me happy when I thought I would never be happy again. And, what's more, he loves me and I love him.'

'Of course he'd say he loved you, they all do. But if you think I'm going to sit back and see my father's hard-earned cash squandered on some bloody gigolo you've got another think coming.'

'Cash! Gigolo!' she spat out, the words seeming to hang in the air above her, refusing to go away as they echoed in her head. 'How dare you! How dare you speak to me like this! It's always the same with you, Peter, it always comes back to money, doesn't it? My God, you've turned into a bitter, money-grubbing little toad. And I was fool enough to think it was me you were concerned about, not the money. Let's get things straight, Peter, I do what I want. I don't feel any guilt at what I'm doing. I'm happy – I know your father would want me to be happy.'

'You reckon?' Peter laughed ironically. 'He would be appalled at your behaviour. But in any case, what he thinks is irrelevant. Certainly it's your life and I suppose, if you want to ruin it, that's your business,' his voice rose shrilly, 'but I don't think you've the right to risk what is by rights mine.'

Within her Ann felt a cold anger that he should talk of her love for Alex in such terms; she wanted to take that love, hold it to her and protect it from her son and his bitterness.

'Look, Peter,' she continued, forcing herself to calm down. 'I want you to meet him. I know you'll think differently once you do. You'll see just how safe I am with him. I'd planned that we should have a family dinner on Christmas Eve at home. You must come. I can't let you think this way.'

'So you're not coming here for Christmas, then?' he asked angrily.

'No, Peter. I want to spend the rest of the holiday alone with Alex, being happy.'

'God, it's disgusting!' His face was distorted with repugnance. 'At your age, Mother, it's ludicrous. Imagine, my mother, cock-struck!'

She winced and leapt to her feet at his ugly words. 'Peter, you disgust me . . . How dare you speak to me like that, use filthy language to me, your mother?'

'Then behave like a mother. I can assure you, your behaviour at the moment disgusts me even more. Cosy, isn't it, all tucked up and in my father's house?'

'*My* house,' she shouted.

'And what happened to all that grief? Disappeared bloody fast, hasn't it? Remember the half-crazed woman you were, wishing you were dead, mooning about? What happened to all that? Or did it never exist? Or have you just bided your time . . . ? God, what a hypocrite you are, Mother.'

'I loved your father, you know I did. I didn't expect this to happen to me, but it has and don't ask me to turn my back on it, because I can't.' She felt a constriction in her throat so that when she spoke the words sounded muffled and came out with difficulty. 'I just can't believe we're having this conversation and that you're speaking to me like this!'

'What did you expect, champagne?' her son sneered.

'You're right about one thing, Peter, I am naïve – I hoped you'd be happy for me.' She stood up to go, but before she left she could not resist turning to her son, with her Parthian shot. 'There's one thing I forgot to tell you, Peter: he's Greek.'

Her son put his head in his hands. 'Christ almighty, that tops it,' she heard him say as she let herself quickly out of the room.

2

Ann's fury was still seething inside her as she put her key into the lock. She heard the telephone ring, and cursed as the key stuck. Wrenching it out of the lock, she rushed to the phone.

She felt overwhelming disappointment at the sound of her daughter's voice. 'Mummy, what the hell's going on?'

'If you believe Peter, the worst, but if you'll listen to me, the best.'

'Peter's in a rare old temper.'

'So am I, Fay. And before you ask, Alex is not a gigolo, and I have no intention of giving him up, so don't even start on me, OK?' Ann said angrily into the receiver.

'OK, Mummy, calm down,' Fay said soothingly. 'But Peter said you don't want to spend Christmas with us.'

'It's not that, Fay. I want to spend it with Alex and in Peter's present mood, Christmas with him would be impossible.'

'But we always spend Christmas together.'

'Correction, Fay. Your father and I always spent Christmas together and latterly, if you or Peter had nothing better to do, you joined us. So, this year, it's my turn – I'm opting out. I've something better to do.'

'Mummy, you sound so angry, I haven't said anything.'

'I *am* angry and Peter has made me very defensive. I just want to make my position clear. Did he tell you about the dinner I planned?'

'Yes, but he says he's not coming.'

'Good, I don't think I particularly want him to come.'

'This doesn't sound like you at all, Mummy.'

'Probably not, but there have been some changes and there will probably be more. Are you coming?'

'Yes.'

'Good, I'll see you then.' Before her daughter could reply, Ann replaced the receiver. She felt too exhausted to discuss the matter any more.

Later, as she prepared for bed in her new room, she looked at her hands, at her wedding ring and the engagement ring with the one diamond, so small because it was all Ben had been able to afford all those years ago. But to her it had been the most precious ring in the world, she thought, touching the small stone tenderly. Slowly she eased both rings off her finger and, wrapping them in tissue paper, placed them in the bottom of her jewel box and closed the lid.

The following morning she was busy making lists for Christmas. Lists of things to buy and lists of things to do. Ann had always made lists for everything: she liked lists because she felt they sorted out the muddle in her head, and this morning they were helping to calm her down. Her task was interrupted by Lydia's arrival, announced by her customary screeching brakes and blaring horn.

'Let's look at you. My God, darling, you look eighteen! I don't believe it!' Ann blushed, embarrassed by her friend's unerring scrutiny. 'Came up trumps, that's obvious, didn't he? Just what you needed!'

'I feel eighteen. Ridiculous, isn't it, at our age?'

'It's never ridiculous at any age.'

They sat at the kitchen table with coffee as Ann told Lydia of her week, about the house, the walks, Alex, but not the nights – those were her own and Alex's secret. Nor could she yet bring herself to tell even her most understanding friend of Alex's proposition.

'So, I'm in love. It's that simple. Madly, crazily in love. I don't ever remember feeling like this in my life.' She hugged herself with glee at the confidence she imparted. 'Had it not been for Adam's birthday, I'd be with him in New York instead of mooning about here. Imagine!' She laughed happily.

'Still, not going will probably make him all the keener. A good ploy really.'

'Lydia, you're a terrible old cynic. We're not playing games with each other: we've gone beyond that.'

'You've led a sheltered life, darling. It never hurts to keep the bastards on their toes,' Lydia said with a flourish of her coffee cup. 'All the same, I'm so happy for you, Ann. It all sounds too lovely for words.'

'Thank God, someone approves. You should have heard Peter last night. I'm disgusting and ludicrous, Alex is a gigolo – and I'm "cock-struck"!'

'Little horror. Mind you, you probably are, cock-struck I mean – but that's what makes the start of an affair so wonderfully exciting.'

'Oh Lydia!'

'It's true. They accept that a man can be pussy-struck. Why should we be different? Sounds to me, though, as if you're reaching the point where you might have to decide between Alex and your darling little son, doesn't it?'

'I know. And it'll be Alex I choose.'

'Thank God for that. That settled, any chance of a tiny weeny drink?'

As Ann started to open a bottle of wine, the phone rang. 'Do this, Lydia.' She handed her the wine as she crossed the kitchen to answer it.

'Anna, my darling. I want you here. Now. Today. The birthday's over, you must come immediately.'

'There's nothing I'd rather do, Alex, but I can't, I don't have a visa.'

'That's no problem. My assistant can arrange everything. Damn, he's in France. Never mind, I will make sure he sees you first thing tomorrow.'

'Yes.' Ann, conscious of Lydia grinning at her over the rim of her glass of wine, could not think what else to say.

'You're not alone, you seem so cold, like a business-woman.'

'My friend Lydia is here.'

'Have you talked about me to her?'

'Yes, incessantly.'

'She approves?'

'Totally.' Ann giggled, and pulled a face at Lydia.

'How was last night?' he said seriously.

'Oh, not too good.'

'What's happened? Tell me.'

'It's not important, nothing really . . .'

'I think there is something. I want to know.'

'I will, I promise, but not now, not on the phone.'

'Very well, my darling. I love you,' he whispered.

'I love you too,' she said gently, replaced the receiver and returned to Lydia.

'Wow, he makes you positively *glow*!' Lydia shrieked.

'You see how it is? Nothing else matters but him. He seems to have taken over my whole existence.'

'Do be careful, Ann.'

'I can't. Right from the start I rationalized I would probably get hurt, but there's nothing I can do about it. Anyhow,' she shrugged her shoulders, 'think of the wonderful memories I'll have.'

'Cold comfort in your old age,' Lydia said sagely.

'Look, Lydia, this dinner I'm planning – if Peter changes his mind and comes, it's likely to be sticky. You and George wouldn't come for drinks beforehand, would you? Help lighten the atmosphere?'

'Like a jester at a wake?' she said with her raucous laugh. 'Of course we'll come, and I'm sure Peter will turn up. I bet his curiosity gets the better of him, if nothing else.'

She was right, Peter had changed his mind. That evening Sally phoned to say they would be coming.

The next day at eight, Ann, still in her dressing gown, was unsettled by the arrival of Alex's aide, Nigel Salisbury. In an expensive suit, Gucci shoes and carrying a large shiny briefcase he had the wideawake air of someone who had been working for hours. Ann patted her hair, tightened the belt of her dressing gown and ushered him into the study, in the same breath apologizing for not being dressed, and offering him coffee. He declined the coffee and, to Ann's embarrassment, waited patiently as she searched desperately through Ben's desk for the passport. She had not thought to explain that she did not have a passport of her own but had always been on Ben's, which was now out of date. They were going to have to apply for a new passport.

'I'm afraid it won't be available until next week, Mrs Grange. That's the fastest I can arrange it. We shall need a form and photos . . .' he said apologetically.

'I think that's very fast. I thought passports took weeks.'

'You and I might think so, Mrs Grange. Unfortunately I doubt if Mr Georgeopoulos will agree.' Ann laughed, thinking he was joking but, seeing the young man's expression, she realized he was serious. Quickly she dressed to go with him for photographs and to fill in the necessary form.

The young man was right. That night, Alex was in a towering rage at the news that she had never had a passport of her own. Not having one seemed the most preposterous thing he had heard. Everyone had a passport, he stormed. She tried to explain that she had never needed one, but it was like explaining to a bee that pollen was bad for it. She finally calmed him by talking of Christmas and how soon it would arrive.

Her plans were far advanced now. Her first decision had been to sell her dining table and replace it with a round one, so obviating the necessity of having to choose which man to seat at the head.

Ann was in a whirl of indecision over food. She bought a turkey, pheasants, fillet of venison and having done that she wondered if he would not prefer goose. She returned to the butcher and bought the goose and then decided perhaps she should get a sirloin. She stocked up with every fruit that she could find, every vegetable. Crackers and chocolates, enough liqueurs to supply a bar. She had a jungle of potted plants delivered and as soon as they arrived she changed her mind again, gave them all to Meg, who by now had decided she was deranged, and instead ordered fresh-cut flowers to be delivered on Christmas Eve.

It took her a whole morning to choose a present for Alex. She was rather pleased with the result – she had another door key cut which was then gold-plated and attached to a gold chain with a fob of his birth sign – Gemini.

Nigel Salisbury, still looking worried, delivered the brand-new passport with its American visa. But, by then, it was no longer pressingly needed. The previous night Alex had told her he was going to a part of Brazil where it might be impossible to reach a phone and in which it was unsuitable for her to travel. He was going to look at trees, he told her cryptically.

Even though he had warned her that he would not phone, as the days to Christmas slipped relentlessly by, so Ann began to worry. She did not know much about Brazil, but she was sure it was a modern country. How could it be impossible to phone? The more she fretted, the more she thought it unlikely. Had he lied to her? Had he met someone else? Was he playing games with her? Perhaps it had all been a dream, one that was over. Each night she changed, made up her face, arranged her hair and hoped he would come. And each night she went more despondently to bed.

The twenty-third had arrived and still there was no word from him. At eight o'clock in the evening she sat in the drawing room, feeling ridiculously overdressed in an emerald green silk chiffon dress that she had bought especially for his return and which, each evening, she had put on – just in case. The bright green suited her fair, highlighted hair. The fine fabric was moulded to her body, emphasizing its shape. She sat in the large wing chair and agitatedly played with the material of the skirt – pleating and unpleating with hands that seemed unable to remain still. Perhaps the colour was too strong. Should she be so rash as to wear a dress that clung so suggestively? It had been far too expensive: the woman she had been would never have lavished so much on one dress. Having destroyed her pleasure in the dress she turned to the next day and the planned dinner. What could she say to her children to explain Alex's absence? She could easily imagine how smug Peter would be if they found her alone.

The doorbell rang.

She leaped from her chair. It was Alex, she was certain. Like magic her despondency vanished.

'I thought you weren't coming,' she cried with relief when she saw him standing on the doorstep.

'I'm so sorry, my darling, I got here as quickly as I could.'

She held the door wide. 'Come in, come in,' she said urgently, taking his hand, dragging him in as if fearful he might disappear. 'Alex, I've been so afraid.'

'Darling.' He was laughing as he kissed her, as if her anxiety pleased him. He leaned against the door, slamming it shut, and held her tightly to him. He stroked her hair, caressed her face, rained short, desperate kisses upon her and spoke a torrent of Greek which she did not understand but did not need to.

3

'A Christmas tree – with lights!' Alex exclaimed as they entered the drawing room. 'Wonderful. You know, my Anna, this is my first English Christmas, I always seem to have been travelling in the past. I've never celebrated this special feast. In Greece, Easter is our big festival.'

'You look tired,' she said, eyeing with concern his face which looked grey with fatigue.

'It was a hellish journey,' he sighed, sitting heavily in an armchair. 'It seems to have taken days to get here. There'd been a freak storm in Portugal, which had knocked out the phones. At Heathrow it was bedlam, so I decided to press on, without waiting to phone.'

'Portugal? Why were you there?' she asked apprehensively.

'Because I prefer to fly from Brazil to London via Portugal, my love,' he explained, smiling at her.

'Oh, I see.'

'Did you think I had deserted you?'

'Well, it did seem a long time with no call.'

'Darling, I warned you – it is a little difficult to find a telephone up the Amazon.' He was laughing now.

'Is that where the trees were?'

'Yes, millions of them, and no women.'

'Oh, Alex . . .' she looked at her hands in embarrassment.

'Admit it. You thought I'd run off with someone else.' He grinned at her.

'No, I didn't,' she lied.

'Ha! And I think you did. You're jealous. That's a good thing, Anna. That makes me feel much more secure with you.'

'I don't think I've got a jealous bone in my body. I wouldn't know what being jealous is like, I never have been.'

'That's because you've never really been in love before,' he said triumphantly.

'Such rubbish you do talk, Alex,' she laughed, but felt slightly uncomfortable at how close to the truth he might be.

He lay back in the chair, closing his eyes, deep lines of exhaustion etched on his face. 'A drink, Anna, please. I'll feel better for a drink.'

'Red or white?' she asked, since he usually drank wine.

'No, whisky, and very large.'

She served him the drink and before she had poured one for herself, he had drained the glass.

'Do you want something to eat?' she asked anxiously.

He held up his glass. 'No thanks, another of these first.'

'Why don't you take this one and relax with it in a bath? I can get dinner ready while you're doing that.'

'We're staying here?' He looked at her quizzically.

'I thought so, if that's all right by you.'

'That would be perfect,' he said with satisfaction.

She led him to their room, showed him which wardrobe was his, and deposited the decanter of whisky by the bath.

'I'm afraid it's not as grand as you're used to,' she said apologetically, looking round the familiar room and wishing again she had had time to decorate it, have new curtains made, a new bedspread, wishing it did not seem so shabby.

'It's far better. It has the feel of you, the smell of you.'

While he bathed, she busied herself downstairs with the last-minute preparations for the dinner. Everything was ready, the venison casserole only needed heating, and the vegetables would take little time to cook. She set the table and stood back, eyeing it critically. She straightened the candlesticks, then moved them into a new position. Disliking that, she moved them back. She fiddled with the flowers, ruining a perfectly adequate arrangement that had already taken her ages to do. She rejected the green napkins that she had painstakingly folded into a lily shape and, from the sideboard drawer, took two thick white damask ones which she folded neatly, no fancy styles, on the bread plates. She was nervous. She wanted everything perfect and was frightened that she had forgotten how to make it so. She smiled to herself, it was probably silly to worry like this. If he was anything like most men, he probably would not even see the table setting. It was odd how men commented if things were not perfect but invariably failed to notice when they were. She frowned. Ben she had meant, that's who she was thinking about really. She quickly turned to check the temperature of the wine; she was loath to have such thoughts tonight.

An hour later he came down, having changed into a black velvet smoking jacket, with an emerald green silk cravat about his neck. The lines of fatigue had all but disappeared from his face.

'Snap!' she laughed, smoothing down the folds of her dress.

'My darling,' he said, softly advancing upon her, his hands outstretched. He took her hands and held her at arm's length. 'You look beautiful. I was going to tell you that you should wear bright colours, they suit you. And how lovely the table looks. Thank you, my darling, this is a perfect homecoming.' He pulled her chair out for her, and expertly flicked her napkin open, placing it with ceremony on her lap. Then with a deft movement he poured the wine. 'You see how talented I am, I could be a waiter if I wanted.'

'You look marvellous and an hour ago you looked done in.'

'Did I disappoint you? Did you think you had an exhausted old man on your hands who wouldn't be able to make love to you?' He laughed.

She blushed. 'Of course I didn't. I was worried.'

'Ah, I bet you've thought of nothing else since I left – bed and you and me in it,' he laughed. 'I know that's all I've been thinking.'

Ann blushed more deeply. He talked unselfconsciously of sex. She could talk to him on the phone, as she had the other morning, but face to face . . . It was a new experience for Ann. She doubted if she and Ben had discussed the sexual side of their life once. And yet this man teased her about it, made her blush, made love to her with words. It was strange, too, how tonight she kept thinking of Ben; she had not thought of him the last time they were together.

'I was worried,' she repeated.

'You shouldn't be. It's miraculous what a drink, a hot bath and the sight of the woman you love can do to a man. And I'm one of those lucky individuals who can sleep for five minutes and it's as if I'd been asleep for hours.'

'So that's how you manage it. That's cheating.' She laughed flirtatiously.

When they had finished dinner they settled themselves on cushions in front of the blazing log fire in the drawing room, large brandies by their side.

'And why, Anna, did you decide we should stay here?'

'I thought you might be too tired for more travelling. But I also felt that it would show my commitment to you.'

'So you have thought of all I said.'

'Yes.'

'And you've no fears?'

'None.'

'And your family?'

'I haven't told them.'

'Why not?'

'I haven't seen Fay, it isn't exactly something you tell your daughter over the telephone, is it? And my son, well, he's being difficult. He's upset just at the thought of my seeing you . . .' Alex frowned at her words and she decided not to tell him the extent of Peter's anger. 'Anyhow, he wasn't in a very receptive mood. I thought we might all have dinner together here, tomorrow, if you have no other plans. I feel that once they've met you, he'll see things differently.'

'Let's hope so. I have no wish to fight with your son, my darling. I've no plans whatsoever: just to be with you. And what about Christmas Day?'

'I've told them I want to spend it alone with you.'

'Good heavens, that is commitment.' He laughed, rumpling her hair. 'Your dress is perfect, are you psychic as well?'

'Psychic?'

From his pocket he took a small box, opening it to reveal a large, square-cut emerald, surrounded by diamonds. The stone matched the colour of her dress exactly.

'Oh, Alex! It's beautiful.'

'I'm glad you like it. Now, let me put it on your finger.'

'Alex! It's too wonderful. But for me?'

'Who else do you suggest?'

'But it's not Christmas yet.'

'This isn't your Christmas present. This is for our engagement.'

'Engagement?' Ann said, confused. 'I don't understand – I mean you haven't asked me to marry you.'

'I did. In Hampshire.'

'You said you loved me,' Ann corrected him gently.

'But when I explained myself, what sharing our lives meant, I thought you understood . . .'

'I didn't. Good Lord, of course I didn't. I thought you were inviting me to be your mistress.'

'My mistress! Oh my darling Anna, you are a lady for marrying, not for making into a mistress. My poor sweet, you really do love me then, for such a respectable lady to contemplate such an action – no wonder you didn't tell your family. I'm not surprised your son is angry if he thinks my intentions are dishonourable. Any good son should be.'

'Do you think so?' she said eagerly.

'I do most certainly. But here, I must make amends.' He sank on to one knee and with exaggerated gallantry asked her to marry him.

'Are you sure?' she asked, not certain if she did so because she was surprised or because of the way he had made the proposal, joking and laughing as he knelt before her.

'What do you mean? Of course I'm sure. I've been sure from the moment we met. Are you having doubts?' he asked seriously.

'No, no. Of course not,' she said hurriedly.

'Then you are going to marry me?'

'Of course, my darling,' she answered quickly, but with her mind in a whirl. Her thoughts were having to change gear too rapidly for ease.

'Then we need champagne. Do you have any?'

'In the kitchen . . .' She began to get up.

'No, allow me. Just tell me where it is.'

Ann sat alone looking deeply into the fire. She felt stunned. She had prepared herself to be his mistress, she was dazed to find herself his future wife. She had never thought of marriage to anyone but Ben . . . There he was again, sneaking into her thoughts.

Alex returned with the champagne and solemnly, on the floor, in front of the blazing fire they raised their glasses in their future.

'Alex, will it always be like this?' she asked wistfully, as if she could not believe that such happiness could last.

'We shall make it stay like this – always, my darling. I promise.'

Disturbing themselves only to throw another log on the fire, or to pour more champagne, they lay entwined in each other's arms. She played with her ring, delighting in the way the firelight set sparks off the diamonds as if the ring were a living thing. It was strange, she thought, when he was beside her, all doubts and worries disappeared.

'What about this house, my love?' he asked suddenly.

'I'm going to sell it. I've decided.'

'You don't have to for me, you realize.'

'I know that. But I've thought a lot about it while you were away. I had thought I would get a small flat in London to be nearer you. But that was when I thought you wanted me to be your mistress,' she chuckled. 'But I still think I'll sell it: it's better to start anew. We could get a house nearer London with the money, if you like?'

'No, that won't be necessary. Invest the money. It will give you a little extra income that is yours alone.' He smiled fondly at her. 'But we're sitting here talking like estate agents when we have far more important duties to each other.' He stood, pulling her to her feet, and with his arm tight about her he led her upstairs to their bedroom.

That night, because it was so late, and he had been so tired and had travelled so far, Ann had thought they would go straight to sleep. He laughed dismissively at her suggestion.

'On our engagement night? Ridiculous idea!'

Ann lay alone in the bed, hugging to herself the memories of last night and this new happiness.

In a way which she did not fully understand, she wished Alex had not asked her to marry him. They had been happy as they were – why change the situation?

When thinking of her ideal marriage with Ben, she had recently found herself admitting how restricted her life had been. If she felt that about Ben, how much more restrictive her life with a demanding man like Alex was going to be. If she refused his proposal he would leave her – he was too proud to accept rejection. And if he left, did she really think she could live without him? That was the crux of the matter. There was no choice.

She dressed hurriedly in jeans and a sweater and ran downstairs, attracted by the sound of laughter from the kitchen. She found Meg beaming with approval at Alex as he enthusiastically waded his way through a large cooked breakfast.

'Darling, at last!' He bounded across the room to plant a kiss on her cheek. 'We thought you were never coming, didn't we, Mrs Meg?'

Meg's smile seemed to know no bounds and it grew even larger, encompassing Ann in its torchlight beam. 'Oh, Mrs Grange, I'm that excited, I don't know what to say . . .' the gap-toothed grin continued, unabated.

'Not as excited as I am, I'm sure, Meg. Look.' Proudly Ann thrust forward her hand with its new ring.

'My goodness, it fair blinds you!' Meg exclaimed, a fat tear emerging and rolling down the great coarse plain of her cheek.

'Heavens, don't cry, Meg. It's a happy day.'

'That's why I'm crying. I'm just so happy for you. And Mr Grange, he would be so happy for you too,' she said.

'Thank you, Meg, you're a dear.' Ann kissed the other woman gently on the cheek, grateful for her simple assurance. But the kiss seemed to plumb new depths of emotion in Meg who let out a great wail, which was interrupted by the sound of the door bell ringing.

'That's my car,' Alex said with more than a shade of relief. 'I'm off to London to shop. And for once, my darling, I don't want you with me.' He kissed her fleetingly on the brow, took one last gulp of this tea, and was gone.

Ann sat over coffee with Meg and listened while Meg repeated how happy for her she was, and Ann assured her how happy she was, and they both agreed what a lovely man Alex was.

As the conversation threatened to repeat itself again, Ann called a halt. 'I've a lot to do today, Meg. It's my important dinner tonight. I just hope the children are as pleased with him as you are.'

'Oh, Mrs Grange, how could they possibly object?'

The day scudded past for Ann, busy with her preparations for dinner. With so much food to choose from it had taken her some time finally to settle on the pheasants. By the time Alex returned, everything was ready, bar the cooking.

'Alex. You look like Father Christmas,' Ann laughed at the sight of Alex on her door step, barely able to see above a pile of gaudily wrapped presents.

'I feel like Father Christmas,' he declared stepping into the hall to reveal behind him a uniformed chauffeur equally burdened. 'Put them there, Kenny,' he ordered indicating the hall floor. 'Leave the Rolls, you take the Maserati. Have a good Christmas, I shan't be needing you until the New Year. Merry Christmas,' he said handing the chauffeur an envelope.

'Thank you very much, sir. A Merry Christmas to you, and to you, ma'am,' He lifted his cap to Ann, who stood holding the door, fully aware that her mouth was open with astonishment, and only just managing to mumble a greeting as he passed.

'Does he belong to the company too?'

'Kenny? Yes.'

'And there's a Rolls out there?' she asked disbelievingly. Following the chauffeur out of the door she saw a silver-coloured Rolls-Royce standing in her driveway. She clapped her hands. 'Imagine what the village is going to say about this. Just how many cars do you have?'

'This is the last.'

'Can we go for a drive?'

'Certainly not. We have much to do!' He took her arm and playfully frogmarched her back into the house.

'So many parcels,' she exclaimed as they laboriously carried them through to the Christmas tree.

'You should see Adam's, a great success if I say so myself . . .'

'You bought my grandson a present? How kind you are.'

'I've bought everybody presents. I've had a marvellous day. But Adam's is best. A wooden fort with hundreds of soldiers. I hope he likes it.'

'And you hope he'll let you play with it?' she said laughing – he grinned sheepishly.

'I got your son a case of wine. It's difficult to buy presents for women you don't know – perfume is such an intimate gift – so I got Fay and Sally each a brooch. Will that be all right?' She nodded, smiling, happy at his boyish excitement. 'Look at this.' He unwrapped one of the boxes revealing a mink hat. 'For Meg,' he announced, balancing it on his head.

'Meg? She'll go mad with excitement.'

'She confided to me this morning that she suffered with the cold on her ears. And you see, ear muffs!' He laughed as he pulled the ear muffs down on to his ears.

'Darling, they're perfect.' She watched him with affection as he attempted to rewrap Meg's present, eventually giving up with frustration and thrusting it at Ann to finish.

'The rest you are to know nothing about until tomorrow, except for this one. Come.' Carrying a large flat box and taking her hand he led her to their room. 'Open it.'

Amidst the sheets of tissue paper lay a bright red silk taffeta dress.

'Alex, a red dress! How did you know?'

'Know what, my darling?'

'That I always wanted one.' Excitedly she unpacked the dress, feeling its smooth silkiness with pleasure, enjoying the rustling sound it made as she held it against her. 'It's beautiful,' she sighed.

'It's a Christmas colour, isn't it?' he said, beaming with pleasure and watching her with an indulgent expression as she cavorted in front of the mirror. 'I don't want to stop your admiration of yourself, but shouldn't we start to get changed?'

Looking at her watch, she shrieked. 'My God, it's past seven!' Ann raced to the kitchen and not for the first time blessed her luck in having an Aga with its permanently heated ovens. She put the parboiled potatoes into the top hot oven. The well-larded pheasants she placed in the lower, cooler oven. The vegetables could cook while they ate the first course. She crossed the kitchen to the refrigerator and removed the plates of smoked salmon and put them on the table to take the chill off them. There was nothing else she could do at the moment, so she raced back upstairs and speedily bathed first. Finished, she ran a bath for Alex.

She was wrapping a towel around herself when Alex, naked, entered the bathroom. He stepped towards her and quickly whipped the towel from her, his hands cupping her still wet breasts, his mouth coming down fiercely on hers.

'Darling, not now, we haven't time,' she gasped as his lips left hers.

'We always have time for this,' he replied, putting his arms round her. Lifting her from the floor and curling her legs about him he entered her effortlessly. Locked in this most intimate of embraces he began to cross the room. The movement coupled with the sensuality of his expression brought Ann too quickly to the point of climax.

'Don't fight it, my love,' he whispered, huskily.

'Together,' she gasped.

'Later.'

Ann lost control. Her hands clasped tight to his neck, her back arched, she held herself taut as an arrow as he moved deeper and deeper within her. She cried out. Her body relaxed. He laughed softly, enjoying her fulfilment, then laid her gently on the bed. 'You see,' he said smiling. 'There's always time.' Quietly he began to make love to her again.

Afterwards she lay, momentarily exhausted, in his arms, wishing they could lie there all evening.

'Now I need another bath,' she said instead, practically.

'Then join me.' He took her hand and led her back into the bathroom. He lifted her into the bath, climbing in beside her, his bulk making the water splash over the sides. She laughed.

'What are you laughing at, little one?'

'I was just thinking how athletic life is with you. I mean most people make love, neatly, in bed.'

'Most people are boring,' he laughed, sliding his hand under the water searching for her.

'No you don't, you insatiable brute.' She hurriedly clambered from the bath.

'Are you complaining?'

'No, no. No complaints, but our guests will be here soon – I can't see my son approving of such activities . . . !' She dried herself quickly and left him soaping himself.

Ann took the new red dress from its hanger and hugged it to her. How wonderful, at last a red dress and even more wonderful that he should have bought it, almost as if he knew. She slipped the dress over her head, afraid at first to look in the mirror in case it did not suit, in case it did not fit.

She need not have worried. The clear primary red made her skin glow, and her hair appear blonder. It fitted perfectly as if made for her. The tight bodice accentuated her breasts. The billowing skirt flaring from the nipped-in waist made her feel graceful and feminine.

She lifted the flat dress box from the floor and for the first time realized that there were matching satin shoes with small diamanté bows on the front. And they were the right size. She wondered how he had known which size she wore.

She studied her reflection. What a change he had made in her: she knew she looked years younger and far more attractive than she would have thought possible – it was not just the clothes and hair, it was that incandescent beauty which is the badge of a woman in love and sexually satisfied.

She hastily applied her make-up and dashed downstairs to put the finishing touches to the dinner.

Alex was waiting for her in the drawing room, a drink poured ready for her. Looking at him in his dinner jacket, Ann could not imagine why, when she had first met him, she had not thought him handsome. Now, to her eyes he was the most beautiful man she had ever known.

'What did you mean, my sweet, that you had always wanted a dress like that?' he said, handing her the drink.

'I always wanted a red silk dress, the brightest red ever made. Silly I suppose.'

'Then why didn't you buy one?'

'Ben liked me best in black and pastel shades.'

'But bright colours suit your colouring so well. You should always have had a red dress.'

'Do you really think so?'

'The minute I saw you I wanted to dress you in shining silk and satins,' he smiled. 'I would have thought that any man would want to,' he added quizzically.

'Well, you see, Ben was . . .' but the doorbell interrupted her. 'That'll be George and Lydia.' She swept excitedly from the room to let her friends in.

'God, Ann, you look wonderful. What a beautiful dress!' Lydia exclaimed, depositing a kiss in the air in the vague proximity of Ann's cheek.

'You look good enough to eat,' George gruffly added.

'Come, both of you, meet Alex.' Ann was laughing with delight at their compliments.

'Lead me to him!' Lydia said, archly.

Lydia took Alex's proffered hand and, standing back, studied him, her head on one side. 'My, my, Ann, you didn't exaggerate one tiny little bit, did you?' She smiled boldly at Alex and Ann felt a tiny tendril of jealousy.

'So, you're Lydia. I have to thank you for all your kindness to Anna. She tells me you are a true friend.'

'Ann, darling, that voice! Who could resist it? I think I shall faint. Perhaps a drinky might just revive me.'

'You make certain you do resist it, Lydia,' Ann teased. 'Darling, Lydia will have a gin and tonic, and George a Highland Park. Is that right, George?'

'Best tincture around,' George grinned back.

Ann felt she couldn't be happier. Alex pouring a drink for her dearest friend, she in her longed-for red dress, and all around her smiling, happy faces.

'Ann!' Lydia's loud shriek made them all jump. 'Good God, George, look at that enormous ring! And note the finger it's on too. Let me look more closely, Ann. Now that's what I call a ring. Congratulations, Alex. You are obviously not only wonderfully attractive but very astute as well. Ann is a gem.'

'I realize my good fortune, Lydia.' He sat on the arm of Ann's chair and put his arm about her shoulder.

'Really looks odd, you with another feller instead of dear old Ben,' said George amiably.

'Shut up, George, you fool,' Lydia said, tapping him briskly on his knuckles. 'You're being tactless, you old buffoon.'

'Sorry,' said George with the resigned patience of a man who frequently says the wrong thing.

'Take no notice of the idiot, Alex, he's always putting his great feet in it.'

'Didn't mean to offend,' George mumbled into his Scotch.

'Nor you did, George. It's a big adjustment for all of us to make.' Ann smiled sweetly while Alex looked from George to Lydia with a puzzled expression.

The doorbell summoned her again. Involuntarily Ann squeezed Alex's hand, hard. Downed her drink in one. Smiled tentatively at everyone, stood and nervously straightened her dress. 'That will be the children,' she said, unnecessarily, in a voice that vainly tried to sound light-hearted.

A sullen group stood on the doorstep, long faces looking incongruous above the brightly covered boxes in their hands.

'Well, you lot don't look very cheerful.' Ann attempted to laugh but her laugh died at the sight of the peeved expression on her son's face.

'You haven't just travelled here with Peter, Mummy.' Fay kissed her mother, slipping off her coat to reveal a smart black cocktail dress. 'He's determined to ruin this evening.'

'You always were one for telling tales,' Peter snapped childishly at his sister.

'Sally, that's a pretty dress,' Ann said, ignoring her bickering children.

'Do you like it? It's only from the market. It's all I could afford.'

'But these Indian dresses are so pretty, and it makes a perfect maternity dress.' Ann smiled sweetly. 'Peter, you haven't changed,' she said, disappointment plain in her voice, as he took his coat off to reveal his customary sweater and cords.

'That's what the row was about. I said you'd be annoyed,' Fay explained.

'But Peter, we always change for Christmas dinners. What on earth got into you?'

'We normally change, Mother, that's when we have a normal Christmas,' he snapped back.

'You're right. Things are different, so why shouldn't you be?' she said briskly. 'Come and meet the others, George and Lydia popped in for a drink.' She led her family towards the drawing room, the happiness of the evening already tainted.

5

Ann fluttered about nervously introducing her children to Alex. There was a forced gaiety about her, a slight shrillness in her voice, as she gamely pretended that it was an everyday event for her to introduce her children to her lover.

Alex bowed, graciously, over the women's hands. Sally giggled at the unfamiliar foreign gesture. For one heart-stopping moment she thought that Peter was not going to accept Alex's outstretched hand. Alex, an almost inperceptible frown on his face, observed the effect of their arrival on Ann as he gravely shook Peter's hand. Apart from a curt 'how do you do' both men stood silently, observing each other. Ann grabbed Peter's arm and asked him to help her serve the drinks, any danger averted for the time being as he busied himself at the drinks tray.

Once the drinks were served, a silence which unnerved Ann settled on the group. Rack her brains as she might, she could think of nothing to say. Her eyes pleaded with Lydia who was busily engrossed in lighting a cigarette, from a lighter that did not appear to work. Smoothly Alex stepped forward and proferred a light from his heavy gold lighter, which, for some inexplicable reason, made Peter snort. Even George seemed to realize he was witnessing a sticky situation for it was he who broke the silence.

'Lydia tells me you're from Greece.'

'That's right.'

'I haven't been to the mainland but I went to Corfu once – holiday, you know.'

'Really? I've never been there myself but I gather it's very pleasant. One of our most beautiful islands.'

'It was a bit too noisy and crowded for my taste.' George thoughtfully sipped his drink. 'Do you own a restaurant?' he suddenly asked.

'George!' yelled Lydia. 'You are ridiculous.' She turned to Alex. 'Trouble with George is, he thinks all Spaniards are waiters, all French are bastards and all Greeks own restaurants!' Everyone but Peter joined in her laughter.

'Well, I like kebabs. Alex might have been able to cook them, don't you see?' Everybody laughed, and Ann allowed herself to relax a little.

'As a matter of fact I do own restaurants, and I too like kebabs.' Alex smiled good-naturedly.

'That your Roller outside?' persisted George, indefatigable in his efforts to make pleasant small talk.

'It's my company's,' explained Alex.

'Lovely car. Best there is. British you see,' stated George, as if being British explained everything.

'It's certainly a wonderful car.'

'They do say,' Peter suddenly spoke, making everyone jump and wheel round in his direction, 'that when the top brass of a company start swanning around in Rolls-Royces, it's time to sell your shares!'

All eyes pivoted back to Alex, like spectators at a tennis match. 'Sound advice,' he agreed, smiling pleasantly.

'They must be successful restaurants,' Sally said simply.

'Oh, I'm in other businesses too.'

'Like what?' Peter asked, abruptly.

'This and that.' Alex's smile was enigmatic.

'What did you say your name was?' George asked.

'I didn't. But it's Georgeopoulos.'

'Is it now?' George smiled, as enigmatic as Alex.

'We were thinking of throwing a party on New Year's Eve. Any chance of you and Alex coming?' Lydia asked.

'I'm afraid Anna and I won't be here, Lydia. We shall ourselves be giving a party. I always do at New Year and I fear the invitations will already have been sent. You are all most welcome to come,' Ann, to her surprise, heard him say.

'Her name's Ann, if you don't mind,' Peter interjected.

'We should love to come, thank you, Alex,' said Lydia, totally ignoring Peter. 'What bliss, I shall be saved the dreariness of organizing one. But sorry, Ann, we must be going. The Smith-Robertsons call – boring old trogs. But there you are, the duties of village life.' Lydia waved her hand languorously in the air. 'I'd much rather be dining here, looks as if this evening is going to develop most interestingly,' she added, looking pointedly at Peter.

Returning to the drawing room after seeing her friends off, Ann found Fay and Alex talking animatedly, Sally collecting the empty glasses, and Peter staring into space.

'Presents now or after dinner?' Ann asked.

'After dinner, please, as always. The anticipation makes it all the more fun. I'll give you a hand with the dinner, Mummy.' Fay jumped up.

'No, darling, you stay and amuse Alex. I can manage. Give me the tray, Sally, you shouldn't be carrying such heavy things. Peter, perhaps you could freshen up the drinks,' and, with relief, she escaped into the kitchen. Once there she poured herself an enormous drink. She leaned against the unit, downing the drink in short, sharp sips, an anxious expression on her face. Peter was going to be difficult, the evening was going to be a disaster. How she wished now that she had asked Lydia to dinner.

She checked her pheasants. Took the plates of smoked salmon through to the table and called everyone to dinner. As her children filed past she pulled Alex back. 'I love you,' she said standing on tiptoe to kiss him. 'Please don't let my son upset you.'

'Upset me? Why should I let anyone upset me?' He kissed her back.

They found consternation in the dining room. 'Where's the table?' Ann was asked by three voices in unison, the minute she entered the room.

'I sold it,' she said, braving their shocked faces. 'I took a fancy to having a round one, so much easier to seat everyone and to talk across, don't you think? Especially when we are odd numbers like tonight. Alex, if you will sit over there between the girls . . .'

'But that table was Hepplewhite, Mother, this is only Victorian!' Peter admonished.

'So it's not such a responsibility, is it? I can upset my wine tonight with impunity.' Ann forced herself to smile at them, annoyed at their reaction. She could not remember either child ever giving an opinion on the table before.

'I hope you got a good price for it, there are such sharks around,' Sally said, running her fingers across the new table's veneer, for all the world like a dealer, Ann thought.

'Yes, Sally, I did. Don't worry. I was quite aware of the table's value,' she answered sharply, making Alex glance quickly at her. 'Now, shall we start?' she added in a businesslike tone.

'You might have offered it to us first.' Peter's scowl seemed to have deepened by inches since they had entered the dining room.

'The insurance on the damn thing was horrendous, and with Adam about, you would have been constantly watching and nagging the child. No, this is a much more satisfactory solution. Now for goodness sake, let's forget about the table, and tuck in.' And Ann began to eat the salmon that suddenly tasted of damp cardboard. 'Stupid me, I forgot the wine.' She jumped up.

'Anna, darling, relax, let me,' and Alex had taken the wine from the cooler and was pouring it for her.

'I don't like arriving and finding Dad's furniture gone like that. You might ask next time, or at least tell us what you're up to,' Peter continued relentlessly.

'I promise. I'm sorry. I should have thought to tell you,' Ann said with studied patience. 'Since I seem to have upset everybody so, I'd better tell you, I've decided to sell the bed.'

'Mummy, you can't sell *The Bed*!' said Fay in a shocked voice.

'Yes I can, quite easily,' Ann replied brightly. Abandoning her attempts to eat the tasteless fish that everyone else had finished, she began to collect the plates. Fay followed her into the kitchen.

'He's super, Mummy. And very sexy. I can see why you're smitten with him.'

'I'm glad you like him.'

'He's not at all what I expected.'

'Well, he wouldn't be if you've been listening to your brother. Can you hold this dish for me?'

'He's not handsome but, well, still very attractive, if you know what I mean. A Mr Rochester, a lived-in sort of face . . .'

'Yes, darling, I know exactly what you mean,' Ann laughed, feeling happy for the first time since her children had arrived.

'I'll be furious if you let Peter break it up, Mummy. You know what he's like when he gets a bee in his bonnet about something.'

'Fay, no one is going to stand in my way. Least of all Peter. I promise you.'

Together they carried the dishes into an ominously silent dining room. Ann began to serve the food and purposely asked Peter to pour the red wine for her. For a while there was silence as they began to eat.

'Darling, this pheasant is delicious. I shall have to tell Pétin she has a rival,' Alex teased her and from the corner of her eye Ann saw Peter flinch at his use of the endearment.

'Who's Pétin?' asked Fay.

'She's a terrifying French woman who runs a restaurant in London. She treats me with great disdain.'

'Perhaps it's the company you keep,' Peter said smoothly. There was a clattering of knives and forks. Ann choked on a morsel of food, but Alex chose to ignore the remark and smiled at Ann.

'Her disdain is a compliment to you, my darling Anna. It shows she sees you as a threat,' he said half seriously.

'I've told you already her name is Ann,' Peter interrupted, his knife poised ominously in his hand.

'And I prefer to call Anna, it's my name for her,' Alex replied pleasantly. 'Anna, shall I open another bottle of wine for you? This one is empty.'

'Oh, do feel free with other people's drink.'

'Peter! Don't be so rude! As it happens, Alex gave me the wine. Now apologize.'

'What's the saying?' Peter looked straight at Alex. 'Never trust a Greek bearing gifts. Isn't that how it goes?' Alex inclined his head in a sardonic bow.

'Peter, are you drunk? You're being thoroughly objectionable,' Ann remonstrated, anxiously folding and refolding her napkin, and then busily moving the salt and pepper pots as if they were chess pieces on an unmarked board. Peter sat in sullen silence methodically chewing his food. Ann looked at Alex, her concern showing in her eyes.

Alex formed a kiss for her and shrugged his shoulders. 'I think I can stand it, my love.'

'Jesus Christ!' Peter slammed his knife and fork on to his plate.

'I'd love this recipe, Ann,' Sally said quickly. 'We occasionally get the odd pheasant from some farming friends. Mine are always so dry.'

'Remind me before you go. You have to cook them slowly,' Ann replied automatically.

Somehow they ate the pudding, the cheese, four of them chattering while Peter sat in sullen silence. Throughout the meal, Ann felt a constriction in her throat that no amount of wine or water would relieve. Nothing she ate seemed to have any taste.

'You sit down, Mummy. Sally and I will do the dishes.'

'We'll all do them,' said Alex, taking a pile of plates in his huge hands.

'Are you going to help, Peter, or are you just going to sit there sulking?' Fay asked her brother shortly. Peter ignored her, continuing to sit stolidly in his chair as if oblivious to the activity around him. 'You always were lazy. As far as I can make out you do bugger all. If you're not going to help, shift . . .' and she roughly pushed him to remove the empty bottles.

The dishwasher loaded, the work surfaces wiped down, Alex put champagne glasses and a couple of bottles on to a tray, and led the way to the drawing room carrying the tray aloft, like a Pied Piper; the rest followed, laughing, with Peter a cheerless last to enter the room.

Ann poured the coffee. 'That's a stunning dress, Mummy. And red too,' Fay said, smiling knowingly at her mother.

'Alex gave it to me.'

'For services rendered no doubt,' Peter muttered, almost inaudibly, but Fay heard and rewarded him with a sharp kick on the shins. Ann glanced anxiously across the room to Alex. He appeard not to have heard as he still busied himself with the champagne.

'Peter, grow up!' Ann hissed quietly with exasperation. She walked towards the window. Before pulling the curtains she paused and watched as a few flakes of snow fell. Reflected in the leaded panes of the mullioned windows was the scene in the room. Repeated many times in the different panes, they looked such a happy, cosy group. The window did not reveal the angry undertones whirling about the room. My last Christmas here, she thought to herself, suddenly overcome with a great sadness for this house that had been her home for so long. She felt Alex's arm about her shoulder.

'Why do you look so depressed, my darling?'

'Oh, it's nothing, that usual happiness mixed with sorrow that Christmas can bring,' she said brightly, a shade too brightly.

'I think you're thinking how sad that this is your last Christmas in this beautiful house.'

'Well . . .' She smiled at him apologetically.

'I understand, my love. It's perfectly normal that happiness should be tinged with moments of regret.'

'How did you know?'

'Because I love you, that's why.' He kissed her gently on the nape of her neck. 'Next year we'll have our own home together and this mood will be no more. It's a transitory thing.'

'Who said something about presents, and what's happened to the champagne, Alex?' Fay called good-naturedly to them and they turned back into the cosy room. 'Bags I be postman,' Fay giggled, suddenly transformed from a sophisticated woman into a young girl again, and swooped on the pile of boxes beneath the tree and began to distribute them, flitting about the room until each person had a respectable pile. 'Who's going to be first?' she demanded.

'A toast first, don't you all agree?' Alex asked, circling the room with the tray of champagne flutes. He stood in front of the fire and faced them, putting out his hand for Ann to join him.

'To this family.' Alex raised his glass.

'To us,' everyone, with the exception of Peter, replied.

'I can only conclude that this entire family is blind,' Alex said, lifting Ann's hand where the emerald ring glinted in the firelight. Three mouths dropped open with surprise, three sets of eyes grew round with astonishment. Two smiled, one scowled. 'So, it is left to me to propose a toast to Anna and myself on our engagement.'

'Mummy!' Fay leapt across the room. 'I didn't notice. Let me see,' she shrieked, grabbing Ann's hand.

'Congratulations to both of you.' Sally smiled a genuine smile and raised her glass to them both, before crossing the room to inspect the ring in turn.

Peter sat isolated.

'What dark horses you are. When are you getting married? Where? asked Fay after a moment's hesitation.

165

Alex looked pointedly at Peter. Silence descended on the room, and Ann felt a snake of nervousness knot her gut. 'Peter, I hope at least you will drink to your mother's happiness if not to mine,' Alex said in a soft voice which, to Ann, sounded too quiet, ominously so. Peter said nothing and looked steadfastly at the floor. 'You obviously don't approve, Peter. I agree with you that I'm not worthy of your mother, but I will endeavour to care for her and make her happy.'

Everyone waited, staring at Peter, each willing him to smile, to approve, to be happy. He sat like a stone, still taking an inordinate interest in the carpet.

'Well, I approve. Welcome to the family, Alex,' and Fay stood on tiptoe and kissed Alex soundly on the cheek.

'Peter?' said Ann looking anxiously at her son. 'Please Peter, don't spoil this evening for me.'

'I'm sorry, Mother. I'll drink to your future happiness, but not with him.'

'Peter, this is ridiculous. You don't know Alex.'

'Exactly.'

'But you should be happy for me that I've found someone with whom I want to share my life.'

'I can't, Mum, and that's that.'

'Would you prefer that I continued to live alone, sometimes afraid of the future?' Ann asked, but from Peter there was no reply. 'But why? You must have some explanation,' she added sharply, beginning to feel irritated by her son's intransigent attitude.

'If you must know, Mum, I don't trust him.'

'You're right to distrust me, Peter, I respect you for that,' Alex said, to Ann's surprise. He continued, 'You know nothing about me. And I can understand your concern that we have known each other such a short time. But you know, as well as I do, that every relationship we enter into is a gamble. Whether one is engaged two weeks or two years, it's still a gamble. But your mother and I, we are – how do you say it? – we are of mature years. Of an age when we know what we seek and having found it we must grasp it with both hands before it's too late.' He paused. Still Peter made no comment. 'We have spent a lot of time together these past few weeks and we've both found that not only do we love each other but we like each other too, which is of greater importance.'

'*Love!*' Peter finally spoke, spitting the word out venomously as if it were lewd. 'Goddamn lust more like.'

Ann noticed Alex stiffen, saw the cold expression of extreme anger flit across his face and loved him for the superhuman effort he was making to continue to talk to her son in a reasonable voice.

'Young man, let me finish. You're making this so difficult. Let me assure you that your mother will have all my love and devotion and, I can promise you, will want for nothing.'

'Fine words. So easily said,' Peter sneered.

'Where will you live?' Fay interrupted, glaring at Peter and attempting to steer the conversation away from him.

'I don't know. We haven't discussed that.' Ann shrugged. 'We've hardly had time to plan anything. Alex only returned from Brazil last night. That's when we got engaged.'

'What about this house?' Sally enquired.

'I'm selling it. I shall be sad of course, but I think it's fairer to Alex, to both of us, to start afresh.'

'Great! Just a month ago you were claiming, emotionally, that you couldn't live without this place,' Peter leapt in.

'I admit I do feel rather stupid about it, but everything's changed, I don't need it any more, you see. I suppose it was a form of security for me. Now I have Alex, he's my future security.' She smiled at him, but the smile was rather wan, for she felt that this conversation, this evening, was far from over.

'Amazing how easily women change their opinions, all for a good lay,' Peter said quietly, but not quietly enough.

Ann sensed more than saw Alex step towards her son. Quickly she grabbed him by the arm. 'Alex, please,' she pleaded. She began to shake and Alex put his arm round her and held her tightly. 'Of course you two can have whatever furniture you want,' she said quickly, deliberately, her voice faint. Alex gently stroked her arm.

'So you'll be buying another house with the proceeds from this one I presume. A little love nest somewhere?' Peter seemed to have gained courage for he no longer spoke quietly.

'That will not be necessary,' Alex answerd coldly. 'I have suggested to your mother that she invests that money to give her some income of her own.'

'Ah! So you have discussed money with my mother?' Peter said almost triumphantly.

'What is your problem? Out with it.' Alex said angrily. 'For God's sake do you think I'm marrying your mother for her money?'

'The thought had crossed my mind,' Peter replied sarcastically.

'Why? Is she rich?' Alex persisted.

'Oh, come off it,' Peter snorted, disdainfully. 'You know damn well she is. You have only to look at this place. And, no doubt, she's been stupid enough to tell you about my father's insurance policies and the other money he left her.'

'Peter! How can you be so insufferable? We've never discussed money, not once,' Ann said, her voice beginning to tremble. She was tired, she was unhappy, she wanted only to left in peace with Alex. She looked at her son and she loathed him.

Peter saw her expression and, sensing he might have gone too far, continued in a far more reasonable tone of voice. 'See it from my point of view, Mother. After all I feel responsible for you still. Why doesn't he tell us what he does? Why does he always have to be so bloody enigmatic? He could be a criminal for all you know.'

'So, am I to take it, Peter, that you would be happier if you knew my financial status?' Alex asked.

'Well, yes.'

'Normally I never divulge the state of my finances to anyone. However, this evening I had hoped to talk to you, Peter, as male head of this family. I wanted to explain to you the settlement I intend to make on your mother, the terms of our marriage contract in fact. But after your behaviour this evening, the intolerable things you have said, your apparent obsession with money, I'm afraid it would not be in your mother's best interest to divulge the facts to you of all people.' Peter's mouth dropped open with astonishment. For once he was speechless. 'Furthermore,' Alex continued coldly, 'I resent your insulting attitude to your mother. Do you really think the only way she can get a husband is by the size of her bank account? I have no interest in how much money she has. I don't want her money. I don't need her money.'

'Well said, Alex. I'm really happy for both of you,' Fay interrupted.

'Thank you, Fay.' Alex smiled at her, the coldness of his expression disappearing as he did so.

'Typical of you, Fay. Great support you are,' her brother taunted. 'I might have guessed that you'd stand back and watch our mother ruin her life and squander our money for a few romantic speeches.'

'There's more to life than money, Peter. Just look at Mummy. When have you seen her look so happy and contented? How can you spoil things for her?' Fay said with spirit.

'I must say, Peter,' Alex continued relentlessly in the cold voice that sent shivers down Ann's spine, 'I hadn't fully understood your father not leaving you anything. Not, that is, until this evening. He was obviously a far more perceptive man than I gave him credit for.'

The women were too slow to stop Peter as he lunged across the room. He lifted his arm to strike Alex, who, almost lazily, caught him by the wrist and held him off, as Peter impotently kicked and spat with rage. Alex frog-marched him across the drawing room and pushed him, with scant ceremony, back on to the sofa.

'For heaven's sake, everyone, stop this!' Ann shouted. 'Dear God, what is happening to this family? Peter, I doubt if I shall ever be able to forgive you for tonight. I'd warned you that I'd not give Alex up for anybody. Why are you doing this? Don't you want me to be happy? Why?' She was shouting.

'Be happy, Mother. What do I care? Ruin your life. But I tell you one thing, if you prefer him to us, then you'll never see Adam again. Ever!'

'Peter, you wouldn't do that. You can't deprive Adam of his family just because you don't approve.' Fay was shouting now.

'I can and I will.'

'Peter,' Alex said icily, 'that quotation you mentioned at dinner – "never trust a Greek bearing gifts"?'

'Yes,' replied Peter. 'What of it?'

'You have it slightly wrong. The correct quotation is *"Timeo Danaos et dona ferentes"*.'

'So, thanks for the classical lesson.'

'It means, "I *fear* the Greeks, even when they are bearing gifts." Should you try to deprive your mother of seeing her grandson whenever she wishes, you will have cause to remember that quotation. I promise,' Alex said slowly and distinctly.

'What's that supposed to mean? Are you trying to threaten me?' Peter was laughing.

'No. I'm warning you.'

'Oh yes? And what do you think you could possibly do to harm me?'

'I'll break you,' Alex said, so quietly that Ann had to strain to hear.

'Ha! You reckon?' Peter sneered. 'Look, I'm quaking in my shoes already. You, break me? Hardly.'

'I can ruin anyone I choose, Peter. I should believe that if I were you.' Alex swung round to face Ann. 'Anna, my darling, your wonderful evening lies in tatters about us. I'm so sorry, I know what it meant to you. But to pursue this conversation would not only be pointless but,

I fear, even more distasteful. If you will excuse me . . .'
He bowed his head to her. 'Fay, Sally, thank you both
for your charming company and for supporting Anna this
evening.' Again he bowed and left the room.

'Bloody cheek!' stormed Peter, but impotently now that
his adversary had left the room. 'Who the hell does he
think he is? How dare he behave like that in my father's
house?' He clambered to his feet, shaking with rage.

'Peter! You pushed Alex too far, he's a proud and
honourable man and you have insulted him deeply. You
have behaved like a perfect shit!'

'*Mother!*'

'Don't like me speaking the truth, do you? You don't
like me using the language you're adept at. I'm sick to
death of you and your tantrums. I have every right to this
chance of happiness. I'd like to involve my family but, if
this is your attitude, I can do without you.'

'I already know what your attitude to the family is. What
sort of loyalty we can expect from you,' Peter snapped
back. 'Fine mother you are.'

'Peter, shut up.' Fay and Sally spoke in unison.

'You're right, Mother, it's your life. Do what you
bloody well want. But don't come whining to me when it
all goes wrong – because I shan't be there. And you can
tell your wop friend that he doesn't frighten me one little
bit.' He laughed a short unpleasant laugh and, without
looking at Ann, began to leave the room. 'You two
coming?' he said over his shoulder.

Sally, for the first time ever, put her arms about Ann
and hugged her. 'I'm sorry your evening's been ruined this
way. Don't worry, Adam's my son too,' she whispered.

'Christ, Mummy, what a fiasco.' Fay tried to smile. 'Will
you be all right? Should I stay?'

'No, darling, I'll be fine. Don't forget your presents
both of you. And Fay, I'll give you a ring, tell you Alex's
address for the party. You will come, won't you?'

'Too bloody right, I'll come. Give us a hand, Peter,'
she called, but there was no response. 'Oh bugger him!

You take these, Sally, I'll carry the others.' And they struggled out to the car weighed down by the gaily wrapped presents. Ann helped to load the presents into the boot. Peter sat behind the wheel looking impassively ahead. She did not speak to him.

As Ann closed the front door she leaned against it feeling an enormous wave of exhaustion sweep over her. She returned to the drawing room where Alex stood waiting for her. He held his arms out and she ran to him and, clinging to him, began to let the pent-up tears flow. He stood patiently, holding her tenderly, stroking her hair, and murmuring to her as if she were a small child. Finally she looked up at him.

'I love you,' she said simply.

'I know that more than ever now. You will never regret your decision, I promise you. But now I need a very large brandy, I think we both do.'

They curled up on the sofa in front of the dying fire, the fairy lights still glowing on the Christmas tree.

'I apologize for my son, Alex. He was evil.'

'I think there's more to this than meets the eye,' he said with the slightly self-conscious hesitation he always had when he correctly used a colloquial saying in his adopted tongue.

'What do you mean?'

'I don't know, but I intend to find out.'

'The worst thing is having to face the fact that I don't particularly like someone I have spent most of my life loving.'

'My poor Anna.' He stroked her hair gently.

That night in bed, however, although he did not know it, Peter had won a small victory. Alex held her gently in his arms; it was not a night for passion.

Ann sat curled up in an armchair, watching through the window the wintry dawn filtering ghostlike into her garden. She had found it difficult to sleep, for the memory of last night's scenes kept filtering back into her mind, insidiously, like a malignant fog. In her throat she still felt the tight constriction. She remembered that feeling from long ago when she had grieved for Ben. As then, it was as if the grief that could not escape had lodged in, latched on to the sides of her throat with vicious talons. As with Ben, so the sadness caused by her son was a physical ache.

Across the room, in the strengthening light, she could see Alex lying asleep. In sleep he looked much younger, for the yard lines about his mouth relaxed. If only Alex were not so mysterious about what he did, she thought, surely that would ease the situation with Peter. Why could he not simply say what his work was, how he made so much money? Why this silly air of mystery?

Ben . . . The thought of him came clearly to her, as if he were in the room with them. She shuddered. Ben would not approve either: she knew that now for a certainty. Alex was everything of which Ben would have been suspicious – he was smart, sophisticated, rich, a foreigner and enigmatic. Perhaps Peter was only voicing what Ben would have said, if he had ever met Alex.

Why should it matter what Ben might have thought? Last night she had said that nothing was going to prevent her happiness, but still she allowed these thoughts to worm their way into her mind, causing suspicions and damage. When she and Alex were alone in the house in Hampshire she had not thought like this. She had been content to live for the moment, grasp each second of happiness. But here in this house, there were too many ghosts of the past.

She uncurled her stiffening limbs from the chair and moved towards the bed to look down at the man she loved. It was extraordinary that a man so strong could be so gentle, so sensuous. She touched his skin: she had not realized that a man could have skin as smooth and fine as his. She loved the feel of his muscles, strong and taut, even as he lay in sleep.

Alex stirred, slowly his eyes opened, and a dreamy smile appeared on his face. 'Hullo.' He stretched his arms out to her, dragging her down towards him. 'Merry Christmas.' And he kissed her. At her lack of response he looked at her, puzzled, and sat up.

'So, what have you been thinking, standing there, my darling?'

'I want to leave here, Alex. This morning.'

'No problem. We'll go.'

'I mean for good,' she stated.

'If that's what you want, my darling. If you are sure then let's pack. But first . . .' He kissed her tenderly but still Ann could not relax in his arms. 'You are right, we must go immediately,' he said firmly.

'I'm sorry. It's just . . . oh, I don't know . . .' She shrugged her shoulders.

'I understand. You cannot stay here in this house of unhappy memories.' It seemed that with Alex there was never any need to explain, he always seemed to understand her feelings.

Just over an hour later they were on the road. As she sat in the warmth and comfort of the Rolls she could feel the tension within her begin to fade.

'I'm sorry, Alex, I'm being very weak. I know I'll have to go back to the house eventually, to sort everything out and pack, but I just felt I had to get out. Last night was a mistake, I see that now. It was also wrong of me, too, to think that I had laid all the ghosts.' She smiled apologetically at him. He took her hand in his, steering the car with the other as he did so. 'And I'm sorry I ruined your English Christmas.'

'You haven't ruined anything. My Christmas is wherever you are, and it has only just started. Look,' he pointed to the large snowflakes beginning to fall, 'it's really snowing now – perfect.'

'Are we going to Courtneys?' She brightened up at the idea, at the memory of the happiness they had shared in the house in Hampshire.

'No, it's full of people. We're going to a flat in London. I think you need peace and quiet and, in any case, I have already shared you with too many people this Christmas.'

The car was soon swishing through the snow-lined streets of London, streets wrapped in that strange, silent calm peculiar to Christmas Day. Like a snake entering its hole, the large car slid into an underground car park. They took the noiseless lift to the top of the tall building. Ann was not prepared for the size of the apartment into which he led her. Alex opened double doors and Ann found herself standing on a balcony, looking down on an enormous room two storeys high. One wall, entirely of glass, led on to a wide terrace. A long way below, and stretching as far as the eye could see, was London. The walls and the furniture in the room were white, the floor was black, the only relief was an occasional touch of grey in a rug or on a cushion. Even the paintings were in the same colours. Bronze sculptures stood in dark silhouette against the walls.

'Heavens!' exclaimed Ann, unsure what reaction he would expect to this starkly elegant room which she found unwelcoming in its perfection.

Alex looked at her, anxiously. 'You don't like it?'

'It's very beautiful. Like a modern painting. The colours are so subtle . . .' She searched for more words to describe it. 'It's very brave, I don't think I could have thought up such, such purity,' she added hurriedly, not wanting to offend him.

'Um . . . You don't like it.' He frowned at the room below them. 'Neither do I,' he added emphatically. 'It's too perfect, isn't it? It lacks soul, like Courtneys. Your

175

house had a soul, a warmth. Come, let me show you the rest.'

Taking her hand, he led her to one side of the balcony and showed her four guest bedrooms, each expensively, luxuriously furnished but each as impersonal as a hotel bedroom; on the other side of the balcony was arranged a group of offices. The sweeping staircase they then descended was a miracle of engineering: it seemed to have no attachment to the wall, a gracious curve of shining steel and black wood.

'My rooms are through here.' He showed her into a large functional study, the room dominated by a huge black desk, plate-glass windows opening on to the same stunning view of London. The fine leather furniture looked little used and consequently stiffly uncomfortable. They passed along a corridor lined with cupboards: 'my things,' Alex airily dismissed them with a wave of his hand. Then they entered his bedroom, another severely furnished room, but this one was dominated by an enormous bed with an exquisite black fur thrown across it which made the bed look even larger against the thick white carpeting. In her beige coat, brown boots, and with her red lipsticked mouth, Ann saw her reflection in the mirror as a garish intrusion into this black and white composition.

'That has to be the biggest bed I've ever seen,' she said, for something to say. She did not wish to tell him she found the room oppressive, almost sinister.

'It was too big, very lonely it could be . . .' he laughed. 'But now. Now it will be the perfect size.' He kissed her gently. He drew away. 'Hungry?' She nodded. 'I'll show you the kitchen, we can find something to eat. Or maybe you'd prefer to go out? Pétin's maybe?'

'No. No. Let's stay here, even if it's just boiled eggs.'

The kitchen in its whiteness and gleaming stainless steel looked more like an operating theatre. 'You see what you can find in the fridge, I'll go and inspect the wine stock.'

Ann opened the door of a giant refrigerator and bent down to study its contents. The light from the interior shone on her as she tried to make up her mind which of the various foods to select. She jumped as she suddenly felt Alex's arms about her unbuttoning her coat, sweeping it on to the floor. She felt him fumbling with the fastening of her trousers; he unzipped them and slid them down her legs and kicked them to one side. Quickly he ripped at her tights, swearing softly at their resistance. His hands crept beneath her sweater, he released her breasts, fondling them, teasing her nipples. His mouth was at her ear, licking, nibbling, and as his hands relentlessly kneaded her breasts, she felt his knee prising her legs open. He pushed her forward so that her arms were supported by the shelf, her head inside the vast cavernous fridge. And he was entering her from behind, his body thrusting urgently.

Ann began to laugh, quietly at first and then her body rocked as much from laughter as from the rhythm of his love-making.

Abruptly he stopped. Ann felt his weight lift from her and she collapsed in a heap on the floor – in one hand a packet of smoked salmon, in the other a pot of caviar – still laughing helplessly. He stood above her, legs widely straddled, and frowned.

'Why, when we make love, do you so often laugh? Do I amuse you?' he asked without a glimmer of amusement in his voice.

Fighting for breath, Ann waved the packet of fish. 'It's just so funny,' she spluttered. 'I've never made love in a fridge before – don't you see how funny that is?' And she collapsed again with another fit of giggles, the pot of caviar rolling from her grasp across the white-tiled floor.

'It was the light shining on you, the bend of your body,' he explained seriously.

'Oh darling, you are divine. Is there nowhere you don't make love?'

'Only in cars, I gave that up years ago. It lacks dignity,' he said seriously.

'About as much as a refrigerator,' Ann shrieked again.

'Agreed.' He smiled and then at last he too was laughing. 'Yes, I see, it is funny. Now I'm really hungry,' he announced.

Ann stood up, conscious for the first time that her tights hung in shreds over the top of her boots and she had only her sweater on. 'Look at me!' she cried.

Gently he removed the shreds of her tights. 'Now you look really sexy – the boots, the jumper . . .' His eyes glinted dangerously.

'No you don't.' She twisted round, grabbing her trousers, and ran swiftly to the bathroom. With her clothes rearranged she returned to the kitchen. 'Food!' she announced eagerly.

They carried their brunch, with a bottle of champagne, back into the large, airy sitting room. Ann sat on the white leather sofa, which was so large that her feet stuck out straight in front. She stroked the soft leather, wondering what animal could produce a skin so silky. Looking up she found him watching her.

'You look very small sitting there,' he said as he handed her a glass of champagne.

'I feel I'm ruining a work of art. We make this room look untidy with our glasses and plates. I don't think it was meant for people and their clutter. It's a room to be photographed for a glossy magazine, not lived in.'

'We shall buy you something else,' he said quickly. 'You're right, this place is not for us. We need a real home to roost in, warm and comfortable and lived in. You must have a garden, and it must be old . . .'

'Alex, really, not for me. I'm sure we can make this more homely,' though as she said it, she knew that homely was the last word to apply to this modern palace in the sky.

'I insist. I want you happy. It must have a fireplace too, so that we can sit at night like we did in your house,' he continued, his face shining with enthusiasm as he described the home they were to find.

'You *are* your company, aren't you?' she asked suddenly.

'Yes,' he answered simply.

'And very rich?'

'Very.'

'Poor Peter. How embarrassed he will be.'

'Yes, poor Peter,' he said thoughtfully. 'Perhaps I should have been more open with you, but you never really asked. You just accepted me. Even when your son was trying to warn you.' He looked at her tenderly.

'Oh, I was very curious at first. I still am if I'm honest. But you obviously didn't want to explain and there were times I was afraid I might not like what I heard.'

He laughed. 'Oh, Anna, your imagination! What things? You know, I can't remember the last time I explained myself to anyone. See how important you are?'

'But if you're so rich how do you manage to stay anonymous? I thought the newspapers loved stories of people like you.'

'They do. But there are many rich, like me, who do not wish to court publicity. It can always be avoided, at a price.'

'Living discreetly, you mean. Going to places like Pétin's?'

'Yes, that. Not going to Annabel's. Keeping a "low profile" publicly. Hiding companies within companies. I prefer it this way.'

'That's very English of you, Alex.'

'English! Me? Never.' He looked horrified. 'No, perhaps circumspect is a better word. It stops begging letters, sycophants. I can move freely without bodyguards, unlike some of my friends. I escape the world's jealousy. I seem to have got the habit of saying that everything is the company's without explaining that I am the company. It makes life easier. Mind you, I can't hide from everyone – your friend is not as naïve as he pretends to be. He knew who I was.'

'I'm glad I didn't know, now. We both know I fell in love with you totally ignorant of your wealth,' Ann said emphatically.

'Maybe I should have been more patient and forgiving with your son though. I was very heavy-handed with him, and look what pain I have brought you.'

'What difference would it have made? If he had approved just because you were rich that would hardly show concern for me. And if he had known and still disapproved we would only be where we are now. I couldn't win either way with Peter.

They both sat in silence for a while.

'You don't want to go back to the village at all, do you?'

'No, but I shall have to. Only I can decide what to sell and what to keep. Perhaps I should get rid of everything, bury the past?'

'Only you can decide that, my love. But you mustn't be alone there, you must have Meg and Fay to help you. I'll arrange the removal and the sale for you, if you wish. Where shall we marry then? In London, Midfield, where?'

'Darling, I just don't know, everything's happened too fast.'

'Then you must not worry about that either. I'll decide for you and make the arrangements.'

'You like arranging things and people, don't you?'

'Yes, then it's done the way I want, when I want.' He turned to pour more champagne.

A small frown crossed Ann's face. In one way it seemed delightful to have her life organized this way, in another she was not sure if she wanted it. She felt a momentary fear that she was being taken over again. She knew she wanted more from life now than just to be an adjunct to someone else.

'Why were you in the Tate that day?' she asked abruptly, wanting to change the subject, not liking the direction of her thoughts.

He looked surprised at the turn in the conversation. He handed her the glass of champagne. 'I had been in a meeting, here actually. It was very boring.' He pulled a face. 'I insisted on a break and I strolled along the Embankment and went into the gallery on a whim.'

'Just like me. I'd had no intention of going there at the start of the day, she said thoughtfully. 'And when did you decide that you loved me?'

'At Pétin's, halfway through dinner, when I was flirting with you, playing the usual game, debating with myself how long it was going to take me to get you into bed. Then suddenly it wasn't a game. And although I desired you, I suddenly realized that I wanted you, longed to possess you in a different way. Not as a conquest. I realized I wanted to protect you, keep you safe.'

He looked at her with such tenderness that Ann felt a sliver of guilt that she could have misinterpreted his desire to organize her life. 'Back at the hotel, that's when I decided something big was afoot.' She grinned at him. 'But where did you go to that night, so late?'

'I went to my mistress.'

Ann felt her skin stiffen with shock and wished she hadn't asked him. The smile slid from her face. He took her hand.

'Don't look afraid, Anna. I went, my darling, to tell her that I was finished with her. You see how convinced I was, how sure I was that we would be right for each other.'

'Poor woman. Was she sad to lose you?'

'Sadder to lose her handsome allowance more likely,' he replied with a cynical laugh.

'Did she live here?'

'No.' He nuzzled her neck. 'I never mix business with pleasure. She had an apartment of her own. And before you pluck up the courage to ask, I haven't slept with another woman since I met you.'

'I wasn't going to ask you,' Ann said with false spirit, knowing she had not asked for fear of his reply.

'You've been thinking it though,' he teased.

181

'I have not. I've had far too many other things to think about.'

'Tut, tut, Mrs Grange, lying to your lover already?'

Ann aimed a cushion at him. 'So what do you do? I really want to know.'

'So, my sex life is of such little interest to you. I shall remember that.' He threw the cushion back. 'What do I do? It really is "this and that". I didn't lie to your family and friends. I started, as I told you, as an engineer in the navy, and then I opened my contraband perfume shop. It was a success so I opened another and so on, but no longer with smuggled goods – I was beginning to have too much to lose. That was a great success. So I bought a small boat, for tourist charter – around the Aegean with a Cordon Bleu cook, that sort of thing. Soon I had a fleet of such boats. Then I bought a hotel and then several of them . . . you know how it goes.' He shrugged.

'No, I don't. I don't know at all,' she laughed, shaking her head, nonplussed.

'I missed engineering. So I started a small factory making replacement parts for cars. All the cars were imported and getting spare parts was often difficult. The engineering side developed so that I was soon making fridges, deep freezers, air-conditioning equipment, boilers. My real-estate interests spread from Greece into the West Indies, the Virgin Islands, places like that. Am I boring you?'

'No. No. It's fascinating.'

'I look at my operation. Each year I spend so much on steel, so I look for a steel plant and manufacture my own. I moved into banking, real estate, I dabble in art. I'm very diversified, you see.'

Ann clapped her hands with glee. 'You make it all sound so simple, but you must have worked incredibly hard.'

'It's been my life until now.' He stroked her leg. 'I have a large staff, I don't do it all myself. You met Nigel, and I have another aide called Yianni, and an army of accountants, lawyers and secretaries.'

'I bet I know one thing,' she said.

'What?'

'I bet you still own the little perfume shop?'

He looked sheepish. 'As a matter of fact I do. You see how well you know me? I always thought that if everything in this mountainous empire I had created collapsed then I could return to it. You know, Anna, when I first started I wanted to be rich, as rich as Niarchos. But that need goes after the first couple of million. Now, making money isn't important any more. No, it's getting a business, making it work, creating jobs, and watching the curve on the graph, that's where the excitement lies. Now, with you . . . maybe I shall retire.' He looked at her, but Ann saw a definite twinkle in his eye.

'I shan't rely on that,' she said indulgently.

He glanced out of the window. 'Look. It's darker already. What a strange Christmas I'm giving you. We haven't even opened our presents. Are you sure you don't want to go out?'

'No, let's stay here, just you and me. Just as it was at Courtneys.'

'I'll fetch the presents from the car.'

Alone she looked about the huge impersonal room, and was glad that he had suggested they move. She thought about what he had told her and she sighed. Ann had never wanted for anything in her life, it had been a comfortable existence. Now she was about to find out what being rich would mean and she was strangely daunted by the prospect.

He returned and presented her with the large parcel that had so intrigued her last night. Beside it, her small parcel to him looked ridiculous. She watched nervously as he opened it. Only as he held the key to the light did she realize that already it was redundant, and seeing it again she began to think it an absurd present to give such a sophisticated man.

'Oh, how stupid, it doesn't mean anything now that I'm going to move.'

'This is the most thoughtful present I have ever received. We shall sell the house but not the door.'

'Perhaps the lock would do,' she said, laughing, as she in turn tore open her parcel revealing a heavily embroidered silk brocade evening coat. She lifted the brightly coloured garment from its rustling nest of tissue paper. The coat glowed not only because of the gold thread used in the stitching but from the red, blues and greens of the brocade. It was as brightly coloured as a stained-glass window and it felt heavy in her hands.

'Alex,' she sighed. 'Alex, it's wonderful.'

'I wanted to buy you a mink coat, but I remembered you said you hated furs. You're so different – the only woman I've met who would refuse a mink,' he said, smiling with disbelief.

'Do you remember everything I say?'

'Everything. That's what being in love is about.'

'I'd love a fur coat, it's my conscience won't let me. The thought of animals being killed just to keep me warm.' she shuddered. She slipped the jewel-coloured coat on. 'How do I look?'

'OK.'

'Only OK.'

'You know how I like to see you.'

'Alex, you always make me blush.'

'Look in the pocket,' he ordered.

From inside the coat's pocket she removed a flat jeweller's box. Inside was a finely worked bracelet and earrings, the emeralds matching her engagement ring.

'Alex, they're wonderful.' Her eyes sparkled with excitement. 'Help me put them on. You're spoiling me, you know,' she added, sitting at his feet, still wrapped in the ornate coat.

'That's what I'm here for. To give you everything you've ever desired. Now, take your clothes off.'

'My clothes?'

'I want to see you sitting here in my coat and I'll know that beneath it you're naked and ready for me,' he said in that soft voice with the husky catch in it that always sent shivers of sexual excitement through her.

It was easier now for her to remove her clothes in front of him. She slipped the new coat about her.

'There's something else you can do for me.'

She looked at him expectantly.

'Don't wear those ugly tights. They make your wonderful pussy look like a burglar with a stocking mask on.'

The image made Ann burst out laughing. 'Darling, you are the sexiest man I've ever known. What a thing to say. Tights are so comfortable. But OK, I promise, suspender belts and stockings from now on – well, perhaps on high days and holidays,' she teased.

Much later, as they lay in the large bed, Ann turned to him. 'Alex,' she whispered.

'Yes?'

'I'm very glad you're rich.'

'So am I,' he said and held her tightly to him.

7

For the few remaining days of their holiday they enjoyed their isolation. Although he frequently suggested that they eat out, Ann resisted. She wanted this time alone with him, she felt instinctively that once this holiday period was over hours alone would become a precious commodity. So they took their meals at the flat, sharing the cooking, the washing-up. It amused Ann to see her virile millionaire, an apron on, a teatowel in his hand, working beside her in a way he had obviously not done for years, and appearing to enjoy every minute of it.

They walked for miles through the snow-packed streets of an unusually deserted London, feeling sometimes that even the city was respecting their need to be alone. They explored parts of London that neither of them knew existed.

Whenever they came across a 'For Sale' sign on a suitable property, Alex was beside himself with excitement, wanting to knock on the door immediately.

'But we can't, darling. We have to wait until after the holidays when the agents are open. You see they all say "strictly by appointment",' she explained patiently, amused by his impatience.

'They either want to sell or they don't. What difference does an appointment make?'

'It's the way we do things.'

'Ridiculous country,' he muttered.

Finally, she could contain him no longer and at a particularly beautiful house in Belgravia, he bounded up the steps, knocked on the door and was confronted by a granite-faced butler, who had no interest in who he was or that he wanted to buy this house. Not even the information that he had the money in cash would move the butler's stony heart. The door was slammed in his face.

'Extraordinary race of people,' he blustered, red-faced with anger as he rejoined Ann on the pavement.

'I thought you liked our quaint ways,' she said, linking her arm through his.

'Not when these quaint ways interfere with what I want to do. I shall write to the owner and tell him just how much his stupid servant has cost him.'

'I doubt if he'll be bothered.'

'Oh yes he will, when he learns just how much I was willing to pay. The man should have gone to ask his boss, not just turned me away like a tramp.'

'Poor Alex, your feathers are all ruffled.' Her gentle teasing finally made him forget his anger.

They window-shopped. They dreamed. They planned. They made love – and they were happy.

On the fourth morning their isolation came to an end. Ann could hear the distant ringing of telephone bells and voices where before there had been silence. With a mounting feeling of unease she realized that life here was returning to normal and that she was going to have to become part of it.

As the bells intruded into this dream world so suddenly she thought of her son. For the first time since Christmas the memory of Peter's bitter face flashed across her mind. She rubbed her eyes with her hands as if to rid herself of the image.

With Alex she had felt like a young girl again, not just mentally, but physically. They had romped on this bed, they had chased each other around the flat like excited children, they had exchanged endearments like love-sick teenagers. Now, with the memory of her son, Ann was helter-skeltered into the present. Her shoulders slumped – she felt her true age again!

She shook herself. No. She would not let him impinge on her happiness. If merely thinking about him made her feel defeated, there was only one solution – she would have to stop thinking of Peter at all.

From the meagre wardrobe she had brought from Midfield she chose a softly pleated grey suit with matching cashmere sweater and tied a red silk scarf around her neck. She looked smart enough, but wished she could look smarter to meet Alex's staff. She felt nervous. She felt sure that they would be expecting a glamorous young woman to appear, not someone like herself.

'Come,' she heard his voice, in brusque response to her knock. She peered around the edge of the study door.

'Sorry to bother you,' she said apologetically.

'My darling, come in.' He leapt from behind the desk, grabbed Ann by the hand and pulled her into the room. 'Fiona, meet my future wife.'

Ann shook hands with an impeccably groomed young woman who looked as if she had stepped out of the pages of *Harpers*.

'Mrs Grange. May I say how happy we all are for you and Mr Georgeopoulos?'

'Fiona hopes you will make me a nicer man to work for, Anna. Isn't that so, Fiona?'

'Well, sir, shall we just say that there has been a marked improvement in the past weeks,' the girl replied, smiling archly at him.

'Fiona does all my social work for me, darling. You must ask her to help you whenever you want,' Alex explained to Ann, who nodded assent, unsure if there would ever be a time that she would require a social secretary. 'Have you seen Salisbury?'

'No.'

'We must join them then. The men are here, you see.'

'What men?'

'The estate agents, of course. They've got details of houses. They're waiting for you.' He turned to leave the room.

'Would it be possible for me to have some coffee, Alex, before I embark on house-hunting?' Ann asked with a grin.

'My darling, I'm sorry. I've been up hours. I quite forgot, you've had no breakfast. Fiona, get Roberts to organize some breakfast for Mrs Grange.'

'Just orange juice and coffee would be perfect,' Ann said quickly to the girl as she left the room.

'You don't eat enough. You should have a big breakfast – I always do,' Alex said bossily; it was an argument they seemed doomed to have every morning. He stretched his hands out to her, and she perched on his desk, her hands in his. 'I can't believe you're here, part of my life. I'm so happy.' He smiled expansively at her. 'Sometimes I think you might just disappear.'

Ann was surprised by the edge of anxiety in his voice. She might spend hours wondering and worrying, but it had never crossed her mind that someone like Alex could be beset by insecurities too. 'No, darling, you're stuck with me now,' she replied lightly. The door opened and a butler appeared with a tray of coffee and juice. Ann was introduced.

'Roberts – the party.'

'Yes, sir?'

'Mrs Grange will want to discuss that with you and Cook as soon as we've finished with the estate agents. We're moving, you see, Roberts.'

There was no reaction from the butler, he merely inclined his head and said, 'Yes, sir,' as if being informed that he was about to be uprooted was the normal thing.

'Another thing, Roberts, Mrs Grange needs a personal maid. Would you set up some interviews for her?'

'With pleasure, sir. Will that be all, sir?' And with his grave little bow he reversed out of the room. The phone rang. As Alex answered it, Ann sat sipping her coffee, stunned by the news that she was apparently in need of a maid. She had no idea what a personal maid would do all day but if it meant no more ironing, no more battles to keep her drawers tidy, no more packing, she might easily get used to the idea. Like many women of a grown-up family, Ann had long ago lost her youthful enthusiasm for housecraft. The image of a comfortable and elegant life was opening up for her; some puritan streak in her rebelled at the thought but she had recently begun to suspect that her puritanism was only skin deep. Alex finished his call.

'Why are you smiling like a well-fed cat?' he asked, stroking her hair as he did so.

'I was just surprised to find that I might enjoy the laziness of being your wife.'

'It's my duty to look after you well when I make you work so hard in bed,' he joked. 'Anyway, there will be little time for laziness – you've a house to find and furnish. I entertain frequently. We shall travel a lot. But have you finished your coffee?' Taking her by the hand he swept her from the room to join the young men. 'It has to be old, large, with a garden and fireplaces . . .' He spoke without preamble as they entered the room. With papers tumbling to the floor, the young men scrambled to their feet. For the first time Ann witnessed the awe and respect, tinged with fear, that Alex engendered. But she was also entranced at how quickly he made things happen.

'Mr Salisbury, how nice to see you again,' she said to the young man who had helped her with her passport and who seemed unaccountably pleased that she had remembered his name. Momentarily the worried look which marred his handsome face disappeard as he smiled at her.

She shook hands with the two negotiators from the estate agents and helped them pick up the brochures.

'Leave those,' Alex ordered. 'Yianni.'

A young man who had been silently standing to one side stepped forward. A slight, almost sardonic smile played about his full mouth, as if he were amused by the estate agents, scrabbling about the floor picking up their papers.

'Anna, meet Yianni. He's my alter-ego. If I'm away and you need anything, ask Yianni.'

'Hello, Yianni.' Ann held out her hand to him.

'Mrs Grange.' He bowed low over her hand, his lips not quite touching the surface of her skin. Ann found herself looking at a luxuriant head of black hair, cut not too short nor allowed to grow too long. 'If I can be of any assistance to you . . .' He smiled at her.

Ann thought he was one of the most beautiful men she had ever seen, tall and slim, dressed in an expensive suit that he wore with effortless grace. From his fine-boned, tanned face, dark brown eyes looked searchingly at her.

'Thank you,' Ann said, feeling slightly flusterd by the attention. Across the room she noticed Nigel Salisbury watching them keenly. Sensing what she presumed was jealousy she smiled at him too, endeavouring to bring him into the circle. 'Two such handsome young men to look after me. How lucky I am,' she said with a laugh.

Alex looked up sharply from the brochure he had been studying. Nigel looked embarrassed and gazed down at his shoes. Yianni bowed graciously.

The brochures having been restored to order, Alex thrust them into Ann's hands. 'You sort through these, Anna. Choose those you wish to see.'

'But Alex . . . Don't you want to choose?'

'No, I've too much to do. It's to be your home too: you search for it,' he said briskly, and swept from the room.

Ann sat on the large leather sofa and quickly sifted through the brochures. She would like a Regency house, she decided, and so rejected anything of a later period. Working on the number of bedrooms, the size of the gardens, Ann had soon sorted them into three piles – those houses she rejected totally, those she might consider, and lastly those she would like to see. The negotiators were quickly on the phone making appointments over the next few days. Alex reappeared after a few minutes and nodded with approval at the speed with which Ann had made her decisions.

'Ann, I must go. I have an appointment in the City, I'll leave you to work.' He planted a kiss on her forehead.

'Aren't you coming to view the houses?'

'No, that's your department now, as are the staff. I should be back soon after lunch.' With Yianni he quickly left the room.

Ann summoned the staff who shuffled into the room, each introduced in turn by Roberts. For a flat, even a large one like this, there seemed an amazing number of people. Apart from the butler, and the chauffeur who had left with Alex, there were two maids, a Greek valet, Demetri, a kitchen assistant and, bringing up the rear, the imposing bulk and tight-lipped face of Mrs Dick, the cook.

'I thought we should discuss the party,' Ann began. 'It's in two days' time, isn't it?'

'These are the menus, Madame,' Mrs Dick handed her a page of neatly written lists. Ann scanned it – smoked salmon, cold beef, cold turkey, salads.

'I had hoped for something a bit different,' Ann smiled but the lips of Mrs Dick compressed even more tightly.

'That's what we normally have for the large buffets,' Mrs Dick said in the voice of one who does not expect to be contradicted.

'Wouldn't it be nice to have a change?' Ann tried a sweeter smile.

'Like what?' the woman snapped suspiciously.

'Oh, I don't know, but cold salad is so dreary.' Ann thought for a moment. Mrs Dick studied the view of London with intense interest. The maids shuffled nervously, the kitchenmaid blew her nose, the Greek watched bright-eyed; only Roberts stood impassive. 'How about a Greek evening in honour of Mr Georgeopoulos?'

'A what evening?' The cook added 'Madame?' almost as an afterthought.

'Well, I've never been to Greece but I've eaten in Greek restaurants delicious things. The Greeks have such lovely hors-d'oeuvres – dolmádes and those lovely little pastry cases filled with cheese and spinach. What are they called?' She looked questioningly at Demetri.

'Bourekia, Madame.'

'And then we could have shish-kebabs, taramasalata and what else, Demetri?'

'Olives of course, Madame, no mézédakia is complete without olives. We could have kokkorétsi, lakerda – there are so many wonderful dishes. And we could finish with baklava.' Demetri's eyes shone with enthusiasm.

'Are those the honey pastries? Yes? I like them. Well, anything you recommend, Demetri. A bouzouki band, that would be fun – on the balcony perhaps. And flowers, all blue and white – those are your national colours, aren't they, Demetri?'

'I don't cook Greek food. French or English only.'

'Oh, Mrs Dick, just this once, won't you, please? I'm sure Demetri will help and advise.' Ann smiled winningly at the woman.

'No, Madame, I won't.'

'Then I shall have to get someone in who will,' Ann replied, still smiling. 'Perhaps you know of someone?' She looked enquiringly at the valet.

'Yes, Madame, I've a friend . . .'

'Not in my kitchen you don't,' the cook boomed at Demetri. A heavy silence filled the room, the others looked from Ann to the cook, all with keen interest.

'Thank you, Demetri, if you would kindly arrange that with your friend for me, then I'll talk to you later. That will be all, thank you. Perhaps you would stay behind a moment, Mrs Dick?'

The others left. The cook stood there, arms kimbo.

'I'm sorry, Mrs Dick, I don't want to upset you. Perhaps if you have your day off that day, then it won't inconvenience you.'

'I said, Madame, I won't have no one else in my kitchen, and I meant it.'

'Oh dear, we seem to be at an impasse, don't we, Mrs Dick? You see I very much want to do this Greek evening.'

'If you do, Madame, then I go.'

'I see.' Ann looked at the large woman standing smugly before her. 'Well then, I'm sorry but you'll have to go, won't you?'

'Mr Georgeopoulos isn't going to like this.'

Ann said nothing.

'I shall speak to Mr Georgeopoulos as soon as he returns, Madame,' the woman said, almost sarcastically, and swept from the room.

Oh dear, thought Ann, she was not doing very well: her first morning and she'd lost Alex his cook. Still, there was nothing else she could have done if she were to be mistress of the house.

Nigel Salisbury knocked on the door. 'Are you ready, Mrs Grange? The car is back. Our first appointment is in half an hour,' he said diffidently.

'I've just sacked the cook, Nigel.'

The worried frown on Nigel's face deepened. 'Oh dear.'

'Yes, "oh dear", she seems to think that Mr George-opoulos is likely to be angry.'

'He does like her cooking, and she has been with him for years.'

'Looks as if he's going to have to choose between me and the cook then.' She tried to laugh gaily, but the laugh had a hollow ring.

Ann set out with Nigel and the two attentive estate agents in the Rolls-Royce. She would much have preferred to be alone to house-hunt, to have done it at her own pace. The first house they were shown was a complete waste of time. The garden was minute; the elegant proportions had been ruined by having walls knocked down to make reception rooms of enormous size. And she felt deeply suspicious of the mouldings which looked too sharp and crisp: she was convinced they were plastic.

Back in the car Ann gave her verdict.

'But the walls could be rebuilt. The mouldings replaced.'

'At what price?' Ann said sharply.

The second house did not meet with her approval either. It was too noisy, though the garden was a good size. But it was so dark that Ann felt no amount of clever decoration would ever relieve it. And there was an atmosphere to the place that quite unnerved her.

But, at the third, Ann fell instantly in love. It had everything that she and Alex had wanted – old, large, with fireplaces and a garden. The mouldings had the worn, slightly rounded shape of originals. It was light and airy, and overlooked Regent's Park, but most important, despite its grandeur, it had a warm welcoming atmosphere.

'This one is perfect,' Ann announced, rather grandly, she thought. The owner looked stunned, Nigel looked more worried and the agents tried to persuade her, unsuccessfully, to look at the remaining house. But Ann was adamant.

'Darling, I've found the perfect house.' She rushed breathless with excitement into his study. 'The mouldings are beautiful. Lovely mahogany doors. A wonderful library. The drawing room is vast and still has its original Regency balcony overlooking the most enormous garden for London. And our bedroom is a dream . . . I nearly forgot, it's still got its original mews house. Not many have them left, you know.' She twirled around in excitement.

'I still think we should look at the others, sir, we might do better,' Nigel said anxiously. 'Unfortunately the owner was present and heard Mrs Grange's enthusiasm. I doubt he will come down in price, sir.'

'Remind me to play poker with you, darling.' Alex smiled at her indulgently. 'In the face of such enthusiasm, Nigel, I doubt if we could do better,' he replied amusedly to the young man. 'Don't worry, Nigel, you must realize that Mrs Grange and I are experts on the subject of "love at first sight".' Nigel looked sheepishly at his feet and then, becoming aware that his boss was teasing him, smiled and the anxious look disappeared again for a second. 'Negotiate, Nigel. Try to get some off the asking price, but don't lose it, we don't want Mrs Grange disappointed, do we?'

'No, sir.' Nigel's habitual expression had become even gloomier with the task alloted him.

'That poor boy is going to end up with an ulcer, he worries so,' Ann said.

'He's good too, he's shaping up excellently. There's no need for his anxiety. So who sacked my cook?' he asked, leaning back in the large, black swivel chair.

Ann looked up sharply and saw a stern-faced Alex looking at her. 'I'm sorry, darling, I had no choice, she refused to do something I wanted done.'

'I know.'

'Did she tell you what?' Ann asked, disappointed that her surprise was now ruined.

'Some garble about not allowing another cook in her kitchen. Why do we need another cook?'

'It's a surprise. Anyhow, I'll cook dinner, it's no problem really.'

'No need, Roberts has arranged a replacement. She's waiting to meet you. I had no idea I had married someone so tough,' he said with a smile.

'You're not cross then?'

'Why should I be cross? The woman was paid to cook: she shouldn't have argued with you. The domestic arrangements are your sphere, not mine – employ who you wish.'

The telephone rang. She waited patiently while he answered it. As soon as he had finished, it rang again. Alex shrugged his shoulders apologetically at her and Ann went to find the new cook.

Charlotte was straight out of cookery school – tiny, pretty and pert with the confidence of a well-connected young lady. She told Ann that she had done a secretarial course and an interior design course but felt cooking might be 'more fun'. Ann had serious doubts that she would last more than a few days and wished she were not quite so attractive. But she was stuck with the problem: she could hardly get rid of two cooks in twenty-four hours.

She wandered to their room, unsure what to do next. She reread the details of their new house several times and wished she had pen and paper so that she could start planning. She did not like to interrupt Alex again and everyone else seemed so busy. Everyone but her.

She removed her make-up, had a long bath and then made up her face again. She looked at her watch. There was not a book or magazine in the room. Come to think of it, she had not noticed any in the flat – would ruin the décor, she laughed to herself. Courtneys had been full of books, like her own house. She went to the window, but it was dark and she soon tired of watching the lights. She looked at her watch, still an hour before she should change for dinner.

Tentatively she picked up the phone, looking puzzled at the large console with its arrays of buttons. She pushed one, got the dialling tone and called Lydia. Lydia was agog to hear her news. She had much to tell her, about Peter, about leaving, about the party. For a good half-hour the friends chatted.

Next she called Fay who was bubbling over with the news that her company had landed a contract to refurbish a large nightclub. Fay had not tackled a nightclub before and was full of outrageous ideas for it. Ann was pleased: the news meant that Fay would be in London for several months. She wanted to see more of her daughter now that she felt she was losing touch with her son.

'Any news of Peter?' she asked, feigning a disinterested voice.

'He's still in a towering rage, Mummy,' Fay said seriously.

'I can't help that.'

'He says he's got an old college friend who works at the Home Office. He's going to get in touch with him to see if he can't get Alex deported as an undesirable alien. He can't, can he?'

'Of course not. What a stupid idea. An alien he might be but undesirable – never!' Ann laughed.

'What did you say? This line's dreadful.'

'I said it was a stupid idea. You sound as if you're at the bottom of the sea too.'

'Shall I call you back, see if it makes it any better?'

'No, don't bother. I was just calling to arrange about the party. Are you bringing a partner?'

'Don't know yet.'

They chatted for another minute, when Ann saw with relief that it was time to change for dinner.

Even then she had a long wait. The telephones never seemed to stop and it was long past nine before Fiona and Nigel finally left. Ann and Alex at last relaxed with a drink before dinner.

'Is it always like this?' Ann asked.

'Usually. It's the time differences, you see. New York is still working and we need to get the telexes to Tokyo where it's almost tomorrow morning. Perhaps today was a little worse, I have been very neglectful of my business lately.' He stroked her face. 'Poor darling, were you dreadfully bored?'

'No, no,' she said quickly. 'We couldn't go on as we were, could we? And once the house is ours, I'll be as busy as you getting it ready. When are you coming to see it?'

'When it's finished,' he answered. Ignoring her protest he went on, 'No, my darling. I want you to surprise me with it, finished, perfect, created by you, for us.'

'But what if I choose things you don't like?'

'You won't, I know.'

'How was your meeting?'

'What meeting?'

'Your lunchtime in the City. I presumed it was business,' she said, feeling slightly flustered, unable to help wondering what it could have been, if not business, which had needed his presence.

'Oh that.' He smiled as if reading her thoughts. 'It's too early to say.'

'What was it about?'

'Oh, my darling, far too boring to bother you with. Ah, Roberts, dinner?'

They had been lucky with Charlotte: the meal was superb. 'We seem to have found a good cook,' Alex said.

'That's what I thought she was supposed to be. Why on earth it was necessary for her to help Roberts serve is beyond me.'

'Probably wanted to see if I was as fascinating as she had been told,' Alex said with a roar of laughter.

'She was ogling you. Don't you dare touch the cook,' Ann lectured Alex half-teasingly.

'I can't help it. Lots of women find me irresistible.' He grinned. 'But you shouldn't worry, am I likely to seduce a servant?'

'Quite honestly I think you're capable of seducing anyone.'

'Then you'll have to keep me amused, won't you? I shall enjoy having this nubile young woman in the house – it will keep you on your toes,' he teased.

'Alex! You are the most appalling chauvinist I have ever met.'

'Complaining?' He turned to her with the dark, piercing look which made her feel he had caressed her.

'No. I'll just get a dishy male one if she dares put a foot wrong.'

'No you won't,' he said in an emphatic voice which Ann knew was in earnest.

'Why can you tease me about other women and I can't joke about me and men?'

'Because women never joke about sex.'

'Of course they do.'

'No. It's too important to them. They use it as a weapon, always.'

'Well, I was joking.'

'Were you joking earlier today when you were at pains to compliment my assistants on their youth and charm?' he asked, glancing sideways at her.

'Alex, don't be silly. I just wanted to make them feel at ease.'

'I didn't like it. Please don't do it again.'

'Alex, really. You are making something out of nothing.'

'It's the "undesirable alien" in me,' he said without smiling.

'Gracious, I meant to tell you. You'll never guess what Fay told me . . .' Ann was laughing as she began to tell him about Peter. But her laughter and her words stopped abruptly. 'You knew?' He nodded. 'You listened?' He nodded, again. 'How dare you!'

'I didn't intend to. You hadn't switched the phones through correctly. My line crossed with yours.'

'That's no excuse. You should have put the phone down at once.'

'Why? What could you possibly be saying that I shouldn't listen to?'

'Nothing. Of course I'd be saying nothing. That's not the point. People just don't listen to other people's phone calls.'

'I do.'

'Then you've no right to. And certainly not to mine.' She threw her napkin on the table and stalked from the room past a startled Roberts.

'Coffee in the drawing room, Madame?' the butler said to her retreating back. Ann did not reply; she marched across the drawing room, along the corridor and slammed the bedroom door with all her strength.

She kicked off her shoes and curled up on the bed, fumbling on the bedside table for a cigarette which she lit with shaking fingers and puffed at angrily. Who the hell did he think he was? How dare he intrude on her private conversations? And then to have the audacity, when found out, not to apologize. She stubbed the half-smoked cigarette out as Alex entered the room carrying a bottle of champagne on a silver tray.

'You angry?' he asked unnecessarily as she glared at him across the fur bedcover. 'I'm sorry, Anna, if I made you angry.'

'It might help if you said you were sorry for listening to my private call.'

'Nothing is or should be private between us.'

'It's an invasion of my privacy, don't you understand? How would you like it if I did it to you? It shows a lack of trust on your part that shocks me.'

He stood at the bottom of the bed looking at her. 'I warned you. I told you I was impossibly possessive and demanding.'

'You didn't tell me you were a snoop.'

'Anna, tell me, do you know what it's like to be jealous? To fear every moment of the day that the object of your love might be unfaithful to you? Do you understand what that does to the spirit? Or are you too English to feel these things?'

'Of course I can be jealous, if there's cause. But I haven't given you any cause. Being English has nothing to do with it. Greeks don't have a monopoly on feelings.'

'Then you don't love as I do.' His shoulders sagged.

'Alex, you do talk such rubbish. Of course I love you.'

'No you don't. To love totally you have also to suffer this intolerable pain of jealousy. It can't be otherwise. And I see you do not feel like this.' He slumped on to the bed.

He looked so dejected, almost beaten, that Ann, her anger fading to be replaced by concern, crawled across the bed to him. 'Alex, what has happened to you in the past to be like this? Please, Alex, don't be upset, don't look so sad. I love you more than life itself. Truly I do. I don't want to see you hurt like this, darling.' She kissed his cheek, his brow.

'Truly?' He looked at her, his grey eyes wide and anxiety.

'I couldn't live without you, Alex.'

'Anna, I love you,' he signed as he engulfed her in his arms and with a desperate urgency began to make love to her.

It was not until later, as she lay in the dark, listening to his regular breathing, that Ann realized he had not apologized.

8

The next morning, New Year's Eve, on Ann's breakfast tray was a small posy of yellow roses, and nestling among them a squat jeweller's box, with a card. 'To commemorate our first real battle,' she read. Inside the box was a large solitaire diamond. She slipped the ring on her finger. The stone sparkled and gleamed in the light. How on earth did anyone acquire a ring like this, so early in the morning, she wondered prosaically. She presumed it was Alex's way of apologizing. How much cheaper just to say 'sorry' – not as dramatic though, she thought. She was still puzzled as to why he should be so insecure, especially with her. She should not have flown off the handle the way she had done. It was the hardest thing of all not to listen to another telephone conversation: she had done it herself often enough when getting a crossed line. How much harder to put the receiver down if one were being talked about. In the light of day, she could understand his curiosity.

In her silk dressing gown she went to find Alex, to thank him for his gift. Searching the flat for him she thought of a problem – if she were to keep the Greek element of the party a secret from Alex she had to persuade him to stay in his study. The trouble was that Alex could not be guaranteed to stay in one place. He tended to work wherever he was. He wandered about the flat, from his study to the drawing room, their bedroom, followed by a coterie of aides and secretaries, notepads in hand, looking like presidential bodyguards with portable phones sticking out of their pockets.

Having tracked him down, she thanked him; then she cajoled, wheedled and bullied him into staying in one place for the day.

Entering the main part of the flat, she heard as much noise issuing from the kitchen as if the party had already begun. There she found Demetri, bossily supervising two large Greeks, Costas and Panos, borrowed from a friend's restaurant, who were noisily and enthusiastically preparing food. Chaos reigned. A somewhat over-excited Charlotte assured Ann it would all be ready in time. Alarmed by the piles of unprepared food stacked on the work surfaces, Ann had serious doubts.

She was distracted from this worry by the arrival of the florists who had to make several trips in the lift with their baskets and boxes of blue and white flowers. When she saw the number of blooms Ann had another worry to fill her mind. Flowers like this, at this time of year, were going to cost a small fortune. Had she gone too far, would Alex be angry at the cost? Perhaps she should have stuck to evergreens, but the blue and white flowers, Alex's national colours, had seemed such a good idea at the time.

With amazing speed, the florists began to transform the stark room. Great vases of flowers billowed, the terrace was turned into a blue and white bower, the banisters were garlanded, and long, twisted fronds hung from the balcony.

In the midst of the scurrying florists, the ebullient Greek cooks, the musicians setting up their stands, Ann had to interview the applicants for the job as her maid. She had quite forgotten that Roberts had arranged the appointment for today. Without difficulty, she chose Elene. At thirty-six she was the oldest, she had the most experience but, more importantly, she was half Greek and spoke the language Ann had resolved to learn. And Ann liked the woman's quiet, gentle expression.

As the apartment was transformed, as plate after plate of delicious food materialized from the noisy kitchen, as the bar was set up, as the band discussed the music with her, Ann's excitement increased – until Fiona handed her a copy of the guest list.

Ann scanned the neatly typed rows of names and her heart sank. 'Oh, Fiona, what have I done?' She looked anxiously at the secretary. 'These people will be appalled. They'll be expecting champagne and caviar, not kebabs and retsina.'

'Mrs Grange, I'm sure they'll be delighted,' Fiona said, sounding doubtful.

Ann looked unreassured as she reread the list of household names. From the worlds of politics, finance, stage, film and TV there was not one name that was not rich or famous, or both.

'But what will Mr Georgeopoulos say?'

'He'll be delighted too. Really, Mrs Grange, I'm sure all these guests are sick to death of champagne and caviar – your party will be a delightful surprise to them.' Ann was sure from the tone of Fiona's voice that the girl was trying to persuade herself that all would be well.

Finally, after an exhausting day, Ann made for her room to have a long relaxing bath and a sleep. She found Alex, lying on the bed, looking at the ceiling with a thoroughly bored and disgruntled expression. 'Can I come out of prison now?' he sulked. 'I want to know what's going on.'

'No. When the party starts. I told you it's a surprise.'

'I hate surprises.'

'You sound like a spoilt little boy.'

'And you sound like a bossy general.'

She laughed at him. 'I feel like one too.'

'Come here,' he ordered.

'No. I haven't time. Neither have you.'

'You can play the general out there, but not in our bedroom. Here I'm in command. Now, come here . . .' he ordered playfully.

She sank on to the bed beside him. There was no point really in even pretending she had other things to do. She always wanted him, always longed for him in her. It never failed to surprise her how constantly ready for him she was sexually.

Eventually, too late for a sleep, she bathed and dressed in the red dress he had given her. Hand in hand they entered the large room and as they appeared the bouzouki band struck up with the tinkling music of the Greek islands.

His glance swept the room, taking in the flowers, the band, the waiters, dressed as evzones. He said nothing. They walked into the dining room and he inspected the large tables of food. His nose twitched as the smells of charcoal-grilled meat coming from the kitchen. Ann waited anxiously for his reaction.

204

With sparkling eyes he turned to her and engulfed her in a hug.

Fay arrived alone. She was dressed in a long, figure-hugging sheath of dark blue crepe. A short, heavily sequinned jacket sparkled in the light as she turned from side to side with excitement at the scene before her. Ann looked at her daughter with pride and with the slight, familiar envy that her daughter's effortless chic always gave her.

'You look marvellous, Fay. So elegant. But you look tired, you know.'

'Oh, Mummy, stop fretting over me. I've been packing for my move. A truly boring way to spend the holiday.'

'You decided not to bring a friend?' Ann asked unnecessarily. Although Fay occasionally talked of the men in her life, it suddenly struck Ann that she had never met any of them. She had looked forward to that possibility tonight.

'He fizzled out, like they all do,' Fay said with a shrug of her shoulders, evidently unconcerned. 'Peter wouldn't come, Mummy, I'm sorry. Sally wanted to and we both tried to persuade him.'

'It doesn't matter, darling. You're here.' Ann hugged her daughter.

'You look wonderful, Mummy,' Fay exclaimed, a note of surprise in her voice, Ann thought. 'You look years younger, and really beautiful.'

'Your mother has always been beautiful, Fay,' Alex admonished.

'Not like this she hasn't, Alex, never. It's amazing the effect you've had on her.'

'I haven't changed her. I've just made you all see what was always there.' He smiled across Fay's head at Ann, and Ann's legs felt weak at the intimacy he could convey in his smile.

Lydia and George arrived. For a second Lydia was speechless as she looked about the enormous room packed with personalities.

'My, my, Ann. Haven't you done well for yourself? Clever little thing. Oh, I do love the famous,' she yelled over her shoulder as she swooped into the room.

The party increased in tempo. The noise grew louder. The food was eaten with relish. More wine was produced. The band played on.

Ann stood by the window, momentarily alone, enjoying the scene, watching Alex, towering above the other men, laughing, gesticulating with a shish-kebab in one hand and a large glass of retsina in the other.

'Are you Ann?' a voice at her elbow asked, making her jump.

'Yes.' She turned to find a tall, willowy woman in her twenties standing beside her. She was dressed in an exquisite, shimmering dress, the colours of which swirled into different patterns, as she moved. Ann wondered if it was a Zandra Rhodes, for it looked more like a work of art than the result of mere dress designing. Her shining dark hair was long, reaching far below her shoulders, and seemed to ripple with a life of its own, as she stood swaying slightly. Ann touched her own hair, as most women do when faced with such luxuriant hair on another woman, and wondered if she should have had it cut so short. The length of the young woman's elegant, well-manicured hands was accentuated by the red nails and the beautiful rings that shone on them. This woman was the epitome of modern style. Beside her Ann felt dumpy and the dress which had so delighted her at Christmas suddenly seemed fussy and unsophisticated.

'Yes, I'm Ann,' she repeated, smiling up at the beautiful woman. The smile disappeared from Ann's face as she saw the malevolent expression in the other woman's large brown eyes.

'You won't keep him, you know. The words were spat out. 'You don't really think a boring, middle-aged hausfrau like you will keep a man like Alex amused for long, do you?'

Ann felt herself redden and involuntarily her hand flew to her cheeks as if she had been hit.

'You can't possibly excite him in bed. Not like I do. Hell, look at you. He's done this before you know, often. But he'll come back to me, he always does,' she hissed. The sway had become more pronounced, and Ann backed away as the woman loomed towards her. Alarmed, Ann looked into the face that had appeared so beautiful and saw only ugliness and hate. Ann looked about desperately for Alex.

'Can I help you, Miss Villa?' Nigel's polite voice asked.

'Piss off, Salisbury,' the woman snarled, her words slurred.

'That's enough, Miss Villa.'

'Sucking up to the new bird are you, Salisbury? Still wetting your pants with terror of the old man? Going to try to get into bed with this one like you tried with me?' Her voice rose, shrill and harsh.

'Miss Villa. I think you should go,' Nigel continued in his calm, courteous voice.

'Fuck off. I'm having a quiet word with the blushing bride, even if she is a bit long in the tooth for the role.'

Ann stood transfixed as Miss Villa swung her arm as if to hit Nigel.

'Who let you in?'

She dropped her arm and swung round to face Alex. She put her hand up and gently stroke his shirt front. 'Alex, darling,' she cooed, miraculously looking beautiful again. 'Been missing me? Do you feel as randy as I do?' She spoke in a low, husky voice, both hands now carressing him, her right leg thrust forward to press urgently against him.

'Nigel, how the hell did she get in? I left explicit instructions she was not to be allowed entry.'

'I'm sorry, sir. I told the guards on the door. She just appeared. I saw her talking to Mrs Grange. I . . .'

'Then get her out,' Alex shouted. Ann noticed the other guests were now watching.

'Alex,' the woman whined, and curled her arm about his.

Angrily he shook himself free and looked at her coldly. 'Leave. Now, and quietly, Sophie,' he said, in an ominously controlled voice.

'I only came to say hullo to your new bride, darling. I was just being polite. When my invitation didn't come I thought there must have been an oversight.'

'I told you, we're finished. I don't want to see you any more. I've paid you off. I've done with you.'

The woman winced at his words, the coldness of his tone only underlining their brutality. She looked from Alex to Ann. Then slowly, so slowly that Ann found herself blushing with embarrassment, the woman's gaze swept from Ann's head to her shoes and back again. She stood very straight. 'I must say, Alex, I thought you only cared for perfection. I think your standards are slipping.'

Alex's hand flashed up as if to hit her. Her head jolted defensively back. His hand hovered in the air, and there was a bleak expression on his face. Slowly he lowered his arm.

'Get out, you whore,' he said through clenched teeth. 'Nigel, get rid of this garbage.'

Ann felt as if she'd been holding her breath for minutes, releasing it only as Nigel manhandled the protesting woman away. Alex turned to the guests who stood watching with interest.

'Cabaret over,' he announced laughing, all anger disappearing from his face. He turned to Ann. 'My darling, I'm so sorry about that ugly incident. What did she say to you?'

'Nothing,' Ann lied.

'She must have said something. Did she annoy you? I'll make her pay.'

'No, nothing. She was so drunk, I couldn't understand the garble,' she continued to lie, feeling inwardly sick. 'Your ex-mistress, I presume.'

'Yes. God knows why she showed up.'

'Perhaps she still loves you.'

'Probably my irresistible charm,' he said with a mocking laugh.

'She is lovely, and so young,' Ann said almost wistfully.

'Are you sure she didn't say something to upset you?'

'Alex, we're letting her spoil the party. Look, people are still looking embarrassed.'

Alex shouted instructions to the band who began a new tune. He jumped into the centre of the room and began to dance; one or two other Greek guests joined him. The others stood in a circle, cheering and encouraging the men as they looped and twisted. Ann watched fascinated at the intricacy of the dance as each man leaped and twirled to the music, each movement a triumph to their strength and masculinity. From somewhere someone threw a plate, then more began to fly through the air, crashing on the floor, the men's feet flashing through the broken shards. Other guests joined in. Those who did not clapped and cheered the others on. There was no stopping them, nobody left, and it was after five in the morning before Ann finally collapsed into bed.

'That was a wonderful party, my darling, thank you,' Alex said as he flopped down beside her, putting out his arm to her.

'Darling, I can't. I'm too tired.'

'Don't ever say "no" to me. I warned you I'd make endless demands on you.' And ignoring her protests he expertly began to awaken her tired body.

Later, as she lay in his arms she sighed.

'Why are sighing?' he immediately wanted to know.

'That Sophie Villa. She said I would lose you. That I wouldn't be able to keep you amused in bed. That you would go back to her.'

'The bitch! I knew she'd upset you. I'll see to her,' he said ominously.

'No, darling, leave it. She's just a jealous woman. I can understand . . . But, what she says . . . I mean, we do make love a lot. It is important to you.'

'Totally,' he grinned.

'Well, she's right. You might get bored with me.'

'And you might get bored with me.'

'Never!' She sat up full of indignation.

'So, you may be convinced of our love for each other, but I may not?'

'But you're so much more experienced than me.'

'Exactly, so I know better than you when I'm on to a good thing,' he chuckled, settling her in the crook of his arm.

'But she's right, I'm old, when you could find someone much younger.'

'I chose you, didn't I?' he said with unselfconscious pride.

'Yes.' She snuggled up to him.

'Then there's no problem. I thought you wanted to sleep.'

'But my age . . .'

'You English,' he sighed. 'You're all obsessed with age. Now, my darling, for once *I'm* tired. I need to sleep.'

She lay in the dark listening to his regular breathing. He made it so easy to believe him but all the same . . . once again she had seen the cold, cruel side of Alex which almost made her feel sorry for that other woman.

9

Right from the start Ann had realized that her Midfield wardrobe would not do. She had made a tentative start at changing it, but the party had shown her she had a long way to go.

She had watched the other female guests with keen interest. Their dresses had made them look like an expensive mannequin parade. Even the simplest had shouted of money and quality. But it was the bitchiness of Alex's ex-mistress which really galvanized her.

Ann dispatched Elene, who had now joined the staff, to buy every fashion magazine she could find. Ann studied them with care, made a booklet of notes and addresses. She phoned her bank, transferred a sizeable sum from deposit to current account and went shopping.

For two weeks she visited designers, shoemakers, lingerie houses, small exclusive boutiques and beauticians. She was quite open about her problem. She needed overnight to become a sophisticated woman with style. She soaked up their advice like a sponge.

Within a month Ann's wardrobe had changed beyond recognition and her bank account was sadly depleted. Alex took an amused interest in this transformation. He approved of most of her choices, but was quite emphatic when something should be sent back. He always complimented her on her looks, always noticed something new: a complete contrast to Ben, who had never seemed aware of her clothes.

Ann sat in her dressing room surveying the new Zandra Rhodes creation she had bought and marvelled at how much she had changed. Or had she? As she now dressed for Alex and his lifestyle, so she had once dressed for Ben and his. She had devoted her life to Ben, fitted into his ways, his wants, exactly as she was doing with Alex – only the demands were different. Whereas Ben had expected a smoothly run house, a neat, respectable wife, a good steak on the table, Alex demanded a beautiful wife and an enthusiastic mistress in his bed.

She tidied the top of her dressing table. She had thought she had come out of mourning a new woman, but now she wondered whether that had been an illusion. She had had a glimpse, a fragmentary flash, that she might, could have been different, but she was losing the independence she had gained. And she found she regretted it.

She had everything a woman could desire. An adoring, rich man who lavished presents and love on her. She lived in luxury, she had no mundane tasks to do. She was sexually fulfilled. What was it then that she wanted?

She looked at herself in the mirror, at the transformed woman reflected there. She thought of Fay, of the way she came and went as the mood suited her. Responsible only to herself, independent of her men. Fay called the tune and made the rules. As she tired of one man she would drop him and then hunt out another.

Even as she thought of her daughter's way of life, Ann knew that this was no solution for her. The ways of a lifetime were too ingrained in her. In any case she loved Alex, wanted to share his future, she could never see men as sexual conquests – she laughed at the very idea. She realized, though, that she felt hemmed in. This great love of his was the tender trap Sinatra sang about. Everything was too perfect. Such perfection cast a shadow, made her worry about 'self' and her identity, hardly subjects that had occupied her mind in the past. And what if it did not last, what if, as that woman had said, he tired of her? She would have scant money by then at the rate she was going through it, and soon no home of her own.

She shook her head at the woman in the mirror, irritated with herself. Why could she not just enjoy herself, live for the present, as Fay did? She unstoppered a perfume bottle and briskly dabbed some behind her ear.

'Anna, where are you?' Alex's urgent voice broke into her confused thinking.

'I'm here, darling.' She smiled: all the thinking in the world was not going to change anything. That would always be her answer as long as he called her. His calling reassured her, made her suddenly aware that Alex needed her as much as she needed him.

A few days later, a letter from her bank arrived and politely informed her that she was overdrawn and that they would appreciate a further transfer of funds.

She did as the bank asked but she began to worry. Alex introduced her to everyone as his fiancée but since Christmas he had not mentioned marriage again. She would look rather foolish back in Midfield, she realized ruefully, with her exotic wardrobe of Rhodes, Bruce Oldfield and Conran. She was certain that Fay, finding herself in the same position, would have asked Alex outright when they were getting married. But Ann was of a generation who would find it impossible to ask Alex what his intentions were.

Her estate agent phoned with news that a buyer for her house had offered the asking price and wanted a fast completion. She replaced the receiver, feeling shocked. She had reached a point of no return. Once the house was sold Ann knew she would be totally vulnerable and completely dependent on Alex. Surely this would be the turning point: he would have to make a decision now about the wedding. Surely he would see that.

'What shall I do?' she asked him over dinner, served exclusively now by Roberts since Ann had told Charlotte firmly that she was not needed in the dining room.

'Accept.'

'Yes, but my furniture and things . . .'

'Darling, you said yourself that only you can decide what you want to keep and what to sell.'

'But what do I do with everything?'

'We shall have our new house long before the sale of yours is completed and if not, then put it in Harrods store,' he replied reasonably.

'But what then?'

'What do you mean, my sweet?'

'Oh nothing,'she said lamely and loathed herself for her lack of courage.

Ann drove down to Midfield.

It was with mixed emotions that she let herself into her house. When she had left it at Christmas she felt she never wanted to see it again. Now she dreaded someone else owning it.

Meg was waiting for her, her face breaking into its

enormous grin at the sight of Ann. 'They're very nice people what are buying, Mrs Grange. With two young children. They want to keep me on, but it won't be the same somehow.'

'Please, Meg. Don't talk like that. I feel so miserable about selling.'

They started at the top of the house and Ann began the sad task of sorting through the debris of her life.

Later she sat in her old bedroom, the four-poster now stripped of its hangings, the bedding folded. Meg had long since gone home to her husband. Ann had poured herself a drink and sat among the boxes they had hauled from the attic full of mementoes, her old school reports, the children's first shoes, their first attempts at drawing.

For several hours she sorted through the boxes. She felt strangely secure and relaxed and with a start realized she had not felt this way for weeks. It was this house, with the past about her, which made her feel like this, a feeling that, in the weeks with Alex, she had lost. Life had been so simple once. She had thought that life with Alex would replace one security with another. Now she was not so sure.

She opened another box and sifted through the papers. She found a bundle of letters from Ben tied with ribbon. Letters he had written to her when he was away at medical school. She pored over them, remembering the heart-hammering tension she had experienced each morning when the postman came – the dreadful desolation when there was no letter, the happiness when there was. A tear slipped down her cheek, a dreadful sadness and loneliness filled her.

She jumped as the telephone rang.

'What the hell are you doing? Why aren't you home?' she heard Alex demand.

'I was sorting through things.'

'I didn't expect you to be gone so long.'

'Darling, it will take at least a week.'

'I meant I expected you back here by evening.'

'What's the time? My watch seems to have stopped.' She shook it.

'It's nine. I've been worried.'

'Darling, I'm sorry. I got engrossed in papers and things.'

'What papers?'

'Oh, the children's old school reports, things like that,' she half lied.

'Well, get back here quickly. I miss you,' he ordered.

She locked up the house and drove through the damp February evening to London – perplexed by the emptiness she felt and the fact that she could have become so engrossed in the past as to forget the time and Alex.

'Don't do that again, ever,' Alex snapped as she entered the large drawing room, which he was pacing up and down like a caged animal.

'Darling, I'm sorry, I just lost track of the time.'

'I'm your time. Nothing else should matter,' he shouted angrily.

'Darling, I don't understand.'

'I can just imagine you alone there getting all sentimental, regretting leaving, remembering the past. Wondering whether you're making a mistake with me.'

'Alex, I wasn't,' she lied, shocked at how close to the truth he was.

'I don't want you going alone again. You'll take Elene or Nigel.'

'But they can't help me pack.'

'Then get Fay or Lydia.'

'Fay's coming tomorrow, and Peter I hope.'

'And be back by five at the latest. I hate it when you're away from me and I don't know what you're doing.'

'Darling, you are silly. I was just packing, nothing else. What on earth could I get up to?' She smiled, touched now by his agitation at her lateness, concerned for his worry, not seeing it as a trap at all. 'Is there any dinner left?' she asked brightly.

'I haven't eaten yet, I waited for you. And I'm starving,' he complained, petulantly.

She ruffled his hair. 'I love it when you sound like a naughty little boy,' she teased.

That night in bed he made love to her with a new intensity that she would not have thought possible. He vowed his love to her a hundred times. Ann sank into a contented sleep.

The following morning as she was about to leave for Midfield, Alex asked her to join him in his study. She was surprised to find her new lawyer, David Student, sitting there with a stranger whom Alex introduced as his lawyer, Mr Howe.

'Ann, we must sign our marriage contract,' Alex announced.

'What contract?' she asked.

'It details what money Mr Georgeopoulos is willing to settle on you upon your marriage, yours outright, and what settlement we have agreed on in the event of a divorce, Ann,' her lawyer explained.

'Alex!' She looked at him shocked. 'How can you even think that way?'

'He didn't, Mrs Grange,' Mr Howe interrupted. 'But as his lawyer I had to advise him to.'

'I don't understand,' said Ann.

'Ann, Mr Georgeopoulos is a very wealthy man. Should you divorce, under English law, you could make a substantial claim on him. If you sign this contract you are, in fact, agreeing not to make that claim,' her lawyer explained.

'It's so you won't ruin me,' Alex laughed.

'I have been over the document, Ann, and it is extremely generous, and, as your lawyer, I can assure you that it is quite in order for you to sign.'

'What does it say?' asked Ann. David Student put on the half-spectacles which made him look like an ageing professor.

'Mr Georgeopoulos has agreed to settle £500,000 upon you on marriage, the income from which you are to use for your personal needs, clothes, that sort of thing. In the event of a divorce you would agree to settle for a once-and-all-time payment of £2,000,000.'

'I'm not signing that!' She turned angrily to Alex. 'I don't want your money. I have enough money for my clothes and to buy you presents, I don't need any more. You don't have to buy me.' Annoyed, she felt she was on the edge of tears. 'And how you could even be discussing divorce when we aren't even married, when you don't mention marriage any more . . .' She stormed from the room, too proud to let them see the tears in her eyes.

Alex found her brushing her short hair vigorously. 'Darling, darling, please don't be cross.' He took her in his arms. 'Please, I've done it for you.'

'I won't sign it, I won't! It makes me feel like an object. All I can think of is us living for ever with each other and here are you making plans in case we get divorced.'

'Anna, listen to me,' Alex said. 'I know you have money, but really it won't be enough for your lifestyle with me. I don't want you coming to me every time you want a new dress because you have run out of money, do I? Heavens, I don't have the time to keep endlessly writing you cheques. And honestly, Anna, of course I don't think we'll get divorced, it's a terrible thought. But – no listen,' he said as she turned away, 'it does happen, you might find you hate the life with me, might yearn to go back to being an English countrywoman. One thing I can assure you, my darling. Once you have experienced this life, then to adjust to a life with less money will be nearly impossible. Do you think that I would want to think of you miserable? No, that's right, but, say we have a terrible fight and we hate each other?' She shook her head vehemently. 'It happens, darling, it does. Then if we hated each other I would fight not to give you a penny, and you would fight to get far more. Don't deny it, I've seen it happen. Human nature is very strange and none of us can say how we will react in the future. You do see, don't you?'

'I won't sign.'

'Please, darling, it is customary, you know, for a man in my position. It will make the lawyers happy, if nothing else. Just sign it. Come, my love, please. I want you to. Will you, for me?' He smiled his beguiling smile at her, and, as always when he did and she smiled back, Ann knew she had lost the battle.

She allowed him to lead her back to his study where the two lawyers looked embarrassed. She signed – at the same time an unworthy but satisfied little thought crept into her mind: she wondered if her late return last night had spurred Alex into action.

When she arrived at Midfield, Fay was already in the house, wearing jeans, her hair in a scarf, helping Meg to empty kitchen cupboards.

'Sorry I'm late. I got held up.' Ann wound up a large alarm clock.

'What on earth's that for?' Fay asked.

'I mustn't be late back to town.' She grinned to herself. 'Is Peter coming?'

'He didn't say. I think Sally's coming, though.'

Instead, both Peter and Sally arrived an hour later. Peter kissed Ann quickly on the cheek.

'Right, I want to go through the house with you three and you can decide what you want. I'm taking my bureau, the porcelain figurines in the drawing room, my books and some of the paintings. The rest I'll sell or you can have. I'm splitting the proceeds of the sale between the two of you.'

'But what about you, Mummy, how will you manage?'

'Alex is looking after me very well, Fay. He isn't the gold-digger Peter feared.' Ann looked pointedly at her son. 'In fact I shan't need any of this money, so it seemed fair to give it to you both now while you're young enough to enjoy it. It'll make things easier, Sally.' She smiled at her daughter-in-law, but while neither Sally nor Peter made any comment, Fay gave Ann a great hug of gratitude.

Peter shuffled behind them as they trooped through the house with pads and pens at the ready. Ann had decided to pretend that the unfortunate incident on Christmas Eve had not happened. If she could forget, perhaps Peter would too.

'Mummy, could I have the bed?' Fay asked. 'That's if Peter doesn't want it.'

'It wouldn't fit in our bedroom,' Sally giggled.

'The bedroom's enormous in my new flat.'

'Take whatever you want, darling,' Ann smiled at her daughter's evident excitement and wished her son would show as much pleasure.

Room by room they made decisions. Sally and Fay good-naturedly coming to agreement. Peter was with them but not part of the proceedings at all.

'Would you like your father's desk, Peter?'

'Not particularly,' he replied shortly.

'Then I'll take it, Mummy. I don't think strangers should have it. Maybe you'll change your mind, brother dear, I'll look after it for you. What about the linen?'

'Choose what you want. I'll give the rest to Meg.'

'Buying everything new then, are you?'

'Something like that, Peter,' she replied lightly, slipping from the room quickly, determined not to lose her temper this time.

She helped her children load the smaller items into their cars. Already the house began to look denuded. Peter and Sally drove off.

'Any booze left unpacked, Mummy?' Fay followed her mother back into the house.

'I think there's a little gin. I meant to give it to Meg.' In the drawing room, Ann poured them both a drink.

'You seem edgy, Mummy. Is it just the strain of packing up the house, or is there something else?'

Ann looked at her daughter, uncertain whether to confide in her, fearful of hearing Fay tell her she was being stupid.

'I suppose it's silly of me, but Alex made me sign some papers this morning. A marriage contract. It gives me a ridiculous sum of money now, and an enormous amount if we get divorced – more like telephone numbers than sums of money. It upset me.' Ann paused, finding it difficult to explain how she felt. 'It made me feel, well, debased, as if he was buying me.'

'I can see that it might. But honestly I don't think you should let it upset you. Alex is enormously wealthy. It's probably the normal thing with people like that.'

'But you see, Fay, I spend hours of every day worrying and wondering. I analyse everything. I never used to be like that: I just used to take things as they came. I wonder if deep down all this questioning is because really I know I shouldn't go through with it.'

'What sort of things?'

'These days I seem to be afraid of everything. After your father died, I began to realize how much of me was subjugated to him . . . I don't want to be like that again but, with a man like Alex, what chance do I stand? And then, as soon as I've decided to keep part of myself back, I realize I can't, that I'm afraid I love him too much. I'm afraid of losing him, of him tiring of me – of something dreadful happening to him. Sometimes I'm afraid of him – he has such a dreadful temper . . .'

'He's not violent?' Fay asked urgently.

'Good God, no. It's just an undercurrent.'

'But I thought everything was so perfect between you two.'

'It is. And that frightens me too. It can't possibly last.'

Fay laughed. 'Oh, Mummy, don't you think all brides think this way, you probably did with Daddy and you've forgotten all about it. You're not losing your identity. You're finding yourself with Alex. God, it shows on your face. I've never seen you like this. And when he's in the room with you, you almost glow with happiness. You deserve someone to love you like this. Let's face it, you had a pretty raw deal from Dad.'

'I only think like this if I'm on my own. It goes the minute I'm with him, I feel completely safe then. But there are times I feel trapped. That alarm clock I brought with me today. I had to, he was so angry when I was late last night. He wants me on hand all the time.'

'Don't you want to be with him all the time?

'Yes, I enjoy it, but it doesn't seem right.'

'That's because you've been used to a husband who went out to work. Now you have to live Alex's job with him. He obviously needs you. It's quite touching.'

'But he doesn't trust me. He dominates me totally, I feel I'm in danger of having nothing left of me. You see the muddle I'm in?'

Fay laughed. 'It sounds to me as if perhaps you need an interest in your own. An absorbing hobby . . .'

'Oh, Fay,' Ann said, exasperated that her daughter did not appear to understand.

'Listen, Mummy, you don't know what you're talking about. I know what you're referring to, that time when you thought you would like to do a course, maybe have a career. Well, do a course, learn a skill if you want. But forget about the career. The big world out there – it stinks, it bloody stinks, Mummy.'

'But I look at you, you're so complete and successful.'

'Oh, yes. I've a good job, loads of money, great success . . . but at what price? I'm tough, when I don't want to be tough, but I've had to learn to be to get on in that male-dominated world. It's true, if you're a woman you have to be twice as good at everything, there is no equality. But complete?' Fay laughed a hollow little laugh. 'I have men by the dozen and you know why? Because I scare the pants off most of them, I'm so bloody successful. I envy you Alex. I envy the love and security he's offering you, the strength. I'd love to find a man strong enough to dominate me, I really would.' To Ann's horror, tears welled up in Fay's eyes.

'Fay.' She stepped forward with concern. 'I'd no idea.'

'It's all right, Mummy. It's my choice, I know it. I'm upset because I see you with all this and you don't seem to realize what you have. Don't you see that he's like this with you because he thinks so much of you. I'm so worried that you might throw it all away and for what? An illusion? I could shake you, Mummy.'

'Oh, dear. You've made me feel rather stupid. I expected you to see everything so totally differently. Gracious, I don't seem to know anybody or anything.'

'It's because you've never known any other way. You and Alex are learning to adjust to each other. He will learn to trust you, let go a little, I'm convinced of it. Enjoy him. Enjoy what life is offering you. Stop cringing behind imagined horrors.'

Ann had much to think of during the car ride back to London. But they were far happier thoughts than those of the night before. Fay was right. If she had lost a small measure of her new-found independence, in return she had gained a self-confidence and a sense of her own worth that she had never known in the past. And, instead of accepting her life unquestioningly, as in the past, she now queried and analysed what was happening to her. She let herself into the flat and searched out Alex. She flung her arms about him.

'I love you so much,' she sighed.

'That's a very affectionate greeting. I love you too.'

'I know. I'm very lucky.' She smiled at him.

'Something's happened?' he said with an edge to his voice that indicated the unease he too suffered.

'Nothing's happened, except I've realized that I worry too much. That I am the luckiest woman alive. And that I'm hungry.' She laughed up at him.

Four

1

One house was sold, one house was bought.

A large sum of money, a ludicrous amount, Ann thought, was deposited in her bank account – her budget for converting and redecorating the new house. She resolved to show Alex just how economical she could be, show him that such an enormous sum was not necessary.

She began to work on her plans for the house with zest. She made detailed, to-scale drawings of every room which she then painted meticulously with her watercolours.

Now her colour sense, restricted by Ben to the garden, burgeoned. She studied every available colour chart avidly. When she could not find the colour she wanted, she would mix her own from her paintbox and then, armed with her personal colour chart, visit the paint manufacturers and persuade them to mix colours for her – an expensive proposition, but Ann was learning, from Alex, about perfection.

By chance, she discovered she had that most elusive of talents, a perfect colour memory. She was ordering red wild silk for curtains when she mentioned to the shop assistant how pleased she was to have found a perfect match for the lampshades she had already bought.

'Are you sure it's a match, madam?' the assistant asked with a voice that clearly indicated he doubted it.

'Oh, yes, exactly.'

'Reds are funny. You may think it's the same but . . . and it's such expensive material . . . perhaps madam would be safer taking a swatch home with her, to check.'

'No, that won't be necessary. It's the same shade, I can see it in my head, you see,' she explained sweetly. 'If I can leave that with you then, and your workshop will send someone round to measure? How long will they take to make, did you say?' Then she asked to see some glazed chintz which had caught her eye in the window. The assistant, with a knowledgeable toss of his head, went to collect a bolt of the chintz from the back of the shop, where he muttered to his colleagues just how difficult customers could be and that that Mrs Grange needn't think he would take the curtains back when she found they clashed with her flaming lamps – she would have to change the lamps.

The man in the shop was wrong, the match was perfect.

Ann, in turn, was wrong, about there being too much money. As the weeks slipped by and daily Ann haunted shops such as Colefax and Fowler, Liberty, or rootled through the floors of Crowthers, visited antique and designer shops by the dozen – so the money in her account shrank at an alarming rate. She bought roomfuls of antiques, reserving others, and paintings by the score. Chandeliers had to be selected. The storage bill for her treasures grew larger as the weeks passed. She commissioned an artist to paint a *trompe-l'oeil* mural in the dining room; she selected china and glass; the kitchens and the bathrooms were to be newly fitted; extra bathrooms were to be added. Unable to find carpets she liked, she had some specially woven. And finally she decided there was room for a swimming pool and gymnasium in the cellars. Now she discovered how quickly money could diminish.

By the time they had possession of the house, Ann's files of ideas were overflowing. Plumbers, electricians and carpenters were briefed and ready. In her mind's eye the house was complete – only the work remained to be done.

She could laugh now at the way she had wondered how she was to fill her time. Supervising the builders, sorting out the problems, and making the decisions that daily had to be made filled her days. On top of all this there remained the necessity of always looking immaculately groomed for her demanding lover, and, with their socializing, she had little time left to herself.

Alex had warned her that there would be a lot of entertaining but even so Ann had been surprised by the amount. Being Alex's hostess was almost a full-time job. Each week they would give at least one large dinner party and attend a couple more. One evening was set aside for the theatre, opera or ballet to which they would take a party and entertain them to supper afterwards. On Fridays they would set off for Courtneys in Hampshire and the house party – a weekly ritual. If she was lucky they occasionally had Sunday evenings to themselves.

Alex, she discovered, never stopped working. Whatever they did, whoever they saw, there was always some business connection involved.

The dinner parties or weekends were always attended by an interesting, ever-changing pot-pourri of people. Alex counted as friends people from many and varied walks of life. With Ben, their friends had been people similar to themselves in status and income bracket who lived in the locality, or medical colleagues. There were no such restrictions in Alex's life. She would watch him in deep philosophical conversation with a bishop or a professor, or enjoying a good political argument with a Cabinet minister, then he would turn and be equally engrossed in a discussion of cam-shafts and cylinder heads with a racing driver or his mechanic – both would have been invited. Artists, writers, actors, engineers, a London taxi driver, all were Alex's friends as well as the endless parade of business associates. Everywhere he went Alex attracted people and he had an insatiable interest in other people's crafts and work.

Always Ann hoped to hear, from one of these guests, some inadvertent remark about Alex's dead wife. Apart from that one time on the beach, Alex had never mentioned her to Ann again. She had looked in vain for a photograph or portrait of Nada, since the less she knew the more her predecessor's looks began to preoccupy her. Packing for the new house she had hoped to find old photograph albums. There was nothing. It was as if Alex wanted to obliterate what had gone before. Ann could only presume that it was still too painful for him to look upon the face of the woman he had loved so much when he was young.

None of the guests ever mentioned Nada and Ann was too shy to ask any of them. Only once had she plucked up the courage to mention the woman to Yianni.

'What was Mrs Georgeopoulos like?' Ann asked him one afternoon, as nonchalantly as possible, appearing to be idly flicking through her magazine as she did so.

Yianni looked at her sharply and his gaze flickered quickly towards the door, a furtive expression in his eyes. Ann was unsure if he did this because he felt trapped by the question or to check that no one was listening. She leaned forward eagerly, convinced at last that she was to learn something.

'She was very beautiful,' Yianni replied shortly, and virtually bolted for the door. So Ann did not try again.

It was inevitable then, given this lack of information, that in Ann's mind Nada became more beautiful, younger and more scintillating as each day passed. There was a new ghost in Ann's life and one she could not compete with, let alone outshine. Insidiously a jealously for his dead wife began to form in her mind.

Although the entertaining was hard work, Ann had the support of an excellent staff. Charlotte the cook, whom Ann had not expected to last, remained with them in London and continued to produce excellent food. In Hampshire a young French chef reigned supreme in the kitchens. She left the menu planning in their capable hands.

When she arrived in Hampshire she would quickly check the guests' bedrooms. It was always unnecessary since the housekeeper, Mrs Beech, had arranged everything to perfection. But Ann felt she ought to do something to justify her position as mistress of the house.

If business was the *raison d'être* of their social life, those guests who were uninvolved were never aware of this. Alex was as subtle a host as he was a lover. At some point during the evening or weekend, as if by a prearranged signal, Alex and whoever it was he wanted to talk to would quietly leave the company. Sometimes they were away for only half an hour, at other times they were not seen for hours. But Alex always returned in plenty of time, before the evening broke up.

'What were you talking to that man about?' she would often ask.

'Business,' he invariably replied.

'What business? I'd like to be involved in your work.'

'Just business.' He would smile at her, the shrug of his shoulders dismissing her question.

Ann could not understand his attitude. She could not make up her mind if it was instigated by a desire for secrecy or because he thought she was too stupid to understand. She had started this relationship with the idea that she would be his helpmeet, act as a sounding board. It had been impossible for her to be included in Ben's medical career, but she had hoped to be a part of Alex's world. She knew she could learn.

There were times when she resented these men with whom he spent so much time. It was not just resentment of the time stolen from them as a couple but that of a woman who sees her man passionately involved and feels herself shut out. These men, she was the first to admit, were charming to her. They brought her flowers, presents. But, maybe fuelled by her resentment, she found that she began to harbour a distrust of some of the most frequent visitors. Among these there was a preponderance of associates in suits that were too shiny, whose jewellery was too large, who seemed to prefer to talk in corners, ringed hands cupping their mouths. Ann began to worry about these business associates in particular but Alex appeared to trust them all blithely. Everyone, it seemed, in Alex's book was a 'good chap'.

But there was one man Ann liked instantly and she wished that all Alex's contacts could be like him. Roddie Barnes was the archetypal handsome, silver-haired, middle-aged, upper-class English businessman. He was always impeccably dressed. His voice was beautifully modulated, he was a delightful companion.

'I like Roddie,' she confided in bed one night after Roddie had been to dinner with his sweet but rather faded-looking wife, and two men who, unfortunately for them, were in the category of which Ann did not approve.

'Implying that you don't like the others?'

'Do you expect me to? Really, Alex, just look at them. Those two tonight looked like extras from a gangster movie.'

'Not everyone is born with good taste, you know,' he replied stiffly. 'Just because they look shady doesn't mean they are – I'm surprised at you, Anna, making such superficial judgements. Those two, Antonio and Mark, are self-made men, they lack Roddie's advantage of birth. I admire them.'

'What do they do?'

'Oh, this and that.'

'That's what you always say. It drives me mad the way you refuse to involve me,' she said, sitting up from the pillow and looking at him earnestly.

'My darling, I don't want you worrying about my business affairs – you worry about our new house. How's it coming along?'

'There you go again – do you know how patronizing you sound? I'm not a child, and I'm not stupid. I want to know. I shouldn't be shut out,' she said angrily.

'Antonio is a property developer in a very big way. Mark started out with a market stall and now owns pubs and clubs throughout the country, among other things. He's very successful. And your favourite, Roddie, isn't in their league. He's the agent for a group of venture capitalists which includes the other two.' He smiled his charming smile and stroked her arm. 'Any wiser?'

'No.'

'I borrow money from them.'

'Why do you need to borrow money?' Ann asked with concern. Ann's Lancashire parents had brought her up to believe that one might borrow for a mortgage, but that any other form of borrowing implied a flippant, irresponsible attitude to life. In Ann's old world HP was the name on a sauce bottle and credit was a dirty word.

'Everyone borrows money,' he said patiently. 'The first rule of business is that you never use your own money if you can use someone else's. It's how things are done. For goodness sake, Anna, don't look so primly shocked. Why, even dear old Onassis borrowed, darling. You see, how can I discuss my business affairs with you when you know so little? It's very complicated and very boring.'

'Boring, I don't believe,' she snorted. 'It fascinates you, you're never bored. I could learn. You think I'm too stupid to understand.'

'Darling, no, I don't. Don't you understand, I spend hours of my day with men like that, juggling figures, worrying over the markets – the last thing I want to discuss in my bed is my work. Come here, you dreadful nagging woman!' He laughed as he grabbed at her, but Ann escaped his grasp.

'These people, are you sure they are OK? Is there no one else you could borrow from? More . . .'

'More respectable – is that what you were going to say? Like Roddie?' He snorted. 'I don't just use them. I'm approached all the time by people like them, hoping to fix up deals with me. Roddie works as the middleman, introducing likely people, his commission is enormous you know. Sometimes I use him, sometimes I don't. At the moment, well, I probably will . . .'

'So where does the money come from? Who are the other people?'

'That's a question I rarely bother to ask. I just want the loot not the history lesson.'

'Then I think you should be careful, it could come from anything – crime, drugs.'

'Anna, what an imagination you have!' He roared with laughter. 'You can't go round harbouring suspicions like this about people. I'll tell you one thing, I'd trust Antonio and Mark further than Roddie any day. In any case this conversation is tedious. I want to make love not talk about them.' And he smothered her next question with a kiss.

They were only ever alone in bed. Everywhere they went they were accompanied by Yianni and Nigel.

Yianni continued to be perfectly charming to Ann. But after all this time she still did not know him. Once or twice she had heard Nigel making personal phone calls, to girls Ann hoped. But Yianni appeared to have no life apart from his work. She doubted if he had any other interests. He worked quietly and efficiently. Watching the younger man working with her husband Ann admired the fact that Yianni was the only employee devoid of sycophancy. He was beyond reproach and yet . . . if Ann had a criticism it was that he never put a foot wrong and glowed with the self-satisfaction of knowing it.

Of the two aides, she preferred Nigel, probably because he was far more outgoing and not nearly so perfect. The last thing anyone could accuse Nigel of was smugness or self-satisfaction. He was always too worried for either. Ann had begun to nag him about his anxiety; not only was she concerned for his health but already a deep furrow on his brow threatened to mar his good looks. His lack of confidence was not helped when Alex shouted at him. After any incident it took hours for him to recover any sort of equilibrium. The fact that Alex shouted at everybody, including Yianni, seemed to offer no comfort to Nigel.

Ann was to see many examples of Alex's awesome temper. From nowhere, and frequently about nothing, a rage would appear, distorting his features. A torrent of words would tumble out, in any of the languages he spoke, rising in a crescendo as his anger expanded. Walls were hit, furniture was kicked, files were thrown, telephones in particular were hurled with ferocity. Then, just as quickly, the eruption would subside. He seemed totally unaware of the devastating effect this had on people as he simmered down, smiled, and the affable, charming Alex returned.

At the first rumblings of discontent his staff would quickly find work to do as far removed from Alex as possible. The poor soul on whom the full force of the anger was directed was reduced to a terrified mumbling. All that is except Yianni, who stood tall and proud, absorbing the abuse and threats, and would invariably, at the end, bow his head to Alex in silent acquiescence and quietly let himself out of the room, a small smile hovering about his mouth. Ann should have respected his courage: instead she found it irked her.

Obviously, Ann thought, these rages were caused by the strain of Alex's work. But since he did not discuss anything with her what these strains were remained a mystery to her, and so she did not know how to alleviate them.

Ann worried about the staff but most of all she worried about Alex. Such uncontrolled explosions could be doing him no good at all. She had suffered the shock of sudden death once: she had to take steps to prevent it happening again.

Things came to a head at the flat in London, the day he threw Fiona's typewriter out of the window, smashing the plate glass to smithereens and breaking a particularly beautiful flowerpot on the terrace. Alerted by the noise of breaking glass and the girl's crying, Ann found the pleasant and efficient Fiona reduced to a sobbing, shaking jelly. She fetched a box of Kleenex, comforted the girl and stormed into Alex's study.

'Alex, this has got to stop!'

'What, my love?' He looked up from the papers on his desk and smiled at her. Ann shook her head with exasperation. How could he change so totally in the space of a minute?

'You know damn well what. These dreadful bouts of temper. Nigel nearly walked out last week and it wouldn't surprise me if Fiona handed in her notice – she's in a dreadful state. You're a bully, Alex.'

'Bah, they're used to my ways, I've been shouting at them for years. It would worry them if I stopped. They shouldn't be so bloody stupid then I wouldn't have to . . .' He shrugged his shoulders as if the whole incident had nothing to do with him. 'I pay them enough anyway,' he added, inconsequentially, and a shade more defensively.

'Just because you pay them, that doesn't give you the right to shout at them. This yelling and bellowing shows a complete lack of respect for them. I hate it.' She stamped her foot.

'I never shout at you, do I?' He looked at her innocently, spreading his hands wide.

'No, and don't you ever start. I promise you I wouldn't put up with it. You're like a spoilt child who can't have his own way. It's ridiculous in a grown man.'

'Yes, Mummy.' He smiled his devastating smile, his grey eyes twinkling mischievously.

'I mean it, Alex.' Turning purposefully away from the smile which always ensured that she lost the argument, she went on, 'I've already had to cope with one sudden coronary, I don't want to go through that again.'

'Am I really bad?'

'Oh, Alex. You're not just bad, you're impossible.' She found herself smiling. 'Why can't I stay cross with you?'

'Because you love me. Come here.' He patted his knee, taking advantage of Ann's apparent change in mood.

'No, I won't. Not until you go and apologize to Fiona.'

'I never apologize to anyone,' he announced arrogantly.

'Then it's about time you started,' she replied shortly.

Seeing her stern expression, Alex got to his feet. Sighing exaggeratedly, he went to Fiona, dutifully apologized, and took Ann to bed.

'You excite me uncontrollably when you're cross with me. Just like my English nanny. What do you think the psychologists would make of that?' He was covering her face with soft sensuous kisses.

'You never take me seriously, do you?' Ann sighed.

'Oh, but I do, my darling, I do,' he said intensely as he searched for her breasts with his mouth, and her anger was lost in their mutual passion.

The next day Fiona received a bouquet of flowers and an expensive pin from Cartier. Peace, for the time being, was restored. But it was an uneasy peace and Ann was not alone in waiting for the next onslaught. Strangely, it did not come, at least not with the same ferocity. Alex still lost his temper but now he was making an effort to control it, usually by slamming out of the room. The bills for broken telephones continued but there was no doubt he was venting his spleen far more often on inanimate objects rather than people.

On one of their Hampshire weekends, Fay came to stay. Not only had Ann longed to see her daughter but she was hungry for news of the rest of her family. Although she relentlessly kept up her approaches to Peter – invitations to dinner, to this house, to Alex's box at the opera – there was a deafening silence from her son.

'How are they?' Ann asked, immediately she closed her bedroom door and was alone with her daughter away from the other guests.

'They're fine. I think Peter's having some difficulties at the college – something to do with research grants and some problem over his fellowship. It doesn't help his temper much. But Adam's fine and Sally's well. I've brought you some photographs.' From her handbag Fay took two envelopes.

Ann took the photographs eagerly. Quickly she flicked through them. And then, more slowly and fondly, she spread them out on the floor, sank on to her knees and studied each one of Adam closely. 'I do miss them, especially Adam,' she said, looking up at her daughter. 'I thought it was something I could cope with, but it's hard. I try to pretend that I don't care any more but I do. I still can't believe that it's happened to me.'

'Poor Mummy.' Fay joined her on the floor and put her arms about her mother. 'Perhaps Peter'll come round. The trouble with him is he's so bloody proud and of course he's feeling pretty stupid about Alex at the moment.'

'About Alex?'

'George and Lydia had them to dinner to try to talk some sense into Peter. Apparently George had known immediately who Alex was and how stinking rich and successful he is. Of course Peter couldn't put a good face on it, could he? Admit he was wrong. No, he got all high-handed and said he'd like to know how. George didn't help matters by saying that high-flyers, like Alex, were very often mysterious about how they had amassed their fortunes. Of course, that gave Peter his chance: he jumped in and said that Alex was probably in the Mafia or drug-dealing. Apparently, according to Sally, George nearly died laughing which only made matters worse.'

Ann started to laugh with Fay but the niggling doubts that Alex's secrecy had created in her wormed their way triumphantly to the surface. Abruptly she stopped laughing. Fay looked at her, concerned. Ann forced a smile that for a second teetered on her face, but slipped quickly away, pulling down the corners of her mouth as it did so.

'You all right, Mummy?'

'Darling, I'm fine.' Ann squeezed her daughter's hand. 'Talking about Peter is enough to wipe the smile off anyone's face.' She laughed nervously.

'Are you sure there's nothing wrong? You're not still spending your time worrying, are you? Do you mean my lecture didn't work?' Fay smiled fondly at Ann.

'No, I listened to you. I've rationalized a lot. It's just that I'm always expecting something awful to happen. Alex says I sound like a Greek waiting for nemesis.'

'You know what that is? You think you're got over Dad dying, but you haven't. It's left you with this awful insecurity. Makes sense, doesn't it?'

'Do you really think it's as simple an explanation as that?'

'Yes I do, and it's time you snapped out of it. You're not being fair to Alex. It's hardly his fault Daddy died.'

'Dear Fay, you talk such sense. You always did, even as a little girl you always saw things so clearly.'

'Me? Don't make me laugh. It's easy enough when it's someone else's problem. I wish I could do it for myself.'

'What's wrong, Fay? I thought the job was going wonderfully and you like the new flat.'

'They are. They couldn't be better.' Fay lapsed into silence and looked at her mother as if deciding whether to tell her something or not.

'Fay?' Ann asked anxiously.

Fay took a deep breath. 'I've had another disastrous affair, Mummy. Another one down the chute.' Ann sat silent, waiting for her daughter to continue. 'I really loved this one, too, that's the pig of it. I even let him move in. Hell, he was the reason I got the flat, to give us more room. I even let my work slip a bit – that's how engrossed I was with him.' She gave a hollow laugh.

'Was that the one you thought you might be bringing to Alex's party?'

'Yes. He'd gone home for Christmas. I'd expected him back for the New Year, but we'd had an argument on the phone that night. He came back, it was perfect again. Then I found I was pregnant, Mummy. Only he didn't want it. He said it was too soon for us, confessed he didn't like children. So I went ahead with it – I had an abortion. And I didn't want to. God, I wanted that baby.' Fay began to cry, and Ann held her tightly: it was her turn to comfort her daughter.

'My poor darling. Why didn't you tell me?'

'Because there's more. He lied to me. His wife turned up, you see, a couple of weeks ago. I didn't know he was married. Not only that, he had three kids too. I couldn't have mine and she'd got three.' Fay blew noisily into her handkerchief. 'He hadn't left her, you see. He'd lied to her and said that he had to spend several weeks in London on a job. He was with them at Christmas and New Year . . . I thought he'd gone to his parents.' Fay began to sob again.

Ann held her daughter close, conscious of how thin she seemed through the fine silk of her T-shirt. She felt frustrated by her inability to do anything but hold Fay and kiss her. She felt ashamed at the way she had been relying on Fay, when all the time she had been holding this great burden of pain and grief within her.

'If only I had known about his wife sooner, I'd have had the baby. I could have managed. I only did it because of him, and because I wanted to keep him.'

'Fay, there's nothing I can say to help you, I wish there was. But I'm always here, darling, if you need me, you only have to call, you know that.'

'Yes, Mummy. I know it's my problem. I know I'll get over it. It's helped just telling you, I haven't told anyone else, you see. I didn't know anyone I could trust.'

Ann smiled at her daughter tenderly, marvelling at the closeness that there was between them these days, a closeness that had never been there before. She might have lost her son, but in his place was this trusting friendship she had built with her daughter.

'Oh, this is silly.' Fay sniffed, stood up and crossed to the dressing table. 'God, I look a bloody mess. Have you set the date yet?' she asked suddenly.

'No, not yet.' Ann played with the silk counterpane, feeling uncomfortable at her daughter's question. 'Alex is so busy these days,' she said vaguely.

'Of course. How's the new house coming along?'

'Oh, wonderfully. It should be finished soon after Easter. It really is going to be super. There's a flat on the top floor, I'm sure Alex wouldn't mind if you came to live there. I'd like that. Would you like me to ask him?'

'It's sweet of you, but no thanks. I love my flat and in any case I'd get jealous seeing you two mooning over each other all the time.' Fay laughed. 'Don't worry, Mummy, I'll get over it.'

'Well, the offer's there. If you're sure you're all right now, I must go down. The Greek Ambassador's due any minute.'

'Nigel seems nice,' Fay said, spraying herself with scent from one of the bottles on Ann's dressing table. 'Is he here?' she asked, trying another bottle.

'Oh, yes. Nigel's always here,' Ann replied, looking searchingly at her daughter.

2

Easter approached and Ann wondered how she should plan for it, knowing now that, to a Greek, Easter was as important as Christmas was to the English.

A couple of weeks before Good Friday Alex woke her with a kiss. This was unusual, he was normally working by six and it was always Elene who woke her and brought her early-morning tea.

'Wake up, lazy bones!'

'No, Alex, go away. I'm not awake.' She pushed him away, limply, still drugged with sleep.

'I wasn't suggesting that we make love!' His loud laugh made her put her head under the pillow.

'Then leave me alone and let me sleep,' she mumbled.

'If you insist, but it seems a pity to miss your own wedding.'

She was awake in an instant and sitting bolt upright. 'My what?'

'One o'clock at the Registry Office,' he announced.

'You didn't tell me.'

'You agreed that I should make the arrangements, so I did. I wanted to surprise you.'

'You've done that. Oh dear, we shouldn't have slept together last night, we shouldn't even have been under the same roof. It's unlucky, you know.'

'It's not a proper wedding, our proper wedding will be in Greece,' he said, brushing her superstitions away.

'It might not be a proper wedding to you, but it certainly is to me. Look at me. My hair, my face.'

'You look lovely. This morning, Madame, you have something to eat. I will not have you fainting and everyone saying it's a shotgun wedding. I'll send Elene in with your breakfast.'

Alone in the room, Ann sat, her arms looped about her knees, and tried to come to terms with his announcement. She might have left the arrangements to Alex but she had not realized that this would entail not being told when the wedding was to take place. She would have liked to have her hair done, to have a facial, a myriad things.

'Madame, isn't it exciting?' Elene said, crossing the floor, carrying her breakfast tray. 'Mr Georgeopoulos says I'm to make sure you eat everything.'

Ann groaned at the sight of the cooked breakfast. 'I could have done with a bit more warning,' she said petulantly.

'Oh, Madame, I think it's so romantic this way. Almost like an elopement. Look,' she said and produced a lovely lace handkerchief from some tissue paper. 'It was my grandmother's, so it can be something old and something borrowed.'

Ann spent the whole morning getting ready. These days she had only to go to the hairdresser's to have her highlights retouched. Elene kept the short cut in shape as well as any hairdresser. Elene gave her a manicure and by twelve thirty she was dressed. She had had her pale grey Yves Saint-Laurent suit hidden away for weeks. She looked at herself in the mirror, turning from side to side, studying herself from every angle. Now she wondered if she should not have chosen something a bit more bridal than this plain suit with its almost military cut. It was too late now, she decided, gathering up her handbag and gloves. If he did not like it, undoubtedly, Alex would tell her.

She presented herself to her bridegroom.

'Such an elegant woman I'm marrying,' he said and kissed her.

As they rode to the Registry Office Ann began to realize how nervous she felt. She had been too flustered all morning for nerves to take hold. But now . . . She felt quite exasperated with herself, wondering what on earth she would find to worry her today. She was growing used to her new self and the endless doubts and suspicious. She sighed.

'You're quiet. Having seconds thought?' Alex asked, taking her hand in his.

'Of course not. What on earth gave you that idea?' she replied defensively.

'I often think you have doubts about our relationship.'

'Oh, Alex, that's not true,' she said quickly, too quickly, she realized.

'Isn't it?' He looked at her. 'I love you, Anna. I shall never leave you, you know.' Gently he peeled back her soft suede glove, kissed her hand and held it to his cheek.

Ann felt shamed by the disloyal thoughts she had allowed herself recently, and smiled at him. 'I love you too, Alex, for ever.'

She had expected the Registry Office to be full of friends. She was disappointed to find only Yianni and Nigel Salisbury waiting to be their witnesses.

The ceremony was over so fast and, with only Yianni and Nigel to congratulate them afterwards, she did not feel married, in fact felt no different at all.

'Where are we going? To lunch?' She asked as they sat in the back of the Rolls-Royce.'

'Lunch? How prosaic. We are off on our honeymoon, of course.'

'Where?'

'To Greece.'

'But I've no clothes. And I meant to phone Fay.'

'Elene has seen to all that. She's at the airport. And I'm sure Fay can survive a few weeks without a telephone call from you.' He smiled.

'But I call her every day,' she said with a worried expression.

'There are telephones in Greece you know,' he teased, but seeing her expression, his changed too. 'Is there something wrong? Is Fay all right?'

'Of course. It's just a habit we've got into,' she lied.

Ann kept in close contact with Fay. Although the girl appeared to be all right Ann was not taking any chances. There were days when she thought she sensed a slight irritation from Fay at her solicitude but it did not deter her. She had thought long and hard about telling Alex what had happened. She had finally decided not to mention it. She knew him now, and was certain that he would have moved heaven and earth to find the man and in some way make him pay for his deceitfulness. Ann felt it was better for Fay if the whole sorry incident were forgotten.

The car arrived at Heathrow. Nothing about Alex surprised Ann any more, so she was not unduly taken aback to find that the plane which was to take them to Greece belonged to Alex, a large AG emblazoned on its fuselage. What a world she had moved into, she thought, that he had not even thought to mention he owned his own jet. Ann looked about the luxuriously appointed interior and decided there and then that this was the only way to travel.

Alex smiled at her as she kicked off her shoes and curled up in the enormous armchair and wished that Lydia could see her now. She clipped the seat belt on and as the plane hurtled down the runway contemplated with pleasure the thought that at last she was to see

Greece, a country which had always fascinated her – even more so now.

A honeymoon. Perhaps once they were there, alone, she would begin to feel properly married.

The plane levelled out. The door at the end opened and bearing trays of champagne and canapés, Yianni and Nigel entered. Ann frowned, vexed at their appearance. Was there never to be any let-up? Were they never going to be alone again?

The plane landed at Athens airport. As the door opened Ann was unprepared for the blast of heat, even at this time of the year, that bounced and shimmered off the tarmac of the runway and enveloped her like a warm embrace. In her wool suit she began quickly to feel uncomfortable. But not for long. Once she was sitting in a large air-conditioned Mercedes she was cool again. The car was soon battling through the hurly-burly of Athenian traffic.

Ann sat forward, eagerly, anxious to see everything.

'Is that really the Aegean?' she asked as they swept along the coastal road past the endless strings of tavernas, nightclubs and outdoor restaurants opening up for the season.

At her first sight of the Parthenon rising majestically over the teeming, dusty city, she gasped as millions of people had done before her.

The car stopped in front of a large apartment block on the Leoforas boulevard. She did not know why, but she had presumed that Alex's Athenian home would be in an old building, not this gleaming, modern apartment block. But then she had not expected Athens to be as modern as it was either.

The doorman in the large, echoing marble hall jumped to attention as Alex approached. They were swept up in a spacious lift and entered a large triplex apartment where marble floors with an astonishing shine spread before them. Alex led her on to a wide balcony – the ubiquitous marble stretched everywhere.

'Welcome to my city,' Alex said dramatically, spreading his arms wide to encompass the view. Across the city the Parthenon loomed, protectively, on its large rock, seeming to glow in the bright sunshine. 'In the old days, before the smog got so bad, you would see the sea and Piraeus clearly, but sadly it's difficult now.'

The roar of the traffic even at this height was deafening. The wide boulevard below was chocked with cars, buses and trucks.

'It's a noisy city.'

'Never sleeps,' he said happily.

She turned back into the large drawing room. Enormous traditional crystal chandeliers hung from the ceilings, at odds with the modern surroundings. The room was a strange mixture of furniture – some antique, some modern – and an assortment of over-carved and overstuffed heavy mahogany pieces. A large bowl of fruit turned out to be plastic as were the flowers in the large vases. Every chair, every table had a crocheted antimacassar on it, giving a homely and cluttered look to the room. It did not look as if this place could possibly belong to Alex.

A short, stout woman with yellow-orange hair appeared in the doorway. She stood rigidly, her body restrained by a tight-fitting corset so that only her head and upper torso moved freely. Above the corset rolls of fat struggled to be free. Her eyes were covered by tinted spectacles which were not dark enough to camouflage their suspicion, or the dark shadows that ringed them. Ann felt uneasy as the woman approached.

'Darling, meet my sister Ariadne.'

Smiling, Ann held out her hand in greeting.

'How do you do.'

'*Kali spera*,' answered a deep gravelly voice, more like a man's than a woman's.

Immediately Alex spoke sharply in Greek to his sister, who answered back at length. Alex began to shout. Ann took his hand in a vain attempt to stop him. He ignored her. The sister screamed words venomously at him. Shaking with anger, Alex turned on his heel and, still holding Ann's hand, without explanation marched with her out of the room, across the hall, up the sweeping staircase and into a large shuttered bedroom. The furniture was covered in dustsheets, the bed unmade. Alex went to the door and roared like a bull. Two young girls dressed entirely in black, large fur slippers on their feet, appeared. Alex shouted and gesticulated angrily at them. Their eyes wide with horror, they scuttled about the room removing the dustsheets, disappearing and reappearing with bed linen while, perplexed, Ann stood in the middle of the room. One girl carried in an arrangement of plastic flowers which Alex snatched from her hands and hurled down the marble corridor, the vase shattering on the floor. He followed the vase and Ann was left alone.

Timidly Elene appeared with Ann's cases.

'What the hell's going on, Elene?'

'Well, I'm sorry but I couldn't help overhearing . . .'

'Don't apologize, Elene, I should think the whole of Athens heard that.'

'Apparently, Madame, Ariadne is insisting you and Mr Georgeopoulos sleep in separate rooms.'

'What?' Ann burst out laughing. 'Separate rooms? Alex?'

'Exactly, Madame. He wasn't very happy with the idea. He doesn't like plastic flowers either, it seems.' The maid smiled shyly at her.

'But Elene, why?'

'It seems Madame Ariadne doesn't regard you as married and what with Easter coming . . .'

Ann was not too sure what Easter had to do with it. 'But doesn't she know we were married this morning?'

'Yes, but not in the Orthodox church and not in Greek law. So, in her eyes you're still not married,' Elene said apologetically.

'I don't believe it.'

'Presumably she's very religious, Madame.'

'Presumably. Ah well. Should we unpack?'

'I don't know, Mrs Georgeopoulous. I will if you wish.'

'Just unpack the blue linen for tonight, and my make-up. Perhaps we'd better wait with the rest.'

Elene began her task and Ann explored their rooms. Not only was there this bedroom, beautifully furnished in white and chrome, but they each had sumptuous bathrooms and dressing rooms. A short corridor led to a large sitting room opening through sliding doors on to yet another marble terrace which interlinked with their bedroom terrace.

But it was the paintings on the wall that most took her attention. Not only was there a Monet but a Pissarro and a Lautrec. Along one wall was a collection of paintings by artists she had never heard of.

Ann knew little about art and its techniques, apart from the little she had taught herself, but this was one area where Ben's self-effacing wife had always had an unerring confidence. These canvases attracted her. There was a boldness in the shapes and the use of colour which, with her own timid use of watercolour, she admired. One, painted in black and white, was relieved only by a great slash of red – the red dripping from a large knife in the hand of a minotaur. But a minotaur who by his stance appeared distraught and ashamed by the blood on the blade. It made her skin prickle as she peered closely at it, studying the technique. As so often, she marvelled that paint on canvas could evoke such emotion in her.

She looked about the room and thought, if this were her room, she would move the Impressionists. These modern paintings were too strong to hang in the same room as the others. It was almost as if they were sucking out of the subtle Impressionists the colour and body with which to stoke their own furnaces of strength.

The maids scuttled back into the room and as they skated across the marble floors on their large fur slippers Ann realized why the floors shone so brilliantly. She could only smile at them, the few words that Elene had taught her had deserted her.

Large vases of fresh flowers in cut-glass vases appeared and were placed around their rooms. Fresh fruit in crystal bowls was brought in.

Still Alex did not appear. Ann decided to bath and change. In the bath she had a fit of the giggles. It was so large, with steps leading down to it, that once it was full she found she could float in the warm water, and had virtually to dive for the soap when she dropped it.

She changed into the long, dark blue linen dress, the blue highlighting the colour of her eyes and making her hair look blonder. Around her neck she slipped several long gold chains, and then clipped on gold stud earrings. It was difficult to know what to wear, how formal Alex's sister was – this outfit, she felt, was a good compromise.

In the cool sitting room Ann sat and waited for Alex. She had explored every nook and cranny of it; there was nothing to do now but wait and worry about whether he and his sister were still arguing.

She had presumed that she would have to make adjustments in this foreign land, that just as his family would be strange to her, she would appear strange to them. However, she had not expected problems to appear so quickly or so dramatically. But worst of all was not knowing what these particular problems were.

She shivered. The air-conditioning was making her feel chilled. She crossed the room and with a struggle opened the sliding glass door, a door which had obviously not been opened for some time. The warm night air rushed in, and as at the airport seemed to take hold of her. She stood for a while on the terrace watching, far below, the noisy traffic which was inching laboriously past so that the air was full of petrol fumes and an unfamiliar smell of resin which would be lodged forever in her mind as the smell of Athens.

It was over an hour before Alex reappeared. 'My darling. I am so ashamed that my sister should insult you in our home. I can't think what to say to you.'

'But darling, it's all right, really, it's not your fault.' She was relieved to see him in better humour.

'You don't understand, my darling. The obligation of hospitality is like a religion in this country. My sister has been insufferably rude, I shall never forgive her completely. But we have had a long talk.'

'Alex, don't worry. Elene explained it all to me. You must respect your sister's religious principles.'

'Religious principles!' Alex snorted. 'She's jealous, that's all.'

'Jealous? Of me?' Ann said in disbelief.

'I'm afraid so.'

'Now we're quits. You with Peter. Me with Ariadne,' she said, shaking her head.

She followed him into the bathroom and sat in an armchair watching him as he stripped to bathe.

'I think you only married me for my body.' He grinned at her, noticing her admiring look.

'Of course. What else have you to offer?' she parried.

Back in their sitting room Alex said they had time for a drink before dinner. Ann was relieved to hear him mention food. She was starving, she had had nothing to eat since their light lunch on the plane. While he poured the drinks she looked again at the paintings. 'These paintings are wonderful.'

'Which, the Monet? The Pissarro?'

'Of course they're wonderful. But it's these which interest me,' she said, pointing at the wall of unknown artists.

'It's my hobby.'

'You paint?' She sounded surprised.

246

'No. I collect. Anyone can buy established artists, I like to search out lesser-known, sometimes unknown painters – help them along. Let them have some money while they're alive. Help to make them famous.' He looked pleased at her interest. 'Do you really like them? Would you like to take them back to London? Would they suit our new home?'

'But what would your sister say if her pictures suddenly started disappearing from the walls?'

'It's all mine, I take what I want.' He gestured with his hand at the paintings, the room, the contents.

'We'll see,' she replied diplomatically. 'The minotaur is my favourite. Such a sad monster, I want to love him better.'

'That's by Renos Loizou, a young Cypriot. He has enormous talent and is doing very well now. He will be very famous one day.'

'Do you buy them as investments?' she asked guardedly.

'Of course not,' he said indignantly. 'I only buy them if I like them. But my darling, it's getting late. Are you hungry?'

'I'm starving. It's nearly ten.'

'Ah, this is Greece – it's uncivilized to eat too early. We'll join my sister.' Quick to notice her change of mood, the expression of disappointment tinged with anxiety, he added, 'She will be over her tantrum by now. After dinner I will take you out to see Athens by night.' He took her hand and reassured her by squeezing it.

They descended the long sweeping staircase. Ann would not have minded in the least if Ariadne were still sulking. They might have been living together for months but she would have preferred Alex to herself on her wedding night. She had heard that Greek families were close but this was taking things to extremes, she felt.

Ariadne was waiting for them in the hallway, her stocky figure still dressed entirely in black, heavy gold jewellery around her neck, her fingers weighed down by equally heavy and elaborate rings. The red gash created by her lipstick contrasted dramatically with her sallow complexion. Ariadne nodded and led the way into the dining room. Brother and sister sat at either end of the long, bulbously carved table. Ann felt isolated in the middle.

'It's so pleasantly warm,' Ann said politely to her sister-in-law. 'I hadn't expected it to be, so early in the year.'

Ariadne replied in a babble of Greek. Alex leapt to his feet, Ariadne followed. Within seconds brother and sister were screaming at each other. Cutlery and glass rattled as they both thumped the table. Anger filled the air. The young maid, wide-eyed, deposited a dish on the sideboard and dashed from the room. Ann looked from one to the other, a perplexed and exasperated expression on her face. They made such a noise that she would have liked to put her hands over her ears. Judging by their expressions they were both saying damaging, cruel things to each other, words that surely would never be forgotten. Ann had never seen such a family row as this. Ben had never shouted in this way. He had been expert at the well-timed word, the sarcastic phrase. She had hated the way he was capable of demolishing her with a comment, leaving her speechless with temper and unable to think of a reply until hours later. Now she thought that method might be preferable to this histrionic exhibition.

'Please. Stop this,' she implored, but neither appeared to hear her, as they concentrated on their verbal destruction of each other.

Alex, with a final, louder bellow, strode towards Ann. He took her hand, dragging her to her feet, her chair clattering backwards on the marble floor, her glass of wine sent flying, and marched her from the room.

Alex ordered the car. All the way down in the lift he muttered to himself in Greek, banging one fist into the palm of his other hand with frustration. Ann did not know what to do or say. If she said something, would it exasperate him more, make matters worse? She opted to remain silent.

He dismissed the chauffeur and drove the car out into the traffic. The other cars might be static in the traffic jam but not Alex, he swung the car on to the pavement, slid into the narrowest spaces, drove the wrong way up one-way streets. The air was thick with car horns blaring, the threats and abuse of the other drivers impotently gesticulating their anger at Alex. She clung to the door handle, closed her eyes, and prayed.

'Would you prefer to go out of town?'

'Sorry?' Her eyes blinked open.

'We can go to the old part of the city, along the coast or up into the mountains.'

'The old part sounds lovely.' She smiled weakly. And not so far to travel, she thought.

He grinned. 'I feel better now. There's nothing like a good tussle with the Athenian traffic to put me in a good mood.'

'I suppose if you survive it, you're just glad to be alive,' she said with feeling. Alex laughed loudly, throwing his head back with delight.

'You'll get used to it,' he said, patting her hand.

They left the car on the edge of the old city, the Plaka, in the care of a young child who, Ann fretted, should long ago have been in bed. Ann clung on to Alex's arm as they made their way up the steep narrow streets, her high heels catching in the uneven stones. The whole area was alive with people, noise, laughter, music, and everywhere the mouth-watering smell of food on charcoal grills.

They finally arrived at the taverna of his choice, and settled on uncomfortable rush chairs. Ouzo was produced, plates of mézé, and bread. Alex studied the menu, the script as strange to Ann as hieroglyphics. The patron was summoned and consulted but unable to decide, Alex led Ann into the kitchen to select from the great vats of bubbling food.

Lydia had told her the food would be awful but in fact Ann loved the marinaded octopus and the stiphádo which Alex finally chose. She was less sure about the retsina, and he ordered her French wine, good-naturedly complaining at the unnecessary expense and declaring her a failure for refusing his national drink. She told him she would do anything for love of him except drink his wine.

Musicians came to play for them, strange music still unfamiliar to Ann's ear, almost, but not quite, Arabic. A gnarled old flower seller sold them flowers. A goat appeared, wandering from table to table like a tame dog. There was no isolation in this taverna, jokes were shared from table to table, witticisms flew back and forth like a tournament in speech. Singing started and everyone joined in. Alex dutifully translated for Ann, but she vowed, more strongly this time, to learn this language, so that she could be a real part of a scene like this.

It was the small hours of the morning when they made their way from the taverna back down the steep roads. On the bonnet of the car the young boy lay asleep. The expression of incredulity on the boy's face at the size of his tip made them both laugh as the child ran swiftly away, obviously afraid that Alex had made a mistake and would want the money back.

Braced for a terrifying return journey Ann was relieved to find that the traffic had thinned and they drove back to the apartment almost sedately.

In their bedroom, Ann sat down wearily on the bed, kicking her shoes off as she did so.

'Wait there,' he ordered.

'I've no intention of going anywhere,' she sleepily replied.

He returned carrying a large leather box. 'For you, my darling wife. Such a disastrous wedding day you have had. Perhaps this will make amends.'

Ann opened the box. Her hand shot to her mouth as she gasped with astonishment. The box was full to the brim with jewellery. Diamonds, rubies, emeralds and sapphires blazed at her in jumbled confusion.

'Oh, Alex, my darling. I feel like the Duchess of Windsor,' she laughed. 'How on earth do you say thank you for something like this? But I have nothing for you.'

'I don't need anything. I have you,' he said, gathering her into her arms.

3

The next morning, when they awoke, it was to find that Ariadne had gone from the apartment. Alex was furious with his sister. Ann was relieved for she had serious doubts that she would ever come to like Ariadne.

Over the next few days Ann met Alex's family. It took several days since the family was enormous. She was to discover that 'family' in this country was not restricted to the immediate members. Second and third cousins and their offspring were as important and as loved as those of closer relationship. If hospitality was a religion here, then 'the family' was the deity.

If Ariadne's welcome had been cold, the rest of the family made up for it with their exuberant warmth. From house to house, from one apartment to another, a gaggle of cousins, uncles and aunts awaited them. In the homes of the older generation they would sit at ornately carved dining tables, always covered with a lace cloth, the chairs hard and upright. At each visit sweetmeats, biscuits and cakes were served with small glasses of sticky liqueurs. It seemed his family could not sit to talk without food and drink before them. It was formal, uncomfortable, but their solicitude was touching.

In the homes of the younger generation they sat on comfortable chairs imported from Italy, with long low tables in front of them, and were served whisky and gin, but still the food appeared and Ann soon learned the offence she caused if she refused it.

Whatever age group was involved, Ann had to become used to an unashamed curiosity about her. There were no restrictions on this inquisitiveness. They asked outright the cost of her clothes, feeling the fabric as if they were professionals. They wanted to know if she bleached her hair. How old was she? Had her first husband been rich? A bracelet was removed and handed around the group and its value discussed in argumentative detail. And from the female members there was an intense interest in her inner workings.

At first she had felt offended by what she interpreted as rudeness. But slowly she began to realize it was a protective curiosity. If they asked the price of anything it was to check that she had not been cheated – a dreadful fate for a Greek. Enquiries about her health were to make certain that she was fit and well and in no need of a doctor. And their expression of admiration at the cost of each item was a form of compliment.

Ann was taken shopping. She had only to say she needed something and an expedition was arranged. Telephone calls were made and other cousins would appear. Noisily they would descend upon the small, exclusive boutiques in Kolonaki. Buying anything became a problem since none of them could agree what was best for Ann and invariably a noisy, but good-natured, argument would ensue. If one cousin remembered one boutique, the others would all suggest another. Consequently the shopping trips were long and frequently Ann returned empty-handed rather than offend.

These sophisticated Athenian women were amazed when Ann insisted that she wanted to go to the shops in the Plaka. She said she wanted to stand in the old Agora where Plato and Socrates might have sat and debated long before the Roman market had been built. Tch! They clicked their tongues against the roofs of their mouths – she would not find any philosophers there now, they laughed; cheating traders, noise, yes, but philosophers no! But Ann was adamant and an expedition to the old part of the city was organized.

As they clattered and chattered their way through the narrow, teeming streets, Ann would have preferred to be alone. Alone she could have dawdled her way about the alleyways, pausing to inspect the wares that tumbled out of the shops on to the pavements, and exploring the dark mysterious interiors. Instead she was led helter-skelter through this kaleidoscope of colour, noise and smells, for these women longed to get back to their own Athens, to have a coffee at Flokas, and watch the world go by, to invade their beloved boutiques on the hills of Kolonaki.

She dawdled behind them at a jewellery store, lingering over the bold distinctive necklets and bangles, toying with the idea of buying presents for Lydia and Fay. Shrieking contempt, her escort swooped back to scoop her up. She was told quite sternly that such rubbish was not for her – that Alex only bought gold from Zoltas, and she must do the same. She was disappointed, she had liked the jewellery, had thought it pretty.

An icon took her fancy. The cousins were even more dismissive than they had been over the bangles. Fakes, they were all fakes, they gesticulated noisily. Alex knew a professor of antiquities who advised him on such matters. Ann should consult him before making such a purchase. Reluctantly she had to leave the shimmering gold, scarlet and cobalt-blue painting which had caught her eye.

At the sight of a pretty rug, the colours glowing jewel-like in the relentless sunshine, Ann was determined she was going to buy it, no matter what they said. The merchant, his keen eyes watching like a bird of prey, stepped smartly forward, smiling expansively. Ann opened her handbag which, with one deft movement, was snapped shut by a cousin's hand and Ann was told imperiously to keep quiet. She watched bemused and uncertain as her entire entourage began to bargain for the rug. The cousins picked it up, examined it minutely, handing it from one to the other. It was found wanting. They sneered at it, threw it dismissively down, stood on it, wiped their feet on it, turned their backs on it. The shopkeeper wrung his hands with distress, tears formed in his eyes. Ann watched anxiously, imagining the ailing wife and children he was no doubt struggling to support. He held the rug in his hands, stroked the pile, held it to them almost in supplication – negotiations were resumed. Palms of hands were hit, hands were shaken – a deal had been agreed. Coffee was called for. It arrived, the copper jug and cups swinging dangerously on a tray suspended on chains from a young boy's hands. The cousins relaxed, elated that their bargaining had reduced the rug to half the price originally asked. Mysteriously the trader was transformed into the overweight, content merchant he really was. He smiled broadly, a mouthful of gold teeth proclaming his true wealth.

As Ann learned a lot from the cousins, she also learned not to admire anything, for if she did, it was immediately unpinned, removed or picked up and given to her. She was confused, rushed, and wished she could see more of Alex. She seemed to spend all her time with his female relations.

One afternoon as the city drowsed in its customary siesta, Ann asked if they could go to the Acropolis.

'Now?'

'Why not?'

'Because the siesta is for making love and sleeping, not clambering over old piles of rocks.'

'Oh, come on, Alex, you philistine. In London you'd have been having business meetings all afternoon – you never have a siesta there.'

He grinned, lazily picked up the phone, made several calls and then turned to her, putting his arms around her. 'It's all arranged, but not now – too many tourists. We'll make love instead.'

The following morning he woke her at four. 'Come, my love, wrap up warm.'

Mystified, Ann dressed and followed him. Outside the apartment block the long black Mercedes waited for them.

They droved through the darkened city but even at this hour there were cars about and lights, proving Alex's claim that the city never slept.

The car snaked through the narrow streets of the old city and stopped at the foot of the Acropolis. Taking her hand he led her to the entrance. A uniformed guard saluted them as he opened the barrier. In the dark Ann stumbled on the rocky ground as they climbed the steep slope to the Parthenon, the white columns glowing luminously in the fading moonlight. At the top they stopped.

'Now we wait,' he said, standing behind her, his arms about her, shielding her from the early-morning chill.

'For what?' she asked as she snuggled closer to him.

'For that.' He pointed as, far away on the eastern horizon, a slit in the darkness of night showed the dawn beginning to break.

The lovers stood silently huddled together, speechless with awe at the beauty of the day defeating the night as the sun rose, playfully flecking the sea with subtle pastel tones while at the same time painting the sky in raucous reds and golds.

The great temple in which they stood let go the ghostly sheen of the night. The silver columns changed from rose to mauve to yellow and gold as if the stone were absorbing the morning's gift.

Ann turned to Alex, tears streaming down her face. 'Alex, my love, I never saw anything as beautiful.'

He held her close to him. 'There are moments in life when the beauty and one's happiness is almost intolerable,' he whispered against her hair and she felt his cheek wet against hers.

His arms about her, his strength, the familiar feel of him and now the knowledge that this great, strong man could weep, filled Ann with a glow of security and peace.

They returned silently to the waiting car where the awakening city seemed to explode around them and the spell was broken. At the apartment they breakfasted on the terrace. The Parthenon was now its normal white, as if Ann had dreamed it was pink and yellow.

'I felt there as if we had reaffirmed our love – only more strongly,' she said.

'It's a magic place.'

'But how did you manage to get us in?'

'Oh, hadn't you realized how important I am?' He laughed self-deprecatingly. 'Anything's possible. I wanted you to see it alone with me, not with hordes of people about. It's a place for the meeting of souls.'

At last Good Friday dawned. Ann was filled with curiosity for the great festival ahead. The noisy city was strangely silent. It was as if a blanket of mourning had settled upon the inhabitants, as if each family had lost someone dear. For once the phones stopped ringing, no cousins noisily clattered about the apartment and, strangest of all, Alex did not want to make love to her.

In the middle of the day Ariadne reappeared in the drawing room – still dressed entirely in black. Ann sat edgily waiting for Alex and his sister to start shouting at each other. Instead Alex crossed the room, his arms outstretched to his sister, who fell sobbing into his arms.

'I couldn't be away from you at Easter,' Ann's astonished ears heard Ariadne say in perfect English.

'Yes, yes, little sister. Don't worry. Everything is going to be all right.' He patted her gently as one would comfort an upset child.

'Anna, I must apologize for my behaviour. It is an emotional time . . .' Ariadne turned her tear-streaked face towards Ann, making no attempt to smile. Her apology sounded automatic, insincere. Ann could only presume that Ariadne had forced herself to say sorry to her in order to ingratiate herself with her brother again.

'Of course, I understand.' Ann smiled at her sister-in-law, understanding nothing, least of all why she had pretended earlier to speak no English.

They ate fish baked with no oil. Drank no wine. The depression within the apartment, that cloaked the city too, began to filter into Ann's mind. She felt a deep sadness. She had mistakenly presumed that a Greek Easter was going to be a happy time, not this unrelieved dejection.

She sat in Ariadne's over-furnished sitting room and listened to Alex and his sister talking endlessly of the past, about their parents, her dead husband, dead friends. Ariadne waded through a box of Kleenex as she wept and sobbed and moaned and cursed the cruelty of life. Ann felt very alien.

But on Saturday the normal cacophony of the city rose to their apartment. Ann, for the first time since she had met Alex, was even relieved to hear the phones ring again. The little maids in their furry slippers again scurried about the huge apartment. The change in Ariadne was dramatic. She bustled about the flat, in and out of the kitchen, noisily issuing orders, but smiling now, and singing, as a great feast was prepared. It was as if the sadness of the day before had never happened.

That night they made the long walk up Lykabettos to the Byzantine church which crowned the top of the little mountain. In the darkened church the chanting sent a chill down Ann's spine. As midnight chimed the priest lit a candle, inviting the congregation to light theirs, those at the front passing the candle to those behind. Soon the church was a blaze of light.

'*Christos anesti,*' they shouted.

'What're they saying?' Ann whispered.

'Christ is risen,' Alex replied, lighting her candle from his.

From the church a happy procession formed, winding its way down the hill like a long line of bobbing glow-worms – sending the message to the city below, to the world.

At the apartment the family had gathered; even the youngest children were shouting with excitement as baskets of red-painted eggs were brought in. Ann watched indulgently as Alex rushed about the room, a red egg in his hand, hitting other people's eggs with it.

'It's me,' he shouted triumphantly. 'I'm the lucky one for this year,' proudly displaying his unbroken egg as his family cheered his good fortune.

They began to eat and drink – without end.

The party went on unabated. Children just slept where they had fallen. By three Ann crept away to bed leaving Alex to enjoy his Greek family.

The whole of that weekend was a party so that there was no beginning or end to the various meals that took place. Visitors came. People slept. Upon waking they carried on where they had left off.

Ann was relieved when Easter was over.

4

'Get Elene to pack, we're getting married again,' Alex announced a few days after Easter.

'Again?' Ann laughed with disbelief.

'Properly this time. In Greek law we're not married, you see.'

'But where?'

'Ah, on my beautiful island, Xeros. Get ready quickly,' he ordered as he left Ann, gaping with surprise at this information, to her packing.

The suit she had worn for her London wedding was far too heavy for this country. And what did brides, who were widows, wear at Greek weddings, she asked herself. On Elene's advice she packed two fairly simple evening dresses: she would choose which one on the trip over. She wished he had told her about this wedding. She would have liked to buy something special, but she supposed she must get used to Alex's habit of wanting to surprise her.

Elene packed her cases in a quarter of the time it would have taken Ann herself. And she knew that, at the other end, everything would come out of the cases fresh and uncreased rather than the crumpled bundles they mysteriously became when she packed for herself.

The car drove them to Piraeus where at the dockside a large gleaming white motor yacht awaited them.

'Yours?' she enquired, quite blasé now at what he might possess.

'No. Borrowed from a friend. A boat is the last thing on this earth this ex-sailor wants to own.'

It was only on the outside that the vessel resembled a boat. Once aboard, in its air-conditioned luxury, it was easy to believe one was still on dry land.

A white-suited steward led the way through a large saloon, the plate-glass windows of which were draped with ornate silk brocade curtains and pelmets. Their feet sank into the plush wall-to-wall sea-blue carpeting. They wove their way between a clutter of occasional tables, each laden with a bric-à-brac – gold snuff and cigarette boxes, what appeared to be Fabergé eggs and, dotted everywhere, smiling photographs in heavily embossed gold frames of their host with celebrities ranging from the Queen of England to Rod Stewart.

They passed through double mahogany doors into an inner courtyard ablaze with orchids around a sparkling fountain spurting from the mouth of a gold dolphin, the water splashing into a lily pond full of sleek carp whose natural golden scales seemed dull beside the glistening sheen of the artificial dolphin.

They were led along chandeliered passages, hung with priceless paintings, until finally they entered their cabin, which was a misnomer for the large, extravagantly furnished room into which they were shown.

She peeped into the bathroom. 'Alex, look at this. Is that mink on the walls?'

'Undoubtedly.'

She lifted an ornately carved soap dish – fat, solid gold cherubs holding the soap aloft. 'Gracious, even the bog brush is gold,' she exclaimed, laughing.

'But of course.' He smiled at her incredulous expression.

She prowled about the suite of rooms. Every surface was of onyx. Wherever possible, everything was heavily gilded. If silk was not used as a fabric then fur took its place. The result was a heavy, claustrophobic feeling. She stopped to inspect a painting over the marble fireplace where a fire burned despite the heat outside.

'Alex. This is a Rembrandt,' she shrieked.

'Lovely, isn't it? Dear old Constantine, he's richer even than I am, but he's no taste as you can see. He's always afraid that people will not realize he's as rich as he is, and this is the result. You should see his villa, that makes this look quite restrained. Do you think you can stand the décor, just for one night? It's time to sail, I must be going.'

'Alex, you're not leaving me?'

'Yes. I shall fly out by helicopter. I want the first time you see my island to be from the sea. It's the only way to see it.'

'But . . .'

'No buts.' Imperiously he held up his hand. 'In any case, it wouldn't be right for us to arrive together.'

'It didn't bother you last time.'

'No, but this is Greece. This is our proper wedding,' he said grandly as he left the stateroom.

Left alone, Ann thought of the paradoxes that were Alex. Here in Greece there was another side to him. Here he drank heavily and frequently became noisily, riproaringly drunk – but in England she could not remember ever seeing him drunk. Here he would lie in bed all afternoon and spend half the night in the company of male friends, at cafés, playing backgammon, arguing politics, gambling – whereas in England they always went to bed together. Here religion seemed to mean something to him, yet previously she had never heard him mention any beliefs he held. And in Greece a family he never talked about in England was an integral and important part of him. And here, she thought, he was even more bossy than he was at home.

In England she had duties, the houses, the guests to entertain. But here, she did not have a set role. She spent more time with his female relations than she did with him.

The apartment was Ariadne's responsibility, and they did not entertain as they did in England.

Back home she had never felt she intruded if she popped in on a business meeting. On the contrary, everyone stood up in welcome as if her arrival were a pleasant interlude; Alex's door was never closed to her. But in Athens his door seemed firmly shut. The couple of times she had ventured in it was to find Alex and his cronies, sitting before cups of sweet coffee, clicking endlessly at their amber worry beads, even Alex flicking the beads back and forth like a personal metronome. Conversation ceased as she entered and no one stood. Business was for men, they seemed to be silently saying. Her role, apparently, was to be beautiful, available, a plaything, nothing more. It was not a role she had envisaged for herself. Here she felt outside his life, an observer. She began to think that, if they stayed, she would lose him. There was so much she did not yet understand about being Greek, and especially being a Greek woman.

The engines of the yacht began to throb and brought Ann back to the present. She opened the sliding door that led to a deck outside her stateroom and watched as the harbour of Piraeus, with the sunbleached pink, white and yellow buildings that cascaded down the hills to the docks, began to disappear to starboard. She stood a long time watching as the city, covered in its pall of dust, disappeared to be replaced by the untidy, free beauty of the coastline as the yacht ploughed serenely through the azure sea. It was a country of paradox – of dirt and dust and crystal clarity. Of noise and tumult and peace and tranquillity. No wonder Alex was as he was, springing from this strange, wild land.

Elene appeared, carrying a sheeted hanger at arm's length.

'What have you got there, Elene?'

Reverently the woman removed the sheet to reveal a rich dark cream, ruched silk dress, the bodice encased in seed pearls, the long full skirt billowing out like a crinoline.

'It's lovely, but it's not mine, Elene.'

'It is, Madame. Mr Georgeopoulos had it made by Devina, that designer who made your blue ballgown.'

'It's exquisite but . . . Elene, I don't think it's me, do you? It looks like a costume from *Gone with the Wind*,' Ann said anxiously.

'I'm sure you'll look lovely, Madame. And in any case, he chose it, so you can't hurt his feelings, Madame, can you?'

'No, Elene, I suppose I can't but I'd rather not have looked like mutton dressed as lamb.' Ann fingered the fine silk dress as Elene produced a large picture hat of the same material, with long ribbons flowing from the hatband. Seed-pearl-encrusted slippers and a matching small clutch-handbag completed the outfit.

Ann looked at the assembled clothes with horror. This was for a tall young girl to wear as she blushingly approached her groom. It was not for a small woman in her forties. What on earth had Devina been thinking of, allowing Alex to choose anything so unsuitable? The designer should have persuaded him to choose another model. But, Ann sighed, in fairness to the woman, who on this planet could dissuade Alex when he had decided what he wanted?

It was not just that the dress was unsuitable, it was more sinister than that, Ann thought. If he wanted her in a dress like this, did that not mean he was dreaming of a young bride? Was he attempting to make her into something she was not? Did it not indicate that subconsciously he wanted a younger woman? Perhaps this dress reminded him of his first wife. Maybe she had worn a dress like this on her wedding day. Good God, maybe he was trying to make her look like Nada. If only she knew what the woman had looked like. She had presumed that, as a Greek, Nada had been dark-haired but she had met blond Greeks, many with Alex's grey eyes. So, was there something in Ann that reminded him of Nada? Was that why he had spoken to her in the Tate, she wondered. Was she to presume that he was trying to recreate the past?

Once again Ann felt a shiver of jealousy for the dead woman. Just recently she had found she had been thinking less of her; was she now insidiously beginning to play an important part in Ann's life again?

This was ridiculous, this not knowing, she told herself. She would phone Ariadne tonight and ask her outright if she resembled Nada. If she did, if there was a glimmer of similarity, then the wedding was off. That was no basis on which to attempt to build a future: such a marriage would be doomed before it started. And Ann had no intention of being a substitute for anyone.

She brushed her hair angrily, hurting her scalp with the bristles. If she had any guts, she would not wear the dress. She should lie and say it did not fit her. She yanked at the hairbrush. But then, why should she lie? Why could she not speak the truth, say she did not like the dress, that it did not suit her? Ann laid the brush on the dressing table and studied her face in the mirror. What a mess she was in. She would probably do none of these things. She loved him. But most of all, she knew the reason: like everyone, she was frightened of Alex.

A steward knocked on her door to announce that drinks were being served in the forward saloon. Ann thought she was sailing alone, but there she found Ariadne and a gaggle of the aunts and cousins assembled and waiting for her. Apart from the crew there was not a man in sight.

As she entered the saloon, the women swooped upon her with cries and clucks of excitement. They fussed about her like hens about a chick. They joked, they made speeches, sang little songs. They spoke to her in Greek, as if they had learned the lines they were saying to her. They chose the food she was to eat. Ann felt she was playing a part in some ancient ritual of which she had no knowledge, which she could never comprehend.

Good-naturedly, Ann let them play with her. But soon the rituals, whatever they were, finished. The meal started in earnest and then Ann began to feel apprehensive.

Later, she could not remember who had started talking about virginity, though she thought it had been Ariadne. All the women joined in. With gusto they told her of rural villages where the guests still assembled under the bridal chamber window, waiting for the bloodstained sheets to appear, the virginal blood being a matter of honour to the bride's family as well as to the groom. They told her blood-curdling tales of vendettas between families when the bride had failed to bleed. They told her of brides murdered because they had previously lost that sacred virginity. She was puzzled as to why they told her, a widow, a mother, such tales.

Then, with great hilarity, they told of clever brides and the tricks they had played. Of sacs of chicken's blood secreted inside them. They spoke of doctors whose speciality was making false hymens to trick the stupid man. She learned of murdered brides, and family feuds when a bride came from a different village, was a foreigner in her bridegroom's tribe, how such marriages were doomed – in rural areas, they kept repeating. She listened to women speaking of men as the enemy. She learned that no man was faithful – only to his mother. They spoke of fierce matriarchal power and pride which seemed alien to her attitude to her own children. She began to realize that the fight for equality had been played for centuries here. That that fight bore no relation to the struggle in the West. She felt confused for none of these women spoke of love. It seemed to them that upon marriage all love ceased.

Sometimes the conversation would shift. But time and again it returned to the subject of virginity, a subject which seemed to fascinate these women far more than it did any man. And all the time they were smiling at her, being kind to her. Ann felt increasingly confused.

She remembered the beautiful dress hanging in her stateroom, thought of Alex, nervously twisted the stem of her glass and eagerly accepted another drink, wanting to staunch with alcohol the fears and doubts which she had thought she had conquered.

'Do I look like Nada?' she asked bluntly.

The clattering women ceased their noise. Several made strange sucking noises as their faces showed disapproval. Several crossed themselves and one cousin spilled her wine. 'Well, do I?' She looked at Alex's family who, as one, turned and faced Ariadne.

'You should not be mentioning Nada on this night,' Ariadne said, her face as rigid as stone.

'It's bad luck. It's sure to bring bad fortune.' An elderly aunt was wringing her hands with anxiety.

'I'm not superstitious. I want to know if I look like Nada. Will one of you tell me?'

'Not in the least,' Ariadne said in a businesslike tone. 'More brandy, anyone?' she asked, bringing the subject to an immediate halt.

Their conversation cranked up again. Ann had had enough. She excused herself and made for her stateroom.

That night she slept little. In the moonlight the dress loomed in the half-light. Marriage was complicated enough without the added complications of different races and cultures, she found herself thinking. Was that their game? Were they trying to tell her, wrapped up in jokes and gossip, that she was a disappointment to them all, that she should have been Greek and a virgin? Were they warning her that such a marriage as this was doomed? All Fay's assurances, all Fay's good sense, slipped from Ann, fled through the porthole and glided away across the Aegean.

She could not go through with it.

And then she thought of him, the way he made love to her, the tingling of her body when he touched her, the weakness of desire she felt when he looked at her, even in a crowd. She thought of the feeling of security she had in his presence, his care of her, his warmth and generosity. Did she really think she could live without him now? She tossed and turned. Go through with what? Was she losing her senses? It was too late for that. They were already married: in English law they were man and wife. This wedding ahead was just another ritual, an elaborate charade. They were already joined together.

In the half-light she lit a cigarette. It was this country which was creating the problems this time, not she. She would not have been worried about tales of virgins and bloody feuds in England; no such thoughts would have crossed her mind there. His cousins might all appear to be Athenian sophisticates but she began to wonder how long they had been like that, how long it was since they had left the villages of which they talked. She had been worried by a crowd of superstitious countrywomen, she decided.

The yacht steamed across the dark purple Aegean. Islands slipped by – large, mysterious, luminous mounds in the moonlight. She longed to be back in England – where he was the foreigner, not she.

5

The following morning the sun streamed into the state-room. It was a glorious day. The sunshine seemed to disperse the fears and shadows of the night before.

Ann stood in front of the full-length mirror while Elene fussed about her, straightening and patting the dress which fitted her perfectly. She slipped on the shoes and perched the large picture hat on her head. Her hair, now bleached by the Greek sun, was completely covered by the becoming hat, which framed her face to perfection. Ann's large blue eyes looked grave as she ruthlessly studied her image.

Certainly the shoes gave her extra height. And the designer had cleverly cut the dress to give her the appearance of being taller. The tight-fitting bodice, rigid with pearls, pushed her breasts high, so that they swelled voluptuously from the low, square-cut neckline.

She turned, the dress billowing about her, swishing and rustling as it did so.

'Well, Elene, what do you think?'

'Madame, you look wonderful. If I did not know better I'd say you were in your twenties.' Elene stood, her hands clasped together on her chest, admiring the woman before her.

Ann looked at Elene sharply for a hint of a sardonic look on her face, but there was none. Ann was far too modest about her looks to realize that the woman spoke the truth. She did look a young woman: it had not been too great an exaggeration. The sun had tanned her a becoming golden brown which glowed against the cream silk. The happiness of the past months had given a bloom to her complexion which totally belied her years. And that same happiness had given her eyes a clear sparkle.

She smiled at herself. All those fears in the night seemed silly now, in the light of morning. They had been an illusion.

Illusion. Ann stopped all movement at the thought. This dress was an illusion – that was what Alex had wanted to create. She shook her head, momentarily dislodging the beautiful hat. Why should he not? What was wrong with wishing to see her as the young bride she undoubtedly was in his heart – the young bride he had made her feel?

She anchored the hat more firmly, took one last look in the mirror, and with confidence stepped out on to the deck.

She stood, surrounded by the other women. All of them, with the exception of Ariadne, were now dressed in long brightly coloured silk dresses. The sea breeze caught at their skirts making them ripplelike multicoloured banners at a medieval joust, the contrast making Ariadne's plain black silk more striking. Ann was not the only woman transformed. The others in their finery had also shed years to become attractive maids of honour.

The island loomed on the horizon. As it drew nearer Ann began to feel nervous but it was the nervousness which any bride feels, no matter what her age.

Alex had been right, this was the best way to approach Xeros. The small island looked almost insubstantial as it floated gracefully on the sea – the strange purple and aquamarine sea she had read of. The grass was green, unburned as yet by the merciless summer sun, and the white-painted houses reflected its rays so brilliantly that it was painful to look at them. The island, with its houses, and the boats bobbing in the port, shimmered in the golden light like a desert mirage.

The boat edged fussily into the small harbour. The local fishing boats set up a welcoming cacophony of sirens and klaxons. Ann was led down the gangplank by her chattering companions. On the dockside stood a group of waiting women. Ann clutched at her hat, which a small breeze was attacking, and screwed up her eyes against the bright light.

'Mummy.' With disbelief Ann heard a familiar voice. She thought it must be her imagination until, from the crowd, she saw Fay pushing eagerly forward. 'You look like a fairy tale.' Fay flung her arms about her mother.

'Fay! What a wonderful surprise.' She hugged her daughter with excitement. 'I'd no idea you were coming. You don't think I look too silly, do you? At my age?' she asked her daughter abruptly. 'Alex had it made for me, I couldn't hurt his feelings,' she explained.

'Trouble with you, Ann, is you've never had enough confidence in yourself. Stop worrying. You look stunning. Positively virginal.' Lydia appeared from the crowd, her raucous laugh making a flock of seagulls panic into the sky.

Ann swung round, the dress billowing about her. 'Lydia! I don't believe it.' She shrieked with excitement, her hat knocked askew as she kissed her friend welcome. 'When did you come? How long have you known? I didn't know I was getting married until yesterday.'

'We've known for months.' Lydia smiled smugly. 'Alex swore us all to secrecy. He had us flown out yesterday, a whole planeload – what a party that was. Even Karen Rigson let her hair down and you should have seen the vicar, I swear he was as pissed as a newt.'

'The vicar? Karen?'

'Oh, yes. We're all here,' Lydia said airily. 'My dear girl, you're so popular in Midfield, a free bash, they've been queuing up claiming to be your best friend.' She laughed. 'Some, like us, came from Athens by boat. Some in helicopters – they've been shuttling back and forth all morning. I tell you, Ann, this is going to be one hell of a wedding. George was a bit green round the gills on the boat. I think he's afraid the sea water will get into his whisky – quite puts him off. But a couple of shorts put him straight.'

'Where *is* George?'

'He's away with the other men. We've been segregated. I tell you it's like being in a bloody harem – it's all too quaint, Ann. The other women are in the church, Fay and I were chosen by Alex to welcome you,' she said, almost proprietorially.

A child came forward shyly with a bouquet of gardenias, her little hands shaking with nervousness.

'Isn't it all romantic, Mummy?'

'I feel terrified. All these weddings, I do hope this is the last one.' She laughed shakily, accepting the bouquet from the curtseying child.

'It's important to us that you are married in my brother's faith,' Ariadne said, injecting a note of seriousness into the chattering welcome. Fay pulled a face behind the sister's back. Ann hurriedly introduced her daughter and friend to the Greek party.

'Is there a car?' asked Ann anxiously, still wrestling with her hat. The mischievous breeze seemed content to concentrate on her and nobody else.

'We walk,' announced Ariadne, introducing the other women on the quay who were from the island.

Supervised by Ariadne, they formed noisily into an untidy procession, the women on the quay lining up behind them. All along the way children ran ahead with baskets, strewing her path with flower petals.

They entered the village and here the procession grew larger. From out of the whitewashed houses, from dark alleyways, from tables in the taverna – leaving drinks half drunk – men and women, young and old, joined in until, by the time they reached the church, the line was several hundred strong.

After the bright sunlight Ann's eyes were momentarily blinded as she entered the dark church. As they became accustomed to the light she saw the little building was packed. Fat wax candles blazed, their light reflecting off the golden icons hanging on the walls, off the jewel-encrusted statues.

Ariadne led Ann by the hand to the centre of the church where Alex stood waiting with four male relations. The ceremony was majestic, moving and long. The bearded priest's incantations, in a fine baritone voice, reverberated round the church. They exchanged their rings. Ariadne placed on their heads golden crowns entwined with flowers and joined by long ribbons. Three times the couple walked around the altar for all the congregation to see Alex's new bride. Babies cried, children played, old ladies wept, and they were married.

Outside, the procession jubilantly re-formed with Alex and Ann leading the way. Children ran about them, little girls shyly putting out their hands to touch Ann – their eyes shining with wonder.

'Happy?' he asked, smiling down at her.

'I know, now, why you insisted on a Greek wedding. Now I feel I'm your wife – a ceremony like that makes one feel really married.'

'Me too. You see, I told you so, I told you this was a proper wedding.'

The procession slowly climbed a hill, the sun now beating down upon them, making it hard work. At the top he paused and, standing behind her, drew her to him.

'Welcome home, my darling,' he said quietly and pointed downwards.

Ann stood mesmerized. Below them in a small green valley, snuggling between two towering cliffs, was an ancient castle keep. Perched on the rocks, the sea swirling at its feet, it seemed to rise from the very depths of the gin-clear water.

'Alex,' she exclaimed at its unique beauty.

'This is what I regard as my true home.'

'It's lovely. But it doesn't look Greek.'

'My father's ancestors built it – they were Venetian merchants – that's why it looks so foreign.'

'Did you spend your boyhood here?' she asked eagerly.

'No, sadly. My father lost it in a card game long before I was born. It took me years of negotiations to get it back, by which time it was virtually a ruin. Now, at last, it's finished. You see, I couldn't bring you here until it was.'

'So that's why you waited to marry me?'

'Of course – it had to be here. I wanted it to be a surprise, so I had to keep it a secret. Did I worry you intolerably? Did you think I would never marry you?' he chuckled.

'I wasn't worried,' she blustered.

'Oh no?' he grinned, kissing her lightly.

Taking her hand he led her down the steep stepped path cut into the side of the cliff. Halfway down he paused. 'See there, I've made a dock for boats and there a helipad, there a swimming pool.'

She smiled at him, finding his pride endearing, and she admired everything.

They reached the building. Ann laughed as she saw, incongruously set in the huge oak door, a Yale lock. Questioningly, she looked up a him.

'Yes, from Midfield. I had it moved.' From his pocket he took the key ring she had given him at Christmas and solemnly opened the door and led her in.

It was one large room only. The rough-hewn walls were covered in jewel-coloured tapestries glowing in the light of great candles standing in large sconces on the walls. The enormous fireplace was full of wild flowers which tumbled out on to the hearth, their sweet scent filling the room.

They stood in the large hall and welcomed their guests. Half the village of Midfield was here, including Meg with her husband. Meg was beaming from ear to ear with excitement, not only at her first trip abroad but at seeing Ann again, and such a happy Ann. All Alex's secretaries, many of his friends, everyone she knew, it seemed, except the other half of her family, she thought.

'I did invite him,' she heard Alex say softly.

She put her hand in his. 'How is it you so often know what I'm thinking?'

'I've told you before, because I love you – because our souls are one. It's how it should be.'

The celebrations began in earnest. Ann had never thought that people could enjoy themselves so much nor make so much noise. Beside the keep Alex had had a modern house built, long, low and white, facing the sea and, in some strange way, the new and old married perfectly. The people spilled out from the great hall, into the open, into the new house, out on the terrace, perched on the rocks, sat in the boats – people were everywhere. The music, the dancing, the eating, the drinking and the toasting seemed set to go on without end.

'Are you tired, darling?'

'No, not at all,' she said. 'I'd really like to change though and get rid of all this money.' She looked down at her beautiful silk dress, probably ruined by now, since it was covered from head to toe in paper money pinned on by the Greek guests as she and Alex had opened the dancing. Alex's suit was the same. No one had warned her of this Greek custom.

'We do look funny,' she said. 'What on earth do we do with it all? I'm sure some of these people couldn't afford to give. This one here,' she indicated a five-hundred-drachma note pinned on her shoulder. 'An old lady gave it to me – she looked so poor,' she said anxiously.

'We can't give it back. They would be deeply offended. In a few months' time we'll get something for the village and then honour will be satisfied.'

He stopped speaking and there, among the noisy crowd, he looked at her with the dark look which penetrated her soul. His expression made the noise of the guests recede and she was aware only of him and the physical longing he had for her which shone in his eyes and which she knew was mirrored in her own. She felt her body responding as it always did to that look, no matter where they were. A pleasurable dull ache began to throb deep inside her.

'Come,' he said, there was no need for him to say more. Hand in hand they made their way quickly through the throng, ignoring the ribald comments of the young men as they disappeared into their suite of rooms and he locked the door against the world.

'Anna, my wife, at last.' He took her into his arms and began to kiss her with a strength that almost made her lose her balance. She responded to his urgent need for her, pressing her body against his. He became frustrated by the rigid pearl-encrusted bodice, the huge skirt. 'I can't feel you,' he said, his voice thick with thwarted passion. He began feverishly to undo her dress.

'Alex, gently.' She pushed him from her and swiftly unzipped the frock that floated to the floor so that she appeared to be standing on a silken cloud.

He stood, silent, looking at her in admiration. Her breasts were bare, her white silk stockings held up by the wisp of a suspender belt he had requested she wear for him.

'Anna.' It was almost a cry as he scooped her into his arms and carried her across the room – a large, airy white room, one wall of which was of plate glass opening on to a terrace which seemed to hover above the sea. The fine white lawn curtains undulated like the sails of a ship pregnant with the breeze from the sea. But she had no eyes for the room, only for him as he laid her on a bed strewn with sweet-smelling herbs.

Hurriedly he undressed; he straddled her body, his fine torso looming over her as he cupped her breasts in his hands and playfully caressed her nipples, laughing with delight as he saw the sparkling response in her eyes. She was already moist and ready for him: it was a response which no longer embarrassed her but rather filled her with pride.

Still he played with her breasts; she longed for him to touch her, feel her readiness, but he delayed. He was enjoying watching the mounting excitement in her eyes as her body began to undulate and rock beneath him.

'Alex, now. I want you in me,' she pleaded.

'No, not yet. This time has to be memorable.'

He leaned forward, his mouth on one nipple, sucking her. First only his soft sensuous mouth and then his tongue, relentlessly sucking harder and harder until she was screaming for want of him. First one breast then the other. She rocked back and forth feeling the hardness of him lying on her stomach, not wanting it there, but down and in her, riding deep, deep within her. She wanted the whole of him within her, to keep him safe there for ever.

Instead his mouth searched for her. Across her taut stomach, across her thighs, kissing, licking, breathing on her and then . . . then she was writhing with passion, holding up her hands, desperate to caress him, to hold him, to give him pleasure, but he resisted her, concentrating totally on giving her joy and gratification as he brought her to a body-cracking climax.

Only then did he penetrate her and he rode into her until she felt her whole body was part of him, just as she wished. Deeper and deeper he thrust into her, bringing her with him, as together they rose to that pinnacle where there is no light, no dark, no heat, no pain, no today and no yesterday, where bodies meet with souls and a whole universe, for a moment in time, disappears. Upon that pinnacle their bodies paused, were shaken by a tempest beyond their control. Together they cried out their love for each other. Together they subsided, exhausted, in each other's arms.

It had been different. After all the times they had made love this one time had been unlike any other – in its intensity, in the way they had plunged into each other's souls.

'I shall love you and care for you all the days of my life, Anna,' he vowed. She enjoyed the warmth of his body against hers, moved even closer to him and wondered why on earth she had wasted so much time in doubt and fear.

They both slipped into the dreamless, rejuvenating sleep that follows such passion.

Ann woke with a start. Her body was chilled. She sat up, her movement waking Alex. Lazily he picked a sprig of rosemary which had attached itself to her back.

'What are all these herbs for?' she asked, laughing as she picked them off both their bodies. 'They're most uncomfortable. You know, I didn't notice them before.'

'I don't know what the different herbs mean, but the village women put them there – to bring us luck, health, to make us fertile, to ensure we made a baby just now,' he said in a dreamy voice.

Ann looked at him quickly from beneath her eyelashes, unsure of the tone of his voice. 'How sweet. Wouldn't that be wonderful – to make a baby here, in this room, on this island?' she said almost breathlessly, never taking her eyes from him, waiting for his reaction.

'What do we need a baby for? We have each other,' he said matter-of-factly, sitting up and brushing the remainder of the crushed herbs on to the floor. 'If you're getting any maternal feelings I'll buy you a puppy,' he added, smiling at her, swung from the bed and crossed the room to the bathroom.

Ann lay, listening to the sound of the water. It had been thoughtless of her to mention a child, reminding him of the child he had lost – and the wife too. She tried to will the thought away. But it would not go. It persisted. Here on their marital bed the memory of his dead wife, uninvited, pervaded the room. Even on her honeymoon, Nada's memory invaded her happiness.

She lay looking at the ceiling. Why should it be this way? Ben rarely came into her thoughts these days, the memory of him was fading with the passage of time. And yet the memory of this woman, a woman she had never met, grew stronger, not weaker, as time went by. Would she always be there?

'And what are you thinking that brings such a frown to your face?' He had reappeared from the shower.

'I was thinking of Ben,' she said purposefully, wanting to hurt him, as the presence of his wife damaged her.

It was his turn to frown. 'Is he a suitable subject, today of all days?'

'I don't see why not,' she said airily. 'He's part of my life just as Nada is part of yours, isn't she?' But seeing his expression, she immediately regretted her spitefulness. The lines on either side of his mouth deepened with disapproval, the bitter look appeared in his eyes. She knew she had made him very angry.

'I think it's time you showered and we returned to our guests,' he said and taking her hand he pulled her roughly from the bed.

They returned to the party. But there was a distance between them which Ann knew was of her making. The party was still careering along at breakneck speed as people became drunker and wilder and, Ann realized, happier. She felt outside the party: a shadow had formed which she could not shake away.

The whole weekend the celebrations continued, stopping only as the participants snatched a few hours' sleep. Ann wanted it to end, she wanted to be alone with Alex, to try to repair the damage she had done. She was certain it was not her imagination that he seemed to be avoiding her.

As soon as the last guest had left, Ann began to try to recapture the mood which she had so negligently squandered.

'I'm sorry I mentioned Ben on our wedding night,' she said, having decided to attack the problem head on.

'It did not seem the right time or place.'

'I know, it wasn't. I was being stupid. Forgive me.'

'He's not part of your life any more, is he, Anna?'

'No, of course not. You fill it completely.'

'Why did you say it then?'

'I was jealous, I think. I'm not sure. You see, until I met you, I'd never been jealous before so I don't really know what it feels like. I just wanted to hurt you, I can't imagine why.'

'That sounds like a true case of jealousy to me,' he agreed. 'But jealous of whom, for God's sake?'

'Nada.'

'Oh, my darling. How ridiculous you are. As if I give her a moment's thought.'

'Honestly? she asked eagerly.

'Honestly,' he replied, so seriously that she allowed herself to believe him.

Another night, tentatively, she broached the subject of her wedding dress.

'How old was Nada when you married?' she asked as they sat on the terrace enjoying the warmth of the evening air and the sounds of the crickets which gave this group of islands their name.

'Eighteen, why?' he asked guardedly.

'Is that why you chose that dress?'

He looked at her, puzzled. 'The dress? I'm sorry, my darling, I don't understand.'

'You wanted me to be eighteen and a virgin.'

He laughed loudly at her. 'Rather an impossibility, I would have thought.' Seeing her serious expression he stopped laughing and he too became serious. 'Anna, I chose the dress because I wanted you to look like a queen. I knew you would never choose such a dress for yourself. But it was how I wanted you to look, romantic, my creation. You also, I might add, managed to look, if not eighteen, remarkably close to it,' he said, smiling proudly at her.

'Wouldn't this imply that that was really what you wanted deep down?'

'Anna, you see shadows where there are none. You invent them. You search for problems and fears to terrify yourself. You live in a past that has gone and should be allowed to die. Come into the present with me, my darling. Listen, I never wanted a young girl as a wife. If I had I would have married one. And as to taking virgins to my bed, I can think of nothing more boring. Where do you get these ideas from?' He sounded exasperated with her.

'Your sister and cousins, on the boat over, kept on about virgins and feuds between villages and goodness knows what else. I think, in a roundabout way, they were telling me that I wasn't suitable.'

'You probably are not to them,' she heard him say to her surprise. 'Marrying a Greek is probably engraved on their hearts. I don't pretend to understand such chauvinism nor the fixation of my countrymen with the virgin state. You didn't marry them, you married me, and to me you are perfect. In fact so perfect, I think I shall make love to you right now and shut all this nonsense out of your head.'

'Alex,' she remonstrated, laughing as he grabbed her and dragged her on to the floor of the terrace. 'Alex, what will the servants think?'

'Anna, I love you. Only an Englishwoman would be bothered about the servants at a time like this,' and he engulfed her in his arms.

For two precious weeks they were alone on their island.

The days drifted by as they swam, lazed in the sun, ate and drank. Ann could not remember a time when she had felt so happy.

They made love in the morning, the afternoon, the evening and at night. The three weeks passed in a cloud of passion, of renewed vows, of sensuous pleasure. Ann seemed to have an insatiable hunger for him which matched his for her.

'I seem to spend all my time on my back,' she laughed, curling her leg around him, toying with the hairs on his chest.

'What's a honeymoon for?' He lay beside her contentedly enjoying her caress. 'Complaining?'

'No, no. It's just . . .'

'What?'

'Oh, nothing.' She slipped from the bed, ran a bath and lay soaking in it. Ann had found herself a new problem to worry about. The trouble was that the more they made love, the more Ann wanted. And when they were not making love she found she was thinking about it all the time. If Alex was across the room, fully dressed, she would find herself imagining him naked, about to take her in his arms again. She was behaving like an oversexed teenager, not a mature woman.

He found her in front of the mirror studying her face. 'Why so thoughtful and serious, my darling?'

'I've got black rings under my eyes,' she said instead.

'Ah, that's good. The sign of a well-loved woman. In this country if your wife hasn't got dark smudges under her eyes then people think her husband is failing her.'

'You are funny.'

'It's true. Sex is a serious subject to us.'

'I think it's becoming so for me too,' she said almost shyly.

'Then you are becoming a true Greek.' He laughed as he gently kissed her.

6

They had been back in London for a fortnight. Ann stood in the newly painted and gilded drawing room of their house and waited nervously for Alex to arrive. As she rearranged a vase of flowers for the third time, she knew it was silly to feel so jittery – the house looked wonderful. But still she needed Alex's approval.

Absent-mindedly she fiddled with the flowers. She smiled to herself, knowing full well what had happened to her. Alex was the centre of her life. Should anything happen to him or their relationship, her own life would have no meaning. Once again she was 'the little woman' albeit on a grander scale. She shrugged her shoulders. Fay was right, she would probably never have survived out in the big world. But all the same, she had created this home on her own. Her choice, her decisions, something Ben would never have allowed. This was an achievement she could be proud of. She stepped back, finally satisfied with the flower arrangement.

The slamming of a car door brought her back to the present. She heard his footsteps running up the steps. Quickly she looked in the Chippendale mirror and patted her hair. Her heart thumped as his door key grated in the lock.

'Anna,' he shouted, appearing in the doorway, his face obscured by an enormous bouquet of his favourite red roses. 'At last, a real "Anna house" to come home to.'

Hand in hand they explored from rooftop to cellar. Each cupboard was opened. Each tap was turned. The china was inspected, the glass was pinged. The curtains were felt. The beds were bounced on, the lighting tested. Ann was glad she had worked so hard for perfection, for Alex's inspection was ruthless.

'It is perfect,' he announced finally. He rang the bell to summon Roberts and ordered champagne. 'Is there something you haven't told me?'

'I'm sorry?'

'That wonderful nursery – such lovely murals, the toys?'

'Oh, that. That's for my grandchildren when they come to stay.'

'Ah. I shall look forward to their visits. I shall enjoy

being a stepgrandfather – if nothing else.' He smiled at her but it seemed, to Ann, a distant smile. And she wondered if it was her imagination or did she hear regret in his voice for the child that might have been? She wished she had the courage to ask him what he was thinking, but as always, when the past might be the subject of his thoughts, Ann was a coward.

The moment passed. They moved into the dining room for their first meal in their new home.

After their Greek honeymoon and the excitement of the new house, they soon reverted to their English routine. The weekdays were spent in London and each Friday they went to the house in Hampshire. Each weekend the house was full of guests. Once again they were rarely alone and their time on the Greek island seemed to Alex like a dream.

Out of the blue, Alex announced that he no longer liked Courtneys. He intended looking for a new estate. The staff sighed, this was his third country estate already. Ann was aghast. She loved this house. Not just because of its architectural beauty and perfection but, more importantly, for the memories that it held of that magical first week together.

Alex, used to an acquiescent Ann, was surprised by the vehemence of her defence of the house as she tore up the glossy brochure of a larger and even grander estate. His sudden dislike of the Hampshire house was Ann's fault – she had been too successful in creating the right atmosphere in their London home; Alex complained that Courtneys was more like an up-market hotel. They finally reached a compromise – Ann was to redecorate and furnish Courtneys. If Alex liked the end result they would stay; if not they would leave.

It was a difficult task he had set her: for how could such perfection be improved? And, since the house was in constant use, it was difficult to fit in the painting and decorating that was required without causing too much disruption.

But as Ann was becoming a perfectionist in her appearance, so she was becoming adept at organizing, and the work was started with the minimum of upheaval.

He had always said that the house lacked a soul. It was its total perfection, she decided, which was wrong – everything to period as if the original owner had gone to the Sandersons and Maples of his day and furnished the house in one fell swoop. Houses evolved over generations. As each generation bought new items, it discarded, or added to those from the past. So Ann decided to make it a mix of styles and ages so that a Victorian chesterfield stood beside a Chippendale card table, in front of a modern Italian coffee table. The paintings became a mixture of the old and the new. It was a bold step to take and one that many purists frowned upon. But the result was a home rather than a museum and Alex approved. The household sank back with a corporate sigh of relief.

Once more the vast tentacles of Alex's business required that each month he had to travel. Remembering his warning that he could not stay faithful, Ann insisted on travelling everywhere with him. She had stopped wondering if the new emotion she felt was jealousy; now, she knew very well that it was. She guarded Alex. It was necessary. She had only to look at him in company to see the way women flocked to him like giant predatory moths about the flame of his wealth and sexuality. She remembered the times she had packed Ben's cases for him and seen him off without a second's thought, not a hint of jealousy. But then Ben had never given her cause for concern so she had never had any need for this uncomfortable emotion. She could not say the same for Alex who flirted outrageously with any female who came his way.

So, with two households to run, the travelling, her appearance to maintain, the necessary socializing and the alterations to the house, Ann was kept permanently busy.

Fay had suggested she take up a hobby but there was no time for hobbies in Ann's new life.

From having been nowhere, Ann went everywhere – Rome, Paris, Bangkok, Peking. She was never sure where each journey would end. Ann and Elene became geniuses at packing for any eventuality.

They were in Singapore when a telex from Nigel arrived telling Ann that Peter and Sally's new baby was a girl.

Ann immediately rang her son's home. Repeatedly she rang but there was no reply. She had to content herself with sending flowers. And she waited impatiently for Alex's business to be concluded so that they could return home.

On their return, Alex was dropped in the City for an appointment, and Ann chivvied the chauffeur to hurry home. She found a note from Sally thanking her for the flowers – there was no mention of the baby, her name, her weight. She listened, drumming her fingers, irritated with frustration, as the phone rang, unanswered, in her son's house. She glanced at her watch, and brightened up – of course, Sally was collecting Adam from nursery school. Without changing, she grabbed her handbag. Calling for her car she made for The White House and Hamleys: she would have time to buy something for the baby and still be in Cambridge by mid-afternoon.

She dawdled too long over her shopping, and it was four-thirty before she was driving at speed up the M11, the back seat of the car piled high with packages of baby clothes, cuddly toys and presents for Adam. She was beside herself with excitement. A baby! No family feud could survive the arrival of a new baby, she told herself.

The car swung into the familiar tree-lined road. The solid Victorian villas had now all been modernized. As her car passed house after house she glimpsed the green of back gardens through two small rooms knocked into one. They had made a good investment for Peter here, she thought. She smiled at the uniformity of the houses, all with Laura Ashley curtains, half with Austrian blinds and virtually all with CND stickers in the front windows. How noncomformist they liked to think themselves: how totally conformist they were.

Ann parked the car, got out, turned round and faced an empty house, a 'S O L D' sign stuck at a crazy angle in the front garden. The windows were curtainless; through them she could see the bare boards, the empty room.

Her slight frame stood rooted to the spot in the suburban street. The odd passer-by stared at her. She was unaware how incongruous she looked in these surroundings in her elegant Chanel suit, a cascade of gold chains glinting in the sunlight, the perfect hair and make-up, the Hermès bag and shoes – such elegance was rarely seen in this Cambridge street. Thoughts tumbled in her head in noisy disorder – something was dreadfully wrong. She felt her stomach churn, nausea begin to rise. Her hands shook as she fumbled in her handbag for her address book. She must have made a stupid mistake, she thought. She checked the number. There was no mistake, of course this was Peter's house, But why, where, when, what could she do . . .? A cat streaked across the road, a car's driver slammed on his brakes. The squealing of the tyres made Ann jump, interrupted the clutter of thoughts. Straightening her shoulders she marched up the path of the house next door.

A young woman opened the door, her welcoming smile disappearing to be replaced by a look of suspicion as Ann asked for Peter Grange's new address.

'Are you his mother?' the woman asked without preamble.

'Yes, yes. I've been away some time, you see. I had no idea they'd sold. Typical of Peter . . . You know how vague he is . . .' Ann said breathlessly, smiling urgently, wondering why she was explaining herself to this stranger.

'Then I don't know where he's gone,' the woman replied unpleasantly and slammed the door in Ann's face.

Bloody cheek, she thought as she hammered on the door which stayed resolutely shut. She stomped down the path, certain that she was being watched, and went up the path of the house on the other side. There the response was the same – the same look of suspicion as she identified herself, the door shut firmly in her face.

Ann got back into the car, fumbled for the key, switched it on, pressed far too hard on the accelerator as she wrenched the wheel round and shot out into the road, causing two other cars to brake and hoot angrily at her. She was too upset to notice either of them. She drove the car, far too quickly, back to London. The nausea had subsided to be replaced with a hurt that rankled. Her throat felt strained, fighting the tears she was determined not to shed. Her face became stony and within her anger took hold.

As the car hurtled down the motorway Ann huddled tensely over the steering wheel, muttering to herself, a litany of anger at her son – 'The ungrateful brat. Quite happy to take my money from Midfield and the furniture, spoke to me long enough to get that!' she fumed. She overtook a Porsche, the speedometer registering a speed she would never normally dare. 'He'd been planning this for weeks. No one sells a house overnight. How could he just walk out of my life when I've done nothing but try and build bridges between us? Did Fay know? Was she in the conspiracy . . . ?' She fumbled with the cigarette lighter, looked up and had to slam on the brakes as roadworks approached. Her heart was thudding, she felt dizzy – 'Calm down, Ann, you'll kill yourself at this rate,' she reasoned with herself, out loud. She continued her journey at a more sedate pace but her new speed did nothing to calm her anger.

At the house the first of the guests were arriving for dinner. They looked astonished as Ann, pausing to apologize, raced up the stairs to find an agitated Elene waiting for her to change. Damn, she thought, if only she had been a few minutes earlier she could have pretended a headache, but she had been seen, she would have to join them now. The dinner seemed to go on for ever.

Ann attempted to make polite conversation but it was difficult: she was too edgy, too furious, the memory of the 'S O L D' sign kept flashing into her mind. To get through the evening she drank too much, too quickly.

It was past midnight before she was at last alone with Alex. 'My brave darling, you looked so tense all evening.' He handed her a brandy. 'You should not have gone alone. Why didn't you tell me what you planned? I would have stopped you. Prevented this shock.'

Ann was too fuddled by drink and emotion to register that Alex knew where she had been. Had she thought she would have remembered she had not had an opportunity to tell him. Instead she launched into an account of what she had found in Cambridge and the sense of shame she had felt that afternoon when the doors had been slammed in her face.

'. . . As if I were a bloody criminal. I know those women know where he is. He'd instructed them not to tell me. How could he humiliate me like that?' she railed.

'Forget him, my love.'

'How? He's my son, for Christ's sake. I want to see my granddaughter. I've a right to see her.' She turned angrily to face him. 'How can you say anything so stupid?'

'But why humiliate yourself? Have you no pride? He has made it perfectly clear he wants nothing to do with us. He's never had the courtesy to reply to your invitations – nothing. You can hardly be surprised, Anna.'

'Pride can be a very expensive emotion,' she replied with spirit. 'But to disappear like that. And Fay's on a trip to Germany. There's no way I can find out . . .' She stood before him, twisting her hands in despair.

'66 Bathurst Terrace, New Town, Edinburgh.'

Ann swung round. 'You know. How do you know?'

'I know lots of things, my darling.'

'But why didn't you tell me? Why keep it a secret from me?' she asked angrily.

'It wasn't a secret exactly. I didn't know how to tell you without your being hurt. I don't want to hurt you, my love, so I avoided telling you. I wish I had now, then you wouldn't have rushed off like that without letting me know. I don't like it when you do that, Anna.'

'So you knew he had sold up?' she said, ignoring his implied criticism. She had no patience tonight with his continued demands upon her.

'Yes.'

'Fantastic. You knew and you hadn't the courtesy to tell me – his mother.'

'I've just explained why not, Anna. And I don't see the point in your being angry with me.'

'How did you know? How do you know so much about my son when I know nothing?'

'I made it my business to find out.'

'And isn't it my business too?' She was shouting at him. 'How dare you snoop about my family without telling me?' Enraged she poured herself another drink, not even bothering to ask him if he wanted one too.

'Darling, you're drinking too much, too fast . . .'

'I'll drink what I bloody well want.' Defiantly she took a large swig of the brandy, which made her cough. 'Why Edinburgh?'

'A new post, I gather, at the university. He became rather unhappy in the last one.' He smiled to himself. 'He got a good price for the old house and was able to buy a far grander one. Don't worry, your dear son is well housed. Your granddaughter weighed eight pounds two ounces at birth and her name is Emma Jane. Sally is well, the birth wasn't difficult. He's on the same salary scale but has an 80 per cent mortgage and so was able to invest money from the sale of the house. He has investments in ICI, Grand Met, Marks and Spencer – all very safe. He seems to be having a little flutter with Australian mining shares.' He laughed at the astonished expression on Ann's face.

'Don't, don't!' she shouted, putting her hands over her ears. 'How can you know these things?'

'It's very easy to find out anything you want about anyone. I thought I should know about your son.'

'Oh, Alex, that's horrible. That's spying.' Ann's shoulders began to shake.

'No, my love, I do it for you. I care nothing for Peter, or what happens to him. He's not worthy of your love. He is despicable to do this to you.' He tried to take her in his arms to comfort her. But Ann shied away from him, her eyes glinting with suspicion.

'You're behind this, aren't you? He never wanted to leave Cambridge, he loved it there. The problem with his grant, it was something to do with you, wasn't it? It was your way of taking revenge.'

'My darling, you talk like a mad woman. How can I influence a great university?' He spread his hands wide, his head on one side, questioning.

'I don't know how, I just know you did. You said that Christmas night you could ruin him if you wanted. I remember.' She turned a tear-streaked face towards him. 'Oh, Alex, how could you?'

He grabbed at her, forcing her into his arms. 'Whatever I do in this life, Anna, it's for you and your well-being. If he's in Edinburgh it will make it better for you. I know it will. Don't cry, my love . . . Try to forget. It's better for you to do so, really. He means only pain to you. Don't find him. Leave him. You have me, now.'

She clung to him, the strength of his arms about her comforting her as it always did. Her anger with him began to fade. She wiped her eyes with the back of her hand, like a child. He produced a handkerchief and gently mopped her face. She leaned against him, exhausted, empty of emotion.

'Yes, Alex. You're right. If this is what he wants, then he can have it this way. I don't have a son,' she said, controlling her tears.

That weekend Ann summoned, rather than invited, Fay to Hampshire.

'Did you know Peter was selling up and moving to

Edinburgh?' she asked before her daughter had time to get out of her car.

'No, has he?' Fay asked in an uninterested voice as she picked her bag off the back seat and swung out of the car. 'Excuse me, Mummy,' she said as Ann barred her way.

'Oh, come on, Fay. You two are as thick as thieves. You must know everything he does.'

The two women started walking towards the house. 'Well, I don't. I haven't seen Peter in months. He doesn't make me privy to everything he does,' Fay said sharply.

'I don't believe you.'

'Thanks. How charming.' Fay dropped her overnight bag on to the gravel. 'You going to carry on like this all weekend? If so, I'm not staying.'

'I need to get to the bottom of what's going on.'

'Accusing me of lying isn't going to help.'

'I'm sorry, Fay. I didn't mean to. It's just . . . I'm so puzzled and hurt. I seem to have done something dreadful and I don't know what it is, and it's driving me mad. On top of everything, I'm sure Alex is behind Peter's move and that disturbs me.' She pushed open the front door and they crossed the hall and began to mount the stairs.

'Bully for Alex if he did get him moved. It's about time my horrible brother got his comeuppance.'

'Fay, how can you say such a thing! You're so close to Peter.'

On the landing, Fay stopped and faced her mother. 'I wish everyone would stop saying that!' she said, exasperated. 'We might be twins, we might once have been close, that doesn't mean we have to continue that way. If you must know, I can't stand him these days. If I'm honest, I love him but I haven't liked him for ages.'

'Good gracious, Fay, that's how I feel,' Ann said, opening her bedroom door.

'Then why all the fuss?'

'I want to see the children. I've every right to see them. Do you know what it is I've done?'

'No.'

'Are you sure?'

'Are you going to accuse me of lying again?' Fay asked as she sat at Ann's dressing table and began to sniff her way through the scent bottles which she always did the minute she arrived.

'No,' Ann said quietly, 'I'd just like to know, that's all.'

'There's no point in asking me anything. Peter and I had a flaming row and I haven't spoken to him for months – that's the honest truth, Mummy.'

'An argument? What about?'

'I'd rather not talk about it. OK?' Fay looked about the room. 'You really have improved this house no end. It's less like a showroom, if you know what I mean.'

'Do you think so?' Ann was neatly side-tracked by her daughter. 'Not everyone approves, you know.'

'Do they matter? It's your home. Did Alex tell you he's offered me a job? Design consultant for all the Georgeopoulos properties – I'd no idea there were so many.' Fay announced this news almost casually.

'Fay, has he? How marvellous. He really is the end, he never tells me anything, but he could have told me this. Are you accepting? I do hope so, perhaps I'll see more of you.'

'Probably. It's a dream of a job. It gives me more scope than now. It's more money – your husband pays very well, you know.' She grinned at her mother, but Ann did not smile back. 'Oh, come on, Mummy. He probably didn't tell you in case I turned it down. Let's face it, you would be disappointed if I did turn it down.'

'Maybe you're right. Will you be living with us like Nigel and Yianni?'

'No, Mummy, I most certainly will not. I can just hear you wittering on at me about my lifestyle.'

'Anyone new?'

'There you go, always nosing about,' but she smiled good-naturedly at her mother. 'Better put you out of your misery. No, I'm footloose. Know anyone interesting? At least you might be constructive in your interest.' She laughed.

'There's always Nigel.'

'Oh, come off it, Mummy. He's quite sweet but he's a bit wet behind the ears for me, don't you think?'

'No. It really annoys me the way everyone puts him down. He's worth more than the rest of your men put together. There's a lot more to that young man than meets the eye . . . But then, you're probably right, he's too sensitive for someone like you,' she added, a shade more sharply than she intended.

'Thanks a lot. Your concern is quite touching.' Fay laughed out loud. 'Is Yianni married?'

'No, but I should leave him alone if I were you.'

'Why? I thought you liked him.'

'I'm not sure. I don't know what it is about him – he's just a little too confident, I find it rather unnerving. Of course Alex won't hear a word against him. Of the two, I much prefer Nigel.' Her daughter arched her eyebrows at her in an exaggerated way. Ann laughed. 'All right, I'll stop. But come on, Fay, stop fiddling with my bottles. We've an enormous lunch party. I want to show you your room. You haven't seen it since it was redecorated.'

7

It had been easy to say 'I have no son' – it was difficult to live with the idea.

During the scant time Ann had alone she would re-run the past few years in her mind's eye. At first she had blamed Peter's attitude to the advent of Alex in her life. But the more she thought and analysed, the more she realized that he had changed towards her long before Alex. But what imagined slight had created such bitterness? It was a conundrum to which there appeared to be no solution. She longed to talk to her son, to sort it all out, but her pride would not allow her to risk further rejection.

She longed to see her grandchildren, to hold them, laugh with them, smell the new-bathed warmth of the baby. Her reaction to being a grandmother had taken Ann by surprise. She had not expected to love Adam as intensely as she did. When he was born she had dutifully gone to the hospital, picked up the child and found herself engulfed with a tenderness and love that at times, she felt, surpassed her feelings for her own children.

At this moment in her life, Ann was lucky that she was kept so busy. Had she not been, her sadness, her endless reviewing of the situation, could have multiplied to swamp her, and damage her life with Alex. She was aware of the danger and fought it, allowing herself only momentarily to grieve and always when alone so that she was sure Alex was unaware of her feelings.

Travelling with Alex could not have been more luxurious – the comfort of his private jet, the speed with which they cleared customs and immigration in any country, the succession of the best hotels the world could provide. But after a year of these travels, a year of receptions and dinners, of new people by the hundred, the journeying began to be a chore and Ann became restless.

At first each new country and city had been an excitement. While Alex was involved with his business Ann would explore the museums, the art galleries, the shops, the markets, but as time slipped by the repetition palled and she spent more time alone in hotel suites waiting for him to return from meetings, and wishing they were home where her own routine was assured.

Alex could not have been more solicitous. He always made certain that trips were arranged to amuse her. He bought piles of books and magazines that might interest her. He was always finding unusual presents to indulge her. These trips were the only occasions when she had time on her hands, so on one occasion she packed her box of paints and began tentatively to do watercolour sketches of the places they visited. Alex was both surprised and excited by the talent these paintings displayed and encouraged her, insisting that in England she ought to have lessons. Ann would look at her attempts with displeasure, certain he was pretending enthusiasm, for she was always dissatisfied with her work, frustrated that she seemed unable to translate the images her eyes saw on to paper as she would have liked.

On these trips, if he ever asked if she were bored, she denied it quickly. She would watch her husband's evident pleasure in flirting with the many women who sidled up to him. She had quickly learned to hide any jealousy for if he were aware of it, his flirtation would become even more blatant. He basked in her jealousy and teased her about it. It was a continuous puzzle to Ann why he, who shielded her from all life's discomforts, should enjoy watching her deal with this most unpleasant of human emotions.

Her best ploy, she discovered, was to be extra charming to whichever young woman he singled out. She found that this completely disorientated them. It was with a sense of triumph that Ann would see a girl turn away from Alex's flirtation, with embarrassed looks in her direction.

Why such games should be necessary was another source of bewilderment to Ann. She wondered if it made him feel more masculine, more attractive to her. Or was the attention of other women necessary to give him some form of security? It all seemed such a waste of effort, especially since she was certain it never went any further than this superficial dalliance. She put it down to his being a foreigner, presuming, in her ignorance of men, that no Englishman would ever play such tricks on her.

She had expected his passion for her to decrease. She repeatedly warned herself that this was what happened in all marriages after the first exquisite passion had passed. But, as in everything else, Alex was different – his need for her was as great as ever. Sometimes she wondered if it was for her or whether his sexual urge was such that he would be like this with any woman. But that was an uncomfortable thought she preferred not to examine too closely.

When she had first met him, Ann had naïvely thought that being a businessman meant sitting behind a big desk, surrounded by papers. But Alex's desk was always empty except for a doodle pad and the ubiquitous telephone; everything, it seemed, was filed away in his head. Times without number he would appear in their room, champagne in hand, to celebrate a new coup he had brought off while out shooting, at a party, on someone's yacht, once in a hot-air balloon over central France. If the travelling began to pall Alex never ceased to fascinate her.

Now that both houses were renovated, Ann's need to find something to occupy her was revived. She did not want to spend the rest of her life, like some of the women she met, working on her appearance. Being beautiful for Alex was important, but she had quickly learned that with organization and Elene's help it took less time as she became more experienced.

Gradually her painting began to fill every moment that was busy elsewhere. While they were in London he arranged for a young woman to come twice a week to teach her drawing and watercolouring. Finally the great day arrived when she was allowed to try her hand at oil painting. Now, she never went anywhere without a sketch-pad. Each week she became more confident with her efforts and each week what had started as a gentle hobby became more important to her.

Fay had settled into her job within Alex's organization. There was no question but that the girl had talent; no one could accuse her of having landed the job by nepotism. Her first big task was the interior of a hotel complex Alex had recently acquired in Florida. Not only were her ideas original but she was economical too. Her estimates were exact to the last dollar. No contractor cheated her eagle eye. All work was completed on schedule. Fay was in complete control from day one.

Alex was impressed but, Ann felt, more with Fay's financial acumen than her artistic talent, which he had taken for granted – he had employed her for that proven talent. Fay would make a good businesswoman, he had said, and coming from him this was the greatest compliment.

Ann had watched with dismay as Fay had 'moved in' on Nigel. 'Moving in' was the only expression she could think of to describe her daughter's behaviour with men, which, since she saw so much of her now, she had been able to observe. Fay eyed the field in a predatory fashion, picked a likely candidate, charmed him into submission, and then, once conquered, immediately dropped him. Nigel seemed to be the current object of the first part of such a campaign. There were many things about her daughter which Ann found admirable, but her attitude to men was not one of them. It was cold, almost ruthless. Ann knew she had been badly hurt but that was no excuse to punish all men as she seemed to be doing.

Ann's concern for Nigel made her tax her daughter with her behaviour. Fay merely laughed at Ann. 'You were the one who said that there's more to him than meets the eye.'

'I also said I thought he was too nice for you,' Ann countered.

'Ha! You think I'll gobble him up for breakfast.'

'I don't want to see him hurt, that's all.'

'Don't be silly, Mummy. I really quite like him. Honest. Have you noticed that when he's not rushing around like the White Rabbit he's actually rather attractive?'

'Fay, you're impossible . . . "I quite like him . . ." There has to be more to a relationship than that.'

'You haven't met some of the shits I've been involved with. We don't all have your luck.'

'If you persist in this flirtation, or whatever it is, please be careful. Can you imagine what Alex will be like if you upset the apple-cart with one of his assistants?'

'God, you do worry, Mummy. I'll treat him with kid gloves.' Fay laughed flippantly and scooped up her folder of sketches.

Yianni continued his serene self-satisfied journey in life. There were times she wished he would make a colossal blunder if only to prove he was human. The habit that vexed her the most was the silent way he wafted about the house like an elegant ghost. He was forever appearing behind her and making her jump. She longed to yell at him to make more noise, to stop creeping about.

Ann was alone in the drawing room, and thought herself alone in the house. On an impulse she decided to change the position of a Ming vase. She gathered the precious object in her hands and crossed the room, carefully. She sensed more than saw a movement in the corner of the room; it made her jump, she tripped on a Persian rug, and the valuable vase crashed to the floor, smashing into little pieces. Swiftly Yianni swooped on the broken shards, tutting at the damage as he did so.

'Why the hell can't you make more noise?' Ann shouted at him in anger.

'I beg your pardon, Mrs Georgeopoulos.'

'I'm sick to death of you sidling about this house. It gets on my nerves. It's as if you're spying on me,' Ann found herself shrieking at a startled Yianni, her shrieks, she knew, out of all proportion.

'Mrs Georgeopoulos, I don't understand,' he said with surprise etched on his face. No one had ever heard Ann shout before.

'What the hell broke? Why are you screaming so, Anna?' Alex stood in the doorway.

'The Ming vase, sir,' Yianni replied smoothly.

'You broke it.' Alex's voice took on a dangerous edge.

'No. I did,' Ann answered. 'Yianni made me jump. He's always creeping about, it's a wonder something like this hasn't happened before.'

'Sir, I apologize if I made Mrs Georgeopoulos jump. I didn't intend to.'

'Of course you didn't, Yianni. It's a shame about the vase. Get Fiona to see if it can be restored. Now leave us, Yianni.'

Seething with anger Ann watched Yianni silently leave the room.

'That wasn't really fair of you, Anna, to break something and then try to blame a member of the staff. I'm surprised at you,' Alex admonished her.

'I wasn't "blaming" him. It was true. It was his fault. He's always making me jump. Wherever I turn there's Yianni, sneaking up, bowing and smiling. He's driving me mad.'

'Darling, don't be so dramatic. If he were noisy you'd hate that even more. Be fair, he's a charming fellow, you know he is. You're overwrought about the vase, that's all.'

'Oh, don't be so patronizing, Alex. Just recently he's begun to irritate me beyond measure. You might think it sounds silly, but I can't help it. If I have to live with your assistants then I think it's only fair that I live with people I can get on with.'

'But I thought you liked him.'

'I did, I don't any more. It's not just that, if you want to know, I don't think he's to be trusted.' There, it was in the open. Not until she said it did Ann realize the true nature of what had been bothering her about Yianni for some time.

'I can trust him implicitly.'

'But he's always so superior, as if he thinks he knows better than you all the time. I wish you would get rid of him.'

'Of course he thinks that. He's a normal ambitious young man. He *should* think like that. No doubt he'd love to usurp me, I admire him for that. In any case I'd be lost without him. He's excellent at his job and after me he knows more than anyone else about my businesses. And making you jump is hardly grounds for dismissal, is it?'

'I don't trust him,' she repeated stolidly.

In reply Alex kissed her, told her not to be a goose and patted her backside.

'Don't do that,' she snapped. He looked at her, surprised. 'I don't like the way you're always patting me.'

'I'm sorry.' He sounded hurt. 'We Greeks, we like to touch those we love. I'll try to remember not to annoy you in future,' he said with wounded dignity and left the room.

Ann slumped down on the window seat and gazed out across the parkland. What on earth had made her react like that and say such things about Yianni? Why had she deliberately hurt Alex in that way? It was not true, she liked the way he constantly touched her as if reassuring himself that she was there. She laid her head back against the shutter. Life had once been so ordered. She had always been a tolerant, equable character; now she was one who flew off the handle. Once she had had a son, now she had only a daughter. She sighed. Peter, the son she claimed to have forgotten, was still malevolently with her.

She slid from the seat and went in search of Alex to apologize.

Although Alex never seemed to mind her interrupting his work, it always made Ann feel guilty. So she had got into the habit of leaving a note pinned to her pillow if she was going out. It would simply say where she had gone and what time she expected to be back – she had long ago learned that he had to know what time she would return.

At first she had put it down to coincidence when twice she bumped into Yianni in Harrods. But the third time, when she saw him peering into Rayne's shop window, she became convinced that he was following her, that her outburst over the Ming vase had not been so far from the truth.

So, she thought, if he wanted to play games, so could she. Now she would sometimes lie in her notes, saying she was going to Harrods and would instead go to Harvey Nichols. It was a silly game but, if she were right, one that pleased her.

She said nothing to Alex of her suspicions for, after their previous conversations and his defence of Yianni, she feared he would think she was being paranoid. And obviously, in Alex's eyes, Yianni could do no wrong.

Proof of her suspicions came by chance.

One morning she had left a note saying she had an appointment with her dress designer. On her way out she remembered that she had left her appointments diary in another handbag. Returning to her bedroom she stood silently in the doorway, stupefied with anger, as she saw Yianni bending over the pillow to read her note. He picked up the phone and dialled a number.

'Ah. Good morning, this is Mr Georgeopoulos's private assistant. He would like to know if his wife has an appointment this morning?' He cradled the phone. 'Thank you. No, no message.' Replacing the phone he turned to see Ann in the doorway. Coolly he totally ignored her expression of anger and crossed the room, smiling at her.

'Good morning, Mrs Georgeopoulos,' he said pleasantly.

'What the hell are you doing in my room, reading my notes and phoning my dressmaker?' she shouted.

'Mr Georgeopoulous . . .'

'You sneaky bastard, you come with me.'

Without knocking Ann stormed into Alex's study.

'Yianni is spying on me, Alex. I've proof now.'

'Darling, do calm down.'

'Calm down? Calm down? He spies! He snoops! He's been in our bedroom reading my notes to you. Sack him!'

'Yianni, if you wouldn't mind leaving us?'

'No, I want him here.' Ann slammed a fist on the desk.

'Yianni,' Alex said in a voice which sounded to Ann insufferably reasonable. The Greek slipped quietly from the room.

'You're going to let that bastard get away with it?' she shrieked.

'Anna, if you will calm down I shall explain. I told him to read the note and check.'

Ann slumped into a chair. 'You did what?' she said with disbelief.

'He was obeying my instructions – do you want to sack me instead?' He smiled confidently at her.

'He's been following me.'

'I know.'

'You?'

'Yes.'

'But why?'

'Because I love you.'

'I've never been so insulted in my life. Have you thought what he must think of me? What the hell do you mean, Alex? Don't you trust me?'

'No.'

'What on earth – I've done – deserve – this sort – treatment – tell me that.' Too shocked to speak coherently, Ann found her words stumbling out disjointedly.

'Nothing.' He smiled.

'Then what excuse can you possibly have? And using that bastard when you know I don't trust him,' Ann stormed, her eyes flashing with fury, tears beginning to form.

He put his arm out to her. She thrust it angrily away. 'Oh, Anna, don't be so upset. Don't cry. I love you angry . . .' With mounting anger Ann saw that he was laughing at her.

'Angry? I'm beside myself with fury. I'm not crying, you needn't think I would. How dare you humiliate me like this! I've done nothing to make you distrust me. I never look at another man, for God's sake.'

'You could be kidnapped,' he said reasonably.

'Kidnapped? Me? In London? Don't be silly. No, this is taking jealousy to an extreme. I can't live like this.'

'I see nothing wrong in looking after what is mine. I know women . . .'

'Then you don't know me.' She lifted her hand as if to strike him. Grasping it he twisted her round her face him and she was trapped by his arms. His mouth crushed down upon hers.

'Oh, my darling, Anna. I only did it for love.'

Feverishly she twisted in his arms, pummelling his chest with her fists.

'Darling, darling.' He swept her into his arms and carried her protesting, impotently hitting him, to their room. He pinned her to the bed. 'Never complain that I love you. Never.' His body crashed down upon her.

'No,' she said, struggling against him. 'No you don't . . .' but he was too strong for her and as always her body betrayed her, even now, when her anger was a great force within her.

She lay beside him, exhausted with passion, despising herself for giving herself to him, for not having the strength of character to make a stand on this issue.

'I apologize, I was wrong to use Yianni.' Suddenly, he spoke, raising himself on one elbow and looking down at her. 'You're right, it was a humiliation for you. But then, you see, he is the one person I employ who would understand my fears. My need to watch and care over you.'

'Why? Why him? What do you mean?'

'A long story, darling, one day I'll tell you. But . . .' He sat up. 'You do need protection. I believe you – you aren't the sort to be unfaithful but times are bad. I shall get you a bodyguard.'

'Darling, don't be daft.' Ann laughed at such a preposterous idea.

'No. It's a good idea. I do have enemies who perhaps would use you to get at me. A bodyguard would be a good idea.'

'What enemies? What sort of people do you know who would harm me? For goodness sake, Alex, this is England. Be reasonable.' But Alex would not listen. He was already on the phone issuing instructions.

To Ann's disbelief the next day she went shopping accompanied by Robin, the most misnamed young man she had ever met, she thought, as his sixteen-stone, six-foot-four bulk shouldered a way through the crowds for her.

Five

1

Ann had been married to Alex for two years when she finally decided what she wanted. A baby.

Her life could not have been busier. Her painting was taking up more and more of her time, but she was sure she had not enough talent for it to be more than a hobby. For a long time, she had been aware of a restless need for something else – and it had taken her all this time to find out what that was. A child.

It was not a decision she reached quickly. She had thought long and hard and weighed up the pros and cons. Maybe, she had reasoned with herself, this need was caused by what amounted to the loss of her grandchildren from her life. And that was not reason enough to have a child. Or perhaps it was that last maternal urge she had heard about from other women – the need of the female body to give life once more before it was too late. And that was too selfish a reason. However, she finally decided, it was a logical progression in her love for Alex. Not only would a baby be a living proof of their love but in having a child she was giving to Alex what no one else had given him, an heir. And that was reason enough for Ann.

She made an appointment to see her gynaecologist and set out with Robin to keep the appointment. She had extracted a promise of secrecy from the young man. It had been easy to do: she had simply said she did not want Alex to know she was seeing her doctor in case it worried him. The large blond hulk sat in the consultant's waiting room surrounded by pregnant women, smiling sweetly at them, settled into the corner with his chewing gum and a magazine on body-building – a new interest which threatened to make him even larger. The other women eyed Ann and her handsome young escort and gave knowing and, in some cases, envious glances.

'Ann, what a lovely surprise.' Michael Rain, her doctor, stood to greet her. Michael had trained with Ben and had risen to the giddy heights of Harley Street, blessed not only with a good brain but the good looks and charm so many women search for in a gynaecologist. 'Why this visit? Nothing wrong I hope.'

'No. I'm as fit as a fiddle. I need advice.' The doctor looked at her questioningly. 'I've remarried, Michael,' she said, strangely blushing.

'I heard. I'm very pleased for you. Ben was a great guy, he wouldn't have wanted you to spend your life alone,' he said reassuringly, as if fear of his disapproval had made her blush.

'The point is – I want to have a baby and I wondered if you think, at forty-six, I'm too old?'

'I see.' Michael sat, smiling, making a steeple of his fingers. 'Do you think you're too old?'

'Gracious, no. I don't *feel* forty-six. I've never felt fitter, and my new life – I'm blissfully happy, I feel like a young girl again.'

Michael smiled his devastating professional smile. 'I would be failing in my duty if I didn't point out that at your age the risks of childbirth are increased for you and the child. Having said that – in my experience, no matter what her age, when a lady decides she wants a baby nothing on this earth will stop her.' He smiled kindly at her. 'Let's examine you and see, shall we?'

A little later he resettled himself at the desk. 'Well, Ann . . .'

She leaned forward anxiously.

His face broke into a broad smile. 'If I'm not mistaken the lecture's a bit late in the day, I think you might already be pregnant.'

'Michael, you're joking?'

'I never joke about anything so serious. I warn you it's a hunch – it's very early, we need to do tests to make sure.'

'How long will they take?'

'A few days. I like to be a hundred per cent certain.'

'Oh Michael!' She clutched her hands together. 'You don't know how happy this makes me.'

'Have you discussed this with your husband?'

'No. I haven't dared,' she said a shade too quickly, and seeing her doctor's frown realized she must explain herself. 'You see he lost his first wife having a baby . . . we've never really discussed it. Once – I'd decorated a nursery in one of our houses for my grandchildren to visit . . .' She twisted her hands in her lap. 'When he saw it he seemed disturbed . . . I wasn't sure if he was disappointed when I said who it was for. Or whether the sight of it had brought back sad memories of what might have been. He still grieves, you see, I'm sure he does.' Her voice held sadness as she confessed to her doctor what she had never been able to confess to anyone else.

'Perhaps it's the best thing for him. A new baby will help him finally resolve his grief, won't it?'

'Do you think so? Sometimes it's a bit like living with a ghost between us, if you know what I mean.' She gave a nervous little laugh.

'I do, Ann.' He smiled at her kindly. 'I think a young wife dying in those circumstances leads to such feelings of guilt in a man. And the memory of a young wife is far harder to expunge.'

'You think so? You think that's it? You see, Michael, I grieved for Ben. It took a long time but it's gone. Of course I'm sad he's no more, he had so much still to give. I can be sad for that, but I have happy memories. I can think of him with affection . . . he doesn't interfere with my present, you see.'

'As it should be, Ann.'

'What does worry me . . . I had planned, if you gave the go-ahead, to discuss this with Alex, make the decision together. But now, I'm not sure if he won't be angry, you know the sort of anger that fear can bring.'

'I'm sure not, Ann. He would be a rare man who wouldn't be thrilled at news like this, since he has no children of his own. If you like I'll have a talk with him to put his mind at rest.'

'Would you really? I'm sure that would help.'

'When will you tell him, tonight?'

'I'll wait for the tests first.'

'That's best. Phone me about five on Friday afternoon. They should be back from the laboratory by then.'

The next few days passed in an agony of suspense for Ann. Each time the phone rang she jumped stupidly – after all, she had arranged to phone Michael so he was unlikely to call her. Her excitement made eating impossible. She was aware of Alex watching her with an anxious expression. She longed to tell him but forced herself to wait for Michael's confirmation. It would have been unfair to worry him or to raise his hopes unnecessarily – whichever was the case.

Friday eventually dawned. Alex had gone to Birmingham and they had arranged to meet at Courtneys for the weekend, Ann travelled down from London with Robin.

She looked about her bedroom. She loved the London house but of all the rooms in both homes this bedroom was her favourite. The room where Alex had taught her the joys of uninhibited love-making. And now, if Michael were right, it would be the room where she would tell him about the baby, watch the happiness she was certain, deep down, he would feel, spread across his face.

It was still only four o'clock. She took a long bath to while away the time until five. Wrapped in her bathrobe she sat on the bed, watched the clock, and willed the hands to move faster. On the dot of five, with nervous fingers she dialled Michael's number. As she waited for the connection, for the first time in a long while she made a silent prayer.

'Ann? Positive,' Michael said without preamble.

'Michael, I can't believe it. How wonderful.'

'You'd better come back next week, say Wednesday at three. We'll give you a thorough medical to make sure you're as fit as you say.'

'Oh yes, Michael. Wednesday at three. Don't worry I'll be there, I can hardly wait . . .' she said breathlessly. She replaced the receiver, smiling to herself, and hugged herself with joy.

'And who is Michael?' Alex's voice made her jump – the thick carpet had muffled his approach; she turned towards him, her face aglow. He grabbed her hand and twisted her body round. 'Who is Michael?' he shouted, his grey eyes icy with anger.

'Alex. You're early,' she said, his anger making her flustered. 'Alex, I've . . .'

'Obviously you weren't expecting me just yet,' he said, sarcastically, twisting her further round, his grip on her arm beginning to hurt. 'How inconsiderate of me,' he went on sardonically.

'Alex, please, you're hurting me.'

'I'll hurt you a lot more if you don't tell me who he is,' he thundered.

'He's an old friend, a colleague of Ben's. Alex, listen . . .'

'So, you can only telephone this old friend when you're here alone, when you think I'm still away.' His shouting pounded into her ears. He lifted his hand as if to strike her. She flinched away from him, horror etched on her face. His hand remained poised in the air for what seemed an eternity. Heavily it fell back to his side. He stood silent for a moment, a strange bleak look on his face, then shook his head violently. 'Who is he? I'll kill the bastard,' he bellowed. Ann recoiled from the expression of hatred she could see in his eyes.

'Alex, stop! You're mad, let me explain.'

'Oh I'm waiting, Madame. Truly I am,' he continued to shout. She moved to the side of the bed away from him. He leaned over and caught hold of her. As she twisted away from him her robe split in two. He grabbed at her, ripping it from her body.

'He's my doctor, for God's sake. His name is Michael Rain. If you don't believe me look him up in the telephone book,' she shouted back angrily. Furious with him for distrusting her, angry that he could make her feel so afraid.

'What's wrong with you?' He took her, roughly, in his arms and shook her. 'For Christ's sake, what's wrong with you? Why didn't you tell me? Why this secrecy?'

With all her strength she pushed him away from her. 'Don't you ever threaten me like that again, Alex. Never. You understand? I hate violence, you know I do,' she shouted, moving away from him across the bed, picking up the remains of her bathrobe and wrapping it about her.

'Please Anna, tell me. Why do you need a doctor?' He put his hands out to her, his eyes pleading with her now.

'I had to phone for the results of some tests. I didn't want to tell you until I knew for certain. But I didn't want to tell you like this. You've spoilt everything.'

'Tell me what? Darling, what?'

'I'm going to have a baby,' she yelled.

Alex stood momentarily stunned. 'A baby?' he repeated inanely. 'A baby?' he shouted. 'Oh my love. Oh my God, my darling, I could have hurt you. Oh my precious.' He took her in his arms and smothered her face with kisses. 'Oh my sweet love, forgive me – I didn't dream, I couldn't dare to hope – I thought you'd found someone else. Christ, a baby, a son . . .'

'It might be a girl,' she said, at last smiling weakly at his genuine pleasure.

'No, no, it will be a boy. I sense it. Shouldn't you be resting?' he asked anxiously.

'No, darling. Don't fuss, I'm fine, really. Nothing's wrong. I'm to go and have a thorough check-up next week. But Michael's perfectly happy with me.'

'Are you certain he's a good doctor?'

'Darling, the best.'

'I shall check, you must have the best care – you two . . .' he said, an unbelieving tone in his voice as he gently stroked her stomach.

'He's in Harley Street, they're usually quite good when they get that far.' She felt light-headed with relief.

'Your stomach's so flat, when will I be able to feel him?'

'Darling, not for ages, I'm only just pregnant.'

'Nothing must go wrong.'

'This time nothing will, I'm sure.'

'Have you lost a baby before?' he asked anxiously.

'No, never. I just meant . . .' Her voice trailed off as she wished that she had not mentioned his lost child. 'I'm as fit as a fiddle,' she added hurriedly.

'You must stop smoking and drinking. You mustn't travel so much, you must rest, take care . . .'

'Darling, women are having babies every minute of the day.'

'Yes, but not my baby,' he declared.

Having told her she must rest he then insisted she get dressed. Everyone must be told. He was beside himself with excitement. All the house guests – who by a lucky coincidence included Lydia and George – were called to the drawing room. The cook was summoned, the gardeners, the stable boys. The weekend passed on a sea of champagne and elation.

Ann passed her medical with flying colours, none of which stopped Alex fussing over her like a broody hen.

Michael declared, in an amused voice, that no father had ever questioned him in such detail: he almost felt he was sitting an examination.

'You were,' Ann laughed at him.

Alex descended on Hatchards and Foyles and bought every book he could find on pregnancy and childbirth. He then proceeded to frighten himself half to death with the pictures of abnormalities they contained, so that poor Michael Rain was bombarded with telephone calls at all hours of the day and night. Eventually, Ann took all the books away from him, threw them in the furnace and forbade him to buy any others.

The nursery began to fill with a barrage of toys bought by Alex who haunted Hamleys.

If she thought she had been loved before, nothing prepared her for the avalanche of affection with which he now showered her. She begged him to buy her no more jewels: she would never have time, in this life, to wear them, she laughed. If she sighed he was at her side immediately, concern stamped across his face. She laughed as he forbade her to lift a teapot. He refused to let her fly – far too dangerous, he announced – and in consequence cut down on his own travelling. Telling Alex not to fuss was as pointless as telling the waves to go back.

Contentedly Ann settled back on this giant, secure cushion of love and adoration.

2

Alex had decided that the fume-laden air of London was bad for Ann and the baby. They closed up the London house temporarily and moved to Courtneys. These days Alex trusted no one to drive her and her precious burden. As a result the chauffeur sulked in his cottage, and Robin had more days off than he had ever hoped for.

Alex had cut down on his travelling but there were still trips he had to make. Ann tried every trick she had learned in dealing with Alex to make him change his mind.

'You can come later in your pregnancy. Not now, you might miscarry,' he stated emphatically.

'But don't you see, darling? Sitting here on my own, worrying and wondering what you are up to without me to keep an eye on you, is likely to be far more damaging,' she argued slyly.

'What on earth am I likely to get up to?' he laughed.

'You know damn well what I mean. All those hungry women sniffing about you. They've been waiting for something like this to happen so they can have you to themselves,' she said petulantly.

'You have nothing to fear, Anna. It's different now.'

'What's different? You're not different – and I should know.' She laughed ruefully. At the start of her pregnancy Alex had moved to another room, declaring he would not touch her again until the baby was safely born. It was only Michael's intervention, assuring him that a life with no sexual relations was likely to harm Ann more, that brought him back to her bed.

'You are to be the mother of my son. That changes everything. I would do nothing to harm you or him. I shall not be unfaithful. You have my promise.'

'Bah,' Ann snorted dismissively, the memory of the flirting women sidling up to him on so many occasions too fresh in her mind.

'I have promised, Anna. I do not break promises.'

Ann looked at him, her exasperation dissipating as she saw the gentle but serious expression on his face. Then she knew she had nothing to fear. She knew the Greeks well enough now to know that as the mother of his child her status in his life was changing. She wished she could believe he would be faithful for her own sake but her feeling of relief at his promise made it easy for her to settle for this second best.

'I believe you, Alex. But what on earth will you do instead?' she asked pointedly.

'I shall get drunk, frustrated and hurry back to you. What else?'

Ann was happiest living in the country. She had lived too much of her life surrounded by countryside ever to be truly content in the city. She liked the London house, was proud of her achievement with it, but it was Courtneys she preferred. Another plus was that Fay, for the duration of Ann's pregnancy, had almost moved in – almost, because her spirit of independence prevented her giving up her flat entirely. So now Fay, frustrated by the difficulties involved in running the business while Alex was so often out of London, would spend as much as a whole week at a time at Courtneys. But, as if to prove her emancipation, every so often she would return to her own flat, if only for one night.

'This arrangement holds only until the baby's born, mind you. As soon as you two move back to London I'm going back, permanently, to my flat. There's no question of my selling it.'

'You would think I was a monster the way you go on about the time you spend here. I really don't mind what you do, Fay,' Ann countered untruthfully. 'It's just it seems silly to me when we have so much room in both houses. You could rent your flat. You would still be independent.'

'There you go, Mummy. Organizing me!'

'You don't understand, do you? I like having you here, close to me, that's all . . .'

'Peter again? Oh, Mummy, try and get him out of your mind. It can't be doing you any good,' Fay said intuitively.

Ann saw the concern on her daughter's face and wondered whether she could ever explain the ache which the loss of part of her family had caused her, how much, with this new baby on the way, she wanted her whole family about her. There was no point, she decided. Fay was not a mother. How could she understand?

With Fay in the house so frequently, Nigel's fate was sealed. Ann watched exasperated as one day Fay was sweetly all over him and the next virtually ignored him. Nigel swung from bliss into despair with a depressing regularity. Ann found herself equally irritated with both of them, Fay that she could be so unkind and Nigel that he put up with it. But then, she thought, he's in love, it's obvious, and what control did one have over one's destiny when love had one by the tail? She of all people knew the answer to that.

One day Alex announced that Fay was to join him, Yianni and Nigel on a ten-day trip first to Athens and then to the Seychelles to investigate a hotel complex in which he was interested. Feeling like Cinderella, Ann stood on the porch steps and waved them goodbye.

She turned back into the silent house and realized that she was almost alone for ten whole days. She decided there and then that it would be pleasant to be completely on her own, for once. Her life these days was dominated by other people: she would enjoy the solitude of once more having only herself to consider. So she sent the cook, housekeeper and a couple of the maids home for a holiday with their families. Just after the others had departed, Robin left too. For months he had been booked on a survival course in Wales. Ann was sure that Alex must have forgotten he was going, otherwise she was certain he would have made the young man cancel his trip.

Ann sat in the small sitting room, the remains of the supper she had cooked herself on a tray beside her. She stretched contentedly, pleased with the prospect of doing whatever she wanted at her own pace. She could watch television if she wanted, an occupation Alex abhorred as a complete waste of time. She could read without interruptions. She could even just go to bed if the fancy took her. She switched the television on, flicked through the channels, and immediately switched it off again when she could find no programme to amuse her. She struggled for a while with some knitting for the baby. But after four dropped stitches she looked with disgust at the misshapen garment and threw it in the wastepaper basket. She had never been able to knit. She finally decided to get on with some painting. Although Alex encouraged her to paint, he would not tolerate the paraphernalia of her painting in the sitting room. It was almost with a feeling of delinquency that she fetched her equipment, shifted the tray, pulled out a small table and neatly laid out her box of paints and pencils. She arranged a small still-life and settled down happily to her task.

For an hour she was engrossed in her work. She stopped and rubbed her back which was aching from the position she was sitting in. It was then that she heard the clock ticking. She listened. This house was never quiet enough to hear the clock; now the noise seemed to fill the room. From a distance she heard a creaking noise which made her jump. How silly she was being. All old houses made noises, she told herself. There was another sound which took her a moment to register as the wind getting up in the trees outside in the park. She realized she was only aware of them because she was completely alone . . . Of course she was, the remaining maids had gone to a dance in the village. The gardener and chauffeur were across the yard in their cottages . . . alone. She shook herself, causing a blob of paint to fall on her picture. She was angry with herself as she tried to mop it up. How stupid. An hour ago she had been happy to be alone. She tore the ruined painting into four, took another sheet and laboriously started lightly sketching out the still-life again. She loaded her brush with paint and began again the relaxing task . . .

With a crash the heavy mahogany door swung open, banging back against the wall. A painting tumbled on to the floor, glass shattering. Two men leapt into the room, dressed entirely in black, stocking masks pulled tightly across their faces. They crouched at angles to each other like a parody of Starsky and Hutch entering a room.

Ann dropped her brush in shocked surprise. She stood up abruptly, the table and her paints clattering to the floor, the water from her paint pot soaking into the carpet. She was speechless and stared with disbelief at the two men – one short and stocky, the other tall and razor thin. The stocking masks were made from tights, their faces in one leg, the other leg tied in a knot and hanging down their backs, making them look like pirates. The stockings flattened their noses, distorted their lips and gave their skin a muddy, pinkish-grey hue. No wonder Alex hated tights, Ann found herself thinking inconsequentially.

'Christ. Nothing was said about her . . .' the shorter of the two growled. He turned as if to run from the room. The tall one stood his ground, grabbed the other by the arm and turned him back.

'Who the hell are you? Get out of my house.' Instinctively Ann took advantage of the fear she felt emanating from them.

'Sit down,' the tall one ordered.

'Sit down,' the short one echoed.

'I will not sit down. What on earth do you mean, barging in here like that with those silly stockings on?' she snapped, indignation making her voice shrill.

'I said sit, you stupid cow . . .' and Ann found herself looking down the black, gleaming short snout of a revolver.

She sat down quickly. Any feelings of anger, indignation and bravado disappeared immediately to be replaced by a feeling that her stomach had suddenly been filled with ice-cold water and her skin invaded by an army of creeping creatures. She wanted to scream and felt certain that if she tried nothing would emerge. And anyway who would hear? Even through the thick curtains Ann could hear the wind gathering force. A storm was beginning, and there was little hope of the gardener and chauffeur hearing anything from the house. At the same time she found her brain seemed to be racing at double speed as she took in the scene. She looked about helplessly for a possible weapon. Wondered if these two were alone. Wondered if they had cut the telephone wires. And decided that the short one was stupid and would not hurt her and that the tall one was in charge and capable of anything. Seconds had passed and it seemed like minutes.

'Who the fuck are you?'

'I'm Mrs Georgeopoulos,' she said and immediately regretted her honesty. Maybe they were the kidnappers whom Alex had feared. More ice-cold water drenched her guts.

'Are you now? Isn't that interesting? Very 'andy. Take your tights off,' he barked ominously.

'I'm pregnant,' she managed to say. She twisted in her chair in a vain attempt to preserve some modesty as with trembling fingers she released her suspenders. The tall man prodded her with the gun to make her face him again.

'Give us a good look,' he sneered. The short one laughed a short, hollow laugh that sounded more like an animal coughing. With a chilling certainty Ann realized she was not safe with either of them.

'I am pregnant. I really am,' she repeated, desperation making her voice uncontrollable, like an adolescent whose voice is breaking.

'They all say that,' he said, peering at her flat stomach.

'But you must believe me, I am.'

'I don't have to believe anything, ducks. Where's the safe? I'm more interested in that than your cunt.'

'I don't know.'

'For an intelligent-looking woman you're behaving like a really fucking stupid bitch.'

'Fucking stupid,' his echo said.

'I'm telling you the truth. I don't know where the safe is.' Even as she spoke she realized how unlikely her words sounded. The problem was it was the truth. When she took her jewels off at night she handed them to Alex, she had never thought to ask him where the safe was. She knew where it was in the London house – she had had it installed – but that was not going to help her in this situation. 'I don't know . . .' she repeated lamely.

'Then I suggest you hurry up and remember.' The tall man's hand flashed through the air and slashed across Ann's mouth. 'Right. Now. Where's this bleeding safe?' He asked her this gently, as if he were speaking to a child, which frightened Ann even more. Her heart was beating so fast that she felt breathless. Her fear was for the baby. She crossed her hands on her stomach and forced herself to take deep breaths to try to calm herself.

'The safe?' he repeated.

'The only place I think it can be is in my husband's study.'

'Good girl. There, I knew you'd co-operate sooner or later.' The man grimaced through his mask. 'Up you get.' He prodded her with the gun. Ann needed no second prod. She quickly stood. 'Tie her up,' the tall man ordered.

'Then she won't be able to walk, show us where it is,' his short companion said smugly, pleased with his own logic. Ann was surprised at what a pleasant and educated voice he had and wondered why he had taken to burglary.

''er 'ands, you bleeding idiot.'

Roughly the stocky man tied her hands behind her back with her own stockings. As he worked Ann was conscious of the acrid smell of his body odour and noticed that he had a bad case of dandruff. She wondered why she kept thinking such unimportant thoughts when her life might be at stake and then she wondered whether her sanity was deserting her.

The prodding of the gangster's gun in her back as she led the way to Alex's study cleared her mind. She was a terrified woman whose legs seemed made of lead, whose mouth twitched and who desperately wanted to go to the lavatory.

Within a couple of minutes the room looked as if a tornado had hit it. The shorter of the two had emptied the bookcase, throwing the books about the room.

Frenetically he ran his hands along the wood; wherever there was a knot he pressed it, cursing as he did so.

'It's not here.' He swore.

'Did you miss any?'

'Of course I didn't. What do you take me for?'

'He must have been mistaken. Try the pictures.'

Paintings were wrenched from the wall. The carpets were torn up in the search for the safe. The tall one stood, his gun pointing at Ann. She stood forlornly amidst the debris, feeling their rising anger as they failed to find the safe.

'You bitch, where is it?' Her captor's hand lashed at her again. A thick gold ring caught the corner of her mouth and Ann tasted the warm and salty taste of her own blood.

'I told you. I don't know,' she screamed at her tormentor. The force of the next blow made her head jerk painfully backwards, catching on the side of the door. 'My husband never told me.' She flinched as a clenched fist came towards her. The fist missed her as the door was flung open and she found herself pushed flat against the wall by the heavy wood.

'Leave her alone, you bastards,' a voice shouted, anger distorting it, and a figure jumped into the room. Cowering behind the door, shocked and in pain, Ann knew that she recognized the voice but her brain which had been racing so fast now seemed to have gone into reverse. She peered gingerly around the side of the door in time to see Nigel swinging a bronze statue through the air and bringing it down with a sickening crunch on the head of the shorter of the two villains.

'Gun ... the other's got a ...' she screamed in warning, beginning to wrestle with the stocking that bound her arms. A bright flame shot from the gun. Nigel staggered back against the wall. There was a look of complete surprise on his face as she looked down to see blood spurting from his shoulder. There were splashes on the wall and on Ann's dress. Nigel shook his head, touched his shoulder as if to check that it was still there.

His expression of surprise changed to one of rage. Ann had never thought to see Nigel so angry.

'You bastards. I'll kill you,' he roared, pushing himself away from the wall and propelling himself across the room after his assailant. The gunman, with swift agility, raced from the room, with Nigel in crazed pursuit.

'Nigel, leave him,' Ann called after him.

'Not bloody likely,' Nigel yelled back.

On the floor the short figure groaned. Ann looked at him closely, at the matted hair sticky with oozing blood. The groan intensified, and he began to move his legs. Desperately Ann twisted her hands back and forth and at last felt the stocking loosen. Free of the bonds she looked about the room and picked up a heavy inkwell that had been swept from Alex's desk. She stood over the prostrate form, closed her eyes, and dropped the inkwell in the region of his head. There was silence again.

Ann stumbled out of the room and along the corridor. She heard the gun go off, followed rapidly by a second shot. Reaching the hall she saw Nigel leaping through the air to land squarely on the tall thin man. As the two men wrestled violently, the gun skidded across the marble floor.

Ann wanted to scream but her brain which had been playing funny tricks all evening played another. Instead of reacting like countless heroines in films who had enraged her by wasting precious moments screaming, Ann dived for the gun, picked it up, raced to the phone and dialled 999. In the seconds she had to wait for the connection, she turned towards the two men on the floor in time to see Nigel land a hefty left hook on the other man's jaw. With a grunt the marauder fell back senseless.

'Oh, Nigel, thank God you came. I thought they were going to kill me,' Ann cried as she swooped to his side. 'But you're hurt, that pig,' she hissed, kicking the senseless man viciously.

'It's all right, Mrs Georgeopoulos, I think the bullet just grazed me.'

'But look at the blood . . .' Ann said anxiously as she helped Nigel remove his jacket, revealing a white shirt scarlet with blood.

'Oh, Christ.' Nigel groaned and promptly fainted.

Ann wrenched off his tie and made a makeshift tourniquet. She was almost too frightened to look in case the bleeding continued, but it had stopped.

From far down the drive she heard the police car siren and the comforting wail of an ambulance. Stumbling to the door she swung it wide open and the light from the hall cascaded on to the driveway. She swayed against the door and found that she was trembling from head to toe, unable to control her movements.

Two policemen leapt from the car. The ambulance ground to a halt and two attendants appeared. One of the policemen immediately put his arm about her, an ambulanceman slung a blanket round her shoulders.

'I'm sorry but I think I've killed a man,' she said. The men looked at her blood-soaked dress and raced into the hall.

With matter-of-fact efficiency the police and ambulancemen took control. Ann was made to sit down. Nigel, conscious again, had his wound tended – it was a graze, there was no great damage. 'These surface wounds often look far worse than they are,' the ambulanceman explained.

'Fancy fainting like that. Bloody stupid.' Nigel grinned sheepishly.

'You'd be surprised how many do, sir.'

Nigel sat slumped against the wall and looked with disbelief at the burglar, still unconscious. 'I was hopeless at boxing at school, too,' he joked lamely.

'Well, you were magnificent when it counted, Nigel. Thank God you came. But what are you doing here?'

'We had almost reached Athens. I made some silly joke about Robin not being so muscle-bound because of having had to cancel his outward-bound course. And suddenly Mr Georgeopoulos asked, "It was cancelled, wasn't it?" Yianni said he'd told me to do it – he hadn't, Mrs Georgeopoulos, he certainly never mentioned it to me. Anyway, Mr Georgeopoulos appeared to believe him and as punishment, I suppose, he made me catch the first plane out of Athens. Thank God he did.' He shrugged his shoulders and winced at the pain.

'Nigel, do be careful.'

The ambulancemen came across the hall carrying the recumbent form of the short man on a stretcher.

'Is he . . .?' Ann could not finish the question.

'No, missus. A nasty messy lump you've made. He'll need an X-ray to check if you've cracked his bonce. Bet he'll have a headache to remember you by!' Both men laughed. One by one the two unconscious bodies were carried out to the ambulance.

The police drove Ann and Nigel to the hospital; Ann had to admit that she was relieved when the doctor insisted she stay in hospital overnight: not only was she shocked but she did not want to sleep in the house without Alex. And once she had told them she was pregnant a whole battery of tests was lined up for the morning.

By the afternoon, assured that the baby was fine, and with instructions to try to rest and be quiet for a few days, Ann returned home accompanied by a bandaged Nigel. They had been in the house only an hour when Alex and his entourage, summoned by telexes, arrived in a panic. They found a placid Ann and an embarrassed Nigel making light of their adventure.

'Good God, Nigel, how can I thank you enough?' Alex took Nigel's good hand in his. 'I am indebted to you for life. I shall have nightmares thinking of what they could have done to Anna.'

'It was nothing, sir. All in the line of duty,' Nigel grinned.

'Nothing! You could have been killed. Oh my God, Nigel. Do you realize? Oh Nigel . . .' and a white-faced and weeping Fay flew into his arms, hugging him as if she feared he would disappear.

'Don't cry, Fay. Honestly, I'm fine.' Nigel put his arm about Fay with a self-satisfied smile playing about his mouth.

Alex and Ann looked at each other in amazement.

Three times they had to tell their story. The study was inspected.

'By the way,' said Ann. 'Where is the safe so that I know next time?' She laughed, secure now that Alex was back.

'There won't be a next time. I'll make certain myself that you are never alone, ever.'

'But where is the safe?'

'This way.' Alex led them from the study and back into the little sitting room which was their favourite room. Yianni, who until now had stood silent, listening to their tale, crossed the room to the bookcase. He pressed what looked like a knot in the wood and the whole bookcase swung open revealing a large steel door which opened into a strongroom.

'They were pressing the knots in the wood in the study.'

'Wrong bookcase,' Alex grinned. 'They could not have been well briefed. The study's too obvious a place so I had it put in here instead.'

'I think I might be safer in an aeroplane, you know.' Ann smiled up at him.

'Neither of us is going anywhere until this baby is born.'

3

Ann was over four months pregnant. She was fully recovered from the shock of the burglary though she doubted if she would ever be able to sleep in an empty house again. At last the slight swelling of her belly proclaimed its inhabitant. She had never felt better. Her face glowed, her hair shone. Her fears had been unfounded, she was approaching this pregnancy like the young woman she felt herself to be.

An American industrialist, felled by a massive coronary, cancelled his weekend visit with his entourage. In turn Alex gave his assistants, including Fay, the weekend off, and put off the other guests he had invited. Ann felt sorry for the poor American, a man she had never met, but she could not stop herself feeling elated at the rarity his misfortune gave them – a weekend on their own.

As on that first week, long ago now, the phones did not ring. Alex opened no files, his briefcase remained closed, he had decided to give his wife his most precious gift, his time.

Saturday slipped by. Like young lovers they talked and planned. They made love.

On the Sunday they sat in their cove, between the rocks, where they had sat that first weekend. It was as if time had stood still, Ann thought, as she watched Alex idly piling pebbles one upon another.

'You know, Alex, since I got pregnant we're much more relaxed with each other. I'm not so afraid of the other women and you are less of a tyrant.'

'Me, a tyrant?'

'Yes, you.' She pushed him playfully. 'So jealous, so suspicious all the time.'

'Ah, but you don't know human nature like I do.'

'But I would never be unfaithful to you, Alex. You're my whole life. You trust me now but is that because I'm pregnant?'

'I suppose so, yes.'

'Oh darling, stay like this after the baby's born. I'd never give you any cause to be jealous. I promised it once, I'll promise it again.'

'I'll try.' He picked up her hand and kissed it gently. 'That's a promise too . . .' They sat staring out over the sea. The soft summer sunshine playing on the water.

'I couldn't bear it if you were ever violent to me again,' Ann said suddenly.

'Violent? What on earth do you mean? I've never been violent to you.' He laughed at the very idea.

'Yes you have. That day when you found me phoning Michael. There was a moment when you looked as if you were about to hit me. Oh Alex, the look on your face . . .' She shuddered at the memory. 'I'll never forget that. It's the sort of scene I never want repeated, don't you understand?'

'Darling, you exaggerate. I would never hit you. I might want to, and have to control myself, but hit you – never! What do you take me for? I'm not the sort of Englishman who beats his wife on a Saturday night. We Greeks respect our women.'

'You don't trust them, though – only if they're pregnant. That's so insulting.'

Alex abruptly knocked his pile of stones to the ground with an impatient gesture. 'For God's sake, Anna, do stop going on about it. I ripped your robe, it was an accident. So, I was angry. I find you making secret phone calls, eyes glowing with happiness . . . Any man would have jumped to the wrong conclusion. What would you prefer, that I didn't care?' He looked at her, with a half-exasperated, half-indulgent expression. 'Maybe I'll trust you when you're seventy and toothless and ugly with age.' He rumpled her hair.

'But to me love and trust go hand in hand,' Ann persisted.

'Oh, Anna, don't be so hypocritical. You hate me being out of your sight.'

'And whose fault is that?' She asked with spirit.

'Touché,' he grinned, but she did not return the smile. 'Come on, Anna, we're both as bad as each other. Only fools trust each other. You watch me like a hawk with other women. I am complimented by your jealous attention. Without it, sooner or later, I would be unfaithful, all men are, it's in our blood.' He laughed but there was no echoing laugh from her.

She looked at the pebbles intently and began to make her own pile. She was angry with herself for spoiling the day and she was angry with him that he would not say the one thing she wanted to hear. On top of everything, she was angry that he had pointed out her own jealousy. It was a conversation she wished she had never started but it was one she was unable to stop.

'Have you?' she ventured, not wanting to ask but the words seeming to form themselves.

'You said you never wanted to know.'

'I want to know now.'

'As a matter of fact . . .' He paused for effect. Ann felt her heart race nervously. 'As a matter of fact, the answer is no. I have not been unfaithful, but I don't promise that it will last.'

'I don't understand you. Everything is so perfect and then you spoil it by making statements like that.'

'I'm not spoiling anything. You started this conversation, I didn't want to. Anna,' he took her hand, 'I love you, I really do. I love you in a way that I never thought would be possible for me. I don't plan to be unfaithful to you, I don't want to be, perhaps I never will, but I'm trying to be totally honest with you.'

'It means you don't love me totally. All men are not unfaithful,' she said angrily.

'Aren't they?' he asked.

'No, there are men who love and respect their wives and their marriages, enough not to leap into bed with other women.'

'You really think so?' he asked, an amused tone in his voice.

'I know so.'

'Really? How interesting. I presume you refer to your precious Ben?' The amused tone disappeared to be replaced with a sharp inflection.

'Yes, and there's no need to sneer at him.' She stopped playing with the pebbles, offended that he should bring Ben into this conversation.

'I wasn't aware I was sneering. I was just thinking how he proves my point!'

'What do you mean?' She looked at him, seeing anger

in his eyes.

'That you are a bloody fool to trust.'

'What do you mean?'

'Nothing.' He began to throw the pebbles he had collected into the sea, not aimlessly, but almost violently.

'Come on, there's something you're not telling me,' Ann persisted while a voice inside her warned her to stop.

'I don't think I'm the right person to tell you.'

'I want to know. I have a right to know.'

He sat for some time in silence, then looked at her closely as if reaching a decision. 'OK, you asked. You think that trust is the most important factor in a relationship?' Ann nodded. 'And you think your marriage to Ben was perfect because you trusted each other?' Ann nodded again. 'And you think that our marriage is not perfect because I don't believe in trust?'

'Your trust would prove you really loved me.'

'And your Ben? Did he love you? Was he honest with you?'

'Totally.'

'Then why didn't he tell you about the affairs he had during your so-called blissful marriage?' He looked at her coldly, leaning back against the rock.

Ann sat in stunned silence. She could not believe what she had just heard. How could he be so vicious? 'You're lying!' she shouted angrily at him.

'Am I?' he answered calmly.

'You're jealous of him – even my poor dead husband.'

'No, surprisingly, I'm not. Your past is nothing to do with me, it's your present and future I concern myself with.'

'If it's true, and I only say "if", how do you know?'

'I made it my business to know.'

'You mean you snooped. Like you did over Peter? You must be proud of yourself, Alex.'

He shrugged. 'If you regard it as snooping – making it my business to find out things about the woman I love – so be it.'

'Tell me then. What do you know? Prove it.'

'I'd prefer not to go into details. There seems little point.'

'There's every point. I want to know how you found out – if you found out.' She gave a brittle laugh.

'The how is easy for someone like me.'

'Someone like you,' she sneered. 'I think sometimes you think you're some sort of god – meddling like you do.' Her voice was rising sharply. 'What you really mean is you employ detectives, in dirty mackintoshes, used to swilling about in filth, no doubt lying their heads off to get paid. Such style you have, Alex.' She laughed again, a dangerously high laugh. He did not answer her. He simply sat and listened to her, absorbing her insults like a punch-drunk boxer. 'Who then? Who is Ben supposed to have been unfaithful with?'

'Heard of Betty Derwent?'

Her shrill laugh rang out. 'Oh, how ridiculous! She was his secretary. You've been misinformed there. The nicest, quietest girl you could hope to meet. They travelled a lot together, they had to, he needed her at conferences. Your dirty snoopers got it wrong there.' She shook her head triumphantly.

'Susan Smithers, a theatre sister, I gather. Rosemary Printer, a staff nurse. Did you ever meet them?' Alex's voice persisted coldly, calmly. 'I gather Rosemary is a particularly busty blonde, almost vulgar, one might say . . .'

'Shut up, shut up.' Ann clapped her hands over her ears. 'Can't you even let the dead lie in peace?'

'Oh? Betty, Rosemary, Susan, are they all dead?'

It was his calmness, the almost clinical way he talked that convinced Ann he spoke the truth. He would not have said anything unless he was a hundred per cent certain. Alex did not work on gossip and innuendo.

'But why tell me?' she cried in anguish, jumping to her feet, as if she could run away from what he had been saying.

Alex too jumped to his feet. Grabbing Ann by the shoulders he swung her round, forcing her to look at him. 'Why, you ask?' There was no calmness in his voice now. He too was shouting. 'I have to listen to you compare me with that bastard Ben and I'm found wanting. He deceived you while I am honest with you. I refuse to have my love for you, my marriage, myself, compared with that man and found wanting. I wouldn't have told you, ever, if you hadn't persisted in your endless, foolish talk of trust!' He lapsed into silence.

Ann slumped miserably against the rock, sliding down it, oblivious to its sharp edges, and crouched on the damp sand, doubling her knees up, putting her arms about them, making herself as small as possible. In her mind was a great gaping nothingness.

Alex took her hand. 'Anna, I'm sorry, I lost my temper. I shouldn't have told you, it was unnecessary.'

She looked at him blankly. 'No, darling, I'm glad I know. I should know.' She began to stand, he helped her to her feet. The sun had disappeared; Ann shivered. 'I'd like to go back now, darling. I feel cold.'

He removed his sweater and draped it around her shoulders, fussing over her. Concerned now that he had gone too far, he kept apologizing. Taking her hand, he kissed the back of it, the palm. 'Forgive me,' he persisted.

She turned to him. 'I don't blame you, Alex. Knowing all that, and listening to me insisting that Ben was some kind of saint. I'm not surprised you let it burst out. Honestly, Alex. It doesn't matter. It was a shock, but if you want to know the truth, I'm angry because I feel stupid. I must have been the only person who didn't know.' She managed to laugh, and squeezed his hand comfortingly. She squared her shoulders. 'You're right. Why spoil such a lovely weekend going on about what Ben got up to? It doesn't matter a jot now, does it?' She smiled up at him.

But later Ann thought long and hard – the earlier emptiness in her mind had been filled by a hundred confused thoughts.

Why hadn't she ever found out, why hadn't she ever known? She had known Ben so well. She was convinced that if Alex were unfaithful she would know immediately, but would she? What a fool she had been – that's where complacency could lead. After Ben had died she had been able to face up to the fact that he had not been as perfect as she thought in other ways. She had acknowledged that he could be a martinet, that she had subjugated herself to him and his demands, so should she really be surprised by his deception? Just because she had never felt the need to stray, why should she have presumed that he had not? Perhaps that was what Peter had been referring to all that time – had he known? Was that why he had hated his father? But then he should have felt sorry for Ann, not loathed her too.

She wished it did not matter, wished she could shake it away as she had pretended to on the beach. But it did matter. After all this time she felt hurt and betrayed. But she did not feel jealous of those women, that was odd. She knew that if Alex were unfaithful she would go berserk. Where Ben had filled her life, Alex consumed it.

It was ironic really. Always thinking her marriage with Ben perfect, always questioning and doubting her relationship with Alex – it began to look as if she had invested faith in the wrong husband.

4

The following weekend Lydia and George were house guests at Courtneys once again. George had put up a business proposition which interested Alex and so, for the past few weeks, Ann had been happy to see far more of Lydia than normal.

This afternoon the two men were happily ensconced in the study, surrounded by plans and papers, making endless phone calls, while their wives relaxed beside the pool.

This pool was Alex's latest toy and replaced the old outdoor one. It was housed in a building whose roof and walls were electrically controlled to swing back when the weather was good, as it was today. It promised to be a lovely, lazy, relaxing weekend.

The two women lay on loungers, Lydia with chilled wine beside her, Ann with orange juice.

'How's Fay? Is she here this weekend?'

'No, she's at her flat. She comes and goes. She's in love,' Ann replied.

'Really? Who with? Tell me all.'

'Nigel, Alex's assistant. Quite honestly I thought she was only playing about with him, nothing serious. Until the burglary. That incident seems to have made her realize that she's really fond of him.'

'Do you approve? I mean, isn't he a bit . . .' Lydia waved her hand vaguely in the air.

'Weak? No, Lydia, after that night that's the last word I'd use to describe Nigel. Actually it was a bit like seeing Clark Kent turn into Superman,' she said with a giggle. 'After the burglary everyone's having to look at Nigel differently, including, it seems, Fay. He's good for her. His gentleness and consideration have made her much calmer and far less brittle. She feels safe for the first time, I think.'

'That's good news then. So is Nigel with her in London this weekend?' asked Lydia, always curious to know all the details.

'I presume so. I would never dare ask. Fay gets ridiculously possessive of her privacy.'

Lydia sat up to refill her glass and stared idly at Robin who was diving at the far end of the pool. Lydia had remarked several times on his fine muscular body shining with droplets of water as he clambered out of the pool. Robin was fully aware of her admiring eyes which inspired him to even more outlandish and gymnastic dives.

'His mother should never have called him Robin, not with a physique like that. Yum-mee,' Lydia drawled.

'Reminds me of our hockey captain at school, legs like beer barrels and she was called Willow – totally inappropriate.' She hooted. 'Why such a gorgeous hulk in your life? I thought Alex kept a tight rein on you with his divine possessiveness.'

'He's supposed to be my bodyguard in case someone gets it into their head to kidnap me. But the one time I needed him he was away acquiring even bigger muscles.' Ann laughed. 'The truth is, he's Alex's spy reporting back as to where I've been, who I've spoken to, even what I've spent for all I know.'

'Ann, you're joking.' Lydia sat bolt upright with shocked surprise. 'That's positively Victorian.'

'I know, it is, isn't it? But that's the price of his "divine possessiveness", as you put it. Poor darling, he can't help being so jealous. I'm jealous too, I understand how he feels.'

'Well, yes . . . but to make you have a minder – that's ridiculous.'

'Oh, I know, I know. You should hear Fay on the subject – that he's treating me like a chattel, etc, etc.' Ann rolled her eyes heavenward. 'But since I've no intention of going off the rails and if it makes him happy . . .' She shrugged her shoulders. 'I've come to terms with him being around all the time. I don't mind enough to make an issue of it.'

'I don't understand it at all. If he's that jealous why on earth employ such a glamorous hunk as Robin? I'd have thought that was asking for trouble.'

Ann shrieked with laughter. 'Oh Lydia, I thought you were so sophisticated nothing escaped your beady eye. Robin's a homosexual, that's why. I'm as safe as houses with him.'

'You're joking! He certainly fooled me. I mean he's so delightfully masculine, and he flirts. I mean look at him now.' Lydia smiled suggestively at Robin, who immediately threw into a double somersault from the top diving board. Thoughtfully Lydia sipped her chilled wine.

'Alex is wasting his money, though. He couldn't have found anyone more faithful than you, Ann.'

'Did you know Ben was unfaithful to me?' Ann asked suddenly.

Lydia choked on her wine. 'Ann, what a strange question,' she said, mopping her bikini where the wine had spilled.

'I'm serious, Lydia. Did you know? It's all right, you can tell me. I know all about it.'

'Who told you?' Lydia asked suspiciously.

'Alex. He went out of his way to find out. He's very good at that sort of thing. He told me everything.'

'Yes, I did as a matter of fact,' Lydia said after a pause.

'And you never thought to tell me?'

'Ann, lovely. No one wants to hear stuff like that. And would you have believed me? It could have led to us having a row.'

'You're probably right. But since Alex told me, I've been feeling such a fool – everyone knowing and not me.'

'I did think to tell you once or twice after Ben died – when you were grieving so. There was a time when I worried that you'd never come out of it. But then I thought, if you knew, it might make you grieve more – who could tell? And I nearly told you when you were rabbiting on about guilt and seeing Alex. Then I thought better "let sleeping dogs . . ." and all that rubbish. After all, you might have gone funny on us and abandoned Alex, and where would that have got you?'

'How did you find out?'

'At first it was just gossip – you know village life. I didn't know whether to believe it or not. Then George and I bumped into him in Bournemouth, of all places, very embarrassed he was too. Swore us to secrecy.'

'Who was she?'

'I don't know – a secretary or nurse from the hospital we presumed. Dreadfully boring-looking female – no style at all. Then George was in London and had to meet a client at the Hilton and up pops Ben with another floosie.

Both were ludicrously young too, quite ridiculous.' Lydia snorted her contempt of errant middle-aged husbands.

'No wonder he never wanted me to go to conferences with him,' Ann said a shade bitterly.

'Without doubt he was the worst shit I ever met. I think he deserved to die.'

'Lydia!' Ann said, shocked.

' "Lydia" me all you like. He was an out-and-out bastard and he never deserved you. I mean Sally was the last straw for me. I found it difficult even to speak to him after that – in fact I rarely did.'

The pool and Robin receded as if Ann were looking at them down the wrong end of a telescope, as if Robin were at the end of a narrow tunnel. The air seemed suddenly chill.

'You're a good friend,' she managed to say, aware her voice came in a whisper. Lydia continued, oblivious of Ann's mounting distress.

'And I mean, that bitch, the least she could have done was to have an abortion. The way you innocently doted on Adam, too – well, it was all too cruel I thought.'

'Adam?' The word slipped from Ann's mouth as the pool and Robin disappeared completely, as the walls of the tunnel collapsed inwards and blackness took its place.

As if from a long way off Ann heard Lydia crying out, a strange echoing cry. She did not want to wake up; she wanted to stay safely in the black cushion of unconsciousness that her healthy body was fighting to escape.

'Christ, Alex, my big mouth. She said she knew. She said you had told her. God, I'm sorry.'

'Phone the doctor, Robin,' she heard Alex shout. 'For Christ's sake, Lydia, stop wailing like that. You've done enough harm as it is.'

'But Alex, I wouldn't harm Ann for anything.'

'Well, you have, you stupid, gossiping bitch.'

'But she said she knew everything, Alex, honestly,' Lydia wailed.

'Of course she didn't know. And I had hoped that getting Peter shifted to Edinburgh would mean she need never know.'

'Oh, God, Alex, what can I do?'

'You can get out my sight, for one thing, before I do something I might regret,' Alex shouted. Ann stirred, she did not want people arguing, shouting about her like this. She had to do something but it all seemed such a dreadful effort . . .

'What happened?' she whispered, opening her eyes to see Alex's anguished face looming above her, and Lydia scuttling away across the lawn, her shoulders hunched, George's protective arm about her.

'You must stay quiet, my love. You must put this out of your mind, don't think about it, any of it.'

'I have to know, Alex.' She grasped his hand urgently. 'Please . . . Alex?' Ann put her hand towards him, feeling confused.

'Lie still, darling. You fainted for a moment, that's all,' Alex said in a bright, encouraging voice to which his worried expression gave the lie.

'It's the heat, I expect.'

'Yes, that's probably it. The doctor will be here in a moment.'

'Don't be cross with Lydia, Alex. It's not her fault,' she pleaded, the memory of what Lydia had said returning. 'I want everything to be as it was before, Alex.' She shivered, feeling a coldness within her which was at odds with the heat of the day.

'There, there, my love, it will be. I promise.'

The doctor examined Ann and ordered her to bed with a mild sedative. He reassured Alex that both she and the baby were fine, but that Ann should be kept quiet for a few days.

Ann lay in the semi-darkened room, her mind reeling. She felt sick. Desperately, deeply sick. But the sickness was a revulsion of the mind. She had been prepared to come to terms with Ben's unfaithfulness. She could never come to terms with this. She had loved Adam as her own flesh and blood and was she now to presume that not one gene of hers was in him? Could she love him less? Could she continue to love him? At last the dark bitter anger of her son was explained. But why did he hate *her*? Why had his grief rejected her when it should have made the bond between them stronger? A glimmer of hope filled her – could it be that if she saw him now and talked to him, his love for her would return?

Alex crept quietly into the room. 'I'm sorry, my love, did I wake you? I thought you were sleeping.'

'No, thinking. Is it true, Alex? Tell me. I have to know all there is to tell. You must be straight with me, Alex.' She took hold of his hand, urgently.

'I'm sorry, my darling. He did have an affair with Sally.'

'But how did you find out?'

'Your late husband was not one for discretion. They were seen together a few times in odd places – London, Bristol, Bournemouth. He seemed to have had a thing about Bournemouth.' Vainly he tried to make her laugh.

'But when, Alex? When did he have this affair with her?'

'It seems to have started when Peter first brought her home to meet you all.'

'Oh, my God. She used to look at me, Alex, with an almost challenging look in her eye. Oh God, it's true then, isn't it?'

'I never wanted you to find this out, darling. It's too dreadful for you,' he said, his voice full of concern for her.

'But hang on,' Ann sat up eagerly. 'Then she married Peter. Then it's all right, Alex. I mean, it's not all right, it's horrible . . . But then, if it was before they married, then Adam can't be his, can he? That was just Lydia repeating evil gossip.'

'Yes, darling,' he smiled. 'Just Lydia gossiping.'

Ann sank back with relief upon the pillows. It was Adam who mattered, the rest was unimportant. 'Oh no, it's not all right.' She turned to look at him, her eyes full of agony. 'I'd forgotten, Sally was pregnant when they married. It didn't seem important – not until now . . .'

'Maybe it's a case of no one knows for sure about Adam,' he said kindly.

'So there's no proof?' she asked, this glimmer of hope making her voice light, almost joyful.

'No, not with Ben dead. Just a rather complicated question mark over poor little Adam's head.'

'So Ben must have wondered about the child.'

'Undoubtedly.'

'God, and he blamed me for their attitude. Oh, Alex, how could he have been so cruel? I didn't know him at all. All those years together – they were meaningless. I was living with a shadow. What might I have been, Alex, what might I have been?' She began to sob at the prospect of twenty-five years of life lying in tatters around her.

'Darling. Hush.' He took her into his arms, attempting to calm her. 'You mustn't get upset, you must think of our baby. There's much for you to adjust to. I'm here. I will help you.'

'What would I be without you, my darling?' She put up her hand and stroked his hair. 'How long have you known?'

'Since that first Christmas. Your son's reaction to me was too extreme. There had to be something else. As if he were punishing you for something.'

'But why me? What did I do? You would think this would make us closer.'

'I asked Fay, she doesn't know – or if she does, she's not saying. Peter won't discuss it with anyone, she says. So that's something even I can't find out.' He half smiled at her.

'Oh God, Fay knows.'

'Yes, my sweet. You were about the only person who didn't, it seems.'

'Dear God. What a fool. How blind I've been. Poor Lydia, she walked right into it. I made her talk.'

'So I gather.'

'Don't blame Lydia, it's not her fault.'

'Once I knew you and the baby were safe I forgave her. She's beside herself with remorse.'

'So you were behind Peter's move after all.'

'You heard that? Yes, I contrived to have him moved. I thought the further away from you he was, the better. I'd have preferred it if he'd gone to the States.'

'But how? How do you do something like that?'

'It's easy. Words in the right ear, promise of money. Money's marvellous stuff. He didn't get his fellowship you see – I saw to that. So in a huff he moved himself, really. I just helped to push him a little.' He gave her a bleak smile.

'I have to see him, Alex.'

'After the baby's born, darling. Afterwards. You can't have any more upsets.'

5

Physically there was nothing wrong with Ann, but mentally she was scarred. For days she lay in the darkened room and sifted through memories. Her mind immersed itself in the past as laboriously she forced herself to face the truth about Ben, looking for clues in their relationship, desperately trying to remember the first signs of her son's alienation.

Her son. Once more her son dominated her thoughts. Once again she worried, made plans for their reconciliation.

She wanted to see no one, not even Alex. She felt too full of shame to face the world. Shame permeated every cell of her body. Shame for Ben's behaviour, shame for her son, her daughter-in-law, for Adam and the burden the child would carry for the rest of his life. But mostly she felt shame for herself – if she had been different, if she had not been so smugly complacent, then perhaps none of this would have happened. What sort of wife had she been to Ben? Dutiful, of course, she had been the epitome of duty, and boring with it. What sort of wife had she been in bed? Unexciting. There had been no uninhibited passion in their bed. Was it any wonder then that Ben should look elsewhere? Her grief and self-blame were such that her tortured mind did not once query how inadequate Ben himself had been in the matrimonial bed. It was as if she wanted to martyr herself, as if her love for Peter and Adam made it essential that she shoulder the total blame. A bleakness possessed her soul from which she could see no escape.

'Anna, I'm sorry this has happened, but you have to pull yourself together – not just for us but for the baby too.' Alex stood at the foot of the bed as, over a week later, the maid removed yet another tray of untouched food.

'I can't.'

'Of course you can. This isn't the end of the world. We have each other.'

'Do we? How can I trust anyone ever again?'

'With difficulty, like the rest of us. You've at last joined the real world, Anna. It's difficult and cruel. I understand your pain, my darling, but lying here a Victorian heroine isn't going to help you,' he said almost sharply.

'I'm not enjoying myself, if that's what you think.'

'I know, I know . . . I'm sorry, my love.'

'You don't know anything. How can you? How can anyone?' Ann blasted at him. She sat up in bed. 'How many people do you know to whom this has happened? Answer me that. It's not as if it happens every day, is it?' she shouted, angry with his sympathy, angry with life that could deal her such a blow and angry with herself most of all that she had not even sensed the wickedness within her own family.

'Shouting at me isn't going to solve anything. Getting up and about, that's what you need. You will really get ill if you insist on mooning about up here.'

338

'Well, who put me here? Who told me? Who ruined my happiness?'

'Anna, that's not fair . . .'

'Isn't it? If you hadn't gone snooping around in things that aren't your concern none of this would have happened. Everything would have stayed the same.'

'It was you who wanted to know. It was you who tricked Lydia. You exasperate me with your contrariness, Anna. You insisted on knowing and then when you find out, you can't take the truth.'

'The truth. Jesus Christ, there isn't a woman alive who could cope with that sort of truth. And if you had minded your own business I wouldn't have to suffer like this.'

'My darling, I understand your anguish. But blaming me for your late husband's sins isn't going to help either of us. I wanted to protect you, that's all. If I knew, then perhaps I could shield you. I failed.'

'Protect me? All you want to do is imprison me, give me a minder.'

'Anna, Anna . . .'

'You ruin my son's career and I'm supposed to thank you for it.' Her voice grew shriller and shriller as her anger mounted.

'Anna, this is getting us nowhere . . . I have to fly to Sweden tonight. Are you coming?'

'No. I don't want to go anywhere,' she snapped petulantly.

'Very well, then I go alone.'

'And no doubt tonight you will be screwing some vacuous creature just like dear old Ben.' Her laugh was more like a screech. Alex looked at her with distaste and turned towards the door.

'I trust you will be in a better humour when I return,' he said coldly and let himself out of the room.

Ann flung herself back on the pillows and began to cry. She was not sure why she was crying – whether it was from anger at the truth, sorrow at what she had just said, guilt at what she had screamed at him, or from feelings of self-pity.

She heard the front door slam. She leapt from the bed and crossed to the window; shielded by the curtain she watched her husband get into the car, saw the cold, angry expression on his face and she felt fear. She had gone too far. She would lose him if she pushed him away like that. She must pull herself together.

But before she could do that there was something only she could resolve.

Hurriedly she dressed, packed an overnight bag and called Robin. 'I've decided to go and stay with my daughter until Mr Georgeopoulos returns. If you could drive me there, then you could take a few days off to visit your friends.' She smiled sweetly at him.

'Mr Georgeopoulos did say I was to stay here with you. That you weren't planning to go anywhere.'

'Oh, Robin, I'll be much better off with Fay. I hadn't made my mind up when my husband left. I told him I might be going. He knows all about it,' she lied.

So Robin drove her to London. At the dock development where Fay lived he had difficulty parking.

'It doesn't matter, Robin. I only have this small case, just drop me off.'

Uncertainly Robin let her out of the car; she was conscious of him watching her walk along the pavement. At the entrance to the flats she turned and waved.

She sat in the foyer for five minutes, assuring the porter she just wanted to rest for a minute, pointedly patting her stomach. Then, looking up and down the street to make certain that Robin had gone, she slipped out, hailed a taxi, drove to Heathrow and caught the shuttle to Edinburgh.

It was early evening when Ann rang the doorbell of the elegant Georgian terraced house in Edinburgh's New Town.

Her heart was thudding as the door opened.

'Good God, it's you!' Sally said in greeting.

'Yes, Sally. I thought it was time I met Emma.'

'You'd better come in. Peter's not back yet and . . .' Sally paused, still standing in the doorway. 'To be honest, Ann, I don't think he'd be too happy to find you here.'

'Why not, Sally? What have I done wrong?' She looked the girl straight in the eye. No smile played about her mouth. There was a new hardness to Ann's expression which made Sally blush. 'Do I have to stand on the doorstep?'

'Ann, I'm sorry, come in.'

Sally ushered her into a long, elegant drawing room. Ann was pleased to see some of her old furniture, and a couple of paintings she'd given them well hung and lit.

'What a delightful room. How well the Midfield furniture fits it. You've obviously far more space here . . . much better for all of you.' With superhuman effort Ann talked inconsequentially.

She noticed Sally begin to relax a fraction as she prattled on. 'Yes, we're enjoying Edinburgh very much. There's so much to do here . . . there's such lovely architecture,' Sally said vaguely, her eyes never meeting Ann's but looking constantly at the clock.

'Where's Adam? It's Adam I've really come to see.'

'The au pair's bathing him. He'll be down in a minute. Gin and tonic?'

'White wine and Perrier please. I'm pregnant, you see.'

'Ann, how exciting for you. Are you all right?' Sally swung round with genuine pleasure on her face.

Sally's natural reaction made Ann, in turn, more relaxed. 'I'm fine – even at my age. And Emma?'

'She's gorgeous. She's asleep. I think she looks like you . . . I did want you to see her you know, but Peter . . . well, he just wanted to cut himself right off.'

This would have been a good moment for Ann to bring things into the open but she stopped herself. She wanted to see Adam. It was important for her to know how she felt about him first. Ann knew she would know immediately she saw the child.

The door opened and the boy entered the room in pyjamas, clutching an old, worn teddy.

'Hullo, Adam,' Ann said gently. The child paused a moment looking at the strange woman, a slightly puzzled expression on his face.

'Granny?' he asked disbelievingly. 'Granny?' His face broke into a broad smile.

'Darling.' She bent down and held her arms open to him and the boy rushed across the room and into her embrace. As she held Adam to her she knew she loved him. Nothing could change that. But more than that, as she held him, she knew with a deep certainty that this child was her grandchild, that her blood flowed in his veins. 'What a clever boy to remember me after all this time.'

'Why haven't you been here before? I've missed you a lot, you know,' he said accusingly.

'Oh, I live a very busy life now, Adam. I travel all over the world in a lovely aeroplane. It's difficult finding time to fit everything in, but I promise I'll find the time in future.'

For half an hour she sat as Adam, now nearly six, told of his school, of his friends, what he wanted to be. She listened entranced as she heard a slight touch of an Edinburgh accent in his voice, while the child chatted on as if her absence had been in weeks not years.

Sally sat on the edge of her chair glancing nervously at the clock, checking it against her watch, toying with her skirt, picking at imaginary threads. Ann found a strange calmness come over her. 'When will Peter be back?' she asked pleasantly.

'He's usually here by now. Any minute . . .' As Sally spoke Ann heard the sound of a key in the lock. Adam catapulted out of the room.

'Daddy, Granny's here . . .' they heard him call.

Peter stood in the doorway. The deep furrows in his face were even deeper than when she had last seen him, and still, she noted, he was dressed in the shabby cords and sweater. He could afford whatever he wanted now, Ann found herself thinking, nonsensically. Silly to dress like that when he could look so much smarter.

'Hullo, Peter,' she said agreeably.

'I thought Adam meant your mother was here,' he said to Sally, ignoring Ann. Crossing the room he poured himself a large drink.

'To what do we owe this honour?' he asked eventually.

'I've come to find out the truth,' Ann replied simply.

'I'll put Adam to bed.' Sally hurriedly began ushering the boy from the room.

'I'd like you here, Sally. I want us all here. Can't you get your au pair to see to him?'

Reluctantly Sally re-entered the room having called the au pair to take care of Adam. Ann stood facing them both.

'So, the truth, please.'

'What truth?' Peter looked at her over the rim of his glass.

'Sally, did you have an affair with my husband?'

Sally looked from Peter and back to Ann. 'Yes,' she said in a half-whisper.

'And is Adam Peter's son?'

'I don't know.'

'Haven't you tried to find out?'

'Father's blood group was the same as mine. It's impossible to prove one way or the other,' Peter interrupted.

'I see. When did your affair with my husband start?' Ann asked, aware that the strange calmness was still with her. She had not, on the plane, ever imagined that she could be conducting such a conversation with her son with such assurance.

'Oh, come on, Mother, don't give us this crap. What's the point in discussing it all now? It's done with, finished. The bastard's dead. Sally and I have worked our way through this and we don't need you stirring things up again.'

'Stirring? I'm not stirring. I'm trying to fit the pieces of this jigsaw together. I have to know for my own peace of mind when things happened. I'm also trying to find out why you hate me so very much.' Her composure was such that her voice sounded as casually interested as if she were asking Sally where she had bought her dress. As she heard her own voice it struck Ann how ludicrous this conversation must sound.

'Shit, what am I supposed to feel, pleasure at seeing you? Throw my arms about my darling, loyal, oh so genteel mother?' Peter sneered.

'You see, Peter. This dreadful bitterness. Why? You have to tell me – I need to know.

'Know what, Mother? You know everything. You've always known everything. I wanted to tell you exactly what I thought of you all those years ago. But you went barmy when the old sod died and, like a fool, I listened to Fay who begged me to leave you alone. That was my mistake. I should have had it out with you then – but I didn't, I let the bitterness fester, and this is the result, Mother.'

'So you only found out just before he died?'

'Yes, if you must know. Though what's the point in raking all this up . . .' He took a long draught of his drink. He refilled the glass, looked at Ann and, shrugging his shoulders, started again almost as if none of it was of any interest to him at all. 'Things had been a bit difficult between Sally and me. We often rowed, Mother, frequently over you and what, in my innocence, I had thought her stupid, jealous attitude towards you. Then one of these rows went a bit too far and Sally said too much. I put two and two together and hey presto, the cat's out of the bag. Just the affair, you understand. But the timing, Mother – I had to know, didn't I, about Adam. I won't go into details of how I got her to confess. I got straight on the phone

344

to Father, quite a row that was too, but with my father's insufferable luck, he died the next day before I could get my hands on the bastard.' He had finished his drink, and turned away to pour another.

'But, Peter, why didn't you come and talk to me about it?'

'I told you, Fay persuaded me not to. You wouldn't have taken it in anyway, not the way you were then. And what was the point, you knew in any case. What got me was how you could continue to say how much you loved him after that.'

'What do you mean, that I knew?'

'Oh, come on. He told me. When I phoned him that night and asked him outright. I threatened to come round there and then to have it out with him and to tell you. He laughed. He bloody laughed. I can remember his exact words – "Good God, boy, your mother and I don't have secrets from each other." He said you didn't mind. Imagine, my own mother didn't mind that my wife had been screwed by her husband.'

'Oh, Peter, my poor darling,' Ann said with feeling.

'Piss off, Mother. I don't need your sympathy. Not yours . . .' He gave a short, bitter, laugh.

'Peter, you must believe me, I've known nothing, not until this past week.'

'Mother, don't pretend. That's not all he said, he told me that for years he'd been having affairs, that you condoned them, Christ, that you used to like to know the sordid details. I gather it's quite common when marriages go stale.'

Ann sat down heavily on the sofa. Her hands were shaking. 'You believe that of me, Peter?'

'When you've just learnt your father's been screwing your wife nothing much takes you by surprise any more. If I'd heard you'd been sleeping three in a bed, that wouldn't have surprised me either. I mean the sexual permutations in our lovely family are endless, aren't they?' Peter laughed humourlessly.

Ann stood up, quickly crossed the room, and slapped her son sharply across the face. 'How dare you, Peter! How dare you say such disgusting things of me!'

Peter slowly stroked his face where the blow had fallen. 'Anything's possible.' He shrugged.

'But I'm your mother, for Christ's sake.' Ann shook her head in disbelief.

'But it was the way you were with Adam. You could go weeks without seeing him and then you were always all over the boy, in a sloppy sort of way. You never treated us as kids like that. It was thinking about that made me believe it was true.'

'Adam's my grandson, of course the relationship is different. I do feel and behave differently with him. I didn't expect to see him every day, I knew I couldn't. As a grandmother you learn to live with that. And if I spoilt him and was "sloppy" with him, that's being a granny too. I still feel like that about him. You can make whatever ridiculous claims you want, but I love him. He *is* my grandson.'

'Can't face the truth, can you, mother?' he sneered.

'Peter, we have to be friends, even more so now. We have to heal this family.'

'I don't think we can ever be friends. I just feel I don't know you or understand you. First the shock of finding out about Father, then his death, and the next thing you're rolling in the hay with that bloody Greek. Somehow that made everything make even more sense. Secondary proof, something like that.'

Ann looked at her son, heard the contempt in his voice and her calmness began to desert her. 'Peter, we have to talk about this and resolve it.'

'There's nothing to resolve, Mother. I love Adam, there's no problem there. I know Emma's mine and I forgave Sally long ago. It's my parents I can't forgive.'

'But Sally, don't you believe me? you know I was innocent of any knowledge – don't you? You of all people must know he was deceiving me. You know I tried to be your friend, for God's sake. At least I now understand why you rejected that friendship.' She managed a short sharp laugh.

Sally looked at the floor for a long time. 'I knew Ben was deeply unhappy with you and had been for a long time. He said you had no mind of your own. It was difficult for him, with his libido . . . I mean, he said you hadn't had sex for years,' she said defensively. 'But, yes, he did tell me he had told you and that you were always pleased if he was having an affair because that way he left you alone in bed. I despised you for that, I must admit.'

'Dear God. I don't believe I'm hearing this. I . . .' Ann laughed a shrill, empty laugh. 'I'm just a normal woman. I loved him the only way I knew how – maybe I wasn't very experienced but . . . I wasn't frigid. That's a lie. It was Ben who stopped wanting me, not the other way around.'

Peter snorted and finished his drink.

'You forgive Sally her actions and yet not me, when I've done nothing.'

'Sally was an innocent, Father a lecher. She didn't stand a chance.'

'So, we're back to your believing anything of me?'

Peter shrugged his shoulders as if bored with the conversation. Ann looked at her son for a long time, the silence oppressive in the room.

'It's you who are the sick one, Peter,' she said slowly, clearly. 'I've lived without you in my life before – if that's what you want I can easily do it again, if necessary. I'm ashamed of you, really ashamed, that you can think such foul things of me.' Anger made her voice shrill. 'I'd hoped that out of this evil knowledge we could be reconciled, that out of bad good could come. But I see you hate me too much.'

'Yes, Mother, I hate you. I hate you for not being what I thought you were. On top of everything else you land up with another shit bastard. You must really like them, Mother, to do the same again.'

'Alex isn't a bastard. Alex is a good man. How could you say such things about him when you don't even know him?'

'Oh yes, a really good man. What's it like being screwed by a murderer, Mother? Does that give you an added thrill?'

'Peter, what the hell are you talking about now? Don't be silly.'

'I suppose you're going to tell us you didn't know about that either.'

'About what, for Christ's sake?'

'His last wife, the one he killed . . .'

Once again Ann felt she was looking down a long tunnel and her son's voice seemed to echo from the sides of the tunnel – boring into her head words she did not want to hear, words she could not comprehend. Slowly and deliberately she picked up her handbag.

'This visit seems totally pointless if you're going to continue your vendetta like this . . .' She started to stand up.

A wave of pain engulfed her, she swayed on her feet. Another pain followed, so strong it felt as if she were being kicked in the stomach. Again the pain. And again. Ann clutched at her stomach, at the precious life within her, and stumbled towards her son, her hands beseeching him. 'The baby,' she screamed and finally was allowed to drop into an abyss of darkness.

6

As she awoke Ann's mind already knew what the pain in her body meant. There would be no baby.

She lay with her eyes closed, as if by not opening them she could delay facing the reality of this emptiness which was now her body.

She knew she was not alone. Without seeing him she sensed Alex's presence. She feared his anger and disappointment. She knew it was all her fault. A tear forced its way between her closed eyelids and ran down her cheek. She felt his lips brush hers.

'Oh, my love, don't cry, don't suffer. I love you,' she heard him say.

Slowly she opened her eyes and through the haze of pain saw him bending over her. 'Alex, my darling, forgive me,' she whispered.

'There is nothing to forgive, my sweet. The Gods decided. It was not to be,' he said gently. She felt a slight prick in her arm and with relief and almost pleasure she allowed the drug they gave her to remove her from a reality she was not ready to face, but she slipped away with the knowledge that he still loved her.

In the night, she again returned to consciousness. Alone she wept for her dead child and for the dreams that she had dared to dream. Alone she fought the bleakness of her soul. Alone she resolved that in this life it was she and the man she loved who mattered.

For two days he said nothing, but on the third day he asked her. 'Why did you go?'

'I had to know for certain. I hoped, foolishly it seems, that out of it Peter and I would be friends again.'

'I could have told you your son's heart is too black for forgiveness.'

'I still love him, Alex. I can't stop loving him.'

'No one expects that you stop loving him. But me? I hate him, I wish he were dead – I could have killed him with my bare hands that dreadful night.' He lifted his large hands, curving his fingers around an imaginary neck.

Ann's womb convulsed. She winced.

'Are you in pain?'

'No,' she lied, 'it's the talk of killing.'

'My darling, I'm sorry, don't let me frighten you.' His long, elegant hands took hers and he lifted them to his sensuous mouth and gently kissed them.

She looked at his hands – hands capable of giving such joy. Were these the same hands capable of destroying life?

She had to ask, she had to know even if the knowledge were to destroy them. Not knowing presented as much danger to them.

'Did you kill your wife?'

He looked up suddenly, searchingly, his grey eyes full of a compassion that she knew in a second could turn to ice. 'What a strange question, my love.'

'I have to know, Alex.'

'And what, or who, put such an idea into your head?' he said lightly, too lightly, Ann thought.

'Peter,' she explained simply.

'I see.' He stood up and went to the window. For a long time, it seemed, he gazed out across the roofs of Edinburgh. Ann felt sick. The longer he stood in thought the more convinced she was that she would hear the reply her mind could not accept.

'I did and I didn't,' he finally replied, sitting back again on her bed. 'Promise me that what I am about to tell you will not make you hate me.'

'How can I promise if I don't know what you're going to say?'

He shrugged his shoulders. 'An impossible request, isn't it? But I hoped you loved me so much that nothing I did would change it – like the love you have for your son. So, I must tell you and I must risk our love for each other. Even more reason to hate that son of yours.'

Ann waited nervously for him to begin.

'At first I loved Nada. Totally. Jealously – more than I love myself. But . . . she never really loved me. And she was unfaithful.'

Ann gave a little gasp.

'Yes, I know what you think – you remember my warning to you . . . But I didn't murder her, though there are many who still say I did. Myself, I don't really know . . . I wanted her dead, I admit that, but the whole nightmare is a vague blackness to me. I would be lying to you if I said categorically that I didn't kill her.' He paused, collecting his words.

'Alex, please, don't talk in riddles. I have to know.'

'I had thought Nada was happy. I gave her everything that any woman could want. But it was all an illusion. An illusion that did not last. After a couple of years it was obvious she was being unfaithful. I could not accept it. My sister warned me. So did my friends. But my pride refused to listen. Eventually even I couldn't ignore it. My love for her was dying, killed by her indifference. Only my stupid pride kept us together, I suppose. I could not face the world witnessing my failure. It was a sham of a marriage and I was as unhappy as it is possible to be.' Ann watched him closely, saw the bleakness in his eyes and shivered.

'I had been away on a trip. I took many trips in those days. I returned unexpectedly and found her in bed with the chauffeur – can you imagine my shame? How he escaped I shall never know. He was faster than me, and he was out of the villa in seconds.' He laughed at some long-ago memory. 'Scuttling down the dusty street clutching his pants to him. Mind you, the bastard has never worked from that day to this – it was a better revenge, really, than killing him. So, I was left with my beautiful, unfaithful wife. From room to room in that villa we ranted and screamed and shouted hatred and vilification at each other. Apparently I had failed her. I did not excite her enough. She was bored with my love-making. I hit her. I hit her several times. The first and only time I have allowed myself to hit a woman. That was when she chose to tell me she was pregnant and that was when she told me she did not know who the father was. She screamed the list of possible fathers – not just the chauffeur, a long list, including friends of mine. We were on the landing. She turned towards me, such a malevolent look in her eyes, she turned, laughed at me and fell down the stairs. She cracked her skull on a large stone ornament in the hall. She was alive when they took her to the hospital. Twenty-four hours later she was dead.'

His grey eyes seemed to turn black at the dark memories he was having to unleash. He took her hand in his. 'To this day, my darling, I don't know if I pushed her or if she fell. At the inquest Yianni stood in my defence and said that he entered the hallway as my wife was turning to go down the stairs. He said she tripped and fell. I don't know the truth – my mind still blacks out the memory. The judge believed him – I was free. But to this day my enemies say I killed her and I'm not certain, in my soul, that if it hadn't happened that way how long it would have been before I did kill her.' He stopped, studying the counterpane intently, as if afraid to look at her.

Ann put her hand out and grasped his. All she could think of, clearly, was that at the end he had hated Nada. That he had not spent these years grieving for her. That his refusal to talk about her had been from fear of her finding out the truth. She felt an immense wave of relief.

'My poor darling . . .'

'You believe me?'

'Of course I believe you, of course, my love.'

'Thank God for that.' He put his head in his hands. 'I've dreaded you finding out. Seeing you afraid of me. Knowing you despised me. Our love is such, Anna, that I cannot contemplate life without you.'

'Alex, my darling. I know. I know just how you feel.'

The next day a nurse told her that her son was waiting outside. Ann refused to see him. She felt a great bitterness towards Peter – not for the miscarriage, for she could rationalize that anything could have made that happen. No, her bitterness was because her son could think such ill of her – that was what she could never forgive. She had told Alex she loved Peter; she was no longer sure. But love him or not, she had reached a point in her life where she had to decide between her son and her husband. How could she expect Alex to receive her son now? And faced with a choice, it was Alex she chose.

Released from the hospital and safely back in their country home, Ann attempted to pick up the pieces of her life.

While she was in the hospital Alex had had the nurseries in both houses stripped of everything, redecorated and turned into guest bedrooms. All the toys he had been collecting were sent to children's hospitals. It was as if she had never been pregnant.

The baby was never mentioned by either of them, but silently Ann grieved for what might have been and there was a wariness about her that had not been there before.

But saddest and most perplexing of all, she had lost her joy in sex. No longer was her body always ready for him. Now he had to coax and wheedle. Now he had to use all the expertize that he possessed. She pretended and acted a pleasure she could no longer feel. As he entered her and his body crushed her she would lie, writhing with simulated pleasure, and long for it to be over. And as he slept beside her she would weep at the memory of how it used to be.

Six

1

The recent events had changed Ann. Her initial wariness intensified – wariness of people, of Alex, of life itself. In many ways she felt as she had when Ben had died, with the same desire to be alone to lick her wounds, to analyse her feelings. She dreaded the nights when, lacking the joy of the past, she felt almost as if Alex abused her body.

She spent hours alone now. In her room, or on long solitary walks in the countryside which in her sad confusion she no longer really saw. She tried to paint again, but her enthusiasm had waned.

Was it simply the miscarriage, and was this a quite normal depressive reaction to it? Or was it her son's betrayal? Or, more sinisterly, did a part of her mind believe Alex had murdered his wife and was it therefore fear of him which held her back – especially when she was at her most vulnerable – in bed with him?

Ann had to admit she was surprised by Alex's reaction to her behaviour. She would have expected, and would have forgiven, exasperated irritation. Instead he was gentle and kind and when he made love to her it was almost with an apology that he should be adding to her burdens. His attitude only confused and muddled her further. In a strange way it would have been easier if he had been angry – that way she could have had a glimmer of justification instead of this added guilt.

When Alex suggested she went to Greece without him, Ann jumped at the opportunity. She needed a short time away from him if she were ever to sort herself out. He also suggested Fay and Nigel accompany her. What could be better for her, Ann thought, than time with her daughter? She still had not discussed Peter with Fay and had a lurking fear that Fay might think the same way about her. It had to be brought out in the open.

Ann felt light-hearted as she kissed Alex goodbye.

'Return to me, Ann, when you have resolved your problems,' he said seriously, taking her hands in his.

'I'll only be away a couple of weeks.'

'No, my love, I want you to stay until you are better.'

'Will you come out?'

'No. I've decided that it is better I don't see you for a while. You need time, my darling. Time to heal yourself. Time to want me again.'

'But Alex,' Ann started, fear clutching at her heart. This was not what she had intended.

'No buts, darling. You are finding life intolerable with me at the moment. And, I will be honest, it is not easy for me either. I have to be away in America for a couple of weeks. When I return, hopefully you will have decided.'

'Decided what, Alex?'

'Whether you want me any more.'

'But I love you, Alex.'

'And I love you, Anna, but I want all of you, not just part of you. I want the magic that was our life together, not this second-hand substitute.'

Ann sat in the helicopter as it approached the island of Xeros. But this time her spirits were not lifted by the sight of the pretty island set in the clear blue sea.

All through the journey Alex had filled her thoughts. She could see she had been so engrossed with her own problems that she had not thought fully of the effect her attitude must be having on him. She had been lulled into a false, self-centred security by his gentle consideration. She should have known better – second best would never be good enough for a man like Alex. If she wanted to stay married she was going to have to use this time without him to resolve the confusion in her mind.

As they entered the villa, Ann was annoyed to see Ariadne hurrying forward to greet them. She had forgotten that Alex's sister invariably came to the island in August to escape the heat of Athens. Ariadne was the last person she needed at this point in her life, she thought, as she forced herself to smile.

The two sisters-in-law embraced each other, politely. She kissed the air by Ariadne's cheek and started to pull away. But she found herself in a vicelike hug from Ariadne who was showering her with little kisses, like a bird pecking for grain. This was not at all the usual restrained, slightly suspicious welcome she normally received from her sister-in-law.

Ariadne finally let go of her but, still holding her firmly by the hand, led them in to the drawing room, insisting she sit down immediately while Ariadne fussed over her with food and drink.

During the next few days the fussing continued, accompanied by a genuine affectionate concern. Ariadne was full of sympathy for her as if it were a case of Ariadne and Ann against the world. It was as if Ann, having suffered, had finally been allowed to join a mysterious society of Greek women. For the first time Ariadne talked to Ann of herself; of the husband of only six months' marriage who had cruelly been taken from her.

'I can love only my Savvas. I am proud of my widow's weeds.'

'So that's why you always wear black?'

'Of course, it is our custom. My life is one of mourning for my husband. There can never be another for me.'

'No wonder you didn't approve of me then – a widow like you, marrying your brother.'

'I did not hold that against you. Your culture, your beliefs are different. I accepted that. You see, how could

I take another man when I know that I shall meet with Savvas in paradise?'

'Dear Ariadne, I wish I could see everything so clearly. I seem to get everything in such a complicated muddle.'

'It's easy for me, life has taught me the hard way. The Gods have not been good to me – so one acquires wisdom. You, for so long, were happy and then the Gods drop shock after shock upon you. Too many shocks in such a short time for a person to deal with.'

'Perhaps you're right. I have had it easy. The hardest part is coming to terms with the fact that for twenty-five years my life had been an illusion of happiness.'

'Why? You were happy then – what you subsequently find out can't alter that – that's not an illusion. It happened. Now you have Alex. Your love and happiness with him is all that matters. Your children have their own lives to lead.'

'You know about my son?'

'Alex told me. He tells me everything,' she said with sisterly pride. Ann felt a minor wave of annoyance with Alex for discussing her problems like this.

'I wish he hadn't. It's very private to me,' she said stiffly.

'But we are family, Ann. Your problems are my problems,' Ariadne explained simply, smiling kindly at her. 'I don't believe this nonsense that your son rejected you because of what your first husband said about you – no son could believe such things. No, he's riddled with jealousy that you found Alex – he probably hoped when your husband died you would go and live with him.'

'Oh, hardly, Ariadne. Jealous? No, that's too silly.'

'No? You mark my words, I know. After all, Oedipus was a Greek. We are wise in these matters, you know.' She tapped the side of her nose with her bejewelled finger.

'Touché,' Ann laughed, at the same time intrigued by the theory. 'You like me now, you didn't, at first, did you?' she asked bluntly.

'I was afraid for Alex. After that whore he was married to I was afraid he might make another mistake.'

'What was she like?'

'I told you, a whore. Nada was the only foolish thing I've ever seen my brother do. She was cheap and common, not suitable at all. But he was besotted by her. Of course she was beautiful and men are stupid where beauty is concerned, aren't they? She took so much from him. Her demands were like a chorus. I told him. I told him of her affairs – I had proof, you see, but he would not listen. He was so angry with me for telling him the truth, he would not speak to me for two years. Oh, the pain I suffered. But I was right in the end,' she said with satisfaction.

'Did he . . .'

'Did he kill her? No, more's the pity, he should have done, years before. Don't you listen to gossip, Ann. My brother is innocent. Yianni was there . . .'

'But he says he can't remember.'

'Probably doesn't want to remember, but Yianni saw it all. There's no question she tripped and killed herself. Good riddance.' Ariadne laughed, but at the same time quickly crossed herself.

Ann had thought that talking to Fay was going to help her; instead it was Ariadne whose no-nonsense approach was of far greater help to her.

She delayed talking to Fay about anything. Over the weeks she had watched her daughter's feelings for Nigel intensify. There was no play-acting now, no teasing, no off-handedness; the girl was in love and Ann did not want to spoil her happiness. She would lie awake at night and through the wide patio doors she could not help but hear them making love, which only intensified her sadness at having lost her own joy in love. But Ann knew she could not delay indefinitely.

Mother and daughter were alone, beside the pool. Ann began to screw up the courage to talk – funny, she thought, that it should be beside the pool: so much had happened as a result of her last serious conversation by a swimming pool.

'Fay, about Peter and me . . .' she started.

'I don't want to discuss it, Mummy.'

'We have to, Fay. I have to know what you think.'

Fay raised herself on one elbow and looking long and hard at Ann. 'I think, Mummy, you were a complacent fool. I think my father was unspeakable and I think my brother is a shit for the way he thinks about you. I've had it with Peter. We're not speaking and I doubt whether I shall ever speak to him again.' She lay back again on her sunbed, closed her eyes and continued to soak up the sun. Ann slumped back with relief.

'Bless you, Fay.'

'I still think you're a fool.'

Ann sat upright with surprise and looked questioningly at her daughter who remained lying with her eyes closed. Ann realized she was holding her breath waiting for her daughter to elaborate.

'You had a lousy relationship with my father which you fondly imagined was perfection. You accepted everything in that marriage unquestioningly – he used you, deceived you, treated you like a live-in servant. Now you have a wonderful man who worships you, who would give you the moon if he could, and what do you do? You spend your time worrying and wondering, distrusting and destroying what could be a relationship so perfect most of us can only dream about it. You don't deserve him. There, I've said it.'

Ann gazed out across the sea. Fay's words had come as a shock. But it was the sort of shock that galvanizes the mind – she felt she had been in a jungle of uncertainty and Fay had shown her the pathway out.

'Thank you, Fay.' She kissed her daughter on the forehead. 'You always were a clever old thing.' She smiled affectionately at the young woman.

Fay sat up and looked at her mother. 'You're not cross with me?'

'How could I be? I needed the truth. Now all that remains is to see my way through the muddle that is me at the moment.'

Fay had helped, Ariadne had helped. They could all point the way, but eventually no one could resolve Ann's problems but herself. In the middle of one night, when sleep refused to come, Ann got up. In the stillness of the Aegean night, to the chorus of the crickets, she began to paint once more.

But these paintings were not the pretty watercolours of before, nor the stilted still-lifes. This time the canvases were splattered with paint, daubed thick with bright pigment. The palette knife was more in evidence than the brush as Ann scooped up great shining globules of paint and layered them on to the canvas. She did not worry about line or balance, perspective she ignored, tonal qualities meant nothing to her – instead she enjoyed the voluptuousness of the pigments, the sensuous pleasure of the feel of paint on the textured canvas. From this haberdashery of colour and shape she created large paintings of swirling, dreamlike people, who floated in an abstract world as ephemeral as flowing water. Frenziedly, silently Ann transferred the agony of the loss of her dead baby, the anger and pain of her son's suspicion, the confusion in her mind, on to the blank white canvases. Out of the agony came pleasure and joy. Out of the pain appeared hope and endurance.

Night after night she painted until her room was full of these canvases, raucous in their colour, screaming loudly of her past despair.

Then one night she did not paint.

She lay in bed, the scent of jasmine filling the air, listening to the sound of the crickets, and suddenly she was assailed by a deep longing for Alex – not only for his presence but a great physical longing, the longing she had often had and had feared never to feel again. She wanted him by her side, she wanted to touch, to caress him.

She lay in the dark full of delighted surprise, uncertain why this feeling had suddenly returned but knowing that all her fears and doubts had evaporated.

The next morning she rapidly packed her bags, left instructions for the destruction of her paintings, ordered the helicopter and kissed the surprised faces of the others goodbye. It had taken her two weeks to come to her senses. She could not wait to get home.

The car slid up the drive of Courtneys and for the first time Ann wondered if she should have phoned first. Maybe he was not even at home – was still in America. With relief she saw his car in the driveway.

It was early evening. She knew he would be having a bath. She raced up the stairs two at a time.

It was not until her hand was on the doorknob that she paused and for the first time realized the risk she was taking. What if he had not waited for her? What if he had taken another woman? What if there was another woman here now, in their room? If it was so, she had no one to blame but herself.

With thudding heart and a sinking feeling in her stomach she turned the handle.

Alex lay in the bath, a glass of champagne at his side, his eyes closed, a Mozart quintet filling the air and deadening the sound of her approach. She stood looking down at his taut, tanned body, then bent and gently kissed him on the lips. His eyes opened, momentarily startled.

'Ah, my Anna. You have returned to me?'

'Yes, my love. I don't know what was wrong with me – but it's gone. I missed you so. Forgive me.'

'Then you have much to prove to me.'

'Gladly,' she laughed.

Quickly he climbed out of the bath and soaking wet he took her in his arms, ruining her clothes as rapidly he tore them from her.

When she was naked, he lifted her, carried her to the bed and began slowly to make love to her. All the old passion swept over her as with ease he drew her to a screaming climax. The relief she felt swamped her body.

'Darling, never let me get like that again.'

'Never, my love. We had so much that was wonderful, and we came so close to losing it.'

She lay in his arms as the dusk settled on the park outside. 'Tell me, Alex. These past months, these past weeks, have you been unfaithful to me?'

He sat up, leaning his weight on one elbow. 'I thought you never wanted to know.'

'I didn't, but I do now.'

'Well,' he grinned. 'You promise not to tell a living soul?' Her heart sank at the meaning of his words. 'It's so ludicrous, me, Alex Georgeopoulos. But yes, my love, I tried to be unfaithful . . . but I couldn't. Can you imagine me – impotent?'

'Oh, Alex.' She laughed with delight. 'I don't believe it. Honestly?'

'Amazing, isn't it? Perhaps I'd better check that everything is still in working order.' Laughing, he took in his arms again.

2

Two weeks later Fay and Nigel returned from the island bronzed, happy and totally engrossed in each other to the exclusion of everyone else. No sooner had they arrived than they disappeared up to Fay's room. Among their baggage were three large wooden packing cases.

'What's this?' Alex enquired curiously of the crates in the hall as he entered the house from the helicopter.

'They're Fay's or Nigel's – they arrived this morning. These cases came this afternoon. Though why they should leave them here cluttering up our hall . . .' Ann felt mildly irritated by her daughter's inconsiderateness.

'What are they?'

'I've no idea. I haven't seen either of them since they got back.'

'Are they staying here?'

'Your guess is as good as mine, Alex.'

'Has it ever crossed your mind that your daughter is beginning to use this place as a hotel? You never seem to know if she's coming or going,' he said a shade tetchily.

'I think it's a sign of how relaxed she is with us both. She treats it like her second home. And certainly, working for you, things are easier if she can stay here whenever she wants,' Ann replied defensively.

'It would make more sense if she moved in permanently.'

'She'll never do that.'

'Are they still together?'

'Very much so, it seems.'

'Good. It's about time they both got married. We need grandchildren, you and I.' He smiled gently at her.

'I'd like that. But I don't know about Fay. She said she would never marry.'

'But then she didn't know about love before, did she? Mind you, Nigel won't be around to marry if he doesn't move these cases by dinnertime.'

As they had drinks before dinner that night, Fay was acting most mysteriously. She seemed edgy that Alex was late.

'Fay, settle down, do. He's got an important deal on. He said these calls might take some time. Have another drink, stop mooching around like that,' Ann remonstrated, but still the girl continued to prowl about the room.

At the sound of Alex's footsteps in the hall, Fay raced out to meet him. She returned, her arm linked in his and arguing with him.

'But can't I have a shower first? I've had a busy day.'

'No. You have to see my surprise first. Come on, Mummy, Alex . . .' Holding Alex's hand and followed by Ann and Nigel, she led them across the hall and into the morning room.

There, leaning against the walls and the furniture, were the paintings Ann had done on the island, all now beautifully framed and looking, to Ann, more like real pictures because of this.

'There, Alex, what do you think of them?' Behind Alex's back, Fay winked at her mother and touched her lips with her finger.

Ann felt herself begin to blush with embarrassment. She had not meant anyone to see this work, not even Alex. It was too personal, not like anything she had ever done before. That was why she had left instructions with the servants for them to be burned. She felt strangely protective towards the paintings, wanting to hide them from others' eyes . . . and yet, she was curious, she wanted to know how other people saw them, to know whether they would understand the emotions she had tried to transfer to canvas. Looking at them again, after a month, she thought to her surprise that they were quite good. She wanted Alex's honest opinion and so she kept quiet.

Alex studied each painting carefully, holding them to the light, peering closely at them, putting them down and standing back from them, an expression of deep concentration on his face. Silently he walked from one picture to the next.

'They are extraordinary!' he eventually exclaimed. 'Such pain in them. It almost hurts to look at them, especially this one.' He picked up the oil Ann had painted for her dead child: strange, distorted, half-human forms swirling against a blue-green background. A great slash of carmine streaked boldly across the foreground.

'Who's the artist, Fay? Where did you find him? Is he someone we should help?'

'You're such a chauvinist, Alex! It's a woman. And yes, I do think she needs help. She lacks confidence, you see. She had arranged to have these burned. I saved them and had them framed,' Fay said proudly.

'That would have been tragic. A woman? They have such a strength in them for a woman painter. I like the almost primitive quality they have. Her name?'

'Ann Georgeopoulos,' Fay announced, grinning broadly from ear to ear and pointing to Ann whose face was now deep red with confusion.

'Anna? My Anna? Darling, I had no idea you could paint like this . . .'

'Neither did I, Alex. They just sort of happened.' His critical acclaim delighted her. 'Mind you, I don't think I could ever do it again.'

'Of course you can and you must. You can't let talent like this lie dormant. We must have an exhibition, immediately.'

'Alex, I couldn't. I painted them for myself, I never intended that anyone should see them. They're too personal, too painful . . .' She tried to explain, fearful of Alex's enthusiasm.

'All creative work is personal and frequently painful. If it's any good you can't escape that fact. No, I insist, darling, you must. I'm so proud of you.' He hugged her to him.

Ann looked at the three eager faces and at her paintings. 'All right,' she said eventually, uncertainly. 'But I want to submit them to a dealer, I don't want an exhibition mounted by you, Alex – that wouldn't prove anything to me. All your business associates would buy them just to please you.'

'Fair enough. But I'm certain a dealer will snap these up.'

'And the one of the baby . . . no one sees that but us.'

'I understand.'

'And I don't want to use your name. People would say I was trading on it. I will sign them, but I'll sign them as . . .' Ann racked her brain for a suitable name.'

'Not Grange, not that name.'

'No, Alex. Ann Alexander. How about that?'

The name was agreed upon as a good compromise. Ann suggested the gallery in the cathedral town nearest to Courtneys. Alex would hear none of it – that place was for amateurs, he airily declared. Ann was aghast when he suggested a famous gallery in Cork Street.

'They won't be interested,' she protested.

'On the contrary, I think Mr Vestas will be very interested.'

'Then you can't come with us, Alex. I'd never get an honest opinion with you – one of their best customers – in tow, would I?'

'But . . .'

'No buts, Alex. We do it my way or not at all,' Ann said emphatically. Alex, for once, acknowledged defeat.

'How do you submit paintings? I mean we can hardly go lugging these paintings around, surely?' Ann asked.

'I think you submit transparencies first,' Nigel volunteered.

The ten canvases were duly photographed and a fortnight later a nervous Ann, with Nigel and Fay in attendance, presented herself for her appointment at the gallery. Alex, a slightly sulking Alex, had been deposited in the bar of the Ritz, to wait for them.

Ann sat awkwardly on the edge of the chair in the severely functional but expensively furnished basement room. She shifted in the chair, the soft leather of the upholstery making her feel hot and uncomfortable through the thin silk of her skirt. She twisted her rings round and round as she made polite conversation with Mr Vestas, the surprisingly young and epicene man who was the owner.

Mr Vestas's assistant took the slides, switched on the projector and doused the lights. Ann's paintings sprang on to the screen, larger than life, seeming to fill the room.

The click-click of the projector as the slides changed and the whirring of its fan were the only sounds in the room, as Mr Vestas studied the images looming above them. At intervals he would raise his hand for the next slide. Some pictures were changed quickly, others he studied for minutes, which to Ann seemed hours.

The show was over. The lights were switched on. Ann searched for her handbag on the floor, eager to make a quick escape.

'Remarkable! Remarkable!' they heard him say.

'Did you like them?' Fay asked bluntly and Ann frowned at her daughter, disapproving of her pushiness.

'And you have no formal education in art, Mrs Alexander?' the dealer asked Ann, completely ignoring Fay, which Ann took to be a bad sign.

'Only O-level.' Ann laughed, but so nervously that it emerged as a giggle. And then she wondered why she had laughed at all since nothing was funny. 'And the past couple of years I've been having lessons when I could fit them in – first watercolours and then how to use oils, that sort of thing,' she added far more seriously.

'And you haven't painted before?'

'Not what you would call painting. Watercolour sketches, still-life, flowers and so on.' Another giggle emerged and Ann despised herself for not being more in control. At this rate the man would never take her seriously and she now wanted very much to be taken seriously.

'Remarkable,' Mr Vestas, infuriatingly, repeated. 'Tell me, could you possibly do, let's see, another half-dozen at least. It's a matter of wall space, you see. Nothing would be worse than an exhibition with too few paintings – overheads being what they are,' he added vaguely smiling kindly at Ann.

'You mean you're going to exhibit them?' Fay pitched in excitedly.

'Undoubtedly, provided Mrs Alexander can come up with a few more. It's just a matter of fixing a date . . .' He rang for his secretary. 'You have an extraordinary technique, Mrs Alexander, so strong and forceful and yet so totally naïve – that of course is their greatest strength. In fact, Mrs Alexander, I suggest that you should cease your lessons forthwith, you've obviously learned how to use the medium. It would be a great shame if you should begin to become self-conscious and lose this delightfully fresh, ingénue style.'

Ann sat momentarily speechless with pleased surprise. Then, 'Do you know anything about me, Mr Vestas?' she asked suspiciously.

'Why no, Mrs Alexander, only what you have just told me. I gather your secretary made the appointment with mine.' He smiled quizzically at her.

'Do you know Mr Georgeopoulos?'

'Of course, a charming man, a valued client. I shall certainly be inviting him to the preview, I think he would appreciate your work. Do you know him too?'

'Yes, yes, I do . . .' Ann said vaguely, still not believing that Alex was not behind this man's acceptance of her work.

'Now our terms . . .' He explained in detail their commission on sales in the UK, sales in the US and, to her astonishment, almost apologetically asked if he could have world rights. Ann happily agreed to everything. From being a happy dauber, she now found herself discussing the sale of work worldwide. It all seemed unreal.

The details finalized, the trio rushed back to the Ritz to find Alex ensconced behind the *Financial Times*, a bottle of Veuve Clicquot on ice and four glasses.

'Alex, you knew,' Ann exclaimed, disappointed at sight of the bottle. 'You fixed it up, didn't you?'

'No, darling. I just presumed that Mr Vestas would have the sense to see what I saw,' he said, smiling as he poured the champagne.

Ann did not have what could be called a studio in either house. Alex immediately organized that rooms in both houses should be fully equipped with every medium that she might require.

For two weeks she did nothing. She was convinced that the paintings were a freak happening, something that she could never repeat. She felt certain that the pictures were the product only of her earlier confusion and unhappiness. Now she was happy and content, it was unlikely that there were any paintings left in her. A phone call from Mr Vestas enquiring how it was going jolted her into action. There were other people involved now: she had a responsibility to try again.

She stood in her studio in Hampshire faced with a blank canvas on the easel and did not know what she was going to do – her mind was completely empty. She picked up her paints and slowly and methodically made up her palette, graduating the blobs of paint by colour. She spent some time admiring the effect of the fat swirls of paint on her wooden palette board. She poured out the turpentine and linseed oil and the smell immediately reminded her of Athens. This necessitated a trip downstairs to select some of Alex's tapes of bouzouki music which she then wound on to her tape deck. Sitting cross-legged on the floor, listening to the music, she wondered why she had ever found it difficult to listen to. She frowned. She knew she had been deliberately wasting time. She could not think of anything else to do to delay the inevitable. Once again she stood in front of the easel studying with a perplexed expression the pristine canvas, so pure, so crisp it seemed almost a shame to spoil it.

She picked up her favourite brush and took a deep breath. The brush hovered momentarily over the canvas and then she stabbed at it, almost jerkily like a novice fencer. It was all that was needed – the feel of the brush on the material and from nowhere her mind was filled with images, which, with mounting excitement, she could barely wait to recreate on canvas.

Happiness, she discovered, took longer to paint than anger and despair. A week later she had produced a canvas of lyrical sweetness and light, the colours translucently subtle. Another followed, and another, until she had six of these new-style paintings.

In a way she was even more nervous as she showed these to Jeremy Vestas, convinced he would be disappointed. Instead he was beside himself with pleasure, exclaiming at the delightful contrast of her styles, at the dramatic effect this would create. She spent the best part of the morning with him deciding on frames and mounts. It was easier to paint the pictures, she declared, than to have to decide how to mount them.

To Ann the whole experience was a puzzle. From painting neat careful scenes of the garden, painstaking studies of flowers, bottle still-lifes – suddenly these new paintings had appeared, as if from nowhere. A long way from being abstract but equally far from representational, they had a mystical dreamlike quality. Ann was creating a world of her own where everything was different, from the colour of the sky to the shape of the trees and flowers. Her waterfalls were just as likely to be pink or orange as green. The animals she painted were unknown to man. All she did was transfer the images, the ready-formed painting which she saw in her mind, on to the canvas – it was really very easy, she decided. She wondered what had influenced her and spent hours in the library leafing through Alex's vast collection of books on paintings. But she never found anything that related to her work. 'Work'; that was how she described it now. 'I'll be working' she would hear herself say and it gave her enormous pleasure to be able to say it.

She had only one theory as to what had happened to her. She felt that in the loss of her baby, the rift with Peter, and in Fay's newfound happiness, she had suddenly been released from the emotional bonds of motherhood. The vast stores of energy required for being a mother were no longer needed. But that energy still existed, it had to be used, so in her case, she thought, it had chosen to emerge in this outburst of painting – a talent which had remained dormant all her adult life.

Her exhibition approached. The first thing to arrive was the catalogue, one of her paintings reproduced in full colour on the front. Inside was a list of the paintings for sale, all named now and with the most terrifying prices beside them. Ann was convinced that no one would buy at that price, the work of an unknown. Who could blame them? Naming the paintings had been an almost impossible task. She had wanted them simply to be numbered but Jeremy Vestas insisted.

'The clients prefer them with names. It helps the poor dears understand them better.' Jeremy giggled at Ann. She had discovered that, in fact, he giggled far more than she did. They had put their heads together and 'Betrayed', 'Lost Love', 'Delight' were the banal results.

The mounting of the exhibition was the next events.

'I shan't be coming, Jeremy. You'll know better than me how they should be hung.'

'Ann, you can't do that. You've got to come.' His small, pink, perfectly manicured hands waved limply in the air. 'All artists make the most dreadful fuss about "the hanging".'

'Well, I won't.'

'But you miss the point, Ann. It's the most marvellous excuse for a party.' Jeremy sounded so disappointed that she finally relented. She was glad she had, for the party which resulted was one of the best she had ever been to. Jeremy Vestas and a bevy of exquisite young men, the gallery staff, Nigel, Fay and herself were the guests. The hanging of each painting necessitated deep debate and everyone's opinion, all helped by copious glasses of wine. It took hours but the result was staggering – there was no sense of unreality now. Ann returned home late, tipsy and apologetic, but it was to be one of the few times when Alex did not complain.

She was still Ann Alexander to Jeremy Vestas and the gallery staff. Not until the night of the private view was her true identity revealed. And then it would have been impossible to keep it a secret as Alex bounded about the gallery telling everyone, whether or not they wanted to know, that the artist was his wife.

The private view was chaos. Jeremy's client list and contacts were vast. Within an hour the long white room was packed with elegant people, all with glasses of champagne in their hands, all yelling at each other to be heard over the hubbub.

Ann stood quietly in a corner and felt immeasurably disappointed – no one, it seemed, was looking at her paintings. Everyone in the room was facing inwards, backs to the picture-hung walls, intent only on their gossiping.

'They're not looking at my picture,' she complained to Jeremy, whom she had managed to grab as he dashed past with a pile of catalogues.

'Oh, dear Ann, don't worry. This lot never do. They wouldn't recognize talent if you rubbed their noses in it. They've no confidence to buy. They've come for the party.'

'Then why did you ask them? Look at the champagne they're soaking up.'

'Tactics, Ann. First wave are the socialites, filthy rich to the last pair of Guccis – they'll be off in a minute to the theatre, dinner, whatever. Then the second wave arrive. They're the serious lot – the collectors, the critics. The press will report, favourably we hope, and that will give this lot the confidence to come back and buy whatever is left. Do you see?'

Ann did not see at all but smiled at Jeremy as if she had. He was right. Within ten minutes the crowd began to thin out. Their places were taken by a new wave of guests. Both men and women were smartly dressed in the understated way of the very rich, the women's jewellery discreet and expensive. They collected their catalogues, their glasses of champagne and began their foray around the gallery. They stood for minutes at a time before each painting, peering closely at them, standing back from them, eyes squinting. One man even had a giant glass with which each inch of every painting was perused.

Ann lurked behind a pillar, intimidated by this intense group. Even Alex was momentarily quietened.

'It's interesting but I really can't find any influences at all in them,' Ann heard one smartly dressed woman, lorgnette in hand, say to another.

'Don't you feel there's a hint of the Pre-Raphaelites...?'

'You mean the other-world quality? I feel more Dali-esque, myself.'

'No. No. Not representational enough.'

The two women moved away.

'The brushwork's powerful,' boomed a large man who looked like a banker.

'Strange linear quality and luminosity,' his companion replied.

'The colour usage is sublime,' said an effete young man with a large floppy bow tie hanging beneath his rotund face and above a rotund stomach. 'Creating by opposites the same dimensions, don't you think?'

'Totally, and a curious metaphysical timbre.'

'Too true, too true . . .' The two men passed out of Ann's hearing, leaving her totally nonplussed.

Jeremy swooped on her with the art critics of a magazine and a Sunday newspaper. 'Mrs Alexander, we wondered if you would kindly explain why you have chosen such a strong allegorical motif?'

Pre-Raphaelite-ish; Dali-esque; metaphysical and now allegorical – Ann looked bewildered. 'Have I?' she replied.

The poised pens halted over their notepads.

'There's a strange static dimension. Was that intentional?' the other one asked.

'I don't know. I just painted them. They came out that way.' Ann smiled shyly at them.

'You see, gentlemen,' Jeremy shouted in triumph. 'I told you, a true naïve we have here. Forget the claptrap, boys, she just paints what's inside her.'

'Jeremy,' interrupted a large man in a pinstriped suit. 'I'm interested in number five, "Betrayed" . . .' and he took Jeremy away with him.

Everything had gone smoothly until that point. Alex

watched the businessman talking earnestly to Jeremy, and as soon as Jeremy flicked his fingers for an assistant to bring him a red sticker Alex pounced.

'You can't buy that,' he said loudly.

All heads turned in his direction.

'None of them are for sale. Sorry.' He shrugged his shoulders apologetically and smiled his most charming smile.

Jeremy went ashen and spoke quickly to the affronted would-be purchaser. Then he flapped his way towards Alex and, despite his slight frame, frog-marched Alex purposefully towards his office, calling over his shoulder, 'Of course everything's for sale. Just a minor hitch. Don't go away.' Then he slammed the office door shut.

Ann could hear the two men talking through the thin wall. The sound level rose. Alex was the first to shout, followed quickly by Jeremy. Then Alex bellowed; Ann waited, surprised to hear Jeremy bellow back. A fist slammed loudly on a desk. Ann slid round the edge of the gallery wall, desperately semaphoring to Fay and Nigel to follow her. The trio entered Jeremy's office to find both men standing belligerently either side of the desk.

'I want them, every last one of them. She's my wife and they're my paintings. I'll pay you for them, I never said I wouldn't.' Alex angrily searched his pocket for the cheque book that he never carried. 'Nigel, cheque . . .' He flicked his fingers in Nigel's direction.

Nervously Nigel stepped forward, cheque book in hand.

'But Mr Georgeopoulos . . .'

'No buts, Vestas. I buy this lot or I never set foot in your gallery again.'

'You make it impossible for me, Mr Georgeopoulos,' Jeremy wailed. 'It's not fair . . . my other clients . . .'

'No!' Ann said loudly. Everyone swung round to face her.

'You see,' Alex said triumphantly, 'Ann wants me to have them, don't you, darling?'

'No. I don't want you to have them, Alex. I want to sell them to those people out there. I didn't paint them to sell them but now I want them on the open market.'

'But I am the "open market". I often buy from here.'

'Not my pictures, Alex. Not this time.'

'Anna.'

'I've made up my mind. Either I'm a working artist or I'm not. If you buy them, I'm just your indulged wife who daubs in her spare time.'

'But Anna . . .'

'No, Alex, I've decided. You can buy *one*, that's all. Otherwise I never paint again.'

Ann stood her ground defiantly and glared at Alex. She had meant what she said. If Alex bought them, in her own mind she would remain forever an amateur.

Everyone looked at Alex who stood, his arms folded, a deep frown on his face. He rocked back and forth on his heels.

'I respect that. You're right, Anna. OK, Jeremy, you can tell your fat friend out there he can buy the picture.'

The reviews were excellent. In the small élite world of art, Ann had caused a stir. She could not have been happier. At last, she had achieved something in her life.

3

'I am retiring,' Alex announced one morning shortly after Ann's exhibition. He was lying on the couch in Ann's studio. He had got into the habit of spending large parts of the day with her, usually lying on the couch surrounded by sheaves of papers, working his way through them as she painted. From the hi-fi system music poured out, non-stop, invariably Greek music to which Ann found she painted best, or Mozart which was Alex's passion.

'I don't believe that for one minute, Alex.' Ann paused, her paintbrush in the air, and smiled across the sunlit studio at her husband.

'Well, semi-retiring is probably more the truth,' he said with a grin.

'And what has bought on this momentous decision?' She put her paints aside, wiped her hands clean and crossed the room to sit beside him.

'I am fifty next month. We've enough money to live like this for the rest of our lives. Why go on, I ask myself. For what? There are books I want to read, music I must study, paintings I want to see. Most importantly, time to spend with you, alone, instead of surrounded as we always are by business associates and staff.'

'It sounds lovely.' She smiled, still uncertain, unable to imagine Alex without his coterie of aides and secretaries, without phones ringing and helicopters clattering.

'While you were away from me I saw how quickly our life together is passing and how little time we have for each other. And then I thought of you on my island. My beautiful island. And I realized we've been there together only once since we married and I got to wondering what the hell do I do it for?'

'And we lost our son,' she said, bowing her head with momentary sadness, for once daring to say what was never far from either of their minds.

'Yes, and that too,' Alex said softly, his voice thick with sudden emotion. 'It would have been wonderful to have him to work for, I admit. But that isn't the whole story. We need to consolidate our relationship so that whatever catastrophe befalls us we can surmount it as a couple. We came too close to parting, you and I, Anna. We must nurture what we have.'

'It wasn't you, Alex, it was me. I've wasted these precious years with you imagining all manner of horrors that didn't exist. I've spent too much time comparing this marriage with my last and finding this one wanting, when all the time it was the other way around and I couldn't see it – was too stupid to realize it. For too long I was afraid just to get on with living.' She took his hand in hers. 'But I know the value of what we have now. I'll never make that mistake again, ever.'

Alex was true to his word. He did relax more. He was home far more often and there were whole months when he did not travel. Yianni, Nigel and, to Ann's surprise, increasingly Fay, took over the bulk of his work. This trio did the travelling for him, the setting up of deals, the negotiations. Alex was consulted at all stages along the way, and when final decisions had to be made.

In working for Alex, Fay had also discovered a latent talent: a quick mind with figures, a brain that could weigh up a balance sheet at one glance and that animal instinct necessary to a good business mind, the ability to smell where a deal was good, where it was bad, where the cracks had been unscrupulously plastered over. She did less and less design work now, delegating the majority, only taking on what really attracted her. And, as Alex did less on the financial side, Fay did more. This suited Alex down to the ground. Greek to the end of his fingertips he explained to Ann that, in the end, the best people to have working for one, the only ones who could be totally trusted, were 'family'. Fay's involvement allowed him to let go even faster than he had planned.

They sold their London house and bought an apartment, which Alex insisted on calling small, but which Ann acknowledged was still, with its nine rooms, a large flat by any other than a millionaire's standards. At first she was sad at the idea of the house being sold. She had created it herself, she was proud of it, and it was almost like selling a well-loved painting. But the old practical Ann could let it go, acknowledging that it made sense since they both preferred this more relaxed lifestyle and the pace of life at Courtneys.

Alex's anger at Lydia's indiscretion had been short-lived and she and George were frequent visitors. Lydia was almost as proud as Alex of Ann's painting success.

Ann never forgot her grandchildren's birthdays and Christmas, sending letters and presents. But she made no attempt to see them. She would wait until they were older, she decided, and could choose for themselves whether they wanted to know their grandmother or not. She banished Peter from her mind, thinking of him only occasionally, usually at night, when sleep would not come. But then she remembered only the good days long ago – nothing of the immediate present.

Ann had matured into a beautiful woman. The pain of the last few years had given her a tolerance and patience with life. She was far more confident, knowing now that she could cope with anything that life might throw at her. She had weathered the onset of middle age, the loss of her son, the loss of her unborn son, the knowledge that even those closest to her could be traitorous and, although there remained a wariness of relationships, in her relationship with Alex there was none at all. With him she had all the confidence of a woman truly loved.

Nothing now interfered with their need for each other which remained unabated. Like young lovers, they eagerly sought each other in bed at night.

A whole year passed in this contentment.

Ann had a second exhibition which was as successful as the first with every painting sold – unusual, Jeremy Vestas had assured her. She could have made a lot more money than she did – with interviews, prints of her work – but she rejected any overtures. She painted because she wanted to, to please herself and Alex; the acclaim from the art world she needed only to prove to herself that she was an achiever.

They had had a wonderful summer. For two whole months they had been on their island. Visitors came of necessity. Ann realized that no matter how 'retired' Alex liked to think he was there would always be this eddy of business contacts in his life, but there had been days at a time when, apart from the servants, they had been on their own. The phones rang, the telexes chattered, the helicopters whirled but Ann wondered now if she would not perhaps miss the bustle if it stopped.

The wardrobes of beautiful clothes hung, for the most part, unworn. The need to be out and about, to be seen, seemed to have deserted Alex. He wanted only to be with Ann.

She had enjoyed that period in her life. She had loved the clothes, the jewellery, and the fact of suddenly finding herself admired. But now she would look back at that time and think that, like a child surfeited on ice cream, she had had enough. It was time to slow down, to relax, and this new lifestyle was more to her liking.

She allowed her hair to grow, and after weeks in the fierce Greek sun she no longer needed the hairdresser's highlights. In Greece she prowled around in shorts and T-shirts, sneakers on her feet. In Hampshire she lived in comfortable tracksuits, her blonde hair invariably tied back in a ponytail. She looked so relaxed and beautiful it would have been impossible for anyone to guess her true age: she looked like a woman in her thirties.

Most of her time was spent painting, but she was not a precious, solitary painter: she was quite happy to work with Alex talking to her, visitors popping in, the endless ring of the telephones. Ann could concentrate in the middle of a riot, Alex used to boast.

It must have been this ability to become so engrossed in what she was doing and her preparations for her third exhibition that prevented her from seeing that the new, relaxed Alex was slipping away from her, was looking tense and becoming edgy. He began to arrive later and later in the studio each day, until some days a whole morning would pass before he came. She decided he had grown bored with the routine, and she continued to paint.

'You getting fed up with this new life style then?' she asked him one afternoon when he finally joined her in her studio.

'I'm sorry? I don't understand.'

'For a year you've spent practically every waking moment with me. Now suddenly you start disappearing. Is there another woman? Retirement over?' she teased.

'No, no. One or two irritating little problems the others needed my genius to sort out for them,' he said with a quick laugh.

Ann looked up sharply. It had been a hollow laugh. She looked at him closely, seeing for the first time a strained expression on his face. 'Anything you want to talk about?' she asked cautiously.

'Nothing I can't handle. And certainly nothing to worry my brilliant artist wife with.'

'If something was wrong, you would tell me, wouldn't you?'

Ann cursed herself for her involvement with her work, and began to watch Alex carefully. She noted he was not eating well. That he was drinking more. His temper, dormant now for many months, began to reappear. She sensed an incipient depression beginning to encroach upon him. To all her questions she always got the same reply: it was nothing to worry her head about. Her suggestion that perhaps he should see the doctor reduced Alex to fits of laughter.

'Me? I'm as fit as a fiddle. Don't I prove it enough to you, night after night?'

But Ann worried. She asked Fay and Nigel but they were as breezy with her as Alex. Of course nothing was wrong, they assured her. Alex was getting back into business; she had not really thought he would stick to his retirement, had she, they laughed. That only left Yianni and while she felt she could ask Nigel, she could not bring herself to ask Yianni anything. Her initial irritation, and distrust of him, had developed to a point where she avoided him as much as possible. She understood the bond between Alex and Yianni, a bond similar to that of one man whose life had been saved by another. She could reason that, had it not been for Yianni, Alex might have gone to prison and they might never have met. She could feel grateful for that. But still, the less she had to do with him the better.

Several weeks had gone by and Ann was still worrying and still in ignorance.

'Mummy, can we talk?'

Ann looked up from her easel to see Fay and Nigel standing, hand in hand, in the doorway. 'Of course, darlings, come in.' She stretched her hands above her head and arched her back. 'I've done enough for one day anyhow. Drink?'

She poured the drinks and the two sat on Alex's couch and for the first time, as she crossed towards them with the drinks tray, Ann noticed that they both appeared nervous. 'Is something wrong?' she asked unnecessarily.

'We think . . . no, rather we know that Alex is in deep financial trouble and is sinking deeper,' Fay said baldly.

'Oh, darlings, no! what? How?' Ann sat down quickly on the chair in front of them.

'The last six months really. That's when we first started worrying. But Alex was convinced it was just a temporary hiccup and that he would be able to solve it.'

'Solve what?'

'It's a bit complicated but, for over a year now, Alex has been losing out on deals, deals he should have been able to stitch up with no trouble. At first we all put it down to his being less involved, that it was our fault – our lack of experience. But it was happening too frequently. I mean we're not that bad, are we, Nigel?'

'I did blame myself at first,' Nigel said, his serious face etched with concern. 'But I'm convinced it's something else now. And you see, Ann, it's not just the deals falling through. For a start, any deal you set up costs money – the lawyers, the architects, projections, etc. Each deal can run into hundreds of thousands – and then if you don't get it . . . Well, you only need a run of those and money is just pouring out with nothing to show in return.' His handsome face was once again lined with the worried expression Ann had not seen for a long time.

'Yes, but Alex can weather the loss of a few million, surely, Nigel?'

'Of course, if there's an end in sight – at the moment there seems no end to see. It's not just this. There have been several disastrous takeovers recently, that at one time Alex would have seen coming a mile off and which he would have manoeuvred himself out of with no trouble at all. He was always one step ahead of anyone – it was his strength. It's as if, now, there's some bastard who knows exactly what Alex is up to, almost before he knows it himself.'

Nigel poured them all another drink. It was not until this moment that Ann realized that Nigel now referred to her husband as Alex. She could not remember when she had last heard him call him by his surname. Had Alex told him to or was it another sign of Nigel's growing confidence in himself?

'And there's worse, Mummy. In the past few months there's been a lot of accidents – at the steel works, the factories, several men have been killed. We can't prove anything, you see, it's just that we're sure it's sabotage. I know it's an ugly word but it's too coincidental to be anything else. Then last week an oil platform in which he is the major shareholder sank. Luckily all the men were rescued that time . . .'

'I read about that. Of course I had no idea that Alex was involved: he never discusses anything with me.'

'I know. And he'll hit the roof knowing that we've come to you now. But we thought we should. The oil rig was the last straw. There's to be an investigation of course. It was so obviously not an accident. Any board of enquiry is going to come to that conclusion – and if they do, and we can't prove who did it, then the insurance company won't pay up and Alex will have to foot the bill. The compensation to the injured alone is monumental: no one can absorb that sort of thing. I know it sounds overdramatic but Nigel and I are convinced there's a conspiracy against him.'

'Do you know who's behind it?' Ann asked angrily.

Fay and Nigel looked uncomfortably at each other.

'Come on, out with it. You have to tell me all you know now.'

'We know how Alex feels about him. It makes it virtually impossible to say anything but, well, Ann, we're convinced it's Yianni.'

'Yianni?' Ann asked automatically, feeling no surprise at all.

'Who else can it be, Mummy? It has to be someone close . . . that leaves Nigel and me, and it's not us. So that only leaves Yianni.'

'I see.'

'But as we say, we can't prove anything, Ann. He's been diabolically clever. What Fay and I don't understand is this – if we can come to such an easy conclusion, why hasn't Alex?'

'He undoubtedly has.'

'Then why doesn't he do something – get rid of him? Stop him before it's too late. Oh, Mummy, I feel so frustrated by it all.'

'He probably thinks he can't.'

'Mummy, I've got to ask this. Does Yianni have something on Alex? That's the only thing Nigel and I can think of – that he's blackmailing Alex.'

'I'll talk to him immediately,' said Ann, ignoring her daughter's question. 'Thank you for coming to me and telling me all this. I knew there was something seriously wrong.'

'He'll be furious with us,' Nigel said anxiously.

'No, he won't. I promise.' Ann smiled kindly. 'And take that silly worried look off your face, Nigel, it makes you look like an old man, and you've managed not to look like that for ages.' He responded to her teasing with a smile.

Ann went immediately to their suite of rooms knowing that she would find Alex taking his evening bath.

He was lying soaking, champagne glass in his hand. To Ann's surprise it was not Mozart but Wagner's *Tannhäuser* which was thundering out of the speakers. She turned the volume down.

'Why did you do that?' he asked fretfully.

'Because, Alex, we have to talk.'

'What about, my darling?' He picked up his sponge and began to soap it.

'About your business problems, and why you are losing money. And what we are to do about it,' she said very calmly.

He said nothing, but continued slowly and methodically to soap his sponge. Equally slowly he began to sponge his arms.

'I asked you some questions, Alex.'

'I've told you there's nothing to . . .'

'. . . worry my pretty head about. Oh, Alex, for goodness sake, this is serious. For once, talk to me about it. I'm your wife. I should be told what is happening.'

'You will never want for anything, my love, I promised you that years ago. So why should I worry you?'

'I didn't mean on that level, Alex,' Ann said, exasperation brimming in her voice. 'I don't give a damn about that. I meant that if you are worried out of your mind then I want to know – to help you, to support you.'

'Got a hundred million?' He smiled lazily at her.

'Alex, you're infuriating. I insist on knowing what is going on – you, Yianni and money.'

He did not answer her. He stood up and she handed him his towel. Wrapping the towel around himself he padded into his dressing room with Ann following him.

'What do you know?' he finally asked.

'I don't know anything, that's the problem. I'm working on intuition. You have problems, serious problems, and I feel that Yianni is at the bottom of it.'

'Clever darling, aren't you?'

'No, I'm not. On the contrary, I'm stupid. I'd noticed you changing, I thought it was restlessness. It didn't cross my mind it could be problems like these. You've always been so successful, I wasn't thinking . . . How serious is it?'

'Serious enough. I'll survive. Young Yianni likes to think he knows everything about my affairs. He doesn't. I would never be that stupid. But he's made massive inroads into my main fortune.'

'So, it will all be all right?'

'It depends what you mean by "all right". I think we may have to change our lifestyle somewhat. Oh, we'll be rich but not this rich.'

'Then it's all right. Isn't it?' she repeated, inanely.

Alex slumped into the chair. He put his head into his hands. 'No. It won't be all right.' He looked up at her, anguish in his eyes. 'Can you imagine how I feel? All those years of working, wheeling and dealing. For what? To lose it all to him. I knew he was ambitious, I stupidly didn't realize just how ambitious. And I trusted him, Jesus, how I've trusted him. And I promised you, I promised you his life . . .'

With horror, Ann realized that he was close to tears. She put her arms about him and held him to her. 'My darling, the money doesn't matter to me. I love you, I'm quite content to live a simple life with you and paint. I don't need the big houses, the trappings. Please, my love, don't upset yourself, we have each other.'

'Anna, don't you see? It's as if all my life has been for nothing. As if without my great wealth I am nothing.'

'Alex, I've never heard such rubbish. You're the most wonderful thing that has ever happened to me. You're you, your money doesn't make you the man I love.'

She put her hand under his chin forcing him to look at her, concern on her face at the despair in his. 'I'd love you, Alex, in a semi-detached in Ruislip.'

'God forbid,' he managed to smile.

'But if it matters so much to you then we'll get that bastard, we'll ruin him. We'll show him he can't do this to you of all people. You must have it out

385

with him. I don't understand why you haven't sacked him already.'

'I have talked to him. God, I even threatened him. There's nothing I can do. He knows too much – my hands are tied.'

'Nada, you mean, his evidence?'

Alex lowered his head again and nodded silently as if he were ashamed.

'So? It was a long time ago. Who cares any more?'

'When I confronted him he told me – you go for me, then I go straight to the police and tell them the truth.'

'And what is the truth?' she asked, her heart beginning to thump alarmingly.

'He now claims he walked into the villa and saw me pushing my wife down the stairs. I have no memory of it, you know I haven't. And he says he's written a statement which is in a safe place so that if anything happens to him, his lawyer will go straight to the police. His ambition is to ruin me totally. It seems he finds me overbearing, has resented me all these years. Not only that, the last straw for him was my bringing Fay in. He felt usurped apparently, and by a woman – it was too much for him. His life's ambition now is to ruin me totally and make himself rich in the process.'

'It seems very convenient that he should suddenly have a different story to tell. A bit late in the day, I should think,' Ann said practically. 'And for goodness sake, Alex, do you really think that people are going to cut you out of their lives after all this time, not deal with you? I don't believe it, I really don't.'

'If only I could remember.'

'You couldn't kill anyone, Alex. I won't let you even think it. I know you better than anyone. You're letting this past drama cloud your thinking. I bet, right now, you're thinking only of that, not of the fortune that's slipping away.'

'I am. I keep going over and over the night in my mind.'

'Then you must stop. This is ridiculous and not at all like you. You have to pull yourself together, Alex, work something out. I can't help you there but I'll support you through it every way I know how. We'll ruin the little bastard so that he never works again,' she ended sternly.

He looked at her sadly. 'See what he's done. He's changing even you, making you sound ruthless. That's not you, Anna. It's not worth pursuing him, if it's going to cause this sort of damage. I don't think I have the energy any more . . .'

'What rubbish, Alex. Of course we go for him, you and I. I'll help you. And if the worst comes to the worst, we have each other, that's all that matters, isn't it? In any case it's ruining our sex life.' She smiled at him.

'God, Ann, I was so lucky that day I went into the Tate. I felt myself going under. But now . . .'

'Perhaps in future you'll let me know what's going on?' she said, laughing.

'Oh, I will. I think I'll send you out to do battle with all my enemies.' At last he too laughed in return.

4

Ann abandoned her painting. She worked with Fay, Nigel and Alex as they sifted through mountains of papers and ledgers, and analysed all the computer print-outs.

One morning, weeks before, Yianni had decamped without warning: perhaps the hostility in the atmosphere had finally pierced even his armour-plated self-confidence. No one knew. Without him around everyone was in higher spirits. Optimism reigned again. And Alex had shed the uncharacteristic depression and was his old dynamic self. Ann would go so far as to say he was enjoying himself as, like a sleuth, he waded through the ramifications of his business empire to unmask Yianni.

'I have to hand it to him, he's done a brilliant job,' he said one day.

'Don't you dare say a good thing about that bastard.'
Playfully Ann threw a cushion at him.

'But he has, he's covered his tracks cleverly. No, his fraud has been masterly, I would go so far as to say he's almost a genius. The problem is he didn't give me credit for being a greater genius. I've found him out . . . It's just a matter of time and I can nail him.' Alex laughed joyfully at his own immodesty. It was wonderful to hear him laughing again.

Ann had loved him before and he her, but in some strange way this danger to their security had seemed to make them even closer, something that Ann would not have thought possible.

She learned so much in these weeks of what Alex's business involved. She had always admired his ability, but now she revered him. His one mistake had been Yianni and was it not a human mistake? Anyone would have felt a trusting obligation to a man who had saved one from certain imprisonment. And as she learned, there was no question but that in the future Alex would be able to talk to her of his work, for now she had a grasp of what was involved.

Three weeks later and they were no further on. Their previous optimism, their feelings of elation began to dissipate. One lead after another came to a dead end. They knew Yianni had defrauded Alex but they could find nothing – no document, no bank account – with which to prove it.

'Brilliant. Absolutely brilliant. I couldn't have done it better myself.' Alex shook his head, slammed the large ledger shut. 'That's it, my friends, there is no way he has left himself uncovered.'

'Oh, come on, Alex. You can't give up that easily,' Fay said indignantly.

'Easily?' Alex laughed. 'No, Fay, I don't give up lightly. But it has become a waste of my valuable time.'

'Bully for you. What about Nigel's and my valuable time? Well, I'm not throwing the towel in. That's the trouble with foreigners, they've no spirit.' She grinned cheekily at her step-father.

'But if he's as rich as you think he is, then that will prove it,' Ann said, anxious as well that they should not give up.

'What has he done wrong? He's done some good deals, picked up some good companies, shares – anyone could have done that. That's not criminal. He hasn't stolen one penny from me.'

'But he stole ideas, your expertise.'

'Ah yes, but even that we cannot trace – he's hidden it all away in companies within companies. It could take years to uncover. It's time we got back to getting this business back into some order. What do you say, Nigel?'

'It seems a shame but I suppose you're right, Alex. I would like to have got him though,' Nigel replied, speaking to Alex as an equal, Ann noted with pleasure. She doubted if Nigel would ever return to the nervous, anxious aide he had been before.

'Bloody wet, all of you,' Fay muttered from the depths of the sofa.

Alex poured them all drinks and the four of them sat despondently sipping them, staring out into space.

'Have any of you bright sparks thought that maybe Yianni had something to do with the burglary? That's criminal enough,' Fay asked brightly, uncurling herself from the sofa.

'You know, Alex, she might be right. You remember I told you that when those men first burst in they said something about nothing having been said about me. And look how they knew about one of the knots in the wood being the button for the safe?' Ann leaned forward.

'Alex, I promise you he never did tell me to get Robin to cancel his trip to the survival course. I presumed he had done it. He must have known Ann was here alone.'

'I believe you now, Nigel. So easy, wasn't it? "Nigel is dealing with Robin, sir." ' Alex angrily hit his palm with his fist.

'That's it then. Call the police,' Fay said, eagerly.

'My dear Fay. You must think me singularly stupid. I have already checked it out with the police. From what little they discovered the whole operation seems to have had shades of Watergate, and Hollywood. Mysterious phone calls to the burglars in a disguised voice, and so on. He wasn't interested in stealing from us. He wanted us frightened. Well, at least I hope that's all he wanted,' and his face darkened at the memory of how close to disaster Ann could have been.

'He had to have a partner. He could never have done it on his own. Where would he have got the money from?' Ann said suddenly.

'Of course he must have had a partner, darling,' Alex agreed patiently. 'But like the deals, where do you start looking? It could be anyone.'

'No. It has to be someone you know. Someone you yourself have done business with.'

'I doubt it, darling.'

'It's the only explanation. Don't you see, darling? Yianni lived here – your world was his life. He never took holidays, or went away for a weekend – I often wish he had,' she laughed. 'Why, I don't ever remember him receiving a personal phone call. It was as if he had no life outside of us.'

'Bloody hell, she's right, Nigel. It has to be . . .'

Ann's theory regalvanized them. It was now time for Alex to call in debts of gratitude from businessmen all over the world, men for whom he had done favours time and again. From innuendo, light and heavy hints, snippets of gossip, a picture began to appear. The jigsaw began to fall into place.

Yianni's partner emerged – Roddie Barnes. The archetypal, silver-haired, charming Englishman who had charmed Ann all that time ago. Then her mind had been full of fears fuelled by Peter's talk of the Mafia. But her suspicion had fallen on the wrong business associates. She had the grace to laugh and swear that she would never rely on female intuition again.

They might have evidence of Yianni's and Roddie's deceptions, but they still had to have legal proof. All they had to go on was that both had acted unethically. Yianni had broken the terms of his contract – but in law they were back to their inability to prove it on paper. As deals were lined up, Yianni had informed Roddie. Since Yianni would know what Alex was prepared to offer, Roddie was always in a position to outbid him. It seemed that a couple of times when Alex had left Yianni to do the bidding for him, Yianni had underbid on purpose – but that was hearsay, the paperwork was in perfect order. The sabotage had been done from unmitigated spite on Yianni's part and a desire to ruin Alex once and for all. Even then he had been clever – on the oil rig he must have bribed an ex-diver, who had been sacked by Alex's foreman, to do the dirty work. At least the insurance company and the police accepted this man was responsible, but no one could break his story that he had acted alone. The quartet's gut feeling was that Yianni had paid him.

Once again the enthusiasm of the other three began to wane but Ann was adamant that they plough on. She would not rest until that man was in prison, she swore. Alex, she knew, would be content just to get his business back on an even keel and hopefully forget the whole unpleasant incident but retribution lurked very close to the surface in Ann's mind now.

The depth of her animosity to Yianni actually shocked Ann herself. She had travelled a long way from being Mrs Grange of Midfield. She was certain that that woman would not have had these deep feelings of revenge, would not have talked in such ruthless terms. But then the woman she was now – poised, successful in her own right, well loved – was a long way removed from the country mouse she once had been. In an odd way Peter had been right, he had not known her but then Ann had not known herself either.

The break when it came was sudden. Ann was waiting with Nigel and Fay for Alex to join them for dinner.

'I've got it!' Alex hurtled into the drawing room waving a sheaf of papers in his hands. 'Look. He's sunk . . .'

He spread the papers on the floor and they crouched on hands and knees as he explained his discovery in detail.

'Look, see, here's the invoice, here's the receipt signed by Yianni, and yet, look at these bank statements, these paying-in books – where is it? Where's the money?' Alex sat back triumphantly on his haunches.

Ann looked at the papers and was disappointed by the amount involved – ten thousand pounds. He was unlikely to go to prison for long for an amount like that – and that's all she wanted: Yianni languishing in jail for as long as possible.

'It's not a lot of money,' she pointed out despondently.

'I agree. But this time he's overplayed his hand. Don't you see where the payment has come from – it must be a grant or something – it's from the Greek government. You can't cheat governments, Anna my darling, they do not like it.' He slapped his thigh and roared with laughter.

'But he's been so clever, Alex, surely he'll have covered his tracks there too,' Nigel said. 'I see what you mean and it should be damning, but you're going to have to get other people to admit to fraud. He must have bribed people to keep their mouths shut when the cheque was cleared to a bank account other than yours.'

'I can work the system too. I've cousins and uncles in far more important positions than anyone Yianni can corrupt. No, we can relax at last. He's been just a little bit too greedy. Foolishly so, it's such a stupid amount compared with everything else. But it's not the amount in this case, the amount is irrelevant – he's committed a crime here.'

The next morning the four of them flew to Greece.

If Ann was angry for Alex it was nothing compared with Ariadne's wrath. She said if she had a gun she would kill Yianni. Ann might laugh but she felt it was true. Ariadne was quite capable of murder on her beloved brother's behalf.

The cousins and uncles and aunts descended like buzzing insects. Anger filled the giant apartment. Like Ariadne, the younger generation wanted blood. 'Yianni should die' was the daily chorus. No, no, Ann argued with them, far better to ruin him – there was more satisfaction to be had that way. There was still enough of Ann Grange left to wonder where all this talk of revenge and retaliation was leading.

Ann had been engrossed only in saving everything for Alex. The money was not important, it was his sense of failure were he to lose everything that she had fought against. But once in Athens, the full ramifications of the disaster they had averted struck her. It would not have been just they who suffered; the whole enormous family would have had to pull their belts in – everyone was dependent on Alex and his fortunes. He had been carrying an awesome responsibility for years.

Here with her limited Greek Ann could no longer be the help she had been. Uncles and cousins took her place in the planning sessions. There was nothing for Fay and Nigel to do, so she suggested they went to the island.

For a week Alex was in meetings with government officials, lawyers and the police. Piece by piece the jigsaw took shape, Yianni's fate was almost sealed. Next week with luck he would be arrested.

On the Friday evening Alex returned from yet another meeting, his bulging briefcase showing the extent of their labours.

'Darling, you look exhausted,' Ann said, concerned.

'No, just a little tired. You know the cure. A whisky, a bath, a little sleep and your wonderful body.' He smiled at her. 'Remember when I first told you that?'

'The night you asked me to marry you properly.'

'A wonderful night that, wasn't it? So many wonderful nights.'

'And days . . .' she laughed. 'I've been thinking, Alex. There's nothing you can do here this weekend. Why don't we go to Xeros, just you and me? You need to relax before next week.'

'But Nigel and Fay are already there . . . I want to be alone with you. Why don't we go to another island?'

'No. Fay phoned yesterday. They've gone to Mykonos to see the windmills. They're returning on Sunday. We would be alone.'

'That drink and your body will have to wait then,' he said, taking her hand and rushing her out of the apartment, into the car and to the airport to catch their helicopter.

It was as if, with the problems solved and almost finally concluded, Alex had shed years. He was like a young man again. They lived in their bed and the whole weekend passed in a haze of the most wonderful sensuous love-making. How could it be, thought Ann, that after all these years he could still surprise her in their bed, could still make her come to heights of passion greater than ever before?

The weekend had been so perfect that she did not want to return to the city. Here she had Alex to herself; in Athens she had to share him with his family and friends. They were enjoying a regenerative and magical time in their life and she wanted to keep it that way.

'Darling, it's so hot in the city. You go, and come back tonight. We'll stay here all week. You're sexier here than in Athens,' she teased him.

'You always accused me of being the insatiable one,' he retorted, agreeing to her suggestion. He had only one meeting that day and could easily return by the evening.

'You promise you'll come back? You won't get tied up with your cousins, out half the night at the taverna?'

'I never break a promise.'

'You broke one,' she said with a chuckle.

'And what was that?'

'That you'd inevitably be unfaithful to me.'

'I haven't given up hope yet,' he teased, kissing her as he left.

She waved as she watched the sleek white helicopter rise into the sky and skim out low over the Aegean.

5

Ann spent the day repairing the ravages of a weekend in bed with Alex. She relaxed in a long rejuvenating bath. She washed her hair, and gave herself a manicure; and she slept. She was exhausted. It amazed her how Alex could be such a demanding lover and still have the energy he had to do so many other things. She was not complaining; she would not have him any other way, she thought, and smiled to herself.

The weekly boat which serviced the island arrived with Fay and Nigel. They had a leisurely lunch while they told her about Mykonos. The young couple swam but Ann opted just to laze in the sun.

The afternoon slipped into evening. Ann went to her room, opened the large wardrobe and wondered what to wear. She would surprise him, she decided, by dressing up, putting his favourite jewellery on, something she had not done in the past weeks. She changed into a long red silk chiffon dress, her diamonds sparkling at her neck and ears, her hair immaculate, a cloud of expensive perfume wafting round her. She poured herself a drink and went out of their room on to the terrace which hung out over the sea. She sat patiently waiting for Alex to return.

From a distance she heard the familiar metallic whirr of the blades and stood up to watch the helicopter approach. It circled over the house and she waved at the machine, as she always did, certain that if she could not see him, Alex would be able to see her in her red dress outlined on the white marble of the terrace. The helicopter swooped out over the sea to come in to land.

She saw the explosion before she heard the noise. She watched as if it were a slow-motion film, as debris lazily arced against the blue sky and drifted down to the sea.

'Not, again.' Her words were almost a sigh. She clutched the balcony with her hands, the stonework cutting unheeded into her palms. She watched the villagers launch the boats and frantically make their way into the flaming sea. She knew they made a fruitless journey. She did not know how long she stood there. She did not feel hot, she did not feel cold, she did not feel anything. She heard running footsteps.

'Nigel?' she said softly.

'Ann,' the young man cried, tears pouring down his cheeks.

'It's over, isn't it, Nigel?'

'I don't know, I came to you. The boats aren't back yet.'

'We'd had a magical weekend, Nigel. At least he died happy. It was so fast, Nigel.' She grabbed the young man's arm. 'I don't think he would have felt anything, it was so fast, you see.'

'Yes, Ann, I'm sure you're right.'

One of the villagers rushed on to the terrace, tears streaming down his face.

'*Kiria, Kiria,*' he shouted. '*Kirios, enai pethanai!*'

'What's he saying?' Nigel asked.

'He tells me my darling is dead.' And it was Nigel who began to cry and Ann who comforted him. 'I should have been with him,' she murmured, more to herself than to him.

The next few hours were a turmoil. The house was filled with people crying and wailing in their anguish. Fay, strong practical Fay, collapsed in Ann's arms, her grief out of control. Ann held her child, stroking her hair, soothing her with consoling words. She summoned the doctor who gave Fay a strong sedative and Nigel led the distraught girl away to bed. The doctor offered Ann the same treatment but she declined emphatically. The villagers stood awkwardly, old men and women, tears coursing down their rough, wrinkled faces; they looked bereft. She moved among them, comforting them, getting them drinks, arranging food for people. She fussed over everyone, helping them in their despair. They looked at her in amazement and marvelled at her calmness and control.

'I think I will lie down now, Nigel. I feel very tired,' she told him, quietly, her composure complete.

'Yes, that's a good idea, Ann. Get some rest. I'm OK now. I'll look after things here for you. Don't worry.'

She entered the room, the beloved room where they had spent so many happy hours, where they had hoped to grow old together. She went to his wardrobe and took down an old jacket that he loved to wear.

She lay on the bed and hugged the jacket to her, his smell upon it. She remembered another jacket, another room, and she saw the emptiness that lay ahead of her. The grief, the madness, the longing.

There were no tears, and she, of all people, knew what that meant. She knew she lacked the strength. Whatever she had expected of life, it wasn't this.

She crossed the bedroom to the bathroom. From the back of a cabinet she took a bottle of pills. Pills prescribed all those years ago at Midfield. Pills she did not know why she had bothered to keep until now.

Methodically she lined the small white capsules up in twos like soldiers on the bedside table.

She poured a large glass of vodka. Then she sat for a long time looking at the pills, outlining their roundness with the tip of her finger. She imagined the blissful oblivion they would give her, longed for the blackness that would caress her. Perhaps Ariadne was right, perhaps there was a life after death. She could be with him again, in his arms in some unimagined paradise.

From afar she heard the telephone ring, she heard the crickets begin their nightly oratorio. She heard a blind clicking like a metronome . . . Those sounds, those bloody

sounds from so long ago. They drummed in her head . . .
soon the bees would start, where was the motor mower,
the smell of roses? And then how long before they were
followed by the pain, the agony . . .?

Who had said something earlier about a bomb? Sabo-
tage? Words she had half heard and had not reacted to.
She did now, though. Only one person could hate and fear
Alex to that extent.

That bastard. It had to be that bastard, Yianni. She
would not give him the satisfaction of seeing her die as
well, not yet. No, she would stay alive and she would make
certain that Yianni never knew another day's happiness
either, as long as he lived.

With a vicious swipe she knocked the white capsules
from the table, the small pills rolling away across the
marble floor. Clutching the bottle of vodka, Ann made her
way to her studio. She manhandled the largest canvas she
owned on to the easel. Violently she squeezed the tubes
of paint, the bright colours swirling on to her palette . . .
She picked up her brush. Almost defiantly she faced the
blank canvas.

Her brush lashed through the air. The colour streaked
across the empty whiteness of the canvas. Again she
lashed with her paint.

Through the night, tears gushing from her eyes, only
the sound of her brushwork breaking the silence Ann,
confidently and with all the passion in her body, painted.

One canvas followed another on to the easel through
that long night. Her revenge and her retribution were
transmitted by paint on to canvas. She was purged of
them. She was free of them. Only her grief remained.

She looked at the paintings. Once before this medium
had saved her sanity. This time it was saving her life.

The painting had exhausted her. Ann lay on the bed, the
bed where he had given her such joy, clutched his jacket to
her and studied the ceiling with unseeing eyes. She smiled

to herself as an army of memories flashed across her mind. So many wonderful memories. What a wonderful life he had given her. A full rich life.

She had grieved for Ben – the imperfect husband – that time she had grieved for an illusion. This time there was no illusion – their love had been so real, so total. It was that which would now give her strength, she resolved, the knowledge that she had been loved so perfectly. How many women could say that?

At last she slept. The deep, dreamless sleep that nature compassionately gives to those whose emotions have brought them close to the abyss.

It was the feeling of someone's weight on the bed beside her that woke her. As soon as consciousness returned, her mind was full of the image of the flaming helicopter. She turned to one side, her eyes tightly closed, and pretended sleep. She did not want to see anyone, speak to anyone, yet.

'Anna.' The voice spoke softly.

'Anna,' the voice persisted.

Ann frowned. She was sure she was awake, but how could she be? She must be dreaming . . . that voice!

'Anna. You're pretending. I know you're awake. You can't fool me.' The voice had a tone of amusement to it.

She stirred. This was too cruel, this was a terrible joke. Gingerly she opened one eye, then the other.

'Alex!' Her voice was half a whisper, half a sigh.

'Anna, my darling.'

'Alex, what is happening? Am I dead? It can't be you. Dear God, I wish it was you.' A tear escaped from her eyes. He leaned forward and gently licked the tear away.

'Precious. It is me. I was not on the helicopter. Wake up, my love. Really, it is me. I'm here. I'm not dead.' He was laughing. 'See, touch me, feel me.'

Ann sat up in the bed, disbelief etched on her face. She touched the hand he offered her, the warm hand she knew so well. She ran her fingers along it.

'But Alex, where were you? Good God, why didn't you phone? Do you know what I've been through?' There was anger in her voice now.

'Anna, you have every right to be angry with me. I'm sorry, my love. You see I broke my promise. I went with my cousin Frixos, you remember the fat jolly one, to the taverna – just for a quick meal, you understand. We started playing backgammon, taking the odd glass of wine. Then we played some more. Then, I'm sorry, darling, but we got totally, completely riproaringly drunk. I slept on the taverna floor.' He grinned at her sheepishly, and for the first time she noticed how dishevelled and crumpled his suit was.

'You could have telephoned. That was cruel, thoughtless of you,' she said with spirit.

'I meant to. I really did. I phoned the airport before I was too drunk. I told the pilot to return to the island, to lie to you and tell you I was held up in a meeting and for him to return with you the next day. I wanted you with me when they arrested Yianni – it's today.' He grinned from ear to ear. The smile was too much for Ann. She hit him with all her force, pummelling his chest with her fists.

'You bastard. You selfish bastard!' she shouted. 'Do you know what hell I've been through, and you were lying in a drunken stupor. You only do it here. Why? You're never like that in England . . .'

'It won't happen again. I promise. You know what I'm like when I get with my cousins.' He caught her wrist so she could no longer hit him.

'You promised before . . .' She stopped dead. Her face went white. 'Jesus Christ, Alex . . . if you hadn't broken that promise . . .'

He gathered her into his arms. 'I know, my love, don't even think about it.' He stroked her hair, kissing her gently. 'But you know what, darling? It really was the only promise I broke – honestly.'

FOLLOW THE PEN OF ANITA BURGH,
AUTHOR OF **DISTINCTIONS OF CLASS**
AND **LOVE THE BRIGHT FOREIGNER** . . .

AND DISCOVER THE STIRRING NEW
ROMANTIC TRILOGY,
DAUGHTERS OF A GRANITE LAND

If you have enjoyed reading **Love the Bright Foreigner**,
you must read **Daughters of a Granite Land**, Anita
Burgh's compelling new trilogy of novels which follow the
triumphs, passions and sacrifices of a Cornish family over
the last hundred years.

Here is an extract from **The Azure Bowl**, the first book in
this exciting new series . . .

THE AZURE BOWL

1

Alice Tregowan's upbringing had been unconventional. Her mother, Etty, hated her. George, her father, seemed unaware of her existence.

It had not always been this way. There had been a time when Etty was as involved with her children as any wealthy young mother was expected to be in England in 1881, that is, she took a dutiful if lukewarm interest in their clothes, manners, health and diet. Each day, at teatime, they were brought to her boudoir to play as she lay, languidly beautiful, on a chaise, resting before the inevitable fatigue of another evening spent with society.

The degree of play was controlled by how exhausted their mother was. If not too tired, she had been known to read to them, to play a game of spillikins or, if she was feeling very relaxed, they might have a round of 'Happy Families'. But often she was too tired and would lie, eyes closed, her hands crossed limply on her body – voluptuous body, released for a few short hours from the constraints of her stays, and now comfortably covered with a lace and embroidered *peignoir*.

At such times the children were expected to 'play', quietly. The problem was that the room held such a jumble of furniture that movement was severely restricted. Small tables proliferated, each with its clutter of boxes, silver-framed photographs and ornaments – all far too precious for the children to touch. It was as if there were not a material or metal known to man that was not represented in this room. Jade and malachite vied with onyx, lacquer with bronze, crystal sparkled, mother of pearl glowed. Iron and brass supported. Lace, chintz, brocade, silk and satin, ruched, bunched and swathed, competed for attention. The curtains at the large windows were half drawn, the shades were down, for Lady Tregowan was afraid lest one shaft of sunlight mar her alabaster complexion and cause a freckle to appear. Always a fire glowed, winter or summer, making the room so hot that even the fronds of the palm in the corner wilted.

Alice was afraid of this room, and of doing damage in it, as she was afraid of her mother. To society Etty was a beautiful, gracious, witty, laughing woman. To her children she was a puzzle. One moment she was engrossed in what they had to say, the next irritated beyond endurance and pushing them from her. One minute she could be laughing, the next screaming at them to leave her alone. Alice did not enjoy her daily visit to her mother.

In their London home, at the top of the house, beneath the great glass dome, the children had their suite of rooms – a day and a night nursery, a schoolroom, their nursemaids' rooms and sitting-room, and a tiny kitchen for making toast and hot chocolate. There were walls, lined floor to ceiling, with cupboards full to bursting with clothes, the best that the White House shop could supply. Every toy that a child could want was there.

Here, in total control, resided their nursemaid Queenie Penrose with her two nursery assistants. Queenie, with her ample body and breasts as soft as the softest feather pillow, whose large good-natured face with round cheeks shone red as any apple. Queenie, whose neck smelt of soap and biscuits, was warmth, security and love.

Very occasionally their mother appeared in the nursery – rustling in her silks, glittering with jewels, expensively perfumed and exuding graciousness with a visiting queen from a far distant land.

From the barred nursery windows, if they stood on tiptoe, they could watch the activity in the square below, the hours of the day marked out by the arrival of the delivery men. First the clang of the churns as the milk, fresh from the cows in Hyde Park, was ladled into tall white enamelled jugs, held by the kitchen maid. The rat-a-tat-tat of the postman. The meat boy with his hand-cart that squeaked. The calls of the old flower seller, the fisherman, the shrimp man, the pretty fruit girls. The rattle of the hurdy-gurdy with the monkey that bit. And, as winter drew in, the bell of the muffin man with his hat as flat as a board.

Most evenings, once Queenie was safely in her room with her jug of stout and her penny dreadful, Alice and Oswald would steal from their beds and crouch on the stairway. They would peer through the balustrade and the wire mesh suspended in the stairwell. The mesh had been placed there the day after Oswald had dropped a toy train over the side, missing a footman's head by inches. Far below, the gas lights in their ornate brass chandelier, hissed. As if through the wrong end of a telescope, the children watched the comings and goings of their parents' friends. The women's dresses swished and swirled, their overskirts frothy with frills, ribbons and flounces of lace which, caught back into full bustles, swayed like giant, brightly coloured bells. The guests formed ever changing patterns on the black and white marble floor like a giant kaleidoscope...

...Once a year, in early spring, the family and Queenie, Etty's maid, George's valet and Phillpott, the butler, would travel across town to Paddington and climb aboard their personal coach for the annual visit to their estate in the West Country.

Their coach was added to the regular train in which less important individuals travelled. Alice loved this journey, the excitement of the great train huffing and hissing in the station, impatient, as she was, to begin. The coach was furnished in red plush and gilt, the woodwork of the shiniest mahogany. Tiny oil lamps glowed, the golden bobbles on their shades swaying with the rhythm of the train. It was like a miniature house on wheels where, in the small galley, Phillpott would heat up their already prepared meals.

Alice enjoyed the journey so much that its completion was only made bearable by the prospect of seeing Gwenfer again. Both she and her brother agreed: Gwenfer was their favourite home of all.

Gwenfer. Had one not known of its existence one would never have realized it was there, tucked as it was between the two giant cliffs which the wind battered and at whose feet the sea lashed and sucked voraciously, hungry to steal more land. On the cliff top there were no trees, for there was never time for them to root deeply enough to withstand the gales of autumn and winter. Only the broom and hawthorn kept a tenacious hold on the poor soil. But by spring and summer, those same barren cliffs were ablaze with the colour of the wild garlic, the periwinkle, foxglove and a hundred other flowers. Then they came alive with bees, butterflies and dragonflies, their improbable colours added to nature's gaudy summer palette. Across the landscape the tall chimneys of the tin mine pump-houses seemed to strut, arrogantly and noisily.

A narrow road criss-crossed the scrub and led through iron gates which never closed, flanked by gateposts surmounted by the great stone falcons which had stood there for centuries. The road snaked perilously down the granite sides of the cliff, twisting and turning to reveal, far below, a valley. Purple, pink and white rhododendrons lined the roadside. Mophead hydrangeas stood waiting their turn to flower and wild rhubarb plants, with stems as thick as an arm and taller than a man, promised shade beneath their giant leaves when the summer finally came.

In the very begnning it had been Gwenfer cottage, then farm. In medieval times it progressed to house and then manor but now, having grown, its size an indication of the Tregowan family's fortunes, it was known the length and breadth of the land simply as Gwenfer. George Tregowan might, like his forebears, have been tempted to extend it further had its position not prevented him. The house filled the head of the valley, embraced protectively on each side by the towering cliffs. Built of the same granite the building appeared to be an extension of the rocks.

Etty came to Gwenfer on sufferance. It was too far away from London and society. It was also too small for her needs. Those intrepid friends whom she could persuade to travel such a distance had to be restricted in number to fifteen, whereas Etty felt that a successful house party needed at least thirty people.

It was fortunate for the house that it was not her favourite – thus it had escaped Etty's 'improvements'. The panelling remained in position, the plasterwork was original and the great stone fireplaces, plainly carved, still stood in the high-ceilinged rooms. She was not sufficiently interested in its interior to refurnish it, so the designing flair of Mr Waring and Mr Gillow had not been called upon and the furniture was much as her husband's Elizabethan ancestors had left it. So great was her lack of interest that Gwenfer lacked the clutter of the other houses. The walls remained white, the only colour coming from the tapestries and family portraits. There was no gas so the great wall sconces remained and oil lamps glowed warmly. The long, mullioned windows to the front of the house faced on to wide terraces of informal gardens which Etty had not bothered to have landscaped. These gardens cascaded wildly down to the floor of the valley where a small river tumbled towards the sea. Even when the ocean was shrouded in fog, even on the calmest day, its sound could be heard in each room of the house, a persistent background noise, as breakers crashed on to the boulders, and spray flew through the air to mingle with the river.

With the sea, the wild gardens and the moors, for Oswald and Alice Gwenfer was a paradise.

2

Ia Blewett was seven. She did not know she was, birthdays were of no significance in her environment. What mattered was one's size and strength and how soon it would be before one could go out to work.

The family was smaller now. Paul, the eldest had sailed away to America to join his Uncle Ishmail. For over a year they had waited for news. Ia's mother had fretted and worried about her son, not knowing if he lived or died. But finally the longed-for letter had arrived. They had had to wait for Mary to return from her work in the Miner's Arms, to learn the contents, for Mary was the only one of them who could read or write. She had to read the letter aloud so many times that it soon became creased and tattered. It was a short letter, misspelled, full of crossings-out and ink blots, but, importantly it told them that Paul was well. He was no longer mining but working in a factory.

'What's a factory, Mam?' Ia asked.

'I'm not sure, Ia but it do sound grand, don't it?'

Then, the precious week, her beloved sister Mary, after a violent argument and a beating from her father, had run away, no one knew where, and that added to the burden of worry which beset her mother.

Issac, her youngest brother, had been ill for months with a bad chest, and was now too weak to work. He spent his days lying on a bed in the small sitting room, coughing and sweating.

The miners' fears had been realized and the mine was long since closed. A mere handful of men were kept to work on maintenance and the futile task of trying to save the workings from flooding. Only Jacob, in the family, was lucky enough to find employment at the mine.

Ia played in the dust in the alleyway between the cottages oblivious of the flies which buzzed about her. With a stick she was drawing patterns in the soil and thinking about her family. If only she were older and bigger, then, with Mary gone, she could have taken her sister's cleaning job at the pub, which would have helped. Instead, she felt useless as she watched her mother becoming older and more bent each month. The stick swished across the pattern she had carefully made. She hated her father. She hated him so much that she wished that the roof-fall, which had smashed his legs to pulp five years ago, had killed him. It was her father's fault that Mary had left. Mary had always been kind to Ia and looked after her: it had been almost like having two mothers. It was Mary who had helped their mother the most, in the house and with money. Not like Jacob who, Ia knew, lied about his money to their mother. The lack of money was always with them. Occasionally her mother would manage to get some washing to do, the odd scrubbing job, but most of the time hunger stalked the family.

When the accident had first happened, Ia had felt sorry for her father as he lay groaning on the bed, the deep wounds in his legs causing him agony as the pus had formed and evil-smelling liquid seeped through the bandages. There had even been talk that one leg might have to be cut off. But it had been saved. After three months Reuben was back on his feet, with a fearful crutch to support him, which he used as a weapon to beat them all. Since he could no longer work, all he did was shout at his family, lie in bed or hobble up to the pub with the few pennies he had beaten out of his wife.

Ia looked closely at a great black beetle, lying in the dirt on its back, its legs waving impotently in the air. She looked at the beetle and thought of squashing it, just as she wished she had the strength to squash her father. She lifted her foot, paused, then bent down and gently turned the beetle right side up, smiling as it scuttled away.

'Ia?' her mother called. Ia turned into the cottage.
'Ia, I'm off to the big house. I'll be back for tea. Tell your dad, when 'ee gets back.'

'Why you'm going there?' Ia asked curiously. She had seen the gates that led to the big house, but she had never seen the building itself.

'I've a job for the day. They needs someone to do some scrubbing.'

'Can I come?'

'No. I don't know as how they'd be too pleased if I turned up with a young 'un.'

Ia watched her mother walk up the alleyway and make off across the scrubland towards the cliff. She settled back to drawing with her stick, but within five minutes she was bored and set off in the direction her mother had taken.

She slipped through the gates and into the lush undergrowth so that no one could see her. She could hear the sea far below her, and made her way towards it.

Down in the cove Alice sat upon her rock and faced the sea, her back to the land. She was twelve and had reached that point in childhood when the adult she was to become made fleeting appearances on her child's face. It was evident that she was going to be beautiful, that her bone structure was fine, that her profile would be perfect and that her large grey eyes were to be one of her best features. Her long hair was thick and silvery blonde and she wore it long and loose. But her fine eyes wore a guarded expression. This was no longer the clear-eyed, innocent look one would have expected in a girl who had wanted for nothing. But then Alice had wanted. She had never suffered materially, but as she had grown so she had become more aware of her parents' abandonment of her. Apart from Queenie, who in the world loved her? Now that so little work was done in the mine, her father had ceased his annual visit; in fact he had not been for two years. Alice had had to come to terms with the fact that Queenie had been right and it was only the mine he had come to see, not her.

Living as she did with the servants, she had learned many things. She had discovered that her father was rich. The mines were his. Six mines he owned, in total. Four he had closed, including Bal Gwen; only Bal Etty and Bal Fair, twenty miles away from here, were being worked. She had learned that her father was feared and hated. This information had not shocked her, when she had overheard it, it was as if they talked of a stranger – for she no longer knew him. She had learned how to recognize, from the sly glance in her direction, when a choice piece of gossip was about to emerge, and know that it would never be said in front of her. So she had resumed her old habit of listening at doors. In that way she had learned that her mother was now totally mad, kept locked in a wing of Fairhall with iron bars at the window. Having the run of Gwenfer's library she had read *Jane Eyre*; she knew of Mrs Rochester's suffering and would wonder how much her mother suffered. Occasionally her feared Aunt Maude visited. It was on one of these visits that she overheard her aunt and Queenie discussing the possibility of madness being handed down to the children of such people and since then, at night, she would lie awake and wonder if she, too, one day might go mad and be locked up with keepers as her mother was. She would wonder what it was like to be mad and completely distanced from people – and she feared it.

This July morning, Alice looked at Oswalds's rock and sighed.

'Oh, Oswald, how different everything could have been …' she said aloud.

The sound of a twig breaking made her turn round. Standing under a large rhododendron thirty feet from her, stood a child, with dirty and bedraggled hair which, had it been washed, would have been as blonde as Alice's own. The frightened eyes were the same grey as Alices's. Her feet were bare and her legs, beneath the short, tattered skirt, were scratched and bloody with weeping sores. The young girl looked shyly at Alice, reminding her of a startled animal. Then, abruptly, she shook her head, flicking her long hair over her shoulder in an almost defiant gesture and stood and stared at her.

'Hallo, who are you?' Alice broke the silence but the girl stood there sullenly. 'Why don't you come and sit here? It looks hard but it's quite comfortable.' Gently Alice held out her hands. She was unused to company and normally did not search it out, but she found that she wanted this girl to join her. Still the child stood silently but one foot was lifted in the air, wavering uncertainly as if she might be about to take a step. 'Would you like some of my lunch?' Alice unwrapped her bundle and spread the food on the rock, using the kerchief as a table–cloth. 'Do come...' The girl looked at the food and then at Alice and then back to the food. Alice picked up a soft buttered roll and held it towards her, very much as she did when coaxing her fox. As quick as lightning the girl ran forward, grabbed the food, stuffed it into her mouth and then began to back away. 'Have some cheese,' Alice said quietly. Again the girl darted forward, her movements as swift as a dragonfly's. This time Alice hung on to the cheese. 'Sit down. Then you can have it' Obediently the child sat on the ground at the foot of the rock. As the cheese followed the bread with equal speed Alice laughed, unaware, in her ignorance of hunger, of its dreadful pain. A chicken breast was quickly gulped. 'My goodness, you are hungry, aren't you?' The child nodded. 'You have the cake. I'm not hungry.' Alice was serious now, at last realizing that the little girl was starving.

The girl stared with disbelief at the sponge, golden yellow and oozing with strawberry jam and clotted cream. She took the cake and looked at it suspiciously, sniffed it, and then a small pink tongue gingerly licked at the jam. Glancing up at Alice she smiled with delight at the taste, stuffed the cake into her mouth, swallowed and then burped loudly.

'You should say, "I beg your pardon",' said Alice, sounding like a miniature Mrs Malandine.

'Why?'

'Because people do when they make a rude noise like that. It's polite.'

'What's rude about it?'

'Well, it just is, you see.' Alice was less sure of herself now.

Ia shrugged her shoulders, grinning broadly. 'Beg your pardon,' she said in her heavily accented voice.

There was another silence. Alice was not used to making conversation and knew even less how to talk to other children.

'My name's Alice. What's yours?' she said abruptly.

'Ia.'

'Ia? I've never heard that name before.'

'It's mine,' Ia said defensively.

'Yes, yes I'm sure it is. You're very pretty.' she added quickly, afraid that her new acquaintance might run away.

'Is I? Mind ee, so's ee.'

'Thank you.' Alice blushed with pleasure at the compliment. 'But you're supposed to say *you*.'

'Whats' wrong with ee? Everyone says un.'

'Nothing's wrong with it except it's not right.' Alice laughed at her own confused sentence. 'Where do you live?' she asked, preferring to change a subject on which she was getting muddled.

'Up along.' Ia jerked her head towards the cliffs.

'What are you doing here?' Alice asked and immediately regretted the question as she saw Ia's alarmed expression.

'I don't mean no harm. I wanted to see where me mam was. She's scrubbing up at the big house.' Ia played with the sand, looking slyly up at Alice as if making up her mind about something. 'Who was you talking to just now? There bain't no one else here.'

'Talking? Me?' Alice blushed fiercely. For a moment she said nothing, unsure how the child would react to the truth. She looked closely at Ia who stared solemnly back, her grey eyes alert with intelligence and what Alice thought was a look of sympathy. 'My brother, Oswald, that's who I was talking to.'

'Has 'e gone to America? My Paul, 'e's gone there, but sometimes I talks to 'e. I stands up on the cliff and I tells him everything.'

'No, my brother is dead. A long time ago ...'

'That's not nice for ee.' Ia stood up suddenly, brushing the crumbs from her skirt. 'I's going now,' she announced.

'Do you have to go?' Alice was disappointed.

'Got ter see me dad.' And as swiftly as she had appeared she left.

The Azure Bowl is now available in paperback from Pan Books.

Anita Burgh
Distinctions of Class £4.99

From backstreet girl to laird's lady, a woman follows her star, for better, or for worse . . .

"Jane sat alone at the back of her private plane. She had a decision to make: one which could change her extraordinary life, once again"

Jane dared to dream as she grew into a beautiful woman in a dead-end world of mean streets, but she never dared dream that one day she'd be the laird's lady, wife to Alistair Redland, future Earl of Upnor.

When that impossible dream became real, she had to wake one day and find her love match wrecked on rocks of class pride and social prejudice.

So, in cloistered Cambridge and elegant Italy, Jane built her life anew. Always desirable, wherever she went there were men who knew just how desirable.

Until her star of destiny drew her north again, to the Highlands, where a twist of fate lay ready to seize again her dreams and test again her courage . . .

Distinctions of Class is a compelling story, a remarkable novel from the pen of an exciting new author, reflecting more than a little of the real life of its creator, Anita, Lady Burgh.

All Pan Books are available at your local bookshop or newsagent, or can be ordered direct from the publisher. Indicate the number of copies required and fill in the form below.

Send to: Pan C. S. Dept
              Macmillan Distribution Ltd
              Houndmills Basingstoke RG21 2XS
or phone: 0256 29242, quoting title, author and Credit Card number.

Please enclose a remittance* to the value of the cover price plus £1.00 for the first book plus 50p per copy for each additional book ordered.

*Payment may be made in sterling by UK personal cheque, postal order, sterling draft or international money order, made payable to Pan Books Ltd.

Alternatively by Barclaycard/Access/Amex/Diners

Card No.   ☐☐☐☐☐☐☐☐☐☐☐☐☐☐☐☐☐

Expiry Date   ☐☐☐☐☐

_____
                            Signature

Applicable only in the UK and BFPO addresses.

While every effort is made to keep prices low, it is sometimes necessary to increase prices at short notice. Pan Books reserve the right to show on covers and charge new retail prices which may differ from those advertised in the text or elsewhere.

NAME AND ADDRESS IN BLOCK LETTERS PLEASE

....

Name _____

Address _____

_____

_____

_____
                                             3/87